D0324375

The Robber Girl

The Robber Girl

FRANNY BILLINGSLEY

CANDLEWICK PRESS

Text copyright © 2021 by Franny Billingsley

Pages ii–iii image copyright © CloudyStock/Shutterstock
Chapter opener image copyright © KsanaGraphica/Shutterstock

First edition 2021

Library of Congress Catalog Card Number pending
ISBN 978-0-7636-6956-0

21 22 23 24 25 26 LBM 10 9 8 7 6 5 4 3 2 1

Printed in Melrose Park, IL, USA

This book was typeset in Joanna.

Candlewick Press
99 Dover Street
Somerville, Massachusetts 02144

www.candlewick.com

A JUNIOR LIBRARY GUILD SELECTION

✳

To Nathaniel, brilliant cultural omnivore,
for introducing me to *Deadwood*

Day Zero

✝ A DAGGER IS MEANT FOR STABBING. It is meant for killing. A dagger has two sharp edges and goes down to a point. If you have a good dagger, the blade is made of iron mixed with carbon. If there's no carbon, it will be too soft. If there's too much carbon, it will be too brittle.

I had a good dagger. A robber girl needs a good dagger.

"*I'm the best dagger,*" said the dagger.

"*You're the best dagger,*" I said.

We matched each other, my dagger and I. We were not too soft, we were not too brittle. I hadn't stabbed anyone yet, but I would. The dagger had stabbed lots of people.

"*More than you can count,*" said the dagger.

"*Not more.*" I could count as high as there were numbers. I could count as low as there were numbers. I could count down to zero.

Yesterday had been Day One. Today was Day Zero. The important part of Day Zero had already started. We'd left the hideout and were riding through the ravine. The path tilted up, the cliffs leaned in on us. Here the horses had to walk in a single line. Later we would have to be quiet, but not yet. Stones went rattling down the path. Hoofbeats and stone falls echoed between the cliffs. The stone was gray, but later, when we had to be quiet, the stone would be pink. It was a long way up to the top of the world, where the stone turned pink.

Here the world was small, the stone walls pressing at us, breathing their damp ancient breath. First in line was Gentleman Jack. He was always first, the ribbons fluttering from his horse's mane, the yellow gloves on his hands.

Primrose. That was the color of Gentleman Jack's gloves.

I came next. Yellow ribbons fluttered from my pinto's mane, but they were regular yellow, not primrose. Primrose was just for Gentleman Jack.

Then came Rough Ricky. No gloves, no ribbons. Just the web of scars on his hands and face. We always came first: Gentleman Jack, then me, then Rough Ricky. The rest of the Gentlemen came behind us, but the three of us were always first.

"And me," said the dagger. "Don't forget about me!"

I would never forget about the dagger.

"I have the sharpest point," said the dagger. "I have two edges, sharp as death."

The dagger was sharp, I was sharp. Together we were sharp, together we were wild.

Soon the ravine would end and the Plains would begin. In the middle of the Plains rose the Indigo Heart, where there would be gullies to leap and mountains to climb. There would be a thousand-thousand tons of pink stone. That's what I'd been waiting for. Today I'd use the dagger. Today I'd get my name.

We threaded the horses through the three great stones that hid the ravine. Here the world burst upon us, a sea of yellowed grass poking through the snow, and in the distance, the earth shrugging its shoulders into the mountains of the Indigo Heart. When you stay in the ravine all winter, you begin to think that's all there is—the cliffs, the cave, the river. It's easy to forget that the ravine is buried in the Plains, like a hollow egg.

Today I'd get a house.

"It's not really your house," said the dagger.

Today I'd get a grandmother.

"She's not really your grandmother," said the dagger.

Gentleman Jack, Rough Ricky, and I still rode first, but now we had enough room to fan ourselves into an arrowhead, with Gentleman Jack making the point. The rest of the Gentlemen rode single file behind. They made the shaft of the arrow.

The wind shrieked across the Plains. It smelled of cold and snow. The wind was fast, and we were fast, but we didn't shriek. We were practicing to be quiet. Ahead rose the mountains, pink above the tree line but dark with indigo trees below.

Nothing could go wrong, not on Day Zero. Day Zero was Now. At last I'd arrived at Now. Now was a yellow ribbon in a pony's mane. Now was a cascade of lace at Gentleman Jack's wrists. Now was a pair of primrose gloves, with the letters GJR embroidered on the cuffs. Now was the glint of a ruby in Gentleman Jack's ear.

Nothing could go wrong, not when Gentleman Jack, Rough Ricky, and I made the head of the arrow.

I knew we were close when we reached the railroad tracks. It was funny how you couldn't see the Indigo Heart as well when you got close. You couldn't see the mountains, pink against the sky. All you could see were the indigo trees and, minutes later, the red clay road that circled the Heart.

"*There's iron in the clay.*" The dagger knew everything about metal. "*That's why it's red.*"

The Indigo Heart was just the way Gentleman Jack had described.

"*Iron is magnetic,*" said the dagger.

The dagger was magnetic, too, which meant it would feel the pull of the road. I wasn't expecting to feel it, but I did, just a little tug when we leapt upon the clay.

"*There's a bit of iron in blood,*" said the dagger.

It was like the tug of sleep when it was time to wake up. You could break the tug but you didn't want to.

"*Magnets are not like sleep,*" said the dagger.

It would be faster and easier to take the road that went winging up the mountain, but it wasn't safe: someone might see us.

We leapt up the embankment, onto the mountainside. Here, among the indigo trees, the horses slowed, crunching over indigo needles and aspen leaves and pockets of snow. It was winter in the Indigo Heart. The birds were silent; there was just the sound of crunching. The horses wound through the indigos, sidestepped jabs of rock punching through the earth. Above, a hawk sailed in descending spires.

"*Watch where we're going!*" said the dagger.

The dagger meant both of us had to watch. The dagger was in the sheath at my waist, and it was also in my head. But it could only see what I saw, so if I wasn't watching, it couldn't watch, either.

"*We have to remember where we're going,*" said the dagger. "*If something goes wrong, we have to get back to the hideout.*"

I couldn't remember a time the dagger wasn't in my head, six inches of carbon and iron, reminding me to be wild. If I ever wished for taming things, like more food or a heavier coat, it would press at my thoughts, cool and sharp. Together we had a blade that cut on both sides. Together we had a spear-point tip.

Together we were wild.

The slopes grew steeper and rockier; we crested a rise, and now we had to take the road. That was the dangerous part. Someone might see us.

The road wound up and up, around rocky outcroppings. We went faster now. There was less snow on the road, and fewer rocks and roots to trip us.

"This is the road," said Gentleman Jack.

I knew what he meant. This was the road where he'd found me, abandoned and left to die.

"I don't calculate the coach will be late," said Rough Ricky.

"Road's not too soft," said Gentleman Jack. Sometimes you couldn't drive on the roads in the Indigo Heart because they were too deep with mud. "Just a little sticky."

We swung around the folds and bends of the cliffs. The sky was low and white, like an overturned eggshell. The land dropped away on the downhill side. We rode between a wall of rock to the left and a plunge into nothing on the right. Sometimes the road narrowed into a lip, pouting round the cliff. It would be easy to swing too far and tumble into the dark.

Gentleman Jack tugged at the reins; our horses slowed. The other Gentlemen passed us. They were a mass of brown except for the scarlet feather in Doubtful Mittie's hat.

"Fool!" said the dagger, and I agreed. We'd all warned Doubtful Mittie, but because he wasn't from the Territories, he didn't believe us: he didn't believe that if you wear a dead man's hat, you'll die, too.

"Not *exactly* that," said the dagger, which was always precise. "*The man has to have died wearing the hat.*"

That's what I'd meant, but there was no point saying so. You couldn't argue with the dagger. It was too un-bendy. You can't argue with iron and carbon.

The Gentlemen vanished up the road, and now it was just the three of us, Gentleman Jack, Rough Ricky, and me.

"*And me,*" said the dagger.

Gentleman Jack had told me about the place I was to hide. He'd told me again and again, and I'd imagined it, but it was different to see it in real life, to see the almost invisible crevice in the cliff. None of the Gentlemen would be able to fit there, but I could. A ten-year-old girl could fit.

"*Maybe ten,*" said the dagger. "*Maybe nine.*"

"*Maybe ten,*" I said. "*Maybe eleven.*"

We slid off our horses, past blue ribbons, past yellow ribbons. Lace flowed over Gentleman Jack's collar. Lace ruffled over the embroidery on his gloves. Gentleman Jack was in motion, his lace blowing in the wind. Rough Ricky was stiff and slow, bound by a webbing of scars. He'd played with fire, which a person should never do. The scars were his Affliction.

"Tell me the plan." Rough Ricky's voice was low and whispery, like ash. He'd wrecked his voice in one of the fires he'd set. "Be careful of smoke and lye," he sometimes said. Lye was something that made fires burn faster.

"I slide myself into that crevice," I said. "I wait until I hear the stagecoach."

"What if they realize you're a girl?" Gentleman Jack reached for the bag of sweets he carried with him always. He had no Affliction—unless, he sometimes said, you counted his sweet tooth. He said it was his one vice, but he meant it as a joke.

"They won't realize," I said. I wore britches; I had stuffed my hair into my hat.

"What if they catch you?" said Gentleman Jack.

"They won't catch me," I said.

"What if they ask your name?" said Gentleman Jack.

"I'll say I have no name," I said.

"What if they ask about the hideout?" said Gentleman Jack.

"I'll say there is no hideout," I said.

"What if she can't speak?" Rough Ricky was talking about my Affliction. I couldn't speak until someone spoke to me first. I could whistle, which got people's attention, but Gentleman Jack wouldn't let me. It was bad luck to whistle.

Rough Ricky was worried the outriders on the stagecoach wouldn't speak to me. That would mean I couldn't speak to them.

Gentleman Jack reached for his strike lighter. It was for lighting cigars, but Gentleman Jack didn't smoke. He made the flame dance on and off, on and off. He said it helped him think.

"They're bound to say something," said Gentleman Jack. "To a kid, alone on the road?" But Gentleman Jack didn't know how easy it was to ignore a plain, scrawny kid.

"I guess," said Rough Ricky.

We both had an Affliction, but Rough Ricky knew what he'd done to get his, and I didn't know what I'd done to get mine.

"Show me the dagger," said Gentleman Jack. He'd taught me to draw it straight and fast. In a second it lay gleaming in my hand. There were its two sharp edges, there was the deadly tip.

"You have kept it clean." Gentleman Jack smiled his best smile. It was the one where you couldn't see his teeth.

I had kept it clean.

"You have kept it dry," said Gentleman Jack.

I had kept it dry.

"You have kept it sharp."

I had kept it sharp.

"It will do," said Gentleman Jack.

I squeezed myself sideways into the crevice. Gentleman Jack and Rough Ricky looked in, blocking the sunlight. Then Gentleman Jack nodded, and they stepped back. Now the sun could enter, but it had to pull in its stomach to fit.

Gentleman Jack and Rough Ricky didn't say goodbye. They simply left; I was alone. Now came the soft thud of horses' hooves in the squish of the road. They were heading uphill to the hiding place. They were leading my pinto. I remembered the yellow ribbons in his mane, I remembered how they blew in the wind. The sunlight was cool; it kept its distance.

"What if they catch you?" said the dagger.

"I use you," I said. "I hurt them."

"How do you hurt them?" said the dagger.

"I cut a tendon," I said. "Then they can't move."

It was good to talk to the dagger. I felt it leaning against my thoughts. It made my mind sharp, it made my thoughts wild.

The crevice was tall and thin, like a broken tooth. Twists and thrusts of indigo branches bristled from fingernail cracks. It was all fingernails and teeth. The wind rustled along the road, but it couldn't enter here. The thick resin smell of indigo lay sticky in my mouth.

"How do you kill someone?" said the dagger.

"I make a sticking motion in the eye," I said. "I make a slicing motion at the throat."

"But will you want to kill them?" said the dagger.

"Only if I have to," I said. "Killing is more sure, but it gets you in bigger trouble."

Now came a rumbling of the stagecoach, faint but clear. Gentleman Jack had said I'd be able to hear it a mile away. The air in the Indigo Heart was good for listening. It was Day Zero, and the stagecoach would not be late.

"I will try not to kill them," I said.

On top of the clatter of the wooden wheels came the thud of hooves. And on top of that came the jingling of harnesses and the whuffling of horse breath.

"Is it time?" I said.

"Almost!" said the dagger.

Day Zero had just begun. At the beginning of today, I had no name and no house and no grandmother. But at the end of today, Gentleman Jack would give me a name. Today we'd go live with Grandmother.

I knew the number for zero had a hole in its middle. But today I'd fill in all the holes.

"It's time!" said the dagger.

I jumped.

Yellow Ribbons

✝ I JUMPED INTO A CONFUSION OF HORSES, huge white legs, shrill whinnies. There were too many legs, plunging and punching the road. I pressed myself against the cliff.

"*You have to go forward!*" said the dagger, which is easy to say when you're made of carbon and iron and can't get trampled.

"Whoa!" cried a great voice.

There was a dreadful space of time in which everything was quiet, save for the scraping of hooves and the jingle of harnesses.

The driver was as big and bright as the horses. I had to talk to him, to this man in the white coat with the long fringes, to this man in the big white hat. He was big, and his mustache was big, and even though there were lots of reins, his hands could hold them all.

"What is it?" he said. Gentleman Jack had been right. The driver would speak to a kid alone on the road. Now I could speak to him—no, to them. There were two of them, the driver and, perched beside him, a man like a little brown mouse. The horses shifted in their traces. Their harnesses shone with silver rings and rivets.

"*Tell him about the outlaws!*" said the dagger.

Gentleman Jack had told me what to say. He said I wouldn't need to say much, he said anyone would rescue a child from outlaws. But I hated talking to people for the first time. They always looked at me funny when they heard my ugly voice.

I said the word "Outlaws." My voice was a closed door. I said, "Stopped our wagon." The pawing and snorting of the horses stomped my voice flat, the bright harness bells rang it out of existence.

"Right on schedule." The mouse man turned to the driver. A silver star shone from his coat. I didn't realize what the star meant. But the dagger did. Something made of iron and carbon would know about metal stars.

"*The Sheriff!*" said the dagger. "*Yell! Warn the Gentlemen!*"

But I didn't have a yelling voice. I could whistle, loud as anything, but that would bring bad luck, which we were having already.

Now there came a click, and now it was too late. Rifles and revolvers clicked when they were getting ready to shoot. Click! It was the mouse man—the Sheriff. He leapt from his perch and twisted with a lithe slimness. A rifle glinted as he threw himself across the stagecoach roof.

The Gentlemen pounded down the road, toward the back of the coach. The mouse man lay on top, looking over the rifle.

Everything happened at once. The rifle cracked. The six white horses whinnied and reared. Crack went the rifle again, bright as lightning.

It was a repeating rifle. The Sheriff could shoot and shoot without pausing to reload.

Now again, sharp enough to crack the eggshell sky. The horses were all jingle and churn, all plunge and whinny. I backed into the cliff, but the horses were still too close. They'd churn and plunge me. They'd jingle and grind me.

I kept my back to the cliff and scuttled downhill, away from the Gentlemen, and the stagecoach, and the horses.

The downhill road was clear. The horses were uphill; everything was uphill. I darted across the road, to where it stumbled over some rocks and fell into the gorge.

So many guns now, so much shooting, you couldn't hear the clicks. The driver held the horses steady. The Gentlemen were firing, the mouse man was firing, and someone else was firing from the gorge side of the coach. The stagecoach door was open. A man used it like a shield, crouching behind it, firing around it.

All I could think of was Gentleman Jack. The man might shoot Gentleman Jack!

I crept along the edge of the gorge, toward the coach. Horses shied and squealed. The air was all lightning bolts and pounding hooves. I had the dagger, though. I'd grab it, but only at the last minute. That was so the man couldn't see me approaching, dagger in hand. That was so he couldn't get ready to defend himself. I could snatch the dagger quick as quick. I'd practiced until I was almost as fast as Gentleman Jack.

A slicing motion at the neck. That was when you wanted to kill someone.

I crept up behind the shooter, who might kill Gentleman Jack. It was better to hurt, not kill. But not when Gentleman Jack was in danger.

A sticking motion in the eye. That was when you wanted to kill someone.

"Behind you!" shouted the Sheriff. He could see everything from the stagecoach roof.

The shooter had folded himself up so he could fit behind the door. He spun around but didn't unfold. More gunshots, the sharp smell of gunpowder. The man grabbed my wrist. A bullet hit a rock beside us. It bounced off, then dove into the squish and drowned.

A horse screamed. A horse's scream is different from a person's scream. A horse's scream is pure nightmare.

I couldn't see the fight from this side of the road, from behind the stagecoach door. I saw only the man, folded like a piece of paper. I saw the man, and the road, and the man's boots on the road. They were black boots, well polished, with silver stitching.

He jerked us against the coach because now the Gentlemen were running, strung in a messy line. They thudded past us, between the coach and the gorge. It took just a moment; I watched them pound downhill. But where was Gentleman Jack?

The Gentlemen raised no dust, it was too sticky for dust. They rounded a bend in the road and vanished. The world grew very small. I looked at the road, at the black boots with silver stitching. Beside them lay a hat with a scarlet feather.

It was Doubtful Mittie's hat. Doubtful Mittie hadn't passed us, had he? Gentleman Jack hadn't passed us, had he?

The man unfolded himself, still holding my wrist. He unfolded and unfolded until he was impossibly tall. But he didn't know I was quick. He didn't know I was used to fighting. When you know how to fight, you take your opponent by surprise. You attack when he expects you to run.

I wasn't tall, but I could jump. I sprang at the man. I wrapped my legs round his waist, I twined my arms round his neck. He wore side whiskers and a high collar. But there was still lots of exposed flesh. I sank my teeth into his cheek.

He slammed the stagecoach door and shook me off, all the while holding my wrist. My hat tumbled to the ground, but that didn't matter, not now. I stood on the road, which stretched out in both directions. It had always stretched in both directions, but now, with the stagecoach door shut, I could see the uphill road. I didn't want to see it; I didn't want to see the things on the road, but my eyes kept getting stuck. They got stuck on the scarlet feather in Doubtful Mittie's hat. They got stuck on a lump of a body wearing Doubtful Mittie's jacket. They got stuck on Gentleman Jack's boots. Gentleman Jack was standing in them. He was alive, but he'd been caught. My hat was lying in the road. My hair tumbled round my shoulders.

"A girl!" said the folding-paper man.

Gentleman Jack had been caught. I'd been caught.

The two of us, we'd been caught. What should I do? What could I do? I couldn't call out to Gentleman Jack. It had been too long since anyone had spoken to me; my Affliction had me by the throat. Gentleman Jack was tall and the Sheriff was a mouse, but still, Gentleman Jack was the one in handcuffs. Gentleman Jack was the one with a revolver pressed to his back. Gentleman Jack was the one who had to listen to the Sheriff saying, "Jack Royal, we arrest you for the murder of Federal Marshal Starling. We arrest you in the name of the Blue Rose."

"A girl dressed as a boy," said the folding-paper man.

Gentleman Jack smiled and smiled. He smiled his best smile, the one that covered up his teeth. He looked just like his last name. He was Royal.

I glanced up at the length of the folding man, past the black creases of his body to the half-moon tooth marks on his cheek.

I saw too much. I saw the silver star on the Sheriff's jacket. I saw the Sheriff force Gentleman Jack toward the stagecoach. Gentleman Jack saw me, but his smile didn't change.

I saw Doubtful Mittie's jacket, wrapped around something that was no longer Doubtful Mittie. He wasn't breathing anymore, so it didn't matter that he was lying facedown in the muck. Still, I wished someone would turn him over.

Doubtful Mittie had flung out his hands, maybe to catch himself. They were the color of raw liver. I smelled them, even from here. They stank of rotting meat. That was his Affliction for having killed a child.

Or children, maybe. Doubtful Mittie might have killed more than one child.

His hat lay in the mud. Doubtful Mittie wouldn't have liked that. He took good care of that hat. I remembered how happy he'd been when Gentleman Jack said he could keep it. Doubtful Mittie had tucked the scarlet feather in the hatband to disguise it. The hat had belonged to the Federal Marshal, and the Federal Marshal was famous, but still, no one would recognize his hat, not with the feather. Gentleman Jack liked it that way. He said the hat was hiding in plain sight.

The folding man dropped my wrist. He no longer needed to hold on. There was nowhere I could go. No one I could save. All I could do was pick up the hat. Doubtful Mittie didn't care about it anymore, but I did.

"Why do you want that?" said the folding man.

"It's Gentleman Jack's," I said. If one of the Gentlemen died, everything he owned belonged to Gentleman Jack.

"I'll give it to him," said the folding man, but I shook my head. I clutched the hat and watched Gentleman Jack. He was going to make a move, I could tell. Yes, there he went!—whirling round, slamming his shoulder into the Sheriff's jaw. But the Sheriff was alert, and smart. He knew the trick of jerking his prisoner's arms, forcing the prisoner to turn to the front or else risk his arms being wrenched from his shoulders.

That was very painful. I knew from personal experience.

The Sheriff and Gentleman Jack disappeared around the far side of the stagecoach. I couldn't see Gentleman Jack, so I'd have to think of him instead. I'd never stop thinking of him. I'd already rescued the hat; I'd give it to him. What if I could rescue the gold on the coach—the five bricks of gold—and give it to him? What if I could rescue Gentleman Jack and—and what?

I'd give Gentleman Jack back to himself.

I buttoned Doubtful Mittie's hat into my coat. Gentleman Jack was just a shadow through the stagecoach window, sitting on the far side of the Sheriff. I hoped he could see me better than I could see him, see me rescuing his property. Obeying the rules, as I always did. I looked over the lump the hat made in my middle; I looked down to my boots. Looking at my boots was better than looking at Doubtful Mittie, looking at his face in the mud, looking at his grasping raw-liver hands.

It was better than looking at the pinto.

But I couldn't ignore the yellow ribbons fluttering from the pinto's mane. Like Doubtful Mittie, the pinto lay in the road. Unlike Doubtful Mittie, he thrashed his legs and struggled his shoulders from the mud.

"What do you think, Sheriff?" said the folded-paper man.

"The pony will never get up," said the Sheriff from inside the coach.

The pinto groaned. He churned the mud with his forelegs; he was lathered with foam. The yellow ribbons fluttered. The pinto's eyes were white. The sky was white. The pinto writhed, but the sky was blank and blind. The pinto couldn't churn himself out of the muck.

The folded-paper man strode toward the pinto. He didn't even look behind to make sure I wasn't slipping away. How could I, with the driver right there?

I closed my eyes. I jumped at the gunshot, even though I knew it was coming. I tasted the gunshot. It left an acid spit in the air.

Now the yellow ribbons lay still. Now the folding-paper man walked back to the coach.

I swallowed hard. I couldn't get sick here, in front of everyone. But the revolver spit made me want to be sick. It would be better if I could be in the coach with Gentleman Jack. I reached for the handle, even though Gentleman Jack was on the far side. But the man pulled me back.

They wouldn't let me ride with Gentleman Jack. That was the Sheriff's job, to ride in the coach and make sure Gentleman Jack didn't escape. It was the folded man's job to make sure I didn't escape. His fingers were long and hard.

"Keep an eye on her, Judge," said the driver.

"Never fear," said the Judge. He held me tight. He was a folded-paper man, but he was also a judge. Gentleman Jack and I had been caught by a sheriff and a judge. They would take us to jail.

The Judge bent toward me. I hadn't quite seen his face until now. His quickness and tallness had gotten in the way. Now I saw that his quickness made him seem younger than he was. There were lines at his eyes, like chicken scratches, and creases running beside his nose and into his mustache. And very red on his cheek were the bright smiles of my teeth.

I would make myself look at the smiles. I'd keep the dagger hidden and remind myself of all the ways I knew how to hurt a person. I had my teeth; I had my fingers. You didn't have to be big to poke your finger into someone's eye.

I looked at the angles and hollows of his face, at his eagle nose, at his cliffside cheekbones. The Sheriff and the Judge must be taking us to jail. At least in jail I'd be with Gentleman Jack.

"What do you reckon to do with her, Judge?" said the driver.

The driver didn't care that I was going to jail. He was too big and relaxed, the reins sliding through his fingers, the fringes of his white jacket blowing in the wind.

"*This is exciting!*" said the dagger.

"I'll take her home," said the Judge.

There came a silence, like a gulp. "Are you sure?" said the driver.

"No," said the Judge. He paused, then said, "We'd better head out, before the snow."

"It's going to blow in hard," said the driver.

I hated the Judge. Before, he had been all long arms and quickness. Before, he had been an unfolding into tallness. But now he stood still, a black paper shadow, blocking the sky. I hated the Judge, with his eagle-nest cheekbones and chicken-scratch eyes.

I hated the Sheriff, so little and scurrying. I hated the driver, so big and easy with himself. I wanted to go to jail with Gentleman Jack. But I couldn't say so. It had been too long since anyone had talked to me. And Too Long was not very long at all. After someone spoke to me, I had to speak within the space of three breaths and a swallow; otherwise my Affliction would gobble up my words.

A wind blew up and with it came a flutter of ribbon. The ribbon was yellow, and if you could see revolver spit, it would be yellow. I swallowed and swallowed, but it was too late. I was sick all over the Judge's boots.

For some reason, that made the men laugh. The Sheriff, the driver, even the Judge.

"They'll clean," said the Judge, and the driver said that, speaking of cleaning, he'd come back to dispose of the bodies. "Not a pretty sight," said the driver, "especially with the hands on that fellow."

He and the Judge exchanged a glance. They understood about Doubtful Mittie's raw-liver hands. They knew it meant he'd killed a child. Or maybe children.

"I'll take the girl on my horse," said the Judge. "The stage is sick-making."

It turned out that the Judge had brought a horse, tied to the back of the stagecoach. Why would the Judge have brought his horse? You don't need a horse when you're on a stagecoach carrying five gold bricks to the railroad station in Buffalo Bend. But here it was, and now we were mounted, with me sitting in front. I craned my neck to look up at him, surprised all over again by my tooth marks.

"What's your name?" he said.

Now I could speak. "I have no name." I hated the Judge. I hated my flat, clopping voice.

"No name?" said the Judge.

"No name."

"We must call you something," said the Judge. But why must he call me anything? And anyway, this wasn't what I'd practiced with Gentleman Jack.

"Where do you come from?" he said.

"I come from nowhere," I said. "Where are we going?"

"We're going to Blue Roses."

I knew Blue Roses was the biggest town in the Indigo Heart. My mother was from Blue Roses, but she'd left me in the wilderness to die. Gentleman Jack found me and brought me back to life.

I had to speak before three breaths and a swallow went by. "What about the gold?" We were going uphill, deeper into the Indigo Heart, and so was the stagecoach. But I'd thought the stagecoach had to go the other way, to get the gold to the railroad, where it could be put on a train and sent out of the Territories.

"There never was any gold," said the Judge.

Of course there'd been gold. Gentleman Jack had heard about it from his reliable source. He'd heard that the stagecoach today was carrying five bricks of solid gold. Together they were worth one hundred twenty-eight thousand dollars.

"There is gold, of course," said the Judge. "The veins of the Indigo Heart run with gold. But there was no gold on the coach, not today."

I couldn't make myself understand. Day Zero was the day the coach was supposed to carry the five gold bricks. We were going to take the gold bricks to Grandmother, and they would make her happy.

"The gold was a trick to catch Gentleman Jack." The Judge craned round to look at me. I saw the bite marks on his cheek, and I saw his coffee-bean eyes. You can't tell what someone's thinking when they have coffee-bean eyes.

Up the road we went, into the Indigo Heart, to Blue Roses. Cliffs rose to the left, and to the right, gullies and gorges fell into darkness.

"Gentleman Jack is a thief," said the Judge, "and a murderer. He killed the Federal Marshal. You know he did."

I had the Federal Marshal's hat buttoned into my coat. Yes, Gentleman Jack had killed the Federal Marshal, and the Federal Marshal's hat had killed Doubtful Mittie.

"There were folks who saw you," said the Judge. "We know you were there."

I'd been there, all right, and I understood why Gentleman Jack had to kill the Federal Marshal. The Marshal wouldn't let Gentleman Jack take any gold from the Indigo Heart, even though he had as much right to the gold as anyone else. I didn't like to remember the Federal Marshal being killed, but that didn't matter. It served the Federal Marshal right to be dead.

We passed under a bluff of red earth; it pressed down on us. It made the air heavy. I couldn't stop thinking about the flutter of yellow ribbon.

"The ribbon's not important," said the dagger. "Paying attention is important. Finding the hideout is important."

I paid attention. I marked the places we passed—the bluff of red earth; a river, high and rushy despite the cold. "The Jordan River," said the Judge. The pinto would have balked at the crossing, but the Judge's horse was used to it. The water wet the Judge's boots. That would clean off the sick.

We passed endless scrabbly indigo, growing almost horizontally from the cliffs. I would remember this, and I would remember the jagged mounds of earth and how the road would sometimes straighten out and let the world burst into view—hillsides dark with indigo giving way to cliffs of pink stone—then winding back into themselves again.

The gray stone of the hideout was in the ravine, which was at the bottom of the world. The pink stone of Blue Roses was at the top of the world.

I wasn't supposed to be here, not at the top of the world. I was supposed to be with Gentleman Jack, riding across the Plains to Netherby Scar and to Grandmother. I'd counted down to Day Zero for so long, I couldn't believe there never was any gold.

The number zero is just the way it looks. It's a big hole filled with emptiness.

The Cottage

UP WE WENT, jolting and lurching; there was nothing but Up in this place. We rode through a valley of twilight and indigo; we rode to where the pink rocks shone with sunset. I hadn't known you could see sunset and twilight at the same time. I looked for something I knew. But it was just the Judge, the horse, and me, and I didn't know any of us.

Gentleman Jack had told me what the people in Blue Roses would say about him. Sometimes the people were called the Rosati, because they were crazy about roses.

The Rosati would say Gentleman Jack was bad. They'd say they had to rescue me from him. But it had been Gentleman Jack who'd rescued me from them.

Where was the jail? That's where I could be with Gentleman Jack. I wished the Judge would say something, so I could tell him I wanted to go to the jail and be with Gentleman Jack. But three breaths and a swallow had passed, and the Judge remained silent.

The light faded. The pink stone had turned gray by the time we slid off the horse. The Judge handed the reins to a man who appeared from the shadows. We walked up steps carved into the rock. They were steep and juddery, sticking out in all the wrong places. Now up a twist of steps and around a bend, now toward a glint of glass. The glass was in a window, the window was in a cottage.

How did I know that word, Cottage?

"Hungry?" The Judge spoke at last.

"I want to go to jail."

"Heavens, no," said the Judge. "You can't go to jail."

"I can," I said. "I've done lots of bad things. I want to be in the same jail as Gentleman Jack." No, not the same jail. I wanted to be in the same cell as Gentleman Jack. A jail was a building full of cages, and a cell was one of those cages.

If I was in a cell with Gentleman Jack, I could escape with him. "There's no jail that can hold me." That's what he always said. We'd be together; we'd make a plan and together we'd escape.

"You're too young to go to jail," said the Judge, "even if you've done bad things. How old are you? About ten?"

"About eleven," I said.

I was wild, and you can't put a wild person in a cottage. I would be sharp and wild, and they would send me to jail.

How did I know this house was a cottage? For one thing, the roof started high on one side and came down low on the other. It slanted almost to the ground. It was a cottage because there were little outbursts of roof everywhere, and windows beneath every outburst, and panes of glass in the windows. The panes of glass were shaped like diamonds.

Chimneys rose from different roof-bursts, but no smoke blew from any of them. That was bad. Gentleman Jack had told me about

Grandmother's house, and everything about it was good. One good thing was that it had eleven chimneys, and during the winter, all the chimneys were warm and puffing out smoke.

That was the right kind of house to have. Who wanted such a small house and one where the two sides didn't match? Who wanted a house that was painted a color like a dream?

"It's yellow," said the dagger. "There's no color like a dream."

But it wasn't yellow. Yellow was a terrible color. Yellow was muddy ribbons and revolver spit.

Everything was wrong. I should have been with Gentleman Jack and our five bricks of gold. We should have been arriving at Grandmother's house, looking at the eleven chimneys and the eleven puffs of smoke.

I pictured it all so clearly. We'd go through Grandmother's door, into a big entrance called a foyer. We'd walk over black-and-white marble. Then we'd come to Grandmother's sitting room. It was called a sitting room, but she would stand up when she saw us. She would come toward us, her arms outstretched. She would put a hand on my cheek and her hand would feel like silk.

"Skin doesn't feel like silk," said the dagger. "Skin feels like skin."

But I knew what Gentleman Jack meant. I'd never touched silk, but I could guess how it would feel.

Then Grandmother would put her hand on Gentleman Jack's cheek and she would say what she always said when he came home.

"This is my boy, returned from the road," she would say. "This is my boy, bright as the sun." Those were the words that showed she loved him.

The stone steps turned into wooden steps, which led to a porch. A carpet lay outside the door. There was writing on the carpet and a picture of a sunflower. I knew Grandmother had carpets inside her house, but I had not known you could have carpets outside a house.

The Judge clicked a key into the door. I knew about doors and keys. Gentleman Jack was interested in them. He liked to open doors that locked him in, he liked to open doors that locked him out. There were no doors to the hideout, of course. There were no doors to a cave in the side of a cliff at the bottom of a ravine.

Click. Now the door was open. It was thick, which meant it guarded the house. Click. Now it was bolted.

The cottage had a foyer, but the floor wasn't made of black-and-white marble. It was made of planks of indigo wood. On it lay a blue carpet with flowers. Wood and carpets were never as good as marble.

There was a curve in the wall, with a little table pressed into the curve. There was a drawer in the table. The Judge opened the drawer. It held a single key. The Judge dropped his key in the drawer. Now there were two keys.

Now it was full.

They had a whole drawer just for their keys. They had a whole table just for a drawer. They had a whole room, which was just for keeping a table, which was just for keeping a drawer, which was just for keeping keys.

There was another door on the other side of the foyer. It was set with a pane of glass. You could look through to a shining stretch of corridor.

"You should know," said the Judge, "that my wife has not been well."

I hadn't imagined the Judge would have a wife. Would she look like him, all cliffs and scratches? I'd show her I was wild. I'd show her

I was dangerous. She'd tell the Judge to send me away, and I'd run and walk and crawl back to the hideout. I wouldn't think about the pinto, I wouldn't think about the yellow ribbons. I'd think about walking and running on my own wild feet. I'd go down the mountain and through the indigo trees, across the Jordan River, over the red clay road.

I'd save myself, then I'd save Gentleman Jack. But first I had to meet the Judge's wife, who was not well.

"Mrs. del Salto will want to know what to call you," said the Judge.

"She can call me the Robber Girl," I said.

The Judge led me down the corridor; we stopped at an opening. "She prefers the parlor," said the Judge. There was no door to the parlor.

It was so dark, I could hardly see the person inside. She was all in black, and the only reason I could see her at all was because she was walking up and down. Her skirts flittered away the dark. The Judge knocked even though there was no door. He knocked at the pale, gleaming wood that surrounded the opening.

The flittering stopped. "I've brought a guest," said the Judge.

"Not a guest," said Mrs. del Salto. "Don't tell me you brought a guest."

That was not what Grandmother would say when we went to her house. First she'd say what she always said to Gentleman Jack. "This is my boy, returned from the road. This is my boy, bright as the sun."

Then she'd touch me with her hand, which would feel like silk, and she'd say, "This is my girl, returned from the road. This is my girl, bright as a star."

The Judge laid his hand on my back. He pressed me into the parlor. In a big, fancy house, like Grandmother's, it was called a sitting room, but in a cottage it was called a parlor. Grandmother's sitting room was bright with crimson velvet chairs and sofas, but the parlor in a cottage was dark.

The Judge stepped into the room. He made something hiss; two lamps burst into light. They hung on the wall, above the fireplace.

"I like the dark," said Mrs. del Salto.

But now I could see the parlor. I saw lace curtains and fat, heavy cushions. I saw a chair embroidered with pale flowers. I knew the word Embroidered because of the embroidered initials on Gentleman Jack's gloves. But how did I know the word Tapestry, which was what another chair was made of?

How did I know the words Tapestry and Cottage? It was as though I'd discovered an extra pocket filled with foreign coins. I knew about foreign coins because Doubtful Mittie had one from the place he came from. It wasn't all one color, like coins in the Territories. It had a silver rim and a gold-colored middle.

Now everything was light, except Mrs. del Salto. She wore all dark; she absorbed the light.

"You brought a child," said Mrs. del Salto.

The Judge said nothing. He bent over the fireplace, laying wood on the andirons, scooping on coal.

"Don't tell me you brought a child."

The Judge didn't have to tell her. She could see for herself. Mrs. del Salto was like my mother. She didn't want me.

"She has nowhere else to go," said the Judge.

That wasn't true. I could go to jail, I could go to the hideout. I'd meet Rough Ricky there and we'd make plans to rescue Gentleman Jack. But the Judge wouldn't let me go to jail, and neither of them knew about the hideout.

The fireplace bloomed with flame. The coal shifted and popped. The coal was noisier than I was. Gentleman Jack had said I must not be noisy in Grandmother's house or I would disturb Grandmother.

That was the way I liked it. I'd had a lot of practice being quiet. It went with my Affliction. When your Affliction makes you unable to speak until spoken to, it means you can't talk about the time before Gentleman Jack rescued you.

"Talking will make you remember," said the dagger.

"Remembering would be a betrayal of Gentleman Jack," I said.

"She needs a place to stay," said the Judge. "It seems she's been living with the Gentlemen."

His voice leaned on the word Gentlemen. You could tell he didn't think it was the right word for Gentleman Jack and his men.

Now Mrs. del Salto would tell me Gentleman Jack was bad and that I shouldn't talk to him. Gentleman Jack had told me over and over what the people in Blue Roses would say.

"What will they try to make you believe?" That's what Gentleman Jack would say.

"They'll tell me you should be caught and hanged. They'll tell me I should live in a regular house and go to school." That's what I would say.

But my mother was from Blue Roses, and she was the one who was bad. I'd been five, or maybe six, and she left me in the wilderness to die.

Gentleman Jack had saved me just in time; he saved me when the buzzards were already circling overhead. I didn't remember it, though. That's why I was sometimes glad about my Affliction. It made me mostly unable to talk, which meant I couldn't talk myself into remembering my mother, who wanted me dead.

But Mrs. del Salto said nothing. She stood so still and for so long that her dress rusted around her. She absorbed all the light of the wall lamps, of the fire in the fireplace. She shrugged. I knew what that meant. She didn't care about me.

It was good she didn't want me, because I didn't want her. I didn't want anything belonging to her, especially not the cottage with its door-knobs and keys.

"The child is picking at her skin," said Mrs. del Salto.

It was my thumb, which was rough and scratchy. I could make the skin come off in flakes. Sometimes I could make it come off in strips.

It was good Mrs. del Salto was hard. It was good she wasn't like Grandmother. I knew what Grandmother looked like because I had a photograph of her. I knew she'd be soft, like this room—like the parlor—all pearl and cream and lace and feathers. She'd be like the wing of a dove.

"The girl may stay one night and no longer," said Mrs. del Salto. "And not in Magda's room or Isaac's room."

"In the attic, then," said the Judge.

"We needn't bother with a bath," said Mrs. del Salto. "Not for just one night."

"Is she to sleep in those britches?" said the Judge.

"It wouldn't be the first time," said Mrs. del Salto.

That was a smart decision. She wouldn't like what would happen if she tried to take my britches. My britches were one of the things I cared about. I also cared about the dagger in the sheath around my waist and about the watch in my pocket. It had belonged to Grandmother when she was young. Gentleman Jack gave it to me because Grandmother's photograph was inside the watch and I liked to look at it. The watch didn't tick, but that was all right. We'd get it fixed in Netherby Scar.

I cared about Gentleman Jack, too—I cared about him most of all— but I didn't care about too many other things.

I was glad to leave the parlor, with its glass windows and the lamps that were set with little half-moon handles. That was so you could turn them on and off. It was all too fragile, the glass that could be broken, the lamps that were too easy to turn off.

I followed the Judge down the corridor to some stairs. There was a carpet on the stairs. They had a carpet outdoors and a carpet on the stairs. I'd been surprised by the outdoor carpet, and now I was surprised by the stairs carpet. After the stairs came a landing with a polished floor and doors and doorknobs. The doors had closed-up faces, but the Judge opened one of them. It grinned onto a twist of stairs. Up we went to the attic, where the floors were painted white. Then into another room, where again the Judge made fire hiss into lamps on the walls.

The attic room was all slants and curls and funny bits of ceiling. There was nothing in it except a cupboard and a table. On the table sat a miniature house. Its roof came as high as my head. I'd seen this house before. I'd seen the roof-bursts, the diamond windows, the way one side of the roof slanted almost to the ground.

The miniature house was exactly like the cottage.

I wanted to ask about it. I wanted to ask how big it was, but that was stupid. It was as big as it was big. Or maybe it was as small as it was small. Maybe I should really ask, How small is it?

The Judge answered the question I hadn't asked. "The dollhouse is one-twelfth the size of the cottage."

"I don't care how big it is," I said.

"Everyone asks," said the Judge. But I wasn't everyone.

Now the Judge was leaving. He was going to leave me in the room, he said. He was going to call me when it was time for dinner.

Once he left, I could run away. I couldn't go out the front door because I'd have to pass the parlor, where Mrs. del Salto was busy being not well. But an indigo tree grew just outside the window. It would be easy to scramble down. Indigo trees have scaly bark, which is good for scrambling. I'd wait until after dinner, though. It wasn't that I couldn't feed myself if I went to the hideout. Of course not. I'd caught squirrels lots of times. I knew how to skin and cook them. I knew how to catch a trout and kill it with a stone.

But it would take hours to get back to the hideout, even on my wild feet.

I would let myself look at the dollhouse. I would let myself have dinner. Then I would leave.

The Dollhouse

THE DOLLHOUSE WAS PRESSED into a bit of wall that wasn't exactly straight but wasn't exactly a corner. It wasn't the kind of corner that made a sharp point with another wall. It wasn't the kind of corner that was in a hurry. It was a place where two walls curled softly into a third. The dollhouse sat on a low table that had been cut to fit into the non-corner.

There were real steps going up to the dollhouse, and there was a real carpet outside the door, with a sunflower, and there was a real door with a real doorknob. The doorknob was no bigger than an apple seed. A human-size person couldn't wrap her fingers around the doorknob. A human-size person would have to use her fingernails. She'd have to click her nails behind the doorknob and pull.

I clicked my fingernails around the apple-seed doorknob. It was made of real metal. It was set solidly into the door. It was a good door and a good doorknob.

I peered through the door into the foyer. Now I knew more about foyers than before. A foyer was where you kept a key.

In the foyer was a little table. In the table was a little drawer. But I couldn't see past the foyer into the rest of the dollhouse. I stepped back so I could see the whole. Maybe there was another door, a bigger door. A seam ran down the front of the house, top to bottom.

I plucked at it. The whole front of the dollhouse was a door. The right side swung open, the left side swung open. In the right side of the dollhouse was the dollhouse door. So there were really three doors, two that opened the front of the dollhouse so regular-size people could look in, and a small one set into the right-hand door. That was the dollhouse door. It was one-twelfth the size of a regular door, so the dolls could walk in and out.

"*Dolls can't walk!*" said the dagger.

I knew that, but I was just imagining it. I was pretending to imagine it.

"*Think about real things!*" The dagger had a real-thing kind of mind.

I saw into the three rooms along the front of the dollhouse. The smallest was the foyer, in the middle. It was exactly like the real cottage: the table, the drawer in the table, the knob on the drawer.

"*The drawer won't open,*" said the dagger.

Would there be a key in the drawer?

"*There won't be a key,*" said the dagger.

I reached my hand into the foyer. I ran my finger along the top of the table. The real cottage wasn't dusty, but the dollhouse was dusty. The knob on the drawer was too tiny to fit your fingernails around. I licked my finger and touched it to the front of the drawer. It stuck to my finger and popped open. I knew from counting money that something light, like paper, will stick to a wet finger.

You had to count money precisely. Otherwise Gentleman Jack got mad.

"I told you there's no key," said the dagger.

I hadn't said there would be a key. The whole point of having the drawer open and empty was that now I could get a key. I could fill up the drawer.

"You can't fill it up when we're leaving tonight," said the dagger.

The dagger was right. I couldn't get a key before tonight, which was when we'd leave.

To the left of the foyer was the parlor. Now, with the front of the house peeled away, I saw the whole parlor at once. It was like the wing of a dove—the embroidered cushions; the feathery chair; the mantel-piece, which had cream-and-rose tiles.

I hadn't noticed the tiles in the regular-size house. They were painted to look like flowers. I saw the dollhouse room better than I'd seen the real room. That was because it was small and concentrated. It was distilled. Gentleman Jack had told me about distillation, how you take a liquid and boil it so that at the end there's less liquid but it's purer. It's more truly its own self.

The dollhouse parlor was the distillation of the big parlor. It was the distillation of feather gleam and dove wing.

If this was a dollhouse, where were the dolls?

"There are no dolls," said the dagger.

"You said the drawer wouldn't open," I said. "But it opened."

"You expected a key in the drawer," said the dagger. "But there was no key."

"I didn't expect a key."

The attic of the dollhouse was almost as high as my chin. It was identical to the attic in the cottage. There was the same cupboard, the same unhurried corner, the same table, and on the table—on the dollhouse table—sat another dollhouse.

It was a dollhouse of the dollhouse. Who could have made it? You would need elf fingers to make such a tiny house. It must be one-twelfth the size of one-twelfth the size of a people house. *"Inside that dollhouse,"* I said, *"there might be another dollhouse. And inside that dollhouse, there might be another dollhouse."* Did the dollhouses keep getting smaller until they were too small to see?

"Ridiculous!" said the dagger.

The regular dollhouse had suddenly become big, and the dollhouse's dollhouse was the thing that was small. I opened the dollhouse cupboard. In it was a bed—a bed in a cupboard! On the bed lay two dolls.

I sat on the floor and laid the dolls on my knee. They were a man doll and a woman doll. They lay with their eyes closed, as though they were dead.

Dolls could not be dead. If I thought the dolls were dead, that also meant they'd been alive. But that was not a sharp, cold thought. I should only have cold thoughts with sharp edges.

Dolls were just dolls. They weren't alive and they weren't dead.

Their faces were dusty. I would dust them, even though they were just dolls. It was all right to want to see their faces. I could be wild and still want to see them. I wiped their faces with the hem of my shirt, but they were still dirty. I licked my finger and drew it over their eyelids. A person should not have dust in his eyes.

"Dolls aren't people," said the dagger.

They weren't people. They were dolls and they were tame. I was a robber girl and I was wild. But I could brush their clothes and still be wild.

I brushed the woman doll's dark-pink dress. The dress had red trim, which was soft and smooth. It was satin.

Satin. The word came to me from the foreign-coin pocket of words. The words were foreign, but I knew I'd used them. I'd spent time in that foreign country.

"Stop remembering the Before Time!" said the dagger. "Remembering is a betrayal of Gentleman Jack."

But how could I stop words from coming into my head? I brushed the man doll's jacket and trousers; they were striped with blue. I brushed his waistcoat and his blue string tie.

"Remembering isn't real," said the dagger.

If they were alive, I'd be a giant to them. I'd be a giant in their world of apple-seed doorknobs and dollhouses within dollhouses within dollhouses.

"Stop thinking they might be alive!" said the dagger.

They weren't alive, which meant it was all right to look beneath their clothes. The woman doll wore a petticoat, and beneath that was some white gauzy stuff that ruffled around each ankle.

The woman doll's foot was attached to her leg with a pin that ran through her ankle. It meant her ankle could bend. Same with the man doll. I looked under their clothes and worked all their joints. It was wonderful how everything could bend, hips and shoulders, elbows and knees.

I sat them upright in front of me. They could sit by themselves. The father doll's eyes opened. The mother doll's eyes opened.

"You're calling them Father Doll and Mother Doll," said the dagger.

It was because of their eyes, I thought. With their eyes open, they looked like a father and a mother.

"Calling them Father and Mother is like playing with them," said the dagger.

Robber girls didn't play with dolls, but it wasn't playing to notice the dolls' eyes looking at me. To notice that the mother doll's eyes were blue and the father doll's eyes were brown.

"Think about Gentleman Jack instead," said the dagger. "What did he say to do if you were captured?"

But I'd already done all that. I'd told the Judge I had no name. I wished the Judge had asked me about the hideout so I could have said there was no hideout. That would have been obeying Gentleman Jack and made him happy.

"*What happens after that?*" said the dagger.

"I go to the hideout," I said.

"*And then what?*" said the dagger.

"*Rough Ricky and I rescue Gentleman Jack.*"

"*What if Rough Ricky's not at the hideout?*"

"I go to Grandmother's house," I said.

"*How do you get to Grandmother's house?*" said the dagger.

"*I follow the railroad tracks to Netherby Scar.*" I reached into my pocket and took out the pocket watch. "*But I will not be able to find Grandmother's house by telling people her name.*"

"*Because you don't know her name,*" said the dagger.

"*Because I don't know her name.*" Knowing her name would be dangerous. If I knew it, I could tell someone—someone like the Judge. I could tell him even if I didn't mean to. That was why I didn't know Grandmother's name, or my own name, either. I only knew Gentleman Jack's name because of the Gentlemen calling him by it all the time.

"*But I have the watch,*" I said. "*I can show it to anyone in Netherby Scar and they'll recognize it. They'll help me find Grandmother's house.*"

The watch covered my whole palm. It had a picture on the lid, called an engraving. The dagger had told me. It knew about engraving because metal is a thing you engrave and the dagger knew all about metal.

The engraving was a bird in flight, whirring like a star. The picture was called an emblem. It was Grandmother's emblem, which was how the people in Netherby Scar would know I was looking for her house.

Later, we'd fix the watch and then it would tick away into the future. In the future, there would be no more Day Zero.

I'd open the lid, I'd look at the photograph of Grandmother. But then my head jerked up, away from the watch. I'd heard a voice; the voice had come from the mother doll.

"She is the one," said the mother doll. Her mouth didn't open and her face didn't change, but the voice came from her.

"She is the one," said the father doll. His mouth didn't open, his face didn't change. "Even though she doesn't look like Magda."

"She can have wild black hair and still be our girl," said the mother doll. "She can have a thin face and pale eyes and still be our girl." That made it sound as though they were talking about me.

"When we heard her voice," said the father doll, "we knew she was our girl."

"Her voice has the sound of piping in it," said the mother doll. They weren't talking about me after all. My voice was the opposite of piping.

"The dolls are talking!" I said.

"Dolls don't talk!" said the dagger.

But they were. And since the dagger could hear what I heard, why couldn't it hear the dolls?

Someone knocked on the door, which made me jump. I wasn't used to knocking because of having no doors in the hideout.

"May I come in?" said the Judge.

"Put the watch away," said the dagger. *"He'll think you stole it."*

I shoved it into my pocket, even though the watch was one of the few things I knew for sure hadn't been stolen. It belonged to Grandmother, but she let me have it so I could look at her photograph. I'd never seen her real face, her in-person face.

The Judge came in, looked at me, looked at the dolls.

"It's been a long time," he said, "since anyone has played with the dolls."

"I am a robber girl," I said. "I don't play with dolls."

"If you're not playing," he said, "then perhaps you won't mind if I invite you downstairs."

"I don't mind being invited," I said. But that didn't mean I had to go.

"Mrs. del Salto and I thought you might want something to eat," he said.

"Iron and carbon don't need to eat," said the dagger.

"I'd also like to ask you a question," said the Judge. "It will be easier over dinner."

I didn't like the way the Judge talked, which was tricky. Why not just invite me instead of wondering if I would mind being invited? Why not just ask me a question instead of saying he wanted to ask me a question?

"I don't answer questions," I said.

"You answered my question about your name," said the Judge.

"I said I had no name."

The Judge didn't exactly respond. "You must be tired and hungry," he said. "You crossed the River Jordan, which is deep and wide. But there's milk and honey on the other side." He held out his hand. "Milk and honey."

I didn't take his hand, but I got up. I looked behind me, just once. There was the dollhouse painted the color I couldn't name—the color that was not yellow—which was also the color of the people cottage. The dolls sat on the floor.

"She's the one," said the mother doll. "She brushed the dust from our eyes."

The Judge didn't turn around at the mother doll's voice. Maybe they were too small for him to hear. Or maybe he was too big. Look at the way his shadow splatted all over one side of the room. He was very big.

But the dagger was small and it heard what I heard. Why couldn't it hear the dolls' voices?

"*Because dolls don't have voices,*" said the dagger.

"She brushed the dust from our eyes and she has piping in her voice," said the father doll. "That means she's our girl."

The Judge walked ahead of me, calling over his shoulder about milk and honey. I followed him; I left the dolls behind.

A Democratic Table

I KNEW SOME OF THE HOUSE ALREADY. I knew the attic steps, grinning up at me with their white teeth. I knew the second-floor landing, with its gleaming floorboards and closed-faced doors. I knew the carpet on the stairs. It was held in place by heavy metal rods lying right where the step turned up to meet the next step. I knew the dove room, all fat and feathery.

I knew the corridor that led to the foyer, but we turned before we reached it. Here was the part of the house I hadn't seen. The Judge led me through a blue-and-gold room, toward a door he said was the kitchen door. But it had no doorknob. How did you open it?

"You push!" said the dagger.

The door swung open. It had no knob or lock. Who would want a door like that, with no knob and no lock? The best doors had locks.

Here in the kitchen, everything was steam and sniff and gleam. It smelled hot and gold. It smelled the way the word Grandmother felt in my mouth. The word Grandmother always fit exactly right on the soft middle of my tongue. I liked holding it there, warm and round.

The kitchen smelled like Grandmother, but it didn't look like Grandmother's kitchen. Gentleman Jack had told me so much about Grandmother's house that I could see it in my mind. Grandmother had a red-and-blue carpet on her kitchen floor. It was called an oriental carpet. She had a blue enamel stove and bright pots and pans.

But except for some copper pans, this kitchen had no colors; it was all black and white and silver.

"*Silver's a color,*" said the dagger.

The floor was plain indigo wood; the stove was black with curved silver legs.

"*Silver is my color,*" said the dagger.

Mrs. del Salto was the most black-and-white of all, with her pale face and pale apron and black hair and rusty-crow dress.

She set three plates on a table covered with a white cloth. Gentleman Jack had described the tablecloths at Grandmother's house. They were damask, he said, which was a fancy kind of material. You could turn damask one way and it would show one color, and then you could turn it another way and it would show another color. But Gentleman Jack had never said Grandmother's tablecloths had fringes dripping off the ends, like these tablecloths. He never said they were too white for food, like these tablecloths.

I didn't sit. Mrs. del Salto set knives and forks beside the plates.

"*They're not real knives,*" said the dagger. "*They have no edges.*"

Mrs. del Salto set a pie on the table. The golden smell came from the pie.

"Sit down." The Judge was already sitting, and so was Mrs. del Salto.

"Even a robber girl may be hungry," said the Judge.

I didn't want to sit at the table. The tablecloth was too white. I didn't want to pick up the knife. It had no edges. I walked around the table because I didn't know where to sit.

"The table has four equal sides," said the Judge. "It's a democratic table, which means you may sit wherever you like."

I sat opposite Mrs. del Salto. The Judge cut the pie. Up drifted feathers of steam. It was not the kind of pie that cut neatly. I didn't know how to eat this pie.

"Chicken pie on Thursday," said the Judge. I'd never had chicken pie. Once Doubtful Mittie had caught a muskrat and brought it to a lady he knew, who made a pie out of it. But it didn't smell like this pie.

It was Thursday, but it was also Day Zero, the longest Day Zero in the world.

I liked eating the way I ate in the hideout, which was alone. I had my own corner and my own bowl and my own tin cup and my own knife, which was also the dagger. I ate like the Gentlemen. If there was meat, we skewered it with a knife and ate it. If there was gravy, we skewered the meat and dunked it in the gravy. But this meat was already dunked.

I tried to do what the Judge did. He picked up his knife and fork. He used his fork to spear the chunks of meat. He used his knife to cut them. He used the edge of his fork to cut the piecrust.

"A fork?" said the dagger. "To cut!"

I couldn't eat the way the Judge did. I wrapped all my fingers around my fork until I noticed the Judge balanced his fork on the edge of one finger. I tried to balance it like that, but the fork tilted to the side and off came a bit of crust, splatting the white tablecloth.

I set the knife and fork on the plate. I looked at the plate, not at the brown splatter on white. I'd only eat with the dagger in Grandmother's house. I'd never make a brown splat on her damask tablecloth. I looked at the terrible knife and fork: they'd made me make the splat. They were silver, with heavy scrolls on the handles.

"*Silver is a good color,*" said the dagger. "*Iron and carbon make the color of silver.*"

No one said anything about the gravy splat. I should never have tried to eat. Not in front of people.

"Aren't you hungry?" said the Judge. "You're nothing but skin and bone."

"Where are the milk and honey?" I said.

"Milk and honey?" The Judge had forgotten about them.

"Because of the River Jordan," I said. You wouldn't need a fork for milk and honey.

"Ah!" said the Judge, and in a series of foldings and unfoldings he set in front of me a yellow cup, a plump brown pot, a basket of bread, a plate of butter, and a small empty plate. I knew about all of them except the small plate.

The cup was for the milk, the pot was for the honey, the butter was for the bread, the bread was for the butter and also for the honey—

But I didn't know what the small plate was for.

The Judge gave himself another small plate, which meant he had two plates and I had two plates. One big and one little. The Judge's big plate was almost empty, except for leftover crumbs and gravy. Mrs. del Salto had just one plate. It was full of chicken pie.

She saw me staring. "Don't mind me," she said. "I eat only ashes and salt."

"Now, Monica!" said the Judge.

I looked at her plate. *"Where are the ashes?"* I said.

"Where's the salt?" said the dagger.

"Now, Marcus," said Mrs. del Salto, and that was that.

Everything was quiet, and I still didn't know what to do with the little plate.

The Judge reached for one of the knives with no edges. It was short and curly.

"Useless," said the dagger.

The Judge reached for the plate of butter and cut a piece about as wide as my thumb. He put the piece on his little plate. He put a piece of bread on the little plate. Last, he cut a bit of butter from the piece on his plate and put it on the bread. So there was the big piece of butter on the butter plate; there was the small piece of butter, the one the Judge had just cut, on the smaller plate; and then there was the still-smaller bit of butter, cut from the smaller piece on his plate, which was cut from the big plate of butter—

"Why not put it right on the bread?" said the dagger.

I didn't want to look at the stain on the tablecloth, but my eyes made me look. I took the yellow cup. It had a handle, like my tin cup at the hideout, but it was the kind of cup that could break. I wrapped both hands around the middle.

When I tilted the cup to drink, the side of the cup cast a shadow on the milk.

"If you will permit me," said the Judge, "I should like to ask you a question."

What a strange place this was. It was strange when people asked about asking questions instead of just asking them. It was like cutting the butter and putting it on a plate, and then cutting the butter on the plate and putting it on the bread. Why not just put the butter right on the bread?

Why not just ask?

The shadow of the cup on the milk turned the milk a color that was not exactly yellow. The shadow turned the milk the color of the cottage. I took a sip. It was cold and creamy. I took another sip. I would find a word for the color of the cottage.

"Or perhaps," said the Judge, "it is more of a request."

The Gentlemen never talked about talking or requesting. They just talked.

I drank my milk, which tasted just the way the cottage looked, thick and comforting. I drank down the milk.

I drank down the cottage.

"Gentleman Jack will go to trial," said the Judge. "We will try him for the murder of the Federal Marshal."

I didn't like the word Murder. I didn't want to remember the sound of the gun or how the Marshal had sat on his horse for a long time, holding his stomach.

"I should like to request," said the Judge, "that you testify at Gentleman Jack's trial."

I waited for him to request it, but he didn't. I set down the yellow cup. The word Murder didn't go with a yellow cup. I couldn't drink down the cottage when the word Murder was in the air.

"You do realize," said Mrs. del Salto, "that the child has no idea what you're talking about."

The Judge hadn't realized. "A trial," said the Judge, "is when some people get together to decide if another person has committed a crime.

If they determine he has, then the Judge decides what his punishment is to be.

"As you know," said the Judge, "Gentleman Jack killed Federal Marshal Starling. That's a crime."

Mrs. del Salto reached for one of the candles. She wore a ring, and even though the stone in it was dark, the candle made it flicker with lights.

Mrs. del Salto pinched the candle flame between her thumb and finger.

I knew it was an opal. The Indigo Heart was filled with opals. You could dig them up just as easily as you could dig for gold.

Opals were for good luck. I wished I had an opal now. I wished I had some good luck.

I wondered if my mother had sat at a democratic table, pinching out everything that was light. Trying to pinch me out. Pinching at everything that was light and life.

"Monica!" said the Judge.

"It's too bright," said Mrs. del Salto. She pinched out the other candle. Her fingertips were stronger than flame. It was better that way. There was still a lamp burning from the wall, but now it was harder to see the stain.

The Judge turned away from Mrs. del Salto and her strong fingertips. He looked at me instead. "Gentleman Jack killed the Federal Marshal only six months ago," he said. "You must remember it."

"I like remembering it," said the dagger.

I poked at the skin of my thumb. I peeled off a strip, I made it bleed. Now that Mrs. del Salto had pinched out the candles, my blood came out black.

"It was the best day!" said the dagger.

"When people see a crime, we ask them to tell us what happened," said the Judge. "It's called testifying."

I licked my thumb. I swallowed down the taste of blood. I couldn't stop remembering the Federal Marshal, and I had to tell myself I was tasting my blood, not his. My blood was black, but it tasted like pennies, which were copper.

"Usually we don't ask children to testify, but this is a special case."

When someone asks you to testify, you shouldn't be drinking milk. Your stomach turns the milk sour, and then it burns you, on the inside.

"We don't tolerate murder," said the Judge, "and the murder of a federal marshal is especially serious. We do everything we can to bring the murderer to justice."

Your stomach does that so you know what you're feeling. The name for this feeling is Worry.

I spoke to the dagger instead of the Judge. "I'd never tell anyone about the Federal Marshal," I said. "Gentleman Jack knows that, doesn't he?"

"Other people have betrayed him," said the dagger with a kind of shrug in its voice. "Maybe someone betrayed him for milk in a yellow cup."

"I have to see Gentleman Jack," I said.

"Pardon?" said the Judge.

"Right now," I said. "I have to see Gentleman Jack."

What if Gentleman Jack thought I'd betray him? That would be the worst thing in the world.

"Not now," said the Judge.

"Now," I said.

"Tomorrow," said the Judge.

"Now," I said.

"Even the Sheriff goes to sleep," said the Judge. "The jail is locked; I don't have a key."

"Can't you see?" said Mrs. del Salto. "The child isn't going to testify." At least she understood me, in her pinchy way.

"Is that true?" said the Judge. "Are you not going to testify?"

"No," I said. Or should I have said Yes? Yes, I was not going to testify? No, I was not going to testify? Even the Judge's questions were tricky.

"Let's get the child to bed," said Mrs. del Salto.

To bed? But I'd just said I wouldn't testify. Wouldn't they send me away?

"They think they can persuade you," said the dagger. *"We can stay the night. It will be easier to find the hideout tomorrow."*

"After I see Gentleman Jack," I said, *"but before the blizzard."*

I knew the house now. The Judge didn't need to bring me to the attic. But he did and he brought some bedclothes with him. Bedclothes is a stupid name. A bed doesn't wear clothes, and anyway, there was no bed.

It turned out I was wrong. The Judge opened the door to the cupboard and said, "Lo!" Inside the cupboard was a bed. Even the dagger was surprised. We'd seen the cupboard-bed in the dollhouse, but neither of us had thought there'd be a cupboard-bed in the regular house. I could tell the dagger wanted to dislike the idea, but it was hard to dislike. It was so neat and compact. So hidden away and high off the floor, like the nest of a bird.

There was a separate space at the end of the cupboard with a rod running across the top. *"For hanging things,"* said the dagger.

The Judge put the clothes on the bed. Now it was dressed. "Ready?"

I nodded. I was ready to be a bird in a nest. I was ready to turn round and round in the nest to make it fit my shape. But first there came a big noise, which made me jump. The Judge wasn't startled, though. Instead, he made a quarter turn, so he was staring at the blank wall behind the dollhouse; and the sound kept going; and after a while, I realized that the sound was made by bells; and that the bells were low and sweet; and that, actually, the bells made a tune; and then at last I heard the Judge muttering something that went to the rhythm of the tune. And now I wasn't startled, but I was still ready to be a bird in a nest.

And then the bells stopped ringing and the Judge stopped muttering and everything went back to normal.

"Not exactly normal!" said the dagger.

On the windowsill was a lamp made to look like a candle. The Judge showed me how to turn it on and off with a switch. It wasn't filled with fire, just with electricity, which waggled in the glass like a fishtail.

But electricity is dangerous. It can turn you into lightning and kill you.

The Judge folded himself out the door. It clicked behind him. I pulled at the door, just to make sure. It didn't open. The door was thick, which meant it guarded the attic. That was good. Without a door, you couldn't have a doorknob. Without a doorknob, you couldn't open or shut a door. The doorknob was heavy; that was good, too.

I fit my palm over the knob, which was a roundness of brass. The Judge's hand would have been too big for it, because it fit perfectly into the cup of my hand. It was an egg in a nest.

"It's not an egg," said the dagger. "It's brass!"

It's better to shut a door than to open it, but I opened the door just so I could shut it again. I liked listening to the way it clicked.

"I know all about metals," said the dagger.

Below the knob was a little handle. It was shaped like the number 8, or maybe it was like a peanut in its shell.

I turned the peanut so it lay on its side. It made a different click from the doorknob click. I turned the doorknob and pushed the door. It didn't open. The little peanut knob was a bolt. I clicked it open and shut it a few times. Yes, when the peanut stood upright, you could open the door. When it lay on its side, you couldn't.

This was not like the hideout, where there were no doors or knobs or bolts. You could open a door with a doorknob, but you could also close it; you could lock it with a bolt. You could lock other people out, you could lock yourself in.

"It's a betrayal of Gentleman Jack to think the cottage is better than the hideout."

"I never said that!" I said.

"It's what you mean."

It was not. The dagger was made of carbon and iron, which made it un-bendy. Sometimes it was so un-bendy that it couldn't understand certain things.

"Gentleman Jack likes loyalty and he likes bolts," I said. "It's not one or the other."

I flipped the peanut onto its side. I locked the Judge out. I locked myself in.

The Three Tasks

✝ THE DOLLS WERE SITTING on the floor where I'd left them. The mother doll spoke as though no time had passed. "We're going to give you a name. A special name for a girl with piping in her voice."

"Gentleman Jack's going to give me a name," I said, even though a robber girl shouldn't talk to dolls. And anyway, I had no piping.

"*Stop talking to nobody!*" said the dagger. "*You're making my edges go cold!*"

"Your voice tells us your name," said the mother doll. "Your voice tells us your name is Starling. Starlings can whistle and warble and make smooth liquid sounds."

I could whistle, but I couldn't warble or make smooth liquid sounds. My voice was as un-bendy as the dagger. And anyway, whistling was bad luck.

"*If you talk to nobody,*" said the dagger, "*that means you're going crazy.*"

"It's a good name," said the mother doll. "Starlings fight for their families. A starling is a warrior bird."

"*I am iron, with carbon added,*" said the dagger. "*If I didn't have enough carbon, I would be too soft. Then I might go crazy.*"

"You brushed the dust from our eyes," said the father doll. The dolls could open and close their eyes. It was good to have eyes that opened and closed.

"You sat us up," said the mother doll.

"If I had too much carbon," said the dagger, "I would be too hard. Then I might go crazy."

"When you're made of china," said the father doll, "your heart is made of china."

"When a person has a china heart," said the mother doll, "it can easily break."

"But I am just right," said the dagger.

"There will be no danger of broken hearts," said the father doll. "Not now that Starling is here to complete the tasks."

"Tasks?" I said. Sometimes Gentleman Jack gave me tasks. It showed him I was useful.

"Tasks," said the father doll. "Like in a fairy tale, you know."

But I didn't know. "If Gentleman Jack asks me to perform a task, I do. I don't listen to anyone else."

"There are three tasks," said the mother doll.

I didn't know about fairy tales, but I knew about tasks, and I knew that two was the right number of tasks. Two was the number of tasks Grandmother gave Gentleman Jack and his no-account brother. Whoever could finish the tasks would get to have her empire. They went like this:

> Fetch unto me the mountain's gold,
> To build our city fair.
> Fetch unto me the wingless bird,
> And I will make you my heir.

Of course Gentleman Jack would win. It was nice of him to have put the tasks in a rhyme to help me remember them.

"And to Grandmother," I said. "I'll listen to Grandmother when I'm in her house."

"You will not go," said the mother doll. "The Indigo Heart is a magnet. It attracts the people it wants to attract."

"It keeps the people it wants to keep," said the father doll.

"You will stay here," said the mother doll. "You will perform the tasks."

"The tasks go in a certain order," said the father doll. "First you bring us a dog."

"A dog for the dollhouse?" I said.

"Not the dollhouse," said the mother doll. "For our house."

It took me a moment to understand. The mother doll thought I'd meant the dollhouse's dollhouse. The word Dollhouse wouldn't mean their own house to her. Of course not. The dolls wouldn't think they lived in a dollhouse. They wouldn't think that any more than I'd think I lived in a people house. They probably didn't even think of themselves as dolls—not the way people thought of dolls—even though when they spoke their lips didn't move and their faces didn't change.

"Then you bring us a collar," said the mother doll.

"A collar for the dog." I glanced through a quilt of shadows into the dollhouse. I remembered a dog with a collar. I remembered holding the dog's collar. It must have been a hollow memory, because inside the memory was a silver echo.

Or maybe someone else was holding the dog's collar and I was watching. Maybe there was a little boy holding the collar.

"*Stop remembering!*" said the dagger.

The dagger was right. Gentleman Jack didn't want me to remember the Before Time.

"*The Before Time is when your mother left you to die,*" said the dagger. The dagger loved talking about how my mother had left me. She left me in the wilderness, and Gentleman Jack saved me.

"It's good for a dog to have a collar," said the mother doll. "It means the dog's not too wild."

"The third task is a baby," said the father doll.

"A baby to play with the dog," I said.

"It would be best," said the father doll, "that the baby not be made of china."

"China is too fragile," said the mother doll.

"China can break," said the father doll. "We don't want our baby's heart to break."

"Our hearts won't break," said the mother doll, "now that you're here. Now that you'll perform the three tasks."

There was no point telling them I couldn't perform the tasks. That soon I would be gone. "The baby can hold on to the dog's collar," I said. "That's how the baby can learn to walk."

That was true—the thought of the baby holding the dog's collar was true—even though there would be no actual dog or collar.

"That's an excellent thought," said the father doll. "Make sure it's a good stout collar."

I thought about the tasks, and they tumbled into a pattern. Sometimes a pattern helped me remember things—like the task rhyme, which helped me remember the things Grandmother wanted. Gentleman Jack didn't like me forgetting, which I mostly did.

"*Except,*" said the dagger, "*you shouldn't remember the Before Time.*"

That was true. There were lots of things I should remember and lots of things I should forget. Sometimes I got them mixed up, and then Gentleman Jack would say I was dull. But maybe I could remember this pattern:

One's for a dog,

Two's for a collar.

Three's for a baby—

Now I'd have to find something that rhymed with Collar. But it didn't matter if I found the rhyming word. It didn't matter if I finished the tasks. What mattered was getting Gentleman Jack out of jail. What mattered was keeping Grandmother's watch polished so it could give me a safe and silvery feeling. That's what Grandmother was like, safe and silvery.

Tonight I would sleep in a cupboard bed. First I'd turn off the electric candle, carefully, so I wouldn't turn into lightning. Then I'd close the cupboard door. Last, I'd turn around and around in the bed. I'd make it into a nest.

I didn't like the night. I was awake for too much of it; there was too much time to worry. I was used to sleeping in the hideout, with other people breathing and turning over and muttering in their sleep, which sounds like clanking marbles. I wasn't used to sleeping alone.

When I couldn't sleep in the hideout, I used to practice throwing the dagger. I couldn't worry when I threw the dagger. The dagger-throwing part of my mind took over. But I couldn't throw it here, not in the cottage.

"Why not?" said the dagger.

"I might hit something," I said.

"That's the whole point," said the dagger.

My memory was holding its breath, just waiting for me to grow careless and start remembering the Before Time. I wouldn't let that happen. I turned over and pressed my knuckles into my eyes. When I did that, I couldn't see anything, not even the things inside my head. It was all a red darkness, which came with a feeling of heat and a feeling of smell.

"*You can't feel a smell,*" said the dagger.

That's where the dagger was wrong. You can feel a smell. Now came the heat and the smell-feeling. They got caught in the cracks of my lips. They made my eyes sting and cry.

I lay there. My eyes were bleeding acid. I listened to the terrible stillness. No birds sang, no squirrels scrabbled through the indigo tree. The air held its breath, waiting for snow.

"*Air can't hold its breath,*" said the dagger. "*Air is breath.*"

But the air was waiting for snow. I was waiting, too, and I was also waiting for morning, when I could go to the jail and tell Gentleman Jack I'd never betray him.

"*Sharpen me!*" said the dagger. It wanted to be sharp and bright for Gentleman Jack.

"*I already sharpened you,*" I said. I wanted to be sharp and bright for Gentleman Jack, too, but I didn't get sharp like the dagger.

"*Polish me!*" said the dagger.

"*I already polished you.*"

Then came the bells that had startled me last night. I wasn't as startled by them this morning, though, which was bad. I didn't want to get used to anything in the Indigo Heart.

It was still dark, but maybe the bells would awaken the Judge. I had to be ready to catch him. I crept down the attic stairs, down to the second-floor landing. Quieter still, on the steps to the first floor, where the bright rods held the carpet in place. And here was a funny thing: there were pineapples on the ends of the rods. I knew about pineapples because once Doubtful Mittie had bought me chunks of pineapple on a skewer. I'd watched the pineapple seller slice through the rind and cut the golden insides into chunks. There's a reason for cutting and skewering pineapples, which is to eat. But what's the reason for a carpet rod of pineapples?

That was where the Judge found me when he came downstairs. "How long have you been waiting?"

"Since dark," I said.

"I guess you're waiting to see Gentleman Jack," he said.

I said I guessed I was.

The Judge asked if I was also waiting for breakfast. I said I guessed I wasn't. But the Judge said we weren't leaving right away, so I might as well eat. He said he was going to fix a tray for Mrs. del Salto.

Fixing a tray is a funny thing. You can fix a tray because it's broken, but you can also fix a tray for someone when you make them food and put the food on the tray and open a closed bedroom door to bring it to them in bed.

I didn't know that people could eat in bed!

And then you have to spend a lot of time behind the closed door, talking to the person in bed.

When the Judge finally came downstairs, I said I wanted to fix a tray of butterscotch for Gentleman Jack.

"He has a sweet tooth?" said the Judge.

"It's his one vice," I said.

The Judge didn't have any butterscotch, but he had something called lemon drops. He said we didn't need to fix a tray of them. He said it would be easier to put them in a bag.

It was almost noon when the Judge turned the good, solid bolt on the good, solid door. We stepped out into the cold, where the sunflower carpet surprised me all over again. I followed the Judge down the porch stairs, then down a clatter of steps carved into the pink rock. We were high in the Indigo Heart. We had to walk downhill to get to the Sheriff's office, which was in the middle of the town of Blue Roses.

The steps rattled in and out of view, falling over themselves for a few hundred feet, then disappearing into the indigo forest. They looked the same when I glanced over my shoulder, except they went up. They dove in and out of the indigo trees, and when they dove out, they went dashing up and down the pink stone. Everywhere you looked were steps. Behind us was west; that's where the sun had set last night. Blue Roses was in front of us, so it was east.

Now came the bells that had startled me last night, but not so much this morning. And now I was so un-startled that I even remembered a bit of their tune. How the tune started low, then leapt high in a way that sounded sad, but the funny thing was that it made you happy to hear the sadness. It was more than just music, I thought. It was a song. If I listened to it hard enough, I'd remember the words.

"*Don't remember the words!*" said the dagger.

The Judge had stopped walking. He turned away from me, and once the bells had played the tune once through, he started talk-singing the song. I understood some of his mutter-talk-singing.

"The bird sang like a star," he said.

"The brightest Sister Seven," he said.

"*Don't remember the words!*" said the dagger.

It was so hard to know what to remember and what to forget. To know what belonged to the Before Time and what belonged to the regular time. That was because I was dull, but Gentleman Jack was pretty nice about it. "A little dull," he'd often say. "But just you wait, we'll sharpen you up."

The Judge's long legs kicked at his coat. It was a different coat from yesterday, long and heavy, with a cape at the shoulders. Why would a person have two coats?

A banister appeared. I didn't need it, though. I was wild, which meant I was sure-footed. It was a good thing I didn't need the banister, because it rocked back and forth when you touched it, and sometimes it disappeared. And just when it seemed gone forever, you curled round a twist of stone, into another patch of indigo, and it sprang back to life.

"It's an unsteady character," said the Judge.

I looked up. Was he joking? I saw only the angles and hollows of his face. You couldn't tell anything from them, except for my tooth marks, which told a story. They said he'd picked a fight with the Robber Girl and come out bleeding.

"I want to ask you to rethink testifying against Gentleman Jack," he said.

He could ask.

"Or rather," he said, "to rethink not testifying. You saw him kill Federal Marshal Starling. That could not have been a pretty sight."

"It was extremely pretty!" said the dagger.

But the Judge and the Sheriff had killed Doubtful Mittie. I remembered how Doubtful Mittie had lain facedown in the muck, one raw-meat hand grasping and gasping, and how I'd wished someone would turn him over.

"He was a fool to have worn the Marshal's hat," said the dagger.

Gentleman Jack had told him not to wear it, and so had Rough Ricky, but Doubtful Mittie hadn't understood. He wasn't from the Territories; he was from the place with the two-colored coin. He didn't understand that if somebody had been killed wearing a hat, and then you wore it, you'd die, too.

It was twice a dead man's hat. Federal Marshal Starling had worn it when he died. Doubtful Mittie had worn it when he died. It was extra unlucky.

"*Dead is dead,*" said the dagger. "*You don't get any unluckier than dead.*"

The steps narrowed here and went all higgle-piggle, like rotten teeth. The banister drew into itself; now it lurched just above the ground. Now it disappeared.

"Off duty again," said the Judge.

For the first time, I wondered about the gold mines. Where were they? I'd seen them in other places, and unless you were sifting for gold in a river, you had to construct an entrance to a gold mine. Sometimes the entrance had a wooden surround. Sometimes metal tracks went into the entrance so you could push a heavy cart. But I saw no openings in the earth, or wooden surrounds, or tracks, or carts. There were only gulches and gullies, which teetered us toward a river and a stone bridge. We went quickly after that. Now some huts sagging into the hillside, now the hills leveling off, now the huts becoming houses, now the spires of the town coming into view. There was a crazy array of roofs, slanted and tiled so snow and rain could slide off. The sun shone off the slants and spires.

"A city that is set on a hill cannot be hidden," said the Judge.

I saw what he meant. The town of Blue Roses was shining in plain sight, but that wasn't all you could see. To the south rose a stretch of steep and twisty stairs. They skittered up and over, leapt pink needles of stone, somersaulted over chasms, and finally landed at what was probably the only flat bit in Blue Roses. On the flat bit rose a great pink building. It had a golden dome that held up the sky.

"Those are the star steps," said the Judge. "On top of them you see the Shrine."

I asked the Judge what a shrine was, and the Judge said it was a holy place dedicated to worshipping a certain sacred person. This particular Shrine was dedicated to the Blue Rose.

"We climb the star steps," said the Judge, "to crave a boon of the Blue Rose."

I glanced up at the Judge.

"It means to make a wish," he said.

The stairs tipped over themselves and made a final downward dash. We tumbled into a confusion of people and oxen and horses.

A pig went squealing through the muck; a little boy ran after it, yelling and waving a stick. Three other boys came running and shouting.

"It's Gentleman Jack's little girl."

"She calls herself the Robber Girl."

"Hey, Robber Girl, I'll give you two bits for one of Gentleman Jack's gloves."

"Back off, boys," said the Judge.

"Hey, Robber Girl, just one glove."

The Judge took my elbow and steered me onto a walkway made of boards. The walkway ran along the pink walls of the buildings, under an upper story that hung out and made a roof.

The Judge and I passed slabs of pink stone, glass doors with gold letters, and windows heaped with bolts of cloth and buckets of nails and baskets of spices.

Now another glass door with gold letters, and set above the letters was a five-pointed star. *"The Sheriff's office,"* said the dagger.

The Judge looked down at me. "Shall we?" he said.

I was about to see Gentleman Jack and make him happy. I'd give him Doubtful Mittie's hat. I'd tell him I'd never betray him.

"We shall," I said.

An Order and a Commission

† THE FIRST SURPRISE was that the Sheriff's office was so still. It was a stillness inside a busyness. It was a stillness inside the jangling, wanting street.

The second surprise was that there were no iron bars. I had expected to see the cell right away, and Gentleman Jack in the cell. Instead, there were piles of yellowed newspapers, half-drunk cups of coffee, ashtrays filled with cold ashes. It was a discouraging place, all leftovers and worn-out news.

I glanced at the wall and—

"Look!" I said.

"Look!" said the dagger.

On the wall hung a drawing of Gentleman Jack. Gentleman Jack, with the lace at his neck and the ruby in his ear. There were drawings of other people, too. Beneath their faces were words, and at the beginning of the words was an amount of money. I didn't understand words, but I understood numbers. I understood dollar signs.

The amount of money was the reward you'd get for capturing the person in the drawing. Gentleman Jack's number was five thousand dollars. It was higher than anyone else's. He was the most valuable. The artist knew all about Gentleman Jack's smile. He knew you never saw Gentleman Jack's teeth.

Rough Ricky's face was there, too, and so was Doubtful Mittie's, but I was careful not to look at Doubtful Mittie. If the Sheriff or the Judge saw me look at him, they'd tell me he was a bad man. They'd tell me they were glad Doubtful Mittie was dead. They didn't know that once he'd bought me a skewer of pineapple; they didn't know that once he'd given me a slice of muskrat pie. They just knew he smelled of rotting copper. It was the blood of the child he'd killed. Or maybe children.

It was blood that never really dried.

The Sheriff was younger than I remembered. Or maybe I'd only really seen his hands before—his hands on the rifle—and his hands were older than his face. He had small dark eyes and a black mustache, with a little side helping of mustache below his bottom lip. He was short, which might make you think he wasn't dangerous. But he'd thrown himself over the stagecoach roof, and he'd shot Doubtful Mittie, and he'd captured Gentleman Jack and wrenched Gentleman Jack's arms when he tried to escape.

I was short and I was dangerous, too.

I already knew I had to show the bag of lemon drops to the Sheriff. The Sheriff needed to make sure I wasn't slipping a knife or a lock pick to Gentleman Jack. The Sheriff shook the bag, stirred the contents with his coffee spoon, then nodded.

He led me to a heavy door. The lock was long and puckered, as though it were screaming. He clicked it open, and now the door did scream as it scraped over stone. Gentleman Jack always said there was no jail that could hold him. But what about a jail with a stone floor? You couldn't dig your way out.

We stepped into a little corridor; there, the smells were concentrated—sweat and damp and rust. I knew the smell of rust, from Doubtful Mittie's hands. It lay heavy on my tongue. Water dripped from the ceiling into a metal pail. Plink, it said into the pail. Plink. Only seconds now until I saw Gentleman Jack. What would he say?

Plink, went the water. Plink, plink.

Would he say, "This is my girl, returned from the road"?

Would he say, "This is my girl, bright as a star"?

The cell block was made up of three cells in a row. Gentleman Jack was in the middle cell, sitting on the edge of a cot. There was the familiar foam of lace, the glint of ruby, but his gloves were soiled and one of his wrist frills was torn. He looked different, but he started with the familiar questions.

"Did you tell them your name?" Gentleman Jack spoke low so the Sheriff couldn't hear.

"I said I have no name." I spoke just as low.

It was good Gentleman Jack asked the same questions. I knew what to say when he asked the familiar questions. It was good his hair was still yellow and his eyes were still greenish-brown, even though he liked you to call them green, because that was the rarest eye color and things that were rare were valuable. He didn't look the same, though, not dirty and torn, not in a cage. And the cage was so bare. Aside from the cot, there was only a chamber pot and a stand with a pitcher.

"Did you tell them about the hideout?" said Gentleman Jack.

"I said there is no hideout."

No one had actually asked about the hideout, but that was all right. The important thing was that Gentleman Jack knew I'd followed the rules. It was the same conversation as always, but the words sounded different. The walls of the jail were too close; they crowded his words together. Gentleman Jack and his words were made for wide-open spaces, not for cells and bars and plinks in pails.

The Sheriff leaned against the opposite wall, probably making sure I wasn't helping Gentleman Jack escape.

I gave Gentleman Jack the lemon drops. Gentleman Jack opened the bag, sniffed it, and closed it up again. "Sour!" he said. "And speaking of sour, the Sheriff took away my Lucretia." Lucretia was his knife. "He took Lucretia and all I got was a dirty penny."

The Sheriff wasn't a fool, not like Doubtful Mittie. He knew that if he took someone's knife, he'd have to pay them a penny. Otherwise, the knife would leap out and hurt him.

"I wish the Sheriff would take me!" cried the dagger. *"Then I'd bite him!"*

"But he'd just give me a penny," I said. The rule of knives and pennies would protect the Sheriff. Once I had the penny, the dagger couldn't leap out and attack him.

"You could run away before he gave it to you," said the dagger. That was an interesting thought. If the Sheriff couldn't give me a penny, the rule of knives and pennies would make the dagger attack him.

They hadn't taken away Gentleman Jack's strike lighter, though. There was the scratching sound when he struck the flint with the wand, the smell of lighter fluid as the wick caught fire. The flame flickered like a tongue. On and off, on and off, to help him think.

That was Gentleman Jack through and through. He had only to say, "Let there be light!" and there was light. The lighter lit up his brain.

"I hesitate to ask, my dear," he said, "and really, I'm sure there's some simple explanation. But it has occurred to me to wonder why you didn't warn us."

I knew what he meant. Why hadn't I warned them on Day Zero that there was a sheriff and a judge.

"Because of my Affliction," I said.

"Ah," said Gentleman Jack, as though he'd forgotten about it. But how could he? It was the biggest thing in my life.

"Not in his life," said the dagger.

I spoke even lower, so that the Sheriff couldn't possibly hear. "The Judge asked me to be a witness in your trial. To say you killed Marshal Starling."

Part of me, though, was still thinking about knives and pennies. I wished I could give Gentleman Jack a knife. How happy he'd be if I gave him a knife.

"But I never would," I said.

Gentleman Jack came close and wrapped his hands around the bars. "Go to the Sapphire Saloon, down Main Street." He jerked his thumb in the direction of the Shrine, which was away from the direction of the cottage. "Ask for Flora. Flora will know what to tell the Judge."

Relief wrung me out like a sponge. I liked it when Gentleman Jack gave me orders. I liked knowing what to do.

"Do you understand?"

I said I understood. I was standing in a pool of relief. Relief was like honey, slow and sweet.

"Show me you understand," said Gentleman Jack.

This was how it always went when he gave me instructions. Gentleman Jack tested my memory. It wasn't that he didn't trust me, not exactly, but it was important to make absolutely sure.

I repeated his instructions, about the Sapphire Saloon, about Flora, about how Flora would tell me what to do.

"Don't let the Judge know you're going to the Sapphire," said Gentleman Jack. "He'd say it's not a fit place for you."

I repeated that, too. I wished he'd ask about Netherby Scar so I could talk about Grandmother and her silken hands and velvet sofas, about the eleven chimneys that rose from her roof, about how her house was always warm.

He didn't ask me about Netherby Scar, but he asked about rescuing me, which was almost as good. "Who rescued you in the wilderness?"

"You rescued me," I said.

Plink, plink went the water into the metal pail. But pretty soon there'd be no plinks. Pretty soon everything would be frozen.

I unbuttoned my coat. "I have your hat." It had become Gentleman Jack's hat as soon as Doubtful Mittie died. Gentleman Jack would see how excellently I was following the rules.

"Oh, my dear child," said Gentleman Jack. "What would I want with a hat? I want my gold. I want a wingless bird. I want my freedom."

I'd been stupid to think Gentleman Jack would care about a hat when he was in jail, wanting gold. I hadn't been exercising judgment. The door between my stomach and chest opened up. That's what happened when I made mistakes. I felt the bitter stomach juice rush into my heart. It's funny how embarrassment starts in your stomach but ends up in your chest.

"Tell me what I want." Gentleman Jack spoke extra gently, which made it worse.

"You want to bring Grandmother five gold bricks," I said.

"What are they worth?" said Gentleman Jack.

"One hundred twenty-eight thousand dollars," I said.

"But who has the gold?" said Gentleman Jack.

"The rich people in the Indigo Heart." It occurred to me suddenly that the Judge probably had some gold, so it was funny that a moment later Gentleman Jack said the exact same thing.

"Like that Judge of yours," said Gentleman Jack. "He has a substantial stake in a gold mine."

Except the Judge wasn't my Judge.

"What do I get if I bring the gold?" said Gentleman Jack.

"You'll get Grandmother's empire, and your no-account brother won't get anything." It was pretty stupid to think Gentleman Jack would want a hat when what he wanted was an empire.

"But only if I bring a wingless bird, too."

Yes, only if he brought a wingless bird.

"Tell me all the things we need to bring Grandmother," said Gentleman Jack. He was testing my memory to help me exercise judgment. It was easy to remember what Grandmother wanted. It's easy to remember things that are in a rhyme.

"Fetch unto me the mountain's gold,
To build our city fair.
Fetch unto me the wingless bird,
And I will make you my heir."

Gentleman Jack wanted to bring Grandmother both things from the poem. There were two things, which was the right number of things.

"Flora and I will make a plan," I said. "Flora and I will get you out of jail and get your gold."

"And the Songbird," said Gentleman Jack. "Ask Flora about the Songbird." Songbird was another name for a wingless bird. "And ask her about getting me an opal. I could use some good luck right about now."

Now the door screeched over stone. It was the Judge, coming in to say we had to leave. There was no time for Gentleman Jack to say, "Show me you understand." No time for him to test my memory.

"Come back as soon as possible," said Gentleman Jack, very low. "Tell me all about Flora. Tell me all about the plan. In the meantime, I suppose I can get used to lemon drops. I appreciate the effort."

The Sheriff rose and led the way. I followed the Sheriff and the Judge through the door with the screaming ghost-mouth. I followed them over the stone floor. I had the same thought as before. Gentleman Jack wouldn't be able to dig his way out of this jail, even though there was no jail that could hold him.

But maybe he could fight his way out. What if I could slip him something small, like the dagger? Then Gentleman Jack could give me the Sheriff's dirty penny and the dagger couldn't hurt him. Then he could take the Sheriff by surprise.

"*It would be excellent to help Gentleman Jack!*" said the dagger.

Into the office again, where the picture of Gentleman Jack stared from the wall. The artist had gotten his face just right: the square jaw, the lightish eyes, which you were supposed to call Green. The Judge had a coat with capes, and boots with silver stitching, but no one was as beautiful as Gentleman Jack.

The stagecoach driver was in the office, sitting in a chair, his long legs on the desk. He still wore his great white jacket with all the fringes, but now he had a star on his coat.

"*He's the Deputy Sheriff,*" said the dagger.

They were all so tricky, the Judge and the Sheriff and the Deputy.

The Deputy had taken off his star so I wouldn't suspect anything when I stopped the stage. No wonder they'd captured Gentleman Jack, with a sheriff and a judge and a deputy sheriff. That was too many people to beat.

"The girl refuses to testify against Gentleman Jack," said the Judge.

"Should we remind her?" said the Sheriff.

"About the Federal Marshal?" said the Deputy.

If I slipped the dagger to Gentleman Jack, he'd have to fight the Deputy Sheriff, as well as the Judge and the regular Sheriff. That was too many people to fight.

"About how he died in agony," said the Sheriff.

"About how Gentleman Jack snuck up on him," said the Deputy, "and didn't give the Marshal a minute to draw his revolver."

But Gentleman Jack hadn't snuck—Gentleman Jack didn't sneak! I was there—I'd seen it all. Gentleman Jack had been on horseback. I'd been beside him, on the pinto. And there'd come Marshal Starling, riding toward us.

"The men of the Territories never take unfair advantage," said the Deputy. "Not even of an enemy."

Gentleman Jack didn't take unfair advantage. He'd even yelled at the Marshal. That was warning him. That was giving him a chance to draw his revolver. Gentleman Jack yelled that he had a lawful claim to the gold in the Heart.

"Gentleman Jack laid a trap for the Marshal," said the Judge. "He never gave him a chance to draw his revolver. He shot him, then ran like a coward."

But Gentleman Jack hadn't run. He'd dismounted and picked through the Federal Marshal's pockets. I didn't exactly watch him, but I knew he was brave not to run away.

Lies, lies, all lies. Gentleman Jack had told me they'd lie about him.

I'd never believe anything they said. Anyway, it was the Marshal who'd acted dishonorably. He'd driven Gentleman Jack from the Indigo Heart because he didn't want Gentleman Jack to have any gold.

"You laid a trap for Gentleman Jack," I said, "with the gold and the stagecoach."

"But—" said the Deputy.

"Wait," said the Judge. "The girl makes an excellent point. Let me explain how the two situations are different. We did lay a trap, but the success of the trap was predicated on—"

"Predicated?"

"Based on," said the Judge. "Gentleman Jack had to do something illegal to fall into the trap. He had to try to hold up the stage. The same was not true of Marshal Starling. Marshal Starling did nothing illegal. In fact, he was upholding the law. He was responding to a report of a disturbance, but that disturbance was created by Gentleman Jack."

I remembered the disturbance. Gentleman Jack had been shooting into the road until Marshal Starling rounded the corner.

"Also," said the Judge, "Gentleman Jack shot him in the belly, which is particularly painful and deadly. If the shot doesn't kill you, infection probably will."

But Marshal Starling should have had his revolver drawn if there was a disturbance. I couldn't say so, though. I couldn't admit I'd been there.

There was nothing more to say. We stepped out from the worn-out leftovers of the Sheriff's office into the clatter and roar of Main Street. And also into the smell of something rich and fatty and salty.

Peanuts! I thought, even though I didn't know I knew the smell of peanuts. I expected we'd turn back the way we'd come, toward the cottage, and I was thinking, thinking about how to slip away from the Judge. But he surprised me by turning left, which was toward the Shrine, and also toward the Sapphire.

The gold dome of the Shrine shone over everything. It reminded me of what the Judge had said about how you couldn't hide a city on a hill. A city on a hill was so different from a cave in a ravine. The Judge must have been thinking the same thing, for he said, "We like to have the Shrine where everyone can see it, and think of the Blue Rose, and worship her and crave a boon of her."

Down the street came a whistling. I stopped and looked around. It was not an ordinary whistle. I heard—oh, I was sure I heard—

I tugged at the Judge's coat.

"Yes?"

"Are there words in the whistle?" I said.

"You understand them!" said the Judge.

I almost understood them, and when the whistling repeated the words, I understood them perfectly.

"Peanuts, peanuts! Fresh, hot peanuts!"

"He's selling peanuts," I said.

"My stars!" The Judge looked at me for a long time. "Not many people understand the Whistling. And only Songbirds can speak it."

"What's the Whistling?" I said.

"It means being able to put words in your whistle, just as he's doing," said the Judge. "It's useful in the mountains in order to reach other people across long distances. But the most special thing about it is that the Blue Rose can hear the Whistling, wherever she may be, so it's the best way to thank her and praise her."

The words from Grandmother's task rhyme sprang into my head. I'd been remembering them a lot today and yesterday.

Fetch unto me the mountain's gold,

To build our city fair.

Fetch unto me the wingless bird,

And I will make you my heir.

"He's kind of like a wingless bird," I said.

"Precisely!" said the Judge.

It was all so beautifully simple. Wingless birds were regular people, except that they could whistle with words. That's why they had no wings.

But then I remembered what Gentleman Jack said about whistling. "It's bad luck to whistle," I said.

"We think it's good luck," said the Judge. "It's considered a rare talent to be able to understand the Whistling."

But it didn't seem rare to me. You just heard the whistle and you understood the words.

"I have to see Gentleman Jack," I said. I had to tell him I'd found a wingless bird. Or I could also call it a Songbird. Would Gentleman Jack like it better if I called it by both its names? Then Gentleman Jack would have one of the things Grandmother wanted. Then he'd be happy.

"You can see Gentleman Jack later," said the Judge.

"Now," I said.

"The snow is coming," said the Judge. "After the snow."

But I couldn't wait until after the snow. I couldn't wait to shine like a star.

The Judge paused at a shop. He pulled at the glass door. Gold letters flashed, the door opened. I looked at him. Didn't we have to beat the snow?

"Mrs. del Salto has given me a commission," said the Judge.

Commission?

"*A commission is something you have to do for somebody,*" said the dagger. "*It's a taming thing.*"

Maybe I could separate myself from the Judge in the store. I could slip out while he wasn't looking and run to the Sapphire and to Flora. Maybe she would help me get back to the hideout.

"But Gentleman Jack told me to go to the Sapphire," I said. "*Isn't that a commission?*"

"*That was an order,*" said the dagger. "*Commissions are tame, orders are wild.*"

The Judge was tame, I was wild. I would get back to the hideout. Rough Ricky would be there, and some of the others, and together we'd plan how to break Gentleman Jack out of jail. Then I'd come back with Rough Ricky and we'd steal the peanut man and make him be a Songbird for Grandmother.

I would go to the Sapphire. I would obey Gentleman Jack's order. I would be wild.

The General Store

† I'D BEEN IN STORES BEFORE, but not one like this. Not where a little bell rang as you entered. Not one that was so warm and huge and quiet. You could hear the smallest sounds, shears snipping and nails clinking and paper crinkling.

It smelled of something sweet—

"*Perfume,*" said the dagger. "*Taming.*"

And of something spicy—

"*Cinnamon,*" said the dagger. "*Wild.*"

Everywhere you looked, there were things to buy, and all of them were bright. Even the ceiling was bright. It gleamed with pots and pans and lanterns. There were two kinds of lanterns. There were lanterns you could buy, and there were lanterns that belonged to the store. The store lanterns lit up the other lanterns so shoppers could see them and want to buy them.

There were tables of fabric in tumbles of designs. Flowers and checks and stripes. Who could have thought up all those patterns? Who could have thought up all those colors?

"*No one thinks up colors,*" said the dagger. "*Colors just are.*"

There was a whole wall of knives. They sat on brackets set into the wall. The knives were old friends, grinning and winking at me. There were cutting knives for meat, with jagged blades and strong tips. There were slashing knives with clean-edged blades.

"*I have a clean-edged blade,*" said the dagger.

"*And a double-sided blade,*" I said.

There were slicing knives with curved bellies; there were skinning knives with dull tips.

"*I have a deadly tip,*" said the dagger. "*That's why Gentleman Jack gave me to you.*"

"*You are just right for me,*" I said.

The dagger's tip was more fragile than the tip of a skinning knife, but it would slice into flesh with little force. That was better for a smaller person, like me, even though the tip was the weakest part of any knife. "Take care of the tip," Gentleman Jack always said, "and the rest of the blade will follow."

Knives were the only things I understood in this place. Knives and footsteps . . . footsteps coming up behind me. I was wild, so I could read a person's footsteps. These footsteps belonged to a child about my age. A girl maybe. I turned around. Yes, a girl, taller than me but about the same age. Maybe ten, maybe eleven.

"You're Gentleman Jack's little girl?" The girl was as bright as everything else. Her dress was the color of poppies, with red-and-white polka-dot trimming.

"It's rude to stare," said the girl, "but you wouldn't know because you're a robber girl. You wouldn't know these are my everyday clothes. They're just flannel."

I'd heard of flannel. You could sleep in flannel. It made you warm. The girl wore flannel because it was about to snow.

"I have lots of special clothes at home," said the girl. "That's because it's my mama and papa's store, which means it's my store." The girl had shiny yellow hair; it made spirals down to her shoulders.

She saw me staring and said, "I have ringlets. Ringlets are a kind of curl. You don't know about ringlets."

"I have ringlets." I took off my hat and shook out my hair.

"Your hair is too messy for ringlets," said the girl.

That was because I was wild.

"Mama is astonished Mrs. del Salto let you spend the night," said the girl. "Mama said you've learned all Gentleman Jack's tricks and that the del Saltos should thank the stars you didn't set fire to their house while they slept."

"Not while they slept," I said.

"What do you mean?" said the girl.

"I'd burn them while they're awake."

I wanted to say that setting fires wasn't one of Gentleman Jack's tricks. It belonged to Rough Ricky. But the girl wasn't listening. She beckoned me deeper into the store. "I'll show you everything that's best." I didn't follow her right away. Shouldn't I be slipping off to the Sapphire? The Judge had a commission from Mrs. del Salto, but I had an order from Gentleman Jack.

"*Not now!*" said the dagger. "*The Judge is watching.*" The dagger saw everything I saw, but sometimes it noticed different things. That was useful.

I followed the girl past a case with a glass top and front, so you could look inside and see that everything was shiny. It was especially shiny because it was filled with opals, which glimmered with under-water colors.

"We call this our good-luck case," said the girl.

I wondered how we could get one of the opals for Gentleman Jack.

"Stealing is always good," said the dagger.

I followed the girl toward a wall of silver—no, not a wall, a mirror, and the girl and I were reflected in it. The girl was tall and strong-looking. I looked smaller than I'd thought. The girl had bright corkscrew curls. I had wild black robber hair. The girl's face was pink and round and freckled. My face was—I couldn't find a word for it. Gentleman Jack always said I didn't know enough words. I could only think of descriptions that began with Not. My face was not freckled. It was not round. It was not pink.

We passed a table of boots, white and gray and black. I'd never seen such clean boots, all polished, with beautiful rows of buttons.

The girl paused and stuck out a foot. Her boots were white; the buttons shone like pearls. I knew about pearls because Gentleman Jack had shown me one. He said Grandmother had a whole necklace of pearls. He said when we lived with her, she would let me try it on. She would fasten it around my neck and show me how it looked in a mirror.

What if—what if I saw my mother while I was in Blue Roses? Would I recognize her? Would she recognize me? Probably not, because she hated me.

We passed a table piled with tools. The wooden handles gleamed; the metal bits were beautifully clean, with no pitting or rust. They were clean and dry and sharp, just the way Gentleman Jack had taught me to keep the dagger. They were even prettier than the buttons. Some of them lay in boxes made to fit them, like little houses. One of the hammers had a red handle.

"My name is Betsy Elton," said the girl. "I know you don't have a name, except for Robber Girl." Betsy stopped at a fat, jolly barrel that came up to my chest and swelled out at the sides. She unhooked a silver scoop from the handle.

"Candy is one of the best things," she said. "But you wouldn't know about it. You don't get candy when you live with thieves and murderers."

"Gentleman Jack's not a thief and murderer!" You don't have to know a lot of words for your words to come out hot.

"He was going to steal the gold from the stagecoach," said Betsy. "That's being a thief." She didn't wait for me to answer. "I can have as much candy as I want." She jiggled the scoop in front of me. "Look how pretty it is."

I'd seen plenty of candy before, because of Gentleman Jack's sweet tooth, but not like this. Not candy that came in all different colors, pink and yellow and green. One of the green candies had a flower buried below the surface. It was like looking through green water into a garden.

"You can pick a piece," said Betsy. "Take it from the scoop."

I looked at the green candy. I already knew how I'd eat it. I'd put it on my tongue and let it melt away. If I was slow and careful, I could melt away the surface, down to the flower.

My hand reached out. I saw my fingers take the candy. I saw the dirt beneath my nails. I held the candy in my palm.

"You're supposed to eat it." Betsy bit into her candy. It cracked between her teeth.

I didn't know how anything worked. I didn't know there could be a candy with a flower swimming beneath its surface. I didn't know candy came in a silver scoop.

"Just the color silver," said the dagger.

"Don't you know how to eat candy?" said Betsy.

But I didn't want to eat mine the way she was eating hers, which was all crack and no melt. I wanted to melt the surface away, down to the flower.

Everyone was watching me not know how to eat candy. When you're wild, you keep track of everyone and everything—people, animals, weapons. I knew about the three women who didn't look at me. They pecked their heads toward one another like chickens, gobbling up their words. I knew about the men in tired-looking hats who didn't look at me, and about the biggish girl on a stepladder, reaching to a high shelf. No one looked at me, but they all noticed me not eating the candy.

The Judge was still up front. I couldn't leave.

"I can have as many pieces as I want," said Betsy. Crack went her teeth. "Come on, I'll show you more of the best things."

I held the candy in the cup of my hand and followed Betsy around the barrels, past buckets and shovels, around a corner—

"Toys!" said Betsy.

Toys were everywhere. At least the candy had been in a scoop. At least I'd known where to look. But there were too many things here. I made my eyes look at one thing at a time. There were baskets heaped with pieces of wood. The wood was cut into different shapes, triangles and arches and blocks, painted in bright, clear colors.

"You build houses with them," said Betsy.

But I didn't need a house. I had Grandmother's house. Grandmother's house was made of yellow brick and it was big. It was bigger than the cottage. Big houses were the best.

I let my eyes look at other things. At a pole with a horse's head on top, at another horse standing on curls of wood, like a sleigh. At a purple yo-yo. At balls of all different sizes. One ball was painted with yellow smiling suns. You could tell it was a ball for kicking.

I let my eyes look at a tiny red ball, exactly the right size for my palm. But I had the candy in my palm. The candy was more important than the ball.

"That's a ball for jacks," said Betsy.

"Everyone knows that," I said, except I wasn't everyone.

There were marbles in jars, and windup toys made in the shape of animals. They were small, with joints, like the dolls. Betsy turned a knob and made a dog dance on his hind legs. Was that the kind of dog I should get for the dollhouse? It might be about one-twelfth the size of a regular dog.

The red ball would also fit into the dollhouse. Maybe the dog could chase it. Maybe when the baby got older, he could kick it.

Behind us rose a glass case, where three brown bears sat on a shelf. The littlest one sat between the medium one and the biggest one. The biggest one was bigger than a raccoon. The bears had outstretched arms that said, "We're soft. Come feel how soft we are."

But I couldn't touch them. The candy was beginning to melt into a little green pool. I wouldn't crack the candy, not like Betsy. I'd melt it in my mouth and get to the flower.

"You're not looking at the dolls," said Betsy. "You have to look at them."

There were lots of dolls, but Betsy jabbed her finger at one, sitting on a lower shelf in the glass case. She was bigger than the mother doll, and she had golden hair and red lips. Her face was painted to look like real skin, all soft and rosy, with lights and shadows. She wore tiny pink shoes and a pink dress with ruffles and lace.

You could tell the doll knew she was beautiful. She wasn't friendly, not like the mother doll and father doll. Her arms stuck straight down, and she didn't look at you.

"There are real buttons on her shoes," said Betsy. "She has real ring-lets, just like me. She's going to be my birthday doll, for when I turn eleven. She's made of china and she came from France." Betsy poked the glass case. "Look at all the things that come with her."

The doll had a trunk, but it had been stood on its end, which turned it into a wardrobe. The lid was open, which was like the wardrobe door being open, with a pole along the top, to hang things. A rainbow of doll clothes spilled from the trunk—lace underthings and coats and shoes and dresses.

"She has a hat with flowers," said Betsy, "and a hat with a veil. She even has shoes for a party." The shoes were the smallest things imagin-able, with lacy sides and tiny bows.

"She's from France," said Betsy. "Didn't you hear me? She's made of china and she came all the way from France."

I stared into my palm, into the little pool of green. I curled my fingers around the candy, but I could see the flower in my memory. I would bring the flower to the surface.

"China is fragile," I said. "That means her heart can break."

"What do you know about china?" Betsy's eyes were brown with yellow flecks. "What do you know about anything?" She pushed her face too close to mine. "Look at the doll dressed in white. She's a bride doll, but a robber girl wouldn't know that."

"Everyone knows that," I said.

"Look at the doll with the crown," said Betsy. "A robber girl wouldn't know she's a princess doll."

"Everyone knows that." But I wasn't everyone.

"A robber girl wouldn't know china is best," said Betsy.

But the mother and father dolls had told me china was fragile and that it was dangerous to be fragile. I knew about china.

"Dolls that come from France are the best of all," said Betsy. "China is the best. France is the best."

"But her heart can break," I said.

"Dolls don't have hearts," said Betsy.

I didn't like not knowing things in the Indigo Heart, like why you'd have a knife with no edge, just to cut butter. Like why the Judge took his hat on and off so often. Like why you took candy with a scoop and not your hands. But I knew one thing Betsy didn't know.

"They do so have hearts," I said.

"You're crazy," said Betsy. "No one likes a girl who's crazy." Betsy's face was red and white, to match her dress. Her cheeks made round red circles, but her mouth made a white line.

"It would be stupid to play with dolls if they had no hearts," I said. "You'd just be playing with something that's dead." I'd never had these thoughts before. They made sharp, uncomfortable shapes in my mind.

"You're an ignorant robber girl. You're not the one with a whole store of dolls."

"Robber girls don't play with dolls." But even as I said this, I saw a baby doll on the topmost shelf. It stood in a wooden stand with a carved-out scoop for its head. That was because babies couldn't stand up by themselves. The baby wasn't cold and unfriendly like the French doll. It held out its arms. "Take me!" said its arms. "Take me!"

Also, a baby could stand up if it was holding a dog collar. "That doll," I said. "The baby doll in the blue clothes—"

"They're only pajamas." Betsy let her lips unpress themselves. "He doesn't have nice clothes. He's not from France."

"He?" The baby was a he?

Would the mother and father doll want a boy baby? They hadn't said which kind they wanted.

"Of course he's a he," said Betsy. "Don't you know anything? Pink is for girls; blue is for boys."

How I hated her, her smooth yellow ringlets, her jutting red face.

"My shirt is blue," I said.

"You're more like a boy than a girl." You could tell she liked saying I was like a boy. She didn't know it was good I was like a boy. She didn't know that Gentleman Jack had always wanted a son.

"What's that doll made of?" I said.

"He's just wax," said Betsy. She made it sound as though wax were a bad thing, but she was wrong. Wax was good. Wax was soft. Wax couldn't shatter like china. Wax was as beautiful as china. The baby's face was all round and soft; it was the color of peaches and cream.

"Peaches and cream isn't a color," said the dagger.

The baby's eyes were blue, just like the mother doll's eyes. Did his eyes close when he lay down? It would be good if his eyes closed.

"He has bare feet," I said. I knew babies caught cold easily. A baby's feet should be covered in the wintertime.

"He doesn't have extra clothes," said Betsy. "Not like the French doll." Her eyes flickered up to someone behind me. My spine prickled.

"She wants the china doll, Papa."

I turned around slowly. I'd forgotten to be alert. I'd forgotten to listen for footsteps. I hadn't realized it would be so easy to forget. But I'd pretend I wasn't surprised. Betsy's papa was a big round man; his head was shiny and bald as an egg.

"The china doll's for me," said Betsy.

"I don't play with dolls," I said.

"She doesn't even know the difference between china and wax," said Betsy.

But I knew about the wax doll in the blue pajamas. I knew he had a heart that couldn't break.

"But she knows a few things." The egg-man grabbed my arm and pried open my fingers. "A few things, eh!"

There in my palm was the candy, lying in a sweet green pool.

"She knows enough to get herself some sticky fingers." The man dragged me back the way I'd come. "Let's see what the Judge has to say about these sticky fingers."

He dragged me past the dancing dog and the marbles. Some of the marbles were like Betsy's eyes, brown flecked with yellow. They were ugly. He dragged me past the red ball that was for jacks, past the yellow ball that was for kicking.

"Let's see what the Judge has to say about a girl who sticks her hand in the candy barrel."

Why didn't Betsy tell the truth? Why didn't she tell him I took the candy from the scoop?

"*I want to bite him,*" said the dagger.

Past the candy barrels, toward the table of tools.

"*Grab the hammer!*" said the dagger. Yes, the hammer with its red handle. But I had no hands free. The candy was in the palm of my dagger hand. The egg-man held my other hand. Quick as quick, I scooped the candy into my mouth.

I couldn't taste the candy. You can't taste anything when your dagger hand is grabbing a hammer. You can't hear anything when Betsy's father is shouting about sticky fingers. You can't hear the candy go crack, crack, crack.

You have to remember what Gentleman Jack told you. He said it was better to attack first, defend later. He said I had the advantage of being small, and of being a girl, so folks wouldn't expect me to attack.

"If someone grabs you," Gentleman Jack always said, "don't struggle to get free. Use that person's strength against him."

Betsy's father was strong, which was good. He held my wrist hard, which was good. It meant his arm was stiff. It's easier to hurt an arm that's stiff.

The red handle was bright. I swung; it arced through the air. The candy had gone crack, and now the hammer went crack. It cracked the egg-man's elbow.

He roared. He dropped my wrist. His arm fell to his side, limp and heavy. The hammer clattered to the floor.

No time to lose, run for the door. When there's a fight, it usually takes people a little while to figure out what's happened, especially if one of the fighters is a maybe-eleven-year-old girl who isn't very big. You have to take advantage of that little while; you have to run.

I leapt past the Judge, who held his hat in his hands, in one of its mysterious takings-off and puttings-on. The Judge was still; the rest of the people were still; the weather was still. I bolted through a stillness of people into the stillness of the coming snow.

Now to the Sapphire, where Betsy could never go because she was tame. But I could go because I was wild. I hated her—how I hated her! Someday I'd—

"I'll let you taste her blood," I said.

"Revenge!" said the dagger. "I love revenge."

Now at last I tasted the candy, the sour-sweet green apple prickling the back edges of my tongue. Later I would lick my palm. Later I would think about the flower I had cracked into careless bits.

But for now, I was running.

Doubtful Mittie's Hat

✝ I HEARD THE SAPPHIRE BEFORE I SAW IT. Music spilled out the big double doors. They were swinging doors, and they were both open despite the coming snow. This was music that didn't care what other music sounded like. It didn't care that you couldn't hum it or guess where it was going. It came sliding out the doors on its shoulder, laughing.

And there was the peanut man, who was also the Songbird. I'd tell Gentleman Jack about him, and I'd be bright as a star. Later, we'd take him with us to Netherby Scar and give him to Grandmother.

Or maybe he was just *a* Songbird. Maybe there was more than one.

"Peanuts, peanuts! Fresh, hot peanuts!" How could a person not understand the words? The peanut smell shouted in the air. It was a smell-shout of fat oozing peanuts and salty steam. The peanut man looked very ordinary to be somebody Grandmother wanted so much. You could hardly even see him. The little cart was tucked between the wall and the slant of one of the open doors. It glowed with hot coals.

I stood in the shout-smell of peanuts. There was too much noise inside, and people would be using curly knives and eating ashes and salt, and I wouldn't understand anything. I wished I could go straight to the hideout. Even if Rough Ricky wasn't there, I could catch a possum by the tail or trap a squirrel. Once, I'd thrown the dagger at a fox. There's a lot of eating in a fox.

The music hooked itself round my ankles, it tugged me inside. I smelled tobacco. It was a good smell. Rough Ricky smoked a pipe, and Rough Ricky would be waiting for me at the hideout. You knew what was going to happen in the hideout.

I knew the tobacco smell, and I knew the sharp ping of whiskey and the thick smell of damp wool. I knew the noise. It was the same noise that was at the hideout, the noise of lots of men in the same space, dealing cards, placing bets, thumping tables, throwing darts.

Someday I'd catch Betsy and bring her here, and she'd be in a place where she didn't understand anything. And I'd take out the dagger and—

"I'll *bite her!*" said the dagger.

I went up to a woman who stood beneath a metal halo suspended from the ceiling. It was set with six candles that dazzled her hair into shades of wheat and honey.

"What brings you here, sweetheart?" she said.

"I'm looking for Flora," I said.

"You have found Flora," she said.

Flora wasn't rusty like Mrs. del Salto. Her honey hair curled around her shoulders, which rose from a purple dress with silver stripes. She put her arm around me, she led me to a table. She wore lace gloves without any fingertips.

"Sit down," she said. But I couldn't sit down, not with the hat buttoned into my coat. I set it on the table.

"Gentleman Jack's hat!" said a voice. That was right; it was his hat, although it had been the Federal Marshal's hat first. Then Doubtful Mittie's hat. But the voices didn't care. They asked for the hat, for the feather, for just one of Gentleman Jack's gloves. But their hands were red and meaty. They'd never fit into his gloves.

"Quiet!" said Flora.

The men fell quiet. Flora lit a candle on one of the tables. It was easier to talk with a candle. It made you want to lean over the table.

"Gentleman Jack wants me to talk to you," I said.

"Here you are," said Flora. "About to do so."

"The Judge wants me to testify at Gentleman Jack's trial." The crazy, curling music poured itself sideways into my ear. "But I wouldn't betray Gentleman Jack."

"Of course not," said Flora.

"Gentleman Jack said you would know what to do."

There was too much to look at in the Sapphire—the moose head behind the bar, the big dollar sign hanging on a wall, the ashtrays, the metal halos suspended above with their burning candles. I'd look at Flora instead. She was so restful.

"You should testify at Gentleman Jack's trial," said Flora.

"What?" I said.

"What?" said the dagger.

"John!" said Flora, not raising her voice. "We need a helping of your famous silver tongue." It was noisy again, but her voice cut through the noise.

"Fold!" said a voice from the card tables. "My lady awaits."

Flora called him John, but it turned out that everyone else called him Lord John. I liked the way he looked. I liked the way he walked and the way he dressed, which was fancy. I liked people who were fancy,

I liked people who wore earrings. His was blue, which meant it was a sapphire.

Lord John explained why I should testify. It was a way to get Gentleman Jack out of jail. I should tell the people at the trial that Gentleman Jack was someplace else when Marshal Starling was killed. If they believed me, then they'd have to decide Gentleman Jack hadn't killed him.

"The Fair was held that day," said Flora. "You could say you'd been to the Harvest Fair with Gentleman Jack."

"I've never been to a fair," I said.

But Flora and Lord John would tell me all about the Fair. I would know so much about it, the people at the trial would believe I'd been there.

"You'd have to say it as though you believed it," said Lord John.

I'd say it as though I believed it, which I did, because I believed in saving Gentleman Jack. "So I won't run away to the hideout?" I said. "I'll stay in the Indigo Heart and go back to the cottage?"

"Yes," said Flora. "If you want to save Gentleman Jack."

All at once, I was very tired. It was tiring not to run away so suddenly. "Gentleman Jack said to ask you about the Songbird."

"Tell him," said Flora, "I have no information on that score."

But Flora was lying. There was a Songbird whistling right outside her front door. Why would she want to keep him secret?

"Gentleman Jack said to ask you about getting a good-luck opal." I thought of the good-luck case in the General Store and the swimmery dazzle of the opals.

"For stars' sake!" said Flora. "He knows he can't get an opal before he gets his gold."

"He also said to ask about getting his gold." Actually, that was the first thing Gentleman Jack had said. If I'd been exercising judgment, I'd have asked it first.

"The way I see it," said Flora, "he won't get his gold until he gets a Songbird."

And did he need a good-luck opal to get a Songbird?

Flora guessed what I was thinking. "Smart girl," she said.

I wasn't smart, but I was determined to get Gentleman Jack what he wanted, which was also what Grandmother wanted. And we already had the Songbird. All we had to do was grab him.

"Tell me quick about the Fair," I said. "The Judge will find me soon."

"He won't find us for a while," said Flora. We leaned into the circle of yellow flame. "First he'll look in the genteel shops and offices."

"Then he'll cross the Line to our side of town," said Lord John. "He'll look in the Den." Doubtful Mittie had crossed a Line to come into the Territories. You crossed a Line when you went into a foreign place.

"And the billiards hall," said Flora. "And the roulette parlor."

The Judge would be going into a foreign place.

We leaned in toward one another, into the pool of candlelight. I looked from Flora's face to Lord John's face. But then something went crack, and I sprang apart from myself.

"No shooting!" said Flora's fierce, clear voice. "This is your last warning, Nilsson."

A big man stepped forward. "Yes, I forget your rules. It doesn't happen again. See, away goes the gun." He set a revolver on the table. There were scratches in the table made by knives. Some of the scratches were letters; some of the letters were probably words.

Flora jerked her head, and a pretty girl came over and snatched up the revolver. She ejected the shell casing; she knew about guns. Did everyone here know about guns? What about the other pretty girls walking around, all of them with long, loose hair?

Mrs. del Salto did not have loose hair. None of the women in Betsy Elton's store had had loose hair. It made the Sapphire women look different.

"But the knife is quiet," said Nilsson. "Now I use the knife."

"Now you do not use the knife." Flora reached for the hat—the hat that was no longer Doubtful Mittie's hat—turned it round, and looked inside. Then she whispered to one of the pretty girls, who hung it from a hook on the wall.

"You may use your knife," said Flora, "when you follow my rules."

Flora didn't raise her voice, but the men quieted. So did the other noises: the clunk of billiard balls, the slap of cards. Even the piano music trailed off the edge of the table and into silence. It was quiet enough that you could hear the double doors whoosh shut.

"This," said Flora, "is Gentleman Jack's hat. I will give each of you a chance to win it. Each of you will stand there . . ."

One of the girls drew an invisible line on the floor with the toe of her slipper.

"And throw your knife here." Flora touched the hatband, beside the scarlet feather.

"Whoever can throw his knife right there," said Flora, "throw it so that it sticks, will get the hat for his own.

"We'll take bets, gentlemen," said Flora. "You can bet on anyone willing to throw." She reached for me, drew me in front of her. "You can even bet on this girl."

"Gentleman Jack's little girl?" said Nilsson.

"Would you be willing to play?" Flora asked me.

I said I guessed I'd be willing.

"Fun at last!" said the dagger.

It got louder now, with the men calling out bets and the girls float-ing around in their airy dresses, taking money, handing out scraps of paper. One of them had a bump in her stomach. I knew about the bump. It was where she was going to have a baby.

The first man stepped up to the invisible line. He reached for his knife, tossed it from hand to hand, quick and hard. Now to his right hand, now to his left.

"*Amateur!*" said the dagger.

"Show-off," I said. A true knife professional stayed still as cold steel.

His knife went wide of the mark. There came laughter, sharp as knives.

"*Nothing's sharp as knives,*" said the dagger. "*Except knives.*"

Next up was a man with a chain across his boiled shirt. Four nug-gets hung from the chain.

"*Gold!*" said the dagger.

"Gold!" I said.

"*But not enough for Grandmother,*" said the dagger.

"*Not enough to get her empire,*" I said.

The gold-nugget man was very fancy, but fanciness doesn't help you throw a knife. There came more laughter when he missed, and the Sapphire was back to its old noisy self. The piano music tilted into my ear.

Another man threw a knife with a curved blade.

"*You can't throw a curved blade!*" said the dagger.

"You can throw it," I said. "But you'll miss."

Why did they want the hat, anyway? It would kill them to wear it. It had killed Doubtful Mittie.

"*Too bad he wasn't more doubtful about the hat,*" said the dagger.

Now came Nilsson's turn. "I hit the hat," said Nilsson, "then I keep the hat, yes?"

"Not a chance," said the dagger, because Nilsson held his knife too hard. You should hold a knife lightly between your thumb and forefinger. That was the only way it could fly true.

"It's not a bad knife," said the dagger.

"It deserves a better owner," I said.

Nilsson was making little jabbing motions. "As though that will help anything," I said. His hand swiveled on his wrist. You needed a solid wrist to throw a knife.

After all his jabbing and jabbering, Nilsson finally threw the knife. It fell short of the wall. There rose the usual laughter, and Lord John brought him something in a glass. "You probably need this just about now."

I stepped away. I didn't want to smell the bitter sharpness.

Nilsson nodded. He had a big bland face, with knobbly bits like a potato. "I did want me that pretty hat."

Now another man, holding his knife with his thumb and three fingers.

"I guess you can hold it like that," said the dagger.

"If you don't care where it goes," I said.

"Funny thing about you, Nilsson," said the gold-nugget man, laughing. "You can carve a thing of beauty with that knife but not be able to throw it for nothing." It was good laughter, though. I knew what bad laughter sounded like, when things could turn ugly in a second.

Flora came up behind me. She smelled of lilacs, even though there were no flowers now, not with the snow about to fall. "You get yourself that hat," she said.

"That little gal of yours, Flora," said a voice. "She got herself a name?"

But I wasn't Flora's little girl. I was Gentleman Jack's, and soon I would be Grandmother's, too.

"What's your name, sweetheart?" said Flora.

"Robber Girl," I said. "Gentleman Jack says you can call me Robber Girl."

There was no laughter at that, not at something Gentleman Jack had said. Everyone knew Gentleman Jack didn't take kindly to laughter.

Mostly, though, the Gentlemen called me Girl.

I slipped the dagger from its sheath. It would be all right to take it out here. These people would let me keep it. I felt the familiar weight of it. I knew just how it balanced. I knew just how it flew.

Lord John examined it. "Clean, sharp, and dry," he said.

I made my ears stop working so I couldn't hear the men stomp and swear. That was one trick to throwing the dagger. You built a wall between yourself and the rest of the world. You didn't think about the egg-man grabbing your wrist. You didn't think about the egg-man talking about sticky fingers. You didn't think about how you had to hate Betsy Elton, and probably Mrs. del Salto, too.

The rest of the world vanished. It was just you and the dagger. When you were throwing the dagger, you couldn't remember anything anyone had said, like Betsy saying thank the stars I hadn't burnt the del Saltos in their sleep.

The only thing I heard was the piano music skittering into a corner, then curling up to sleep. The piano player was going to watch me throw the dagger. I heard the absence of piano music. That was all.

I held the dagger by the handle. It warmed to my touch. It lay in the cradle of my thumb and first finger. Now everything was straight, everything was orderly.

I raised the dagger. The blade faced the back wall. That was the best way to throw it. That way it would somersault through the air.

I flicked my hand forward.

The dagger flew.

It didn't make much of a thunk, but that was all right. A six-inch blade doesn't thunk, but it sticks. If it has a sharp tip, it sticks. It took the men a moment to notice that the dagger had truly struck and that it had struck true. Then they were shouting that Flora was a sly fox to have bet money on me. That they wished they'd bet money on me.

I realized Flora must have talked about me with Gentleman Jack. That was why she'd bet on me; she knew I could throw a knife. Gentleman Jack must have talked about me when I wasn't there—what a strange thought.

Nilsson had reached the wall before I did. He was already examining the hat, and the dagger, and guessing how far the dagger stuck into the wall.

"Deep enough, I guess," he said gloomily.

"I have the sharpest tip," said the dagger.

I pulled the dagger from the wood. The hat fell, Nilsson caught it. Yes, the dagger had a sharp tip, but the wall was made of indigo, which is soft. It's easy to throw deep into indigo. I wouldn't say that now, though, not with the dagger so happy and proud.

"Nilsson," said the bartender, "you ain't going to get that pretty feather, now, are you?"

"I give the little lady the hat, yes?" said Nilsson.

"Yes!" said a sea of voices.

"Water is a sea," said the dagger. *"Not voices."*

Now, for the fourth time since I'd come to Blue Roses, came the reeling, pealing bells. I glanced to the window. It had gotten dark without my noticing. But of course, we'd left late because of all the tray-fixing.

Everyone stopped and listened. The bells played the tune once through, then started again. Was it possible that I remembered the tune? Not from the three times I'd heard it already, but from long ago?

"Not possible!" said the dagger.

But now the piano joined the bells and everyone turned to face the same direction. They sang the words the Judge had muttered last night. I knew the tune, and now I heard the words.

"The bird sang like a star,
Exalting near and far
The brightest Sister Seven.
With grateful joy we raise
Our voices in her praise:
A melody to heaven."

"You don't know the tune," said the dagger. "You don't know the words."

But I knew some of the words, like Sisters Seven, and Grateful Joy, and Melody to Heaven. They rang a soft silver bell, which meant I'd known them in the Before Time.

"Yes," said the dagger. "But that's betrayal."

Five minutes later, it was over and everything went on as before. Nilsson knelt on the floor in front of me. His knobbled potato face floated in the air. "Fair and square," he said, and set the hat in my hands.

With Nilsson kneeling and me standing, we were about the same height. I leaned forward. "You carve things from wood?"

Nilsson nodded. "Best woodworker in these parts."

"If you carve me something," I said, "I'll give you the hat."

"You will?" said Nilsson. "Little Robber Girl, you will!"

"I need a dog," I said. "A dog carved of wood."

"How big will he be, this dog?" said Nilsson.

"It needs to fit into a dollhouse," I said. "A dollhouse is one-twelfth the size of a regular house." I measured a space between my thumb and index finger. Then I made it a little bigger. It had to be a big dog, big enough for the baby to grab onto its collar and pull himself up. Big enough to support the baby when he was learning to walk.

"But it shouldn't be made of indigo," I said. "Indigo is too soft." I needed a dog that wouldn't break. I needed a dog with a good, strong heart. "And he should have joints, because he'll need to run after the ball."

"I make him of oak," said Nilsson. "White oak is stronger than red. Its pores are smaller, so it rots slow. I make him of white oak."

Lord John took the hat from me. "I'll play middleman. Nilsson, when you give me the dog, I'll give you the hat."

"But don't wear the hat," I said. Nilsson wasn't from the Territories; you could tell by the way he spoke. He'd had to cross a Line to get here. He might not know he shouldn't wear a dead man's hat.

"The snow is coming." Nilsson lumbered to his feet. "I bring the dog after the snow."

One of the double doors swung open. There was something about the way it opened that made everyone look up. It was the Judge, who would never slam through a door. Already, I knew this about him. He would open it quietly and deliberately, and he would close it the same way.

The Judge waited just inside the door. I walked toward him. The floor was sticky. I knew the floor at the cottage would never be sticky. The floor at the cottage was smooth and pale. The planks fit together with hardly a seam. The planks in the Sapphire were rough and widely spaced. The burnt end of a cigar lay in one of the spaces.

The Judge and I left the Sapphire together. The air turned our breath into clouds; the peanut man's song made a cloud in the air, and his coals made steam, and it smelled like butter and ash. All up and down the street, flames leapt from great metal bowls attached to the columns that held up the roof that hung over the sidewalk.

"Do you want to go home?" said the Judge.

"No!" said the dagger.

"Yes," I said.

Buttercream Cottage

"TELL THE JUDGE YOU'LL TESTIFY," said the dagger.

But he'd have to speak to me first. Three breaths and a swallow had already passed. Anyway, I couldn't tell the Judge until I told Gentleman Jack. Gentleman Jack might hear I was going to testify and think I really meant to do it. I couldn't bear that.

I had time to notice Main Street now. A few stunted indigo trees grew here and there along the boardwalk. We crossed a big square with buildings on four sides, and then we were on the fancier part of Main Street. We must have crossed the Line. I looked behind me, once, and saw the star steps climbing to the Shrine, and the Shrine shining above all of Blue Roses. You could always see the Shrine and the Shrine could always see you.

And then a thought came to me that the direction everyone faced when the bells rang was the direction of the Shrine. That made sense: the words worshipped the Blue Rose and the Shrine worshipped the Blue Rose.

The Judge said nothing. Not about me and the candy. Not about me and the hammer. Not about me and the egg-man and how I'd cracked his elbow.

The Judge waited to speak, and the snow waited, too. It waited for us to return to the cottage. Return. That was another good word, like Grandmother. It meant we had left the cottage and now we were going back. You have to leave before you can return.

I was glad the Judge didn't speak. Then I couldn't, either. That was restful. What would be unrestful would be explaining that Betsy had given me the candy but her father thought I'd stolen it. How I'd had to crack-crack-crack the flower in order to grab the hammer.

I'd been thinking about saving Gentleman Jack from jail. I would always save Gentleman Jack. But I'd never save Betsy. I'd only un-save her.

"*That's when I'll taste her blood!*" said the dagger.

We turned up the path that led to the cottage. The higher we went, the more the steps misbehaved, stumbling here, crumbling there, changing their mind about whether to go up or down.

"*If steps go up,*" said the dagger, "*they also go down.*"

"Look at the stars," said the Judge. "The Seven Sisters are very bright tonight."

I'd only ever heard about the Seven Sisters from the song the Rosati had sung along with the bells. The Judge said they were seven stars, all nestled together, and that he could show them to me. In order to find them, first you had to find the Orion constellation. The Judge said a Constellation is a group of stars that makes a pattern people can easily recognize. I said I knew that already. The Judge pointed out the Orion constellation, which is one of the most recognizable, so it was easy to find. Then you look at the three stars that are in Orion's belt. They're also pretty easy to find. You follow the line they make—which is Up—to another star, with a reddish color, and you keep your eyes going in the same Up direction and hop your eyes over to the Sisters.

They were the brightest stars, which meant they were easy to count. They made a blue cluster in the sky. "Not seven," I said. "Just six."

"Yes," said the Judge. "The Seventh Sister is the Blue Rose, who has come from the heavens to help us here on earth. If ever you see the seventh star, you'll know the Blue Rose has returned to the heavens to visit her star sisters. It's the time you're most likely to discover whether she granted the boon you craved."

"Does she come back to earth?" I said. "After she visits her sisters?"

"Always," said the Judge.

We rounded a curve, and there was the cottage. In the parlor window shone a candle. The flame reflected itself in the glass. The cottage was lighting our way. It was different from returning to the hideout.

"Of course it's different," said the dagger. "You can't see a hideout—that's the whole point!"

The cottage was expecting us. The cottage knew about snow, which was why it had a long slanting roof that would make the snow slide to the ground. It was waiting for us to go inside, and then the snow would fall.

"A cottage doesn't wait!" said the dagger.

It was too dark to see the color of the cottage, but I remembered it. I remembered the trim, which was like a blue ribbon holding the walls together. I remembered the walls were the color of a dream.

"That's not a color," said the dagger, but the dagger was wrong. It had also been wrong in the General Store when it said people didn't think up colors. When it said that colors just were.

"A little faster, please," said the Judge. "Mrs. del Salto will be worried."

Now I could speak. "What color is the cottage?"

"We call it buttercream," said the Judge.

Buttercream. That was not a word in my foreign-coin pocket, but I knew what it meant. Buttercream was soft and glimmering. Buttercream was the color of cream mixed with sunshine.

The Judge wiped his feet on the outdoor carpet with the sunflower. I wiped my feet on the sunflower. It would be quiet inside; it would be even quieter when it snowed. Sunshine is loud. Snow is soft.

When you return to a place, you know what's going to happen. You know the Judge will take the key from his pocket. You know the key will fit into the keyhole, that the door will swing open, that there will be a shining indigo floor.

So much floor, just for a key.

"Mrs. del Salto will be waiting," said the Judge.

You know the Judge will open the drawer of the little table. But this is the first time you notice the inside. You notice it's lined with soft green material. That's so the keys can be comfortable, the Judge's key and Mrs. del Salto's key, lying side by side.

It was a long time ago since I'd first come into the cottage. It was a long time ago I'd been surprised they'd built a whole room just for some keys. Now I wasn't surprised.

"*Keys don't have rooms,*" said the dagger. "*People have rooms.*"

But I went ahead and thought it anyway. What if the keys had come before the room? What if the keys had come first, and then the drawer to hold the keys, and then the table to hold the drawer, and then the room to hold the table, and then the house to hold the room?

"You don't need keys if you don't have a house," said the dagger.

The Judge knocked at the opening to the parlor. In the parlor was a window, beneath the window was a ledge, and on the ledge burned the candle.

"To light your way," said Mrs. del Salto. "In case it snowed."

"Thank you," said the Judge.

"Still," she said, "I like the dark."

I felt how walking into the room was like walking beneath the wing of a dove. The Judge made the fire whoosh into the lamps. He bent over the fireplace and made the coals crackle and burn.

"You said it was just for one night." Mrs. del Salto flitted up and down, her old-crow dress rusty in the firelight.

She meant me. The Judge had said I was going to stay just one night.

"The snow is coming," said the Judge.

"Inarguable," said Mrs. del Salto.

We were quiet a long time. It was hard to say exactly when it started to snow. Just a few flakes at first, matching up with the room. The room was feathery on the inside—not real feathers, just the idea of feathers—and now there were feathers on the outside. The feathery flakes were sticking to the windows.

"If the girl's going to stay until it stops snowing," said Mrs. del Salto, "she must at least have a name."

I had no name.

"What did that man call you?" said Mrs. del Salto. She meant Gentleman Jack. Maybe she couldn't say his name. Maybe she was afraid it would make the inside of her mouth too rough.

"Gentleman Jack?" I said. The inside of my mouth was already rough.

Mrs. del Salto's skirts slithered and whispered. They were waiting for my name.

"Gentleman Jack's going to give me my name," I said.

I scratched at the rough skin on my thumb. It came off in flakes. I had to stay in this place until the trial, even though Mrs. del Salto didn't know that yet. I had to stay in this place, where everyone had real names. I didn't have a real name. Robber Girl was only a job name, like the Sheriff, whose job was to be the sheriff. Or the Judge, whose job was to be a judge. But they had real names underneath.

"We shall have to find you a name," said the Judge.

I had a job name but no real name. Beneath the job name was emptiness.

"Maybe a bite of dinner will help us with the name," said the Judge.

I thought of the stain on the white tablecloth. I thought of the oily splat, I thought of how I couldn't use a fork.

"I don't want any dinner," I said.

"Macaroni and cheese on Friday," said the Judge.

"She's awfully scrawny," said Mrs. del Salto. I wouldn't look at her. I'd only look at her beautiful ring. The stone was the opposite of her, all layers and depths. She existed only on the surface.

"*Later,*" said the dagger, "*we'll creep into the pantry and get something to eat.*"

What was a pantry?

"*It's a place to keep food,*" said the dagger. "*Grandmother's house has a pantry.*"

After the trial, I would go to Grandmother's house. After the trial, I would get my name.

It was a dark night to find a pantry. The snow made ferns on the windows, and the stove made a big black hunching in the dark. I remembered where Mrs. del Salto kept the candles and the matches. The flame made the shadow of the stove jump up the wall.

The pantry was a little room off the kitchen.

"There will be chicken pie in the pantry," said the dagger. "It's called leftovers."

Chicken pie on Thursdays—that's what the Judge had said. But it was Friday, and there was macaroni and cheese on Friday. You could eat chicken pie on Friday, though. You could eat it if you stole from Thursday.

The pantry was filled with doors and drawers. There was glass in the doors and latches on the doors. But you could flick the latches sideways and open them. Bolts were better. I looked at the shelves through the glass—here a stack of plates, there piles of tablecloths, and everywhere the reflection of the candle.

"There are bolts all over Grandmother's house." The dagger was old and had been to Grandmother's house lots of times.

The drawers were set in rows below the doors. Between the doors and the drawers was a shelf, and on the shelf sat the chicken pie. The first drawer was filled with glass jars and metal tops and the biggest spoon in the world.

"What are these for?" I said.

"They're kitchen things," said the dagger. "They're taming things."

"But you told me about the pantry," I said. "That's a kitchen thing. You told me about leftovers."

"You're supposed to raid pantries," said the dagger. "Raiding is the same as stealing. Leftovers are for stealing. Stealing is wild."

The next drawer was filled with a mound of whiteness; it glistened in the candlelight. "Sugar!" I'd had sugar before, in the hideout. When we had sugar, Gentleman Jack would let me have coffee. He let me put in as much sugar as I wanted.

I licked my finger and stuck it in the glistening mound. Imagine, a whole drawer of sugar. The hinges of my jaw ached with sweetness. Sugar was for stealing, so it was wild, too.

"Grandmother has two drawers of sugar," said the dagger. "One for white sugar, one for brown."

I set down the candle; I sliced the dagger into the pie. I set the slice on my hand. There was no fork to trip me up, no plate to make the fork clink, no tablecloth to stain. My hand would be a plate, the dagger would be a fork. I could lick my hand clean, I could lick the dagger clean.

But I had no time to do either. There came a low whiffling sound—

"The kitchen door!" said the dagger. "It has no bolt."

It didn't even have a latch. I couldn't stop the door whiffling open, or the feet padding into the kitchen, or the fire whooshing into the lamps.

I shoved the dagger into its sheath. The other hand was full of pie. The light had not whooshed on in the pantry, but the candle still burned. I stood in the semidarkness, beside the open drawer of sugar.

"Hungry?" said the Judge.

I hated his voice, so reasonable and pleasant. You couldn't tell what a person felt with a voice like that. At least you knew what Mrs. del Salto felt.

His voice stabbed me in the stomach.

"That's not what stabbing feels like," said the dagger.

The dagger didn't always understand the way words worked. This wasn't an actual stab. It was a stab that started in my mind and ended in my stomach.

"Let's set you a place," said the Judge.

I didn't know how to set a place, but the Judge was already turning away. I had to leave the dimness of the pantry. The Judge held a plate; he slid the pie from my hand onto the plate.

I licked my palm. I wiped it on my britches.

"Sit down," said the Judge.

He meant I should sit at the table with the white tablecloth. The stain was gone, but I didn't know how to sit; I didn't know how to eat. I had been stealing the pie—no, raiding the pie. A judge wouldn't like that.

"Tell him you'll testify!" said the dagger. *"Then he won't care about the pantry."*

Now there were two plates of pie on the table, and two forks and two knives. "I wish you'd eat," said the Judge. But the pie had too much gravy.

"I'm going to eat, if you don't mind."

Why should I mind? He knew how to use the points of his fork to stick the chicken. He knew how to use the side of his fork to cut the piecrust. He knew how to get the meat and the crust and the gravy onto his fork all at the same time.

When the Judge was done, he slanted his knife and fork across the upper part of his plate. *"The knife is dull,"* said the dagger, *"but it's made of silver, which means it's valuable."*

The Judge rose. "I'll lay a fire in the library."

Now it would come.

"What will come?" said the dagger.

But I didn't know.

We pushed through the door that had no knob. The library lamps hissed and flared; the fireplace hissed and flared. There was a big table with a chair behind it, but the Judge did not sit there. There was a child's rocking chair in front of a wall made of books, but the Judge did not want me to sit there. He sat in a chair in front of the fire and waved me to a matching chair.

"Tell me," said the Judge. "What would you like to happen?"

My thoughts skittered around like bugs. They didn't know where to go. My thoughts had been underneath a nice, quiet rock—thinking about raiding the pie and what my punishment would be—but then the Judge kicked the rock aside and let in too much light. My thoughts were surprised.

"*Tell him you want to testify!*" said the dagger.

"I want to see Gentleman Jack," I said. I had to tell Gentleman Jack about Flora and our plans. I had to tell him I was going to save him, not betray him. I had to tell him that we'd found a Songbird. That would make him happy.

"But the snow has come," said the Judge.

"After the snow."

"Here's what I propose," said the Judge. "After the snow, you will go to school. After the first day, you may see Gentleman Jack."

"*School is a taming thing,*" said the dagger.

"I won't go to school," I said. "Gentleman Jack wouldn't like it." Gentleman Jack wouldn't want me to be tame.

"You will go to school," said the Judge. "You will show the towns-folk, like Mr. Elton—"

Mr. Elton was the egg-man, I thought.

"You will show him you're not wild."

"I am wild," I said. "I made the red marks on your cheek."

"You will show him you're not vicious."

"I am vicious," I said. "I hit him with a hammer."

"You will show him you do not steal."

"I do steal," I said. "I was stealing the pie."

"It's lucky," said the Judge, "that you didn't much hurt him. It's lucky, too, that he was also in the wrong, having accused you of stealing. We spoke about it and we decided to embrace the Blue Rose's first precept."

"What's a precept?"

The Judge said it was a sort of rule, intended to make people live more happily and more righteously. The Blue Rose's precept went like this:

Accept your sorrows,

If you cannot change them.

Embrace your joys,

So you don't estrange them.

"The Blue Rose said that!" I said. "It doesn't sound fancy enough."

The Judge explained that hundreds of years had passed since the Blue Rose led them to the Indigo Heart, and that they no longer really knew the exact words she used, and the rhyme kept changing and getting more modern, and maybe even a little bit funny, but the sense of it remained the same.

I asked him about Estrange, and he said it means to grow distant, or cold. "Perhaps you've had a fight with a friend and now you and the friend no longer talk."

I was estranged from Betsy—

"You can't be estranged unless you were friends first," said the dagger.

"I'll be estranged if I want to!" Or, could I be Stranged from Betsy?

"What this all means," said the Judge, "is that we'll be friends again, and not be estranged. We will not say he wrongly accused you. He will not say you should not have hit him."

"I wish I'd hit him a thousand times," I said.

"You show commendable enthusiasm," said the Judge.

I looked past the Judge. In the corner stood a grandfather clock; it was even taller than the Judge. I looked from the face of the clock to the face of the Judge and back again. You could tell the Judge was alive because of my tooth marks.

"You stung him," said the dagger. "You mortified his flesh."

A person doesn't get tooth marks when he's dead. He doesn't bleed when you stick him, he doesn't bruise when you kick him. Gentleman

Jack told me so when Marshal Starling was lying in the street. If I'd bitten the Marshal, he wouldn't have gotten any tooth marks.

The clock was dead, too. I could tell because the pendulum didn't swing, and there was no ticking sound, and the hands didn't move. The Judge's clock was dead, and my pocket watch was dead. But we'd fix the watch when we got to Netherby Scar.

There was a grandfather clock at Grandmother's house, but it was alive and ticking. I liked the word Grandfather. It was almost as good as the word Grandmother, which was the roundest, warmest word in the world.

There was no grandfather clock in the dollhouse, though.

"Your clock doesn't go," I said. I felt Grandmother's watch, heavy in my pocket. Gentleman Jack had let me keep it so I'd never forget that Grandmother was waiting for us.

"No," said the Judge. "Here in the cottage, we have let time die."

"Time can't die," I said.

"You'd be surprised," said the Judge. "Mrs. del Salto killed it."

I wasn't that surprised.

But I couldn't let time die, not for me. I could only get to Grandmother's house if time passed. Once I knew the date of the trial, I'd start counting the days again. I'd push time forward. And later, when the pocket watch was fixed, I'd make time come alive by winding up the watch's heart.

I looked at the wall made of books. I looked at the tiles around the fireplace. They were blue with yellow tulips. On the mantelpiece stood a gold frame holding a photograph.

"Gold paint," said the dagger. "Not valuable."

The photograph showed a girl holding a little boy. Their mouths were straight lines. The girl looked at me. I looked back.

"Magda and Isaac," said the Judge. "Magda would have been about your age."

"*He means Magda died*," said the dagger.

I wished Betsy were in a frame, squeezed into a wooden box. Then she'd be dead. The Judge and I sat quietly in that room where no clocks were ticking and no children were growing.

"*You're growing*," said the dagger.

I wondered how I'd look in a frame. But Magda had light hair and a plump face and I had black hair and a thin face. It was hard to imagine, and anyway I didn't want to be like Magda and Isaac, stuck in their frame, forever the same size. I didn't want to be dead.

"You want to see Gentleman Jack." The Judge was good at stirring up the conversation, poking at it like hot coals. "What else do you want?"

"I want to know about jacks," I said.

A New Day Zero

✝ THE MORNING WAS DARK. The snow made a gray flutter at the window, like doves. It was different to be in a cottage than in a hideout. It was different when it snowed. The cottage huddled in around you. The cottage pushed away the wind, the cottage pushed away the snow.

The attic door was closed. Its tongue slid back and forth when you turned the peanut handle. I'd jiggled the door last night to make sure its tongue was securely in its mouth. It was good to be locked in an attic when it snowed.

The electric candle stood in the window. I could light the candle. Or I could not light the candle. I could do whatever I wanted.

"*Except not go to school,*" said the dagger.

Sometimes I wished the dagger couldn't hear all my thoughts.

"*I heard that,*" said the dagger.

The snow was quiet, which made the outside world bigger. It made the inside world smaller. The cottage huddled in around me. The door was quiet and the bolt was quiet. They kept other people out; they kept me in. I hadn't known what it would feel like not being able to move. The snow drifted against the windows and doors, which meant you couldn't open them. The bolt kept the door closed, which meant I had to stay still.

The snow breathed feathers against the window. This was my second time sleeping alone. There had always been Gentlemen in the hideout.

But I wasn't quite alone. There was the dagger. There were the dolls. Were the dolls still in the dollhouse, alive and talking?

"*Not alive!*" said the dagger.

Yes, alive, for they weren't in the dollhouse parlor, where I'd left them. They must have walked on their little joints to the back of the dollhouse. The kitchen must be in the back, where the human-size kitchen was. I wondered if they ever went to bed. Their bedroom was just above the parlor. If their eyes could close, they could probably sleep.

"*Dolls aren't awake!*" said the dagger. "*Dolls aren't asleep!*"

I'd let myself be trapped by the soft corners of the cottage and by the bolt at the door. I could turn round and round like a bird in a nest, making the room fit my shape. Later, when I was in Netherby Scar, I'd wind the pocket watch, and my fingers would go round and round.

It would be in Netherby Scar that I would come alive and the watch would come alive. We'd each of us help the other come alive.

I fished the watch from my britches pocket.

There was a little knob on top, just for winding. The watch was made of silver, beginning to grow dull. Silver was valuable, even if it was dull, which meant you could sell it for a lot of money. But things could be valuable for different reasons. I didn't care about the money— I would never sell the watch!—but the watch was valuable because it meant Grandmother was waiting for me. I ran my fingers over the engraving of a bird in flight. The oils from my fingers would tarnish the silver, but I'd had the watch for sixty days. That was enough days to have learned how to polish it.

"Iron and carbon don't get tarnished," said the dagger.

They could get tarnished, but you could never win an argument with the dagger.

I flicked the tiny clasp at the bottom of the watch; the case opened. The watch face was on one side of the case. On the other side was a photograph of Grandmother when she was young. She was very beautiful, her black hair pulled back from her face, a few tendrils curling down the sides. Her eyes were long and her eyebrows made upward slashes, which doesn't sound pretty, but it was.

In her arms lay a baby in a white smock. The baby wore a little white bonnet, on to which were stitched some letters. The letters were too small for me to read, but that didn't matter: I didn't know how to read, and anyway, I already knew the baby was Gentleman Jack.

The photograph made a kind of echo-memory in my mind. But I didn't know what sound it was echoing. It was snowing, but there was enough sun to cast a slanted shadow from the electric candle. The echo-memory was like that shadow. You can't see the sun because of the snow, but you know the sun is there because of the shadows.

"After the trial," I said, "Gentleman Jack and I will come home to you." It was silly to speak to a photograph, but I did anyway.

I always spoke to Grandmother's photograph.

The dagger and I went downstairs. "Pay attention to the exits," said the dagger. Exits were important, Gentleman Jack always said.

"There's one exit," I said.

"*The front door is one*," said the dagger. "*The door into the kitchen is two.*"

"*A door's not an exit if you don't know where it goes.*" That was one of Gentleman Jack's rules. "*Do you know where the door at the other end of the kitchen goes?*"

The dagger didn't know.

If I could turn the dollhouse around, maybe I'd know where the kitchen door led. So far, it looked as though the dollhouse was just the same as the cottage, except for a few details—like the grandfather clock. There was no grandfather clock in the dollhouse.

Down the polished corridor and through the library we went. There was the fireplace—blue tiles, yellow tulips—but there was no fire. There was always a fire in Grandmother's fireplace.

"*Fireplaces,*" said the dagger. "*Grandmother has lots of fireplaces.*"

And here was the funny thing I'd seen last night. The walls were made of books.

"*Not made of books.*" The dagger loved knowing more than me. "*There are bookshelves on the walls and books on the bookshelves.*"

The dagger was old. It had been into lots of houses when it belonged to Gentleman Jack. It knew about things like walls that were made of bookshelves.

I'd seen the Judge's table last night, but now I saw how long it was, with lion's feet on the legs. I saw the things on the desk. A wooden box, painted the bright blue of cornflowers, and painted on that, purple irises. I opened the box and I closed it. I opened it and closed it. Each time, the lid fit squarely on the shoulders of the box.

If I were a box, I'd always want to wear my lid.

"*That's a taming thought,*" said the dagger.

But I wanted to keep thinking it. Maybe I could think it sideways, so the dagger couldn't hear.

"*I can hear sideways,*" said the dagger. "*I can hear upside down.*"

The box was full of thumbtacks with little cloth heads and tiny patterns on the cloth. I would take the most beautiful ones. There— pink, green, yellow.

"*They're only made of brass,*" said the dagger. "*Not as good as cold iron and carbon.*"

There was a scatter of coins on the desk, and an inkwell.

"*The inkwell is made of silver,*" said the dagger.

"I'll take the inkwell when we leave," I said. "I'll take the coins."

"*But not the photograph,*" said the dagger. "*The frame isn't valuable.*"

I put the lid back on the box. I didn't want the dagger to know what I was thinking, which was that the box could be happy now that it wore its lid. The dagger would say that boxes and lids were taming. It was wearisome to have the dagger always listening in.

I remembered the Blue Rose's first precept. First it said, "Accept your sorrows." Then it said, "Embrace your joys." The words seemed clear, but the idea behind them was kind of bendy. It was the kind of idea the dagger wouldn't understand. The dagger would say you should never accept your sorrows. But I'd taken off the box's lid, which was a sorrow to the box. Then I'd put it back on, which meant the box could be joyful.

Accept your sorrows, I thought. Maybe the dagger wouldn't understand.

The dagger said nothing.

Embrace your joys, I thought.

The dagger said nothing.

I turned my back on the library, on the bookshelf walls and the box and the frame, on the coins and the inkwell, which was made of silver. I pushed through the kitchen door into the smell of coffee and bacon. The Judge and Mrs. del Salto sat at the table.

"Where do we send the girl?" said Mrs. del Salto. She looked at me. "Where do we send her after it stops snowing?"

The Judge lifted the yellow cup off a hook beneath a shelf and put it on the table. He was going to give me milk; he was going to give me honey. But what if Mrs. del Salto told him to send me away first?

And suddenly the reason I hadn't told the Judge I'd testify at Gentleman Jack's trial seemed like the stupidest reason in the world. It would be terrible if Gentleman Jack thought I was going to tell the truth at his trial, but it would be even more terrible if they sent me away so I couldn't testify at all.

I had to tell the Judge I was going to testify. I had to tell him now, but no one had spoken to me since last night. I had to get them to speak to me first. The yellow cup sat on the table. I remembered how its shadow turned the milk the color of the cottage, but that didn't matter now.

I took two steps to the table. I snatched up the cup, I dashed it on the floor. Now they'd have to say something.

At first there was only silence. I looked at the Judge. My tooth marks were red on his cheek. I looked at Mrs. del Salto, eating ashes and salt.

"What was that about?" said the Judge.

"I want to tell you I'll testify—testify in court—about Gentleman Jack."

"Breaking a cup is a peculiar way to do so."

I looked at the cup. It lay in pieces on the floor. It wasn't as strong as my tin cup in the hideout. Things made out of metal were the best. Another best thing was eating and drinking in the hideout. There I ate by myself.

"I'll get some glue," said the Judge, "so you can repair it."

"Did you hear what I said?"

But the Judge was already swinging through the kitchen door to his library. Then he returned moments later with a small glass bottle. "Please count the number of pieces into which you have rendered the cup."

Rendered? I didn't know that word, but I knew what he meant. I counted. There were eight pieces.

"You will go to school for eight days before you may see Gentleman Jack." The Judge placed the bottle before me.

"So many days," said Mrs. del Salto.

The bottle of glue was shaped like a gourd. When you unscrewed it, there was a brush attached to the inside of the lid. That was smart. I glued the pieces; the Judge and Mrs. del Salto watched.

Eight whole days, I thought. For once, Mrs. del Salto and I were thinking the same thing.

The Judge was looking at the cup. "You have restored its bloom."

Here were more words I didn't understand, but the Judge explained: it was when something needed to grow, like skin, say, after you'd scraped it—

"Or," said Mrs. del Salto, "your heart after you'd broken it—"

"Monica!" said the Judge, and they both fell silent.

But I didn't need to hear any more. Restored its bloom. I understood what it meant.

"Let's start over," said the Judge. "Good morning."

I knew what to say. "Good morning."

"I'm glad you're to testify at the trial, but I wonder what changed your mind."

Mrs. del Salto interrupted. "How long until the trial?"

"The trial is set for May sixth," said the Judge.

I thought a moment. "Ninety-three days." I'd had practice figuring out days. I would start counting backward again until I got to another Day Zero. Day Zero had always been the day Gentleman Jack and I were going to start living in Grandmother's house.

"You count fast!" said the Judge.

"That's a lot of days," said Mrs. del Salto. She didn't want me in the cottage, casting my shadow on the memories of Magda and Isaac. You could tell by the way she looked at me with her black-button eyes. She didn't want a living girl in the cottage, when her own two children were stuck in a frame.

"He's to be tried in the capital," said the Judge. "You know how crowded the trial calendar can be."

"May sixth is good," said the dagger. *"You can eat grasshoppers in May."* The dagger was right. I might have to get to Netherby Scar by myself. But I could always find things to eat. There'd definitely be daisies, which were almost lettuce, and grasshoppers. You could eat anything, if you'd a mind.

"You'll need a name," said the Judge. "For us to use, of course, but especially to use in school. I'll give you one if you'd like."

The dolls had given me a name. It was better than Magda or Isaac. I didn't want the Judge to give me a dumb name like that. "My name is Starling."

"What a terrible name," said the dagger. *"Starlings are small and plain."*

"What a lovely name!" said the Judge. "Starlings are fierce fighters. Starlings are feathered iridescence."

I'd never seen a starling, but I could tell the name was good. A name was good if the first name went with the last name. I couldn't read, but I knew letters and their sounds. I knew the words Starling and del Salto went together. They both had the S and the L sounds, which were soft. They both had the T sound, which was like a little jump to help get your tongue to the next sound, which was soft again.

"It's too long," said the dagger.

It was exactly the right length.

"It's longer than Gentleman Jack," said the dagger.

There were four sounds in Gentleman Jack. There were five sounds in Starling del Salto. "It's just one sound longer," I said. "That's like a quarter inch longer."

"A quarter inch is too long," said the dagger.

"Not in a knife," I said. "In a knife fight, an extra quarter inch might mean winning."

"Starling," said Mrs. del Salto. "A murmuration of starlings."

I didn't know what that was.

"It's when they all fly together," said Mrs. del Salto. "Each starling turns and swoops at exactly the same time, as though they're in a ballet."

I didn't know about a ballet, but it was such a pretty word, it must be taming.

"Can I have some cleaning things?" I said.

"Oh?" said Mrs. del Salto.

"I want to clean the dollhouse." I really just wanted to polish the watch, but I couldn't say that.

"You approve of cleaning, don't you?" said the Judge.

"In moderation," said Mrs. del Salto. "In extreme moderation."

"Can moderation be extreme?" The Judge laughed, and even Mrs. del Salto smiled. I'd never seen her smile before.

The cleaning things were through a door that led to some narrow stairs. "Stairs to the cellar," said the Judge, "where the butter waits and dreams."

"Butter doesn't dream!" said the dagger.

Before you got to the cellar and the dreaming butter, there was a little landing with some shelves. I recognized cloths for dusting and brushes for scrubbing and soaps for rubbing. Mrs. del Salto gave me wet cloths for washing and dry cloths for drying. I let Mrs. del Salto tell me about spirits of ammonia and spirits of turpentine, even though I already knew about them. I would mix them together to clean the watch.

I hadn't known about beeswax, though, which was for polishing furniture. I hadn't known it smelled of honey, which was from bees, mixed with the smell of fresh wind. The fresh-wind smell was from lavender oil.

Mrs. del Salto took me through a door from the kitchen that led into a dining room. Its walls were the color of cream, with painted roses and ribbons making swoops along the top. Mrs. del Salto said that the swoops were called a Garland. The carpet was strawberries on cream.

In the middle stood a great table. "It shines like that because of the beeswax," she said. I looked at the table, and then at the wall, where the garland looped up toward the ceiling, making an arch. In the arch, on the wall, was something that might have been a picture, but it was covered by a cloth.

"A mirror," said Mrs. del Salto.

But mirrors are for looking, and you can't look through a cloth.

"One must always cover the mirrors in a house of death," said Mrs. del Salto. "Otherwise, the souls of the dead might get stuck."

But I thought Mrs. del Salto would want the souls of her children to get stuck. She didn't like it that they'd died and gone away.

It was good to learn about beeswax. Then I'd know about it when I got to Grandmother's house, which was sparkling clean. Gentleman Jack said that every day they washed the windows with newspaper and water. The newspapers were so old, they'd gone gray and soft as powder.

Mrs. del Salto wanted me to smell the bottle of lye. She said if I smelled it, I'd never drink it by accident. But I refused. I already knew how lye smelled, even though I'd never sniffed any. I knew the smell from my imagination. It smells like gravy that's been bled from a tablecloth, which was how she got out my gravy stain. It smells like eyeballs stewing in hot sauce; it smells like throats on fire. The idea of fire makes sense because when you mix lye with certain other things, it can explode.

Mrs. del Salto said I must never drink lye. She said it would eat through my insides and kill me. She didn't know that my imagination had been poached in the smell of lye.

I asked Mrs. del Salto why there was a tablecloth in the kitchen and not the dining room. Weren't tablecloths fancy, and wasn't the dining room fancier than the kitchen?

She shrugged. "The dining room is for entertaining, but I no longer care to entertain."

I went back to the attic smelling of lye.

The Judge had been to the attic while I'd been learning about beeswax and lye. He said he'd realized I couldn't see the back of the dollhouse, so he'd set the dollhouse on a plate. It wasn't a plate for eating, though, not the kind of plate you'd sit in front of, at a table, your eating hand limp and heavy as a dead bird.

It was an enormous plate, the kind you could push with one finger and send spinning round. The dollhouse spun round with it, so the back of the dollhouse went flashing by and then the front again. Round it spun, easy as anything, from the front to the back, from the back to the front.

"It's pleasant to go spinning round," said the voice of the mother doll.

"Very pleasant indeed," said the father doll.

I dragged my finger against the edge of the plate. It slowed, then stopped. The dolls were in the back of the dollhouse.

"You won't forget about the tasks?" said the mother doll.

"The three tasks," said the father doll.

"I'll be here for ninety-three days." It was good the trial calendar was crowded. It meant I could travel when it was warm and eat daisies and grasshoppers.

"First the dog," said the mother doll. But I'd already talked to Nilsson about the dog.

"Then the collar," said the father doll.

"Then the baby," said the mother doll.

"*Stop talking to the dolls!*" said the dagger. "*They're not real!*"

Why couldn't the dagger hear the dolls? It could hear things inside my head, like the things I was thinking. And it could hear things I heard, like people talking.

"*Maybe you're the one that's not real,*" I said.

"*I am six inches of carbon and iron,*" said the dagger. "*I have two edges and a deadly tip. When you have edges and a tip and carbon, you're as real as anything.*"

The dagger felt real, but the dolls felt real, too. Look at them, moving around on their stiff little joints. Of course they were real. Look at them, walking to the back of the dollhouse.

The front of the dollhouse went like this, left to right: parlor, foyer, library. The back went like this: dining room, kitchen. There was a door between the dining room and the kitchen. It was a door that wasn't an exit.

The mother doll and father doll stood in the dining room, which was almost identical to the human-size dining room I'd just seen. There were the red roses and ribbons, the strawberries-and-cream carpet.

"The table is bare," said the mother doll. "It wants a tablecloth."

The mother doll had found the words I hadn't quite found when

I'd asked Mrs. del Salto about the tablecloth. I saw it now: the dollhouse table was too bare. It was gritting its teeth.

"It should be a lace tablecloth," said the mother doll.

"There should be a mirror on the wall," said the father doll. "The dining room wants a mirror."

There was no covered-up mirror in the dollhouse dining room, just an empty space where the garland looped up, making an arch.

"The dining room is a happy color," said the father doll. "People eat more when they eat in a room the color of crimson."

Not red, I thought. Crimson. I knew the color Crimson, but I'd forgotten I knew. It was the color of Grandmother's velvet chairs.

"The dining room is dusty," I said. "So is the kitchen." The second floor needed cleaning, too: the mother and father dolls' bedroom in the front, above the parlor; and the two bedrooms in the back, staring at each other from either side of the landing.

"One for the sister," said the mother doll.

"One for the brother," said the father doll.

Magda and Isaac, sister and brother, the children in the photograph, squeezed into the frame so they could never grow. The rooms were so dusty, the carpets had gone gray. I would clean them, but first I'd polish the watch. That was the important thing. If I kept it polished, I'd get to Grandmother's house.

I got all the tarnish out of the bird engraving, which isn't easy, because it gets down in the tiny lines. But when it was clean and sparkling, it made me think of what the Judge had said: "Feathered iridescence."

Iridescence, I thought, had something to do with shininess. The watch was shiny and starlings were shiny, and my name was Starling.

I knew that Gentleman Jack thought I was dull, even though he didn't always say so. But maybe with a new name, I could start to shine.

Now came the bells, the midday bells, reeling and pealing and singing and ringing. Should I stand up? I knew which direction to face. But I wasn't sure about singing the song—I had such an ugly voice. Better think about more important things. Better think about hiding the watch.

I knew from Gentleman Jack that it was best to hide things in plain sight. I'd hang it from the library wall in the dollhouse. That's where the grandfather clock stood in the human-size house. I pushed one of the thumbtacks into the wall and hung the watch from a link of chain. The bird flew against the library wall.

Now the watch shone, but the rest of the house was dirty. That was unfair to the watch. I'd clean the house, and the house and the watch would match. It would take me a long time, but I had all day. I couldn't leave the attic. The corners curled around me and kept me still.

"Do you see," said the mother doll, "that you came back to the cottage, just as we said you would?"

"Do you see," said the father doll, "that the Indigo Heart is magnetic? It keeps the people it wants to keep."

"I'm not here because of magnets," I said. "I came back because I have a new plan for getting Gentleman Jack out of jail. I'm here because the snow won't let me leave."

"*Gentleman Jack is your magnet,*" said the dagger. "*You'll follow him out of the Indigo Heart.*"

"The Indigo Heart will draw you back again and again," said the father doll.

I remembered the lightning fizz I'd felt when I crossed the red clay road. That was because of the iron in my blood. But the fizz wasn't strong. I could break it anytime.

I started by cleaning the kitchen. I took out the tiny pots and pans. They didn't have blackened bottoms like the ones in the human-size kitchen, but they looked real and were surprisingly heavy.

"Cast iron," said the dagger. "I know my metals."

I took out the oven and the stove and the table and the cabinets with their little drawers. I dusted them and wiped them on a damp cloth. Then I dusted the kitchen and scrubbed it with soap. I put everything back, but before I put the cabinets back, I opened some of the little drawers.

They were empty. But I knew where the sugar was. I would fill them up.

Eight Days of School

† I HAD TO PUT ON A DRESS before I went to school. Mrs. del Salto said so. But where would I carry the dagger? In a sheath beneath the dress? But then I'd have to fling up my skirts to grab it. "You may not go in those britches," said Mrs. del Salto.

"Gentleman Jack lets me wear britches."

"I am not Gentleman Jack," said Mrs. del Salto.

"I will go in my britches," I said.

"Then you shall not go to school," said Mrs. del Salto. "Then you will not see Gentleman Jack."

But I wore her down—that's what she said—and I came downstairs wearing both britches and dress.

"An interesting look," said Mrs. del Salto. "All I can say is I've done my best."

But that wasn't all she could say. She told me there was no time left to brush my hair, but that I'd have to eat breakfast. And that next time we'd brush my hair and that I'd have to eat breakfast seven more times before I could see Gentleman Jack.

The Judge and I paused in the foyer on our way out. There was the table, there was the drawer. The drawer slid open like butter.

"Butter?" said the dagger.

"Smooth, you know," I said.

"Butter can't be a drawer!" The dagger didn't notice the drawer was lined with green felt. It didn't understand that the felt made a bed inside the drawer so the keys could rest. I wouldn't tell the dagger; it wouldn't like me thinking such thoughts. I remembered how, after I'd mended the cup, the Judge had said I'd restored its bloom. I'd think about that. I'd think about how the keys could rest on the green felt and restore their bloom. The dagger couldn't understand what words like that meant. I'd hide my thoughts beneath the Judge's words.

I thought about how I didn't have a key.

"You don't need a key if you want to go out," said the dagger. "You only need a key if you want to come in."

The Judge took his key from the drawer. Now there was only one key. He'd put it back when he returned. Then there'd be two again. When I went to Grandmother's, I'd have a key to her house. But I didn't have a key to the cottage.

How would I get back in? Would there ever be three keys?

When I turned to leave, my spine was aware of the table and the single key in the drawer.

Outside, it was very bright. The sun bounced off the snow and made you squint. I wished it would snow again. You couldn't go to school when it snowed. You had to stay inside because of the way the house curled around you.

"If you wish for snow," said the dagger, "you can't see Gentleman Jack."

The dagger was right. Wishing for snow was a betrayal of Gentleman Jack.

Our feet squeaked on the snow. Rough Ricky had once said that snow squeaked when it was very cold.

"*Snow is always cold,*" said the dagger.

"*Are you contradicting Rough Ricky?*" I said.

"I *guess not,*" said the dagger.

I thought about how in eight days I'd see Gentleman Jack and tell him the story about the Fair and also that I'd found a Songbird for Grandmother. I thought how happy I was that Gentleman Jack was in trouble, because I could save him. But then I thought that being happy about Gentleman Jack being in trouble was a betrayal of Gentleman Jack.

But I was still happy.

I heard the peanut man's whistle before we reached Main Street. "Peanuts! Fresh, hot peanuts!" But we turned away from him, away from the Sheriff's office and the General Store and the Sapphire and the Shrine.

We hadn't far to go. First we came to a great blackened ruin of a house. It had been burnt and no one had built it up again.

The house bulged at my eyeballs; it made me cough, and once I started, I couldn't stop. The Judge turned and folded an arm around me; his free hand patted my back. He patted out my coughing.

"Better?" he said.

I couldn't really be better, because the house was breathing, even though it was so dead. It breathed out ashes and something that could burn you if you breathed in deep. The indigo trees behind the house were all burnt. There were no green needles, no indigo tang. Instead, they made a skeleton forest. Through their outstretched bones, you could see, in the distance, four grave markers rising from the parched ground. Three were stone; the fourth was a wooden star, painted white.

I thought of Rough Ricky and his Affliction, and I wondered, not for the first time, how you got an Affliction. Could you just set one fire and you were suddenly covered in scars? Or did you get an Affliction by setting fires over and over, each time getting more and more scars, until one day your face was cemented into place and you couldn't smile?

The school was just a couple hundred feet farther on, across the street. It was made of the same pink stone as everything else. The Judge said that first it had been built of indigo, but after the house burnt, they'd rebuilt the school to keep the children safe. It had a hard face, like Rough Ricky. It had two window-eyes and a long nose-door. The three steps below the door made a mouth. Children were playing in a yard beside the school. The yard was plain and messy; it wasn't all sneery and looking down on you the way the school was. The boys played on one side of the yard. The girls played on the other.

"*Robber girls don't play*," said the dagger.

The girls went round in a circle, singing. I wished I didn't have to see Betsy in the circle. I wished she didn't have ringlets and that the sun didn't make her hair so bright.

"I must tell you," said the Judge, "that Mrs. Elton is the schoolmistress."

The sour-apple taste of green candy rose in my throat.

"You must respect her and follow the rules."

We were quiet a little while, watching the girls go round in their circle. They sang some regular words and then they sang some words that didn't make any sense.

"You'll need this." The Judge handed me something in a frame.

There was no picture in it, though, not like the picture of Isaac and Magda. There was just a smooth expanse of gray. The gray looked soft, but when I touched it, it was hard. My finger left a little mark on the hardness.

"And this." The Judge handed me a white stick. I took it; I flexed my fingers around it. It broke. I looked up at the Judge. Would I have to wait another day before I could see Gentleman Jack? Would it be nine days?

"It's all right," he said. "It works just as well in two pieces. It's chalk, for writing on the slate."

I stood while the children played and the school stared at me with its Rough Ricky face. I had a slate and chalk. But I had already broken my chalk and I didn't know how to write.

The Judge handed me a pail. "Your lunch."

Would he give me a key to get back into the cottage?

"Don't think about the cottage," said the dagger. *"Think about Gentleman Jack's questions."*

That was smart. Gentleman Jack's questions always filled my mind. Sometimes, when I couldn't understand something, he'd tell me to recite his questions over and over. It would help me concentrate, he said.

"What will they try to make you believe?" That was one of the questions.

"They'll tell me it's forbidden to dig for gold in the Indigo Heart," I would say. "They'll tell me the Blue Rose is a star and that the Indigo Heart is made of stardust, so when you dig in the Indigo Heart, it's like you're hurting the Blue Rose."

"Will you believe them?" Gentleman Jack would say.

"I will not believe them."

"You have found a lovely name for yourself," said the Judge. "But you will also need a last name."

The Judge didn't know I'd already borrowed del Salto. It was just for now, though, until Grandmother and Gentleman Jack gave me my real name. "The name del Salto goes with the name Starling." My voice was filled with used-up coughs, so it was uglier than usual. "Because of the L's and the S's."

"I quite agree," said the Judge.

Maybe the Judge would think I knew how to read because I knew some letters and the sounds they made. He was hard to fool, though.

Now the door opened and Mrs. Elton appeared. She held a bell and she looked a little like a bell herself, with her narrow waist and big skirts. She rang the bell, and when she had finished, it dangled from her hand like a teardrop. It was strange to think of how many things Mrs. Elton owned—the wax baby in the blue pajamas; the candy with the floating flower; the red ball, which was for jacks; and the bears with the outstretched arms that said, "We're soft. Come feel how soft we are."

"*Don't think about softness,*" said the dagger. "*Think about sharpness!*"

The Judge and I went up the mouth-stairs and up to the nose-door. The nose-door had a knob, but I couldn't tell if it was a knob that opened or a knob that closed.

The Judge took off his hat. He said, "Ma'am," to Mrs. Elton and that he was happy to present her with a new pupil. "Starling del Salto," he said.

"*Too long,*" said the dagger.

I picked at the side of my thumb, out came the blood. My thumb had been ready for blood, it wanted to bleed. Other children came up behind me. When Betsy Elton had come up behind me in the General Store, I'd been able to read her footsteps. But even though I was still wild, I couldn't read all these footsteps. They tramped all over one another and got confused and stamped one another out.

The Judge asked very low if I had any questions. But you can't ask questions if you don't understand anything. You can't ask questions when the footsteps stomp one another out.

You can't ask, "How does everything work?"

The school smelled of newness. It smelled of wood shavings and wet paint. The walls and floor were raw and painful. On either side of a central aisle stood rows of desks with benches attached. They shone with varnish. Varnish smelled sharp. It smelled like the idea of not understanding anything.

The bigger children sat in the back, the smaller children in the front. "Sit down, Peter," said Mrs. Elton, and a little boy in a red shirt sat in the front row and kicked his legs. There were no desks attached to the front-row benches.

"Stop squirming!" Mrs. Elton stepped onto a platform at the front. Behind her on the platform sat a desk, and on the wall behind hung a gigantic slate. She told everyone to be quiet, then beckoned me up. She was very tall on the platform.

I stood in a great silence, with Mrs. Elton looking at my front and the boys and girls looking at my back.

Mrs. Elton wrote a word on the big slate. Mrs. Elton said she wondered if I knew what the word meant.

I said nothing. Mrs. Elton's desk gleamed at me. I swallowed varnish.

"If you don't know," said Mrs. Elton, "you must say, 'I don't know, ma'am.'"

"I don't know, ma'am."

Mrs. Elton wrote again. "What about this word?"

"I don't know, ma'am."

"Or this?"

I didn't know.

"That spells Book," said a sharp little voice behind me. "That new girl don't know nothing."

"Quiet!" Mrs. Elton's voice was terrible. There came a snap, snap, snap. That was Mrs. Elton hitting a stick against the palm of her hand.

"Mind your grammar, Agnes," said Mrs. Elton. "As for Starling, she must sit in the front row, between Peter and Molly. She must be in the youngest class."

I sat. There was no desk, so I had nowhere to put my slate. Peter sat on my left, his legs dangling above the floor. Molly sat on my right. Molly had soft brown hair, and her legs dangled, too. But I was too big. My legs didn't dangle.

I had the same gravy-splat feeling I'd felt at dinner with the Judge and Mrs. del Salto. It was the same feeling I had when I thought about my mother leaving me, probably because of my Affliction. The feeling smelled of varnish.

"Quick," said the dagger. "*Think of Gentleman Jack!*"

"Who saved you?" Gentleman Jack would say.

"You saved me," I would say.

I wondered if the dolls would say that to me. I'd bring them the dog and the collar and the baby, which would be like saving them. Then I'd say, "Who saved you?"

"You saved us," the dolls would say. Maybe today even, I'd bring them the dog, and they'd say, "How happy we are!"

Gentleman Jack didn't care if I could read or write the alphabet on my slate. What he liked was that I could read people's footsteps. He liked that I was soft-footed and that I could draw the dagger almost as fast as he could draw his Lucretia.

Mrs. Elton wrote more words on the big slate. She said that the first-level children should copy the words. I was a first-level child and I had a slate, but I didn't know how to copy words.

Molly dangled her feet. She made some marks on her slate. Her hands were clean, her nails pale and shiny as moons. I put my hands in my lap. My hands were rough; my nails were broken. My fingers couldn't make those marks.

I breathed through my mouth so I wouldn't smell the sharpness. School smelled of varnish, and varnish smelled of shame. I looked at Molly's hands so I wouldn't see anything else.

Maybe I didn't know how to write words on a slate, but I knew how to speak like Gentleman Jack. He was a gentleman. He was Royal. He'd never say, "Don't know nothing." I spoke like the Gentlemen, except for my ugly voice.

Peter wasn't writing on his slate. He was drawing something that was probably a horse. You could tell by the mane. But Molly was writing. Molly, with her soft brown hair and moon fingernails. She was smaller than me, but she was making marks on her slate.

Smack! Peter yelped. The stick had come down on his fingers. "Are you supposed to be drawing on your slate, Peter?" said Mrs. Elton. Her voice was bleached, like old bones.

"No," said Peter.

"No, what?" said Mrs. Elton.

"No, ma'am," said Peter.

"What are you supposed to be doing?" said Mrs. Elton.

"Writing," said Peter.

"See that you do so," said Mrs. Elton.

Mrs. Elton bent over me. "You are not writing on your slate." Her face was too big to see properly, her features all squished flat. "Have you been paying attention?"

I hadn't been paying attention.

"What was I just saying?" said Mrs. Elton.

Mrs. Elton had told Peter to write on his slate, but that couldn't be the right answer. I looked away from her face, flat and hard as the school. My eyes got stuck on her skirts, swinging side to side. I'd think about how Gentleman Jack always helped me remember, even though I wasn't that smart. "We must work with the materials we have," he'd say.

But Mrs. Elton wasn't going to help me. Her face was too close. She opened her mouth, it made a black hole. I saw her teeth. I saw her tongue. A great silence pressed at my ears. I couldn't hear her speak.

There was only the black hole of Mrs. Elton's mouth and the silence.

Even the dagger was silent.

Now I couldn't think about the dog or the collar or the baby. I picked at the skin of my thumb, which was wanting to peel itself away. I'd lick off the blood. Then I'd know I was alive.

If I'd been sitting in the back, I could have slipped out through the door. But I was sitting in front, one a too-short bench that had no desk. If I left now, I'd have to walk along the front, brushing past the knees of the first-level children on one side, and on the other side the edge of Mrs. Elton's platform. I'd have to turn and walk up the aisle of desks, where everyone could see me.

The door was at the end of the aisle.

Mrs. Elton's enormous face backed away. Now I heard her again. She called the fourth level to the front. Up came Betsy, a red-haired girl named Tilda, and a boy named Gabriel.

Betsy, Tilda, and Gabriel were supposed to show Mrs. Elton they knew a history lesson. They took turns reciting what they had learned, which was about the Indigo Heart.

Here's what Betsy said: "In the beginning, when the earth was created, it was given a heart. The Blue Rose sang it out of stardust. That heart is the Indigo Heart and it's the center of the world. If you listen, you can hear it beating."

"What does the Blue Rose bring us?" said Mrs. Elton.

"She brings us marvels," said all the children together. "She brings us the gift of children."

Here's what Gabriel said: "For many years we, the people now known as the Rosati, wandered the world, for none of the inhabitants of the rivers and seas, mountains and deserts, would permit us to settle in any of those places. The Blue Rose saw our wanderings, and understood and appreciated the values by which we ordered our lives; and when she fell to earth as a shooting star, we followed her through forty days and forty nights until at last we reached the Indigo Heart, which was the Blue Rose's to keep or lend, as she pleased. There, in the snow, the Blue Rose caused seven blue roses to bloom. It was this marvel that showed us we'd reached our true home."

"What does the Blue Rose bring us?" said Mrs. Elton.

"She brings us marvels," said all the children together. "She brings us the gift of children."

"Does the Blue Rose always bring us what we crave?" said Mrs. Elton.

"She is wiser than we," said all the children together. "She brings us what we need."

"How, then, must we receive her marvels?" said Mrs. Elton.

"We must accept her marvels with an open heart," said all the children together. "We must seek to know why we need them. They will otherwise turn against us."

Here's what Tilda said: "The Blue Rose taught us to care for our new land. We learned that she, the Blue Rose, is made of stardust, and that the Indigo Heart is likewise made of stardust, and that should we ever dig into the Indigo Heart, we would also be digging into the Blue Rose. We must maintain our new home inviolate. No matter how many precious metals lie buried in the stardust, we may never dig into the stuff of stars."

"Remember," said the dagger, "that the Judge has a substantial stake in a gold mine. Don't just sit there, letting them lie to you!"

Sometimes I did just sit there. Gentleman Jack said the same thing. It was good that the dagger reminded me to be wild. Six inches of carbon and iron would remind you to be wild.

I stood up so Mrs. Elton would ask what I wanted, so that then I could speak. She waited a long time; I waited a long time. "What is it?" she said at last.

"That's a lie," I said. "People like the Judge and the Federal Marshal made it up to explain why they don't want other people digging for gold. The Federal Marshal ran Gentleman Jack out of the Indigo Heart." I was trembling, but it was the good kind of trembling. It's what happens when you save up all your wildness and anger and you let them off their leash.

"The Federal Marshal was jealous that Gentleman Jack found so much gold. He didn't make him leave because of stardust."

"Get out of here," said Mrs. Elton. "You're nothing more than a filthy savage. Your britches are barbaric."

I leapt at Mrs. Elton; I snatched her stick. The stick was easy to break because I was strong with trembling. The snap was very loud, or maybe the school had gone very quiet.

"Get out!" said Mrs. Elton.

I pushed past Betsy, Tilda, and Gabriel, clumped by the front edge of the platform. I turned up the aisle. The aisle had too many rows of desks. It went all the way from the first-level children to the biggest children in the back.

It was the longest aisle in the world. My mouth was full of fire. The doorknob turned. It was a knob for letting you out.

The whole world spread itself, shining, before me. I remembered what the Judge had said, that a city set on a hill cannot be hidden.

I turned down Main Street. I couldn't avoid the burnt house, but I could hold my breath so the smell of fire wouldn't scorch my throat and wouldn't pinch off my breathing. I didn't turn up the path to buttercream cottage. I kept along Main Street. Mrs. del Salto would not want me back after I'd been savage and barbaric at school. She'd be sitting in the cottage, eating ashes and salt.

And because I had no key, the door wouldn't let me in.

The Sapphire Saloon

✝ THIS WAS THE SECOND TIME I had run to the Sapphire. The streets were piled with snow. I took the boardwalk so I could go fast. I ran past the pillars that supported the overhanging roofs. I ran past the stores and the signs that hung in the store windows. They all said Open. I knew the word Open because it started with the friendly letter O, which invited you to step through its round mouth.

The store windows caught at the reflection of my hair. It was savage, which was good. When you're savage, you can make Betsy Elton be sorry. I wished I could make everyone be sorry—everyone who says you can't dig for gold in the Indigo Heart, but then goes ahead and digs when they think no one's looking.

The street opened up into the square, where the buildings faced one another from four sides. That must be where the Line was, because here began the disreputable part of town. If you kept following Main Street through the disreputable part, you'd reach the star steps, which went skittering up and up—up the mountain to the Shrine. There were stairs everywhere you looked, leaping up the sunset face of the mountain, falling all over themselves down the sunrise face, down the tangled streets and into the valley. A new wind suddenly sprang up. I knew the wind; it even had a name: the Chinook. When it came, winter had to leave. The ground was piled with snow, but the Chinook smelled of spring. It stirred up the smells of dirt and wet and indigo. It smelled sharp and watery, it smelled of the promise of green and growing things.

The Chinook came fast in the Indigo Heart. Gentleman Jack said that the weather changes more quickly in the Indigo Heart than anywhere else. It had been so cold this morning, the snow had squeaked. Now it was warm enough to melt the snow, and the squeak along with it.

I ran past the spindly indigos. They didn't grow well on Main Street—on the disreputable end of Main Street, where they probably drank lots of coffee and smoked lots of cigarettes. When I'd told Mrs. del Salto that Gentleman Jack gave me coffee sometimes, she'd said that coffee would stunt my growth. And then she said, "Cigarettes, too."

If Nilsson had carved the dog, maybe I'd get it today. What if I could get the baby before May sixth? What if there was time to watch the baby learn to walk? The baby would hold on to the dog's collar and stagger and laugh, and the dolls and I would laugh, too, and the mother doll would say, "Such a big boy, walking!"

The bells rang. I kept running, but everyone else stopped. It was interesting to watch them, to see how they all turned to face the Shrine. The Rosati wanted to face the Shrine when they sang the song of praise to the Blue Rose because the Shrine was dedicated to the worship of her.

The bells faded, and I heard the piano now, the sideways music from the Sapphire. It tugged me down the street, past an infinity of stairs tumbling downhill, panting uphill. The music was familiar and so was the whistle of the peanut man: "Peanuts! Fresh, hot peanuts." I stepped into the sharp smell of the saloon. It was quieter than before. I knew the sound of cards slapping on the tables. I knew their smell, too. They smelled of mildew and damp, and of the color yellow.

Last time I was here, I'd seen Flora, first thing. But this time I saw only Lord John. He beckoned me to his card table with a jerk of his head. I stood beside him until he'd finished dealing, then he reached into his jacket pocket. "Nilsson made you that dog."

He pressed something into my hand. It felt right, warm and wooden, but I looked at it through squinted eyes. If it wasn't quite right, I didn't want to see it all at once.

But it was absolutely right. It was a rough brownish dog with just enough spiky fur at the shoulders. The dog was big but not too big. He was as high as my longest finger. His legs were jointed, and his tail . . . he could wag his tail! He didn't have a collar, but when he did, he'd be big enough for a baby to hold it and stagger around.

He stood on my palm, looking a little off to the side. He was a shaggy dog. You could prickle your finger onto his coat. He was a good dog.

I looked around the Sapphire for Nilsson.

"There's no Nilsson here," said Lord John. "You'd have to travel awfully far to find him."

I thought for a minute, then I knew. "Dead?"

"Dead," said Lord John. "It looked like mountain fever."

We looked at each other. "You get mountain fever when it's hot," I said. "He shouldn't have worn Doubtful Mittie's hat."

Poor knobble-faced Nilsson. I could hardly even picture him; I mostly just remembered his knobbles. He'd put on the hat two men had died in, and he'd died, too. All that was left of him was the dog.

Then it occurred to me that he'd died so much faster than Doubtful Mittie . . . or maybe the right word was Sooner. He'd died so much sooner. I tried to explain. Doubtful Mittie had worn the Federal Marshal's hat for months before he died, but Nilsson hadn't even worn it for a week.

Lord John understood. "We live in a place of power," he said. "The Blue Rose is made of stardust, and the Indigo Heart is filled with stardust. Boons craved of the Blue Rose are granted more quickly and more fully than they are in the rest of the Territories. The same is true for breaking the rules—the consequences of your actions come faster and hit you harder."

"There's nothing harder than death," said the dagger.

Nilsson was gone, but he'd left a good dog. White oak was better than indigo, better than red oak. Its pores were smaller, it was stronger.

A clatter of icicles fell from the roof. The Chinook was setting the water to running and the snow to shifting. It was different outside the Sapphire from how it had been before, and it was different inside, too. For one thing, there was no Nilsson. And the light was different. Now it came purring through the front, stretching itself slantwise, kneading its paws into the floor.

Lord John took me to see Flora. We went up a broad staircase, down a corridor, and into a dark room. There lay Flora, asleep in a big bed. Lord John just whispered her name and she woke up.

"It's awfully early, John," she said. Then she saw me and pushed herself up against the pillows. Her arms were long and pretty, and so was her hair, all in a tumble.

A derringer lay on a little table beside the bed. I'd never seen one before, but Gentleman Jack had told me about them. They were guns for ladies, he said, because they were small enough to be strapped into a garter and because they couldn't shoot straight. Then he'd laugh.

I always wanted to laugh, too, but I didn't know what was funny, and I couldn't ask. It would just make Gentleman Jack look at me and remember how dull I am.

I set a finger on the derringer.

"Careful," said Flora.

"Do you wake up at night and kill people?" I said.

"Sometimes," said Flora.

"Gentleman Jack says a derringer doesn't shoot straight," I said.

"Gentleman Jack's the one who doesn't shoot straight," said Flora.

But Gentleman Jack had shot straight at the Federal Marshal: straight enough that the Marshal had sat on his horse, looking surprised; straight enough that the Marshal had held his belly, the blood leaking around his fingers. Then I remembered backward, to why Gentleman Jack had shot the Marshal, which was that the Marshal stopped Gentleman Jack from digging for gold. That he chased Gentleman Jack out of the Indigo Heart.

But that talk about stardust and digging up Blue Roses was just lies so the people in charge could keep the gold to themselves.

"She needs to practice her story," said Lord John, "so the jury will believe Gentleman Jack was at the Fair and could not have killed the Marshal."

"I want to tell Gentleman Jack we have a plan," I said. "I want to make him happy."

"You'll need to practice saying you were at the Fair," said Lord John, "and describe what you did at the Fair, to make the jury believe you."

"Start with the date," said Flora.

"It was August twenty-sixth," said Lord John, "but you can't be expected to know that. It will sound rehearsed."

August twenty-sixth. I wished Lord John would let me remember August twenty-sixth. I could remember it; I wanted to remember it.

"Just say you were at the Harvest Fair," said Lord John. "That will sound natural, coming from a child." Lord John told me what Gentleman Jack and I were supposed to have done at the Fair. He told me about the pink lemonade Gentleman Jack had bought for me. He said it was cold and tart. He told me about the tall man with three shells and one pea, and how the man put the pea under one of the shells and switched the shells around so quickly, you couldn't tell where the pea was.

He told me about the huge horses from Belgium with calm dark eyes and hair growing down over their feet. Gentleman Jack had given me carrots to give them, but I had been too afraid of their massive heads.

"I was not afraid!" I said.

"You were afraid," said Lord John.

He told me about the enormous tent where they served dinner. He told me how I had eaten turkey and dressing and apple pie.

"No apples in August," said Flora.

Lord John paused. "Blueberry pie."

I liked the way they were serious about the story. I liked the way they made all the imaginary details line up with real-life details.

There came a pause, into which came the familiar whistle. "Fresh, hot peanuts!"

"You went back to the lemonade barrel," said Flora, "even though they were almost out. Gentleman Jack paid five cents for another cup, but it was watery because all the ice had melted."

I nodded. I had never had lemonade, but I could guess how it felt, expecting a cold, tart explosion but getting only warm, sugary water.

"At the end of the day," said Lord John, "you had a piece of gingerbread and you were sick."

"I was not sick!" I said.

"You were sick," said Lord John.

"I was not sick!" I said.

"She was not sick," said Flora.

"Fine," said Lord John. "She was not sick."

Lord John and Flora laughed. "Now you can tell Gentleman Jack we have a plan," said Flora. Her gown was filmy and covered with white embroidered flowers. White on white. I liked the way it looked. "Now you can make him happy."

"But I can't see him," I said, "until I've gone to school for eight days."

"Have you gone to school?" said Flora.

"Once," I said.

Or maybe half of once. I prickled my fingers onto the dog's fur. There were prickles on the dog, and prickles on my insides. The inside prickles were because I knew the Judge would find out what happened today at school. The outside prickles were because of the dog's good, strong fur.

"He can wait eight days to be happy," said Flora.

I didn't want Gentleman Jack to have to wait, but at least I'd have two happy things to tell him. There was the story about the Fair and the news about the Songbird for Grandmother.

Now Flora stood up. And you could see now—now that she was standing up—

"You have a baby bulge!" I said.

"I do," she said.

"Is it a baby craved of the Blue Rose?" I said.

"I asked the Blue Rose for a baby girl," said Flora, "if that's what you mean."

A girl? Why would anyone want a girl!

I thought back to what the children at school had said about the Blue Rose. "But the Blue Rose brings you what you need," I said. "Not what you want."

Flora and Lord John were quiet a moment, then Flora said I was absolutely right. "We hope it will be a girl," she said. "But it is good to remember that we must be prepared for either flavor."

"And to receive the child with an open heart," said Lord John. "Because otherwise—"

And here Lord John, Flora, and I spoke at the same time. "Otherwise, it will turn against you."

Then we laughed. It was nice to know what to say—to know it so exactly, you could say it with other people, like a song. Then you knew you'd said the right thing. But I had to be careful with Flora. I couldn't start liking her too much, or trusting her. She'd lied about the Songbird. She wanted to keep him for herself.

I passed the peanut man when I left. "Peanuts! Peanuts!" he said in the Whistling. "Hot roasted peanuts!"

I wished I were a Songbird and could whistle to Gentleman Jack. He'd hear me from his jail cell, across the Line, in the genteel part of town. Then I wouldn't have to wait eight more days, or even nine, to make him happy. I'd whistle that I'd found his Songbird.

I passed into the thick, oozy smell of peanuts. "Fresh, hot peanuts!" It was amazing how you could understand the peanut man. He couldn't whistle the hard sounds of the words, like the T in Hot or like the P in Peanuts, but his whistle could capture the other sounds, like the Ah in Hot, the Eee and Uh in Peanuts. And when you thought about the words, they went up and down in a certain way—there was a music to them—and the whistling words made the same music. If the lowest sound were the Number One, and the highest sound were the Number Four, then the song he sang went like this: Three-One-Four-Three.

I wondered about the rules of the Whistling. If someone whistled to you, was that like speaking to you? Did it mean you could speak? Did it mean your Affliction wouldn't silence you?

It did.

"I want to whistle something to Gentleman Jack, in the jail," I said.

"He won't understand," the peanut man whistled.

"Why can I understand?"

"It's a gift to be able to understand the Whistling. Besides me, there are only two people in Blue Roses who understand. First the Sheriff, now you."

"But why can a few people understand when most people can't?" This was the first time I'd seen the peanut man close up. His face looked a little like a peanut shell, sort of—crinkly, with squished-in cheeks.

No, Crinkly wasn't the right word. I wished I knew more words so Gentleman Jack could be proud of me and say I was shiny.

"No one really knows," said the peanut man. "It often runs in families."

It took me a minute to realize that I'd asked the peanut man to whistle our plans for Gentleman Jack down Main Street, where the Sheriff would hear and understand. That gave me a sick sort of feeling. I had to be very careful not to underestimate anyone, especially the Sheriff. He looked like a mouse man, but he was really a cat.

"But the Sheriff can't speak the Whistling?" I said.

"He doesn't have a gift for it, like you," said the peanut man. "He asked me to teach it to him, so he could understand as many people as possible in the Indigo Heart."

"I don't have a gift for it," I said.

"But you didn't ever have to learn to understand. And you have piping in your voice."

That's what the dolls had said, too. But I didn't understand how an ugly voice like mine could have piping.

Now I was glad I had to wait to tell Gentleman Jack when I saw him in eight days. I'd tell him about the Songbird. Then I could see his best smile. Then I could see how happy he was. I'd make him so happy, he'd say I was the brightest star. He'd say I was brighter than any of the Seven Sisters. When I told him about the Songbird, I would shine like a star—how I would shine!

The stores were all closed. I knew the word Closed because it was so different from the word Open. The word Closed started with the unfriendly letter C that made you bang yourself against its outside curve. It made a hard, choking sound when you said it.

Closed. The door to buttercream cottage would be closed, and I didn't have a key. The Chinook still blew. I breathed in the sharp, watery smell. I breathed in the promise of mud. The snow still lay on the street and on the railings and windowsills of the buildings, but only on the shady side. On the sunny side of the street, the snow was melting and trickling down the sides of the buildings.

It's funny how, when you step away from your thoughts, you make room in your brain to find the just-right word. You can find it even though you don't know enough words. I knew the word for the peanut man's face. Corrugated. That's what his face looked like and that was also what a peanut shell looked like.

What if Gentleman Jack knew that I knew the word Corrugated?

It was in the square that I saw a swirl of rusty-crow skirts moving toward me. It took me a moment to recognize the skirts and the rusty-crow hair. They rustled toward me; they knew where I would be. Inside those skirts was Mrs. del Salto, and inside Mrs. del Salto was a person, waiting.

Layers of Memories

✝ MRS. DEL SALTO HAD BEEN FRANTIC. School had ended, and I hadn't returned. "Frantic!" she said.

I could hardly answer, I was so surprised to see her in the sun, in the Chinook, with the snow melting all around. I hadn't thought she could exist outside. Then came the words I'd been thinking over and over. "I don't have a key."

Mrs. del Salto's mouth slipped sideways. "Did you think I wouldn't let you in?"

I didn't want to say what I thought. I didn't want to make her mouth slide off her face.

"For star's sake!" Mrs. del Salto grabbed my hand. She turned it over, then looked me up and down. "I've never seen such a grimy child."

"Are you barbaric when you're grimy?" I said.

"What makes you ask?"

"Mrs. Elton," I said. "She said I was a filthy savage. She said my britches were barbaric."

"I'll fix that," said Mrs. del Salto. "I'll fix it if it kills me." She was silent a long time, before she said, "Which it probably will."

It was getting dark, but none of the metal bowls were filled with fire. I asked Mrs. del Salto why.

She said tonight was the night of the Dark Moon. She said they didn't light the bowls because they wanted to see the night sky. "It's harder to see the stars," she said, "when the moon is shining in the sky and fires are burning on earth."

"There's no moon?" I said.

"There's always a moon," said Mrs. del Salto, "but this is one of the nights you can't see it. You'll see the sun set at five forty-two, but you won't be able to see the moon rise."

But Mrs. del Salto had killed time. How did she know about five forty-two?

"Why do you want to see the stars?" I said.

"Because then we can see if the Blue Rose has returned to visit her sisters. You can see the Seven Sisters best when the sky is dark."

"Why do you care if she's in the sky?"

"It is said," said Mrs. del Salto, "that that's the best time to crave a boon of her." On we went, into the almost dark. "Or," said Mrs. del Salto, "to discover if she's granted a boon you've not yet craved."

Time was all jumbled up when it came to the Blue Rose. How could you ever understand it?

"Not that I care," said Mrs. del Salto. "I'm done with the Blue Rose."

This was the second time I'd returned to the cottage.

"Third time," said the dagger.

"Second time returning," I said. "Returning is different from coming the first time."

When you returned to a place, it could be familiar. It could give you a warm feeling, as though you'd swallowed the Chinook and it were melting you inside.

Now to the foyer, Mrs. del Salto opening the drawer of the little table, putting her key into the drawer, where it lay on the green felt lining. It seemed so long ago that I'd discovered you might build a drawer to hold a key, and a table to hold the drawer—

"Not this again!" said the dagger.

And a room to hold the table, and a house to hold the room—

"What are you waiting for?" said Mrs. del Salto.

"I'm waiting for the Judge."

"Suit yourself," said Mrs. del Salto.

Quick as quick, while I could still speak, I whispered to the dog, "You'll see what happens when the Judge comes home." Even the dog's tail and ears had pointy wisps of fur. He was a perfectly dog-like dog.

It seemed a long time we waited, but it was hard to tell because of no time passing. Then came the Judge, pounding his feet on the porch stairs, shuffling his boots on the sunflower carpet, turning his key in the front door.

"Now you'll see," I said. "The Judge will put his key in the drawer."

The Judge paused when he saw me and looked down his granite-cliff cheekbones. "What are you doing here?"

"Waiting," I said.

"Waiting for what?" The Judge put his key in the drawer.

"See?" I said to the dog, but only inside my head so the Judge couldn't hear. "You know what's going to happen in the cottage."

"I have something to say to you," said the Judge. "It will be easier in the kitchen." He went through the glass door into the corridor, and I followed.

The Gentlemen never said they had something to say. They just said it. They didn't have special places to make it easier.

We went through the library, passing the photograph of Magda and Isaac, the coins, the inkwell, the box taking joy from its cornflower lid. We swung through the door into the kitchen, where it was easier to say things.

The Judge gave me milk and bread and butter and honey, which I now knew was called a Snack. A snack is something quick and gobbly. "You didn't stay a whole day at school," said the Judge.

Should I nod or shake my head? Yes, I hadn't stayed?

No, I hadn't stayed?

"You still have eight days of school before you visit Gentleman Jack."

"But—" I said.

"You may not be violent," said the Judge.

"I am violent." You could tell from the marks of mortification, which were beginning to fade from the Judge's face. "I will sting. I will mortify."

"You must follow the rules."

"Only if they're Gentleman Jack's rules."

"Then you may not see Gentleman Jack," said the Judge. "Even though he's been asking for you."

"Asking for me!" I said.

"Asking for you."

Was that good or bad? I couldn't tell. Why did a person feel worried when a thing might just as easily be good? Why was the feeling of bad-ness stronger than the feeling of goodness? The Judge handed me a piece of bread, butter, and honey. I took it but I wouldn't eat it. That would be like agreeing with him. That would be like saying I was willing not to be violent.

"You may not be disrespectful."

"I will be disrespectful when people lie to me," I said. "Mrs. Elton said no one's allowed to dig for gold in the Indigo Heart, because that's digging into stardust, which is like digging into the Blue Rose. But I know you dig for gold. Gentleman Jack said you have a substantial stake in a gold mine."

"I do," said the Judge, "but the difference is that I don't dig into stardust. All working gold mines are located outside the Indigo Heart."

Could that be true? I was pretty sure a Judge always had to tell the truth. That would explain why I'd seen no wooden surrounds or metal tracks or just plain openings in the rock.

"We think it reasonable," said the Judge, "to banish a person who doesn't respect our land and our laws. To banish a person who has a disagreeable tendency to burn us in our beds."

"Gentleman Jack doesn't burn people," I said. That was Rough Ricky's job.

"It seems that both you and Mrs. Elton violated our agreement," said the Judge.

What agreement?

"The agreement Mr. Elton and I arrived at after your visit to the General Store."

"When Mr. Elton accused me of stealing," I said. "And I hit him with a hammer."

"Do you remember what we agreed?" said the Judge.

I remembered it exactly.

> *"Accept your sorrows,*
> *If you cannot change them.*
> *Embrace your joys,*
> *So you don't estrange them."*

"You have an excellent memory!" said the Judge. Sometimes I could fool people into thinking I had a good memory, but I could never trick Gentleman Jack.

"Did you accept your sorrows?" said the Judge.

I'd never thought about sorrows. Did I have them? Did Mr. Elton dragging me through the store count as a sorrow? I didn't like remembering it. It gave me a varnish-smell feeling, the feeling I'd had in school when I didn't understand how anything worked. I remembered that dreadful moment with Mr. Elton: the store, silent, except for Mr. Elton yelling about sticky fingers; the crack-crack-crack of my teeth on the candy; the Judge, caught in the middle of his hat takings-off and puttings-on.

Maybe the varnish-smell feeling was a sorrow. That was a new thought. And then I had another new thought. I would see if I believed it when I said it.

"But Mrs. del Salto doesn't want to accept her sorrows," I said. Mrs. del Salto had said she was done with the Blue Rose. "When you stop time, you don't accept your sorrows. When you stop time, you want everything to be the way it was before."

The Blue Rose was about new beginnings, and Mrs. del Salto didn't want any new beginnings.

"That is a most perceptive observation," said the Judge. We looked at each other for a long time, and then the Judge became judge-like again.

"The Indigo Heart only welcomes people who obey our laws," said the Judge. "Our laws protect the Blue Rose, which means they protect us, too, because the Blue Rose breathes spirit into all creation."

"Breathes spirit?"

"Brings to life," said the Judge.

"But Gentleman Jack breathed spirit into me." Gentleman Jack had brought me to life when he found me in the wilderness. I wanted the Judge to realize he didn't know anything about Gentleman Jack. Gentleman Jack didn't burn people in their beds. He hadn't burned Marshal Starling. I'd seen the Federal Marshal, sitting on his horse, looking surprised. Holding his stomach, the blood leaking around his fingers.

"Mrs. del Salto said there's a Dark Moon tonight," I said. "Are you going to see if the Blue Rose is in the sky?"

"Yes," said the Judge. "Maybe I'll discover she's granted me a boon."

"Did you already crave one?" I said.

"I don't have to have done so. The Blue Rose exists in the future and the present and the past. She can see in all directions. She is our Guide to endings and middles and beginnings."

That was kind of what Mrs. del Salto had said. That on a night of the Dark Moon, you could discover whether the Blue Rose had granted your boon even if you hadn't made one.

"Another piece of bread?"

I glanced at my hand. I'd decided not to eat the bread because that would be like agreeing with the Judge. But I'd eaten it without noticing. I'd been a traitor to myself. The taste of honey lay on my tongue. I scraped it off with my teeth.

I remembered something from school today. "But to get a marvel, your heart has to be open to whatever the Blue Rose brings you. What if the Blue Rose brought you Gentleman Jack? What if he's the marvel and your mind has to be open to him?"

The Judge smiled inside his mouth. You could tell by the way his eyebrows moved up. "An excellent argument."

But Gentleman Jack said girls shouldn't argue, which was how I knew I hadn't. "I never argue." I always obeyed Gentleman Jack.

"Good to know," said the Judge.

Gentleman Jack had told me about taking a bath in Grandmother's house. There, water came rushing from a pipe in the wall into a copper bathtub. The water came out hot, sometimes too hot, said Gentleman Jack. You had to wait until it was just bearable and you got in and your skin turned red.

It was different from a bath in the hideout. There, you jumped into the river at the bottom of the ravine. We didn't do it very often.

Mrs. del Salto boiled water on the stove and poured it into a wooden tub in the kitchen. Then she told me to give her my britches.

"You'll take them away," I said.

"Certainly," she said.

I wouldn't give Mrs. del Salto my britches. She'd see the sheath at my waist; she'd see the dagger in the sheath. She'd see the dog in my pocket.

"You can't have them," I said. "I will claw and bite."

"Dear me," said Mrs. del Salto.

"And sting and mortify."

"Most invigorating," said Mrs. del Salto. But she decided to leave me alone to take my bath and explained about the soap and the washcloth and also about washing my hair. She said that if there was a speck of dirt on me, she'd put me in the bath again and scrub me with a brush.

The water was almost too hot, even though it didn't come rushing from a pipe. I eased myself into the tub; I felt the house settle in around me. The walls breathed in and out. Their breath smelled of indigo. The fire shifted and sighed.

"*Don't forget about Grandmother's house,*" said the dagger. "*What will Grandmother do when you get there?*"

"She'll say, 'This is my girl, bright as a star.' She'll let me sit in one of the velvet chairs."

"Crimson velvet," said the dagger.

"I'll sit in crimson velvet," I said. "Grandmother will brush my hair."

In buttercream cottage, you had two cloths, one for washing dishes and one for washing yourself. So many cloths! Mrs. del Salto had left the dishcloth to scald on top of the stove. We scalded gently together, the dishcloth in its pot, the washcloth and I in the tub, and when I got out, I was red all over.

The light was dim. The bar of soap and the washcloth were white, and so was the nightgown Mrs. del Salto had left draped over a chair. I liked the way the nightgown felt on my skin. I liked the way it felt to be clean inside a soft, clean nightgown. It was all right to put on the nightgown because it was after five forty-two, and it was dark.

I talked to the dog as we climbed to the attic. "These are the stairs. There's even a carpet on the stairs. The carpet is held down by rods with pineapple decorations."

"A wooden dog can't hear you," said the dagger.

"There's no carpet on the attic stairs," I said. "The attic is different from the rest of the house."

"A wooden dog can't see the stairs," said the dagger.

"Neither can a dagger," I said.

There was something new in the attic. The children's rocking chair from the library now sat in front of the dollhouse. The Judge couldn't have brought it. He'd been away all day. Maybe Mrs. del Salto had brought it when she was frantic. Maybe she was frantic for someone to sit in it and play with the dolls. But she didn't know the dollhouse was alive and playing on its own.

"This is the dollhouse," I told the dog. "See how it looks just like the people house?" I opened the two big doors in the front of the dollhouse. The mother and father dolls sat in the parlor. They leaned against embroidered cushions. The sight burst upon me like the flesh of an apple.

I reached for the dog.

"*He won't come alive,*" said the dagger.

"*Stop stepping all over my thoughts!*" I said.

"I don't step," said the dagger. "*I don't have feet.*"

The dagger was too un-bendy to understand words that compared one thing to another. It wouldn't understand about the Blue Rose breathing spirit. It even complained when Gentleman Jack said Grandmother's hands felt like silk. "*Hands feel like skin,*" it always said.

The dolls leaned forward, away from the embroidered cushions. I set the dog on the carpet. The dog shook himself. He wagged his tail. The mother doll whistled, a nice, easy whistle. "Here, boy!"

The dog rocked forward on his little legs. He set his chin on the mother doll's knee.

"Oh, Starling," said the father doll. "You have brought us our dog!" The father doll patted the dog. His china hand made a little thunk-thunk-thunk on the dog's wooden head. "We are so happy."

"He's perfect," said the mother doll. "He's especially perfect because he's made of wood."

"Instead of china," said the father doll.

"China can easily break," said the mother doll.

"Wood cannot easily break," said the father doll.

Of course the dog would come to life in the dollhouse. Nothing was as alive as the dollhouse. The dollhouse had breathed spirit into the dog.

"He's made of oak," I said. "Oak is stronger than indigo. He's made of white oak, which is stronger than red."

"He'll need a strong name," said the mother doll.

The dog made funny little pounces onto his front legs. Nilsson had given him wonderful joints. Look at him, wagging his tail! He bounded off to the library and sniffed all around. His barks were sharp as needles.

"Barks aren't needles," said the dagger.

"Oakheart," said the mother doll. "Wouldn't that be a good name for him?"

Oakheart was a good strong name. And then I remembered the rhyme that helped me remember the tasks.

> One's for a dog,
> Two's for a collar—

But now the dog had a name:

> One is for Oakheart,
> Two's for a collar.
> Three's for a baby—

Now the first line had one extra sound, which made it better.

I sat in the rocking chair. It was just the right size for a child who was ten years old, or maybe eleven.

"That's Magda's old rocking chair," said the father doll.

"It's made of willow," said the mother doll. "Willow's not as strong as oak."

"But willow is supple," said the father doll. "That's good for a rocking chair, which is made of bendy strips of wood."

A rocking chair was the exact opposite of a dagger.

"A rocking chair doesn't need a heart made of oak," said the mother doll.

I watched Oakheart run around the house, sniffing in all the corners. He ran to the back of the dollhouse, where I couldn't see him without swinging the house around on the giant plate. I imagined him sniffing at drawers full of sweetness. I imagined him sniffing at the cellar door. Maybe he could smell the butter waiting in the dreaming dark.

I thought how funny it was that I was sitting in a chair that had once been a willow. I thought of how things could be transformed— a willow tree into a chair, a white oak tree into a dog. I thought of Nilsson, a live man transformed into a dead man just because of a hat with a scarlet feather.

But I wouldn't think about that now. I was inside the cottage, with knobs that closed and bolts that locked, and I had brought a dog to the dollhouse, and the dollhouse had breathed spirit into the dog.

Later, though, Mrs. del Salto made me click open the door and go to Magda's room. I slipped the dagger into one of my boots. That way, I could avoid the endless fuss about wearing britches, but still bring the dagger.

I needed the dagger to explain things to me.

I'd seen Magda's room in the dollhouse, but that was the concentrated version. Here, in the human-size version, the shades were closed. I knew sunlight made paint and curtains fade. That must be why the shades were closed, to protect the colors of Magda's room. There was no ten-year-old girl living in the room who needed sunlight.

Magda's room was mostly green, with dabs of yellow. I didn't like Magda, but I liked her room. Green and yellow are restful on the eyes.

A wardrobe took up one of the walls. It was painted a beautiful sharp-ish yellow, like the taste of a dandelion. Mrs. del Salto opened it. There came the smell of sweet and spicy trees. They smelled of memories.

"You can't smell memories," said the dagger.

Inside was a burst of whiteness—

"Hardly anything's white!"

"It's just the idea of whiteness," I said. It was because the wardrobe was filled with waterfalls of fabric, pale and sheer, and heaps of light lacy things, and soft woolen things, and the whole of it left an overall impression of whiteness, like a sliced almond.

"I'll alter some of Magda's dresses for you," said Mrs. del Salto. She didn't want to, though. You could tell by the way she knelt, looking into the wardrobe. "Two will be enough for now." She was probably thinking that I'd make them dirty. That I'd make them savage.

"She's right," said the dagger.

It was a wardrobe of memories, memories of Magda. It was a shrine to Magda, bursting with almond whiteness. The layers of fabric were folded around the memories of Magda.

Mrs. del Salto took out one dress, then another, shaking her head, putting them back. Her ring stood out against the whiteness—beautiful and lively and filled with possibilities. It was hard to believe she'd been frantic.

She reached for a dress with stitching on the chest that made a pattern—

"Smocking," said Mrs. del Salto.

There was a dress with a pink sash—

"Silk," said Mrs. del Salto.

Silk? I wouldn't touch it. I only wanted to know the feeling of silk by touching Grandmother's hands. And then I had a big thought: of course! Grandmother would have made a shrine to Gentleman Jack. She'd have made sure his lace was beautifully clean, she'd have folded it just so and laid it on a special shelf, overflowing with whiteness. Maybe she'd have pinned a little ruby brooch onto his neck ruffles, as a bright surprise. She'd have made sure he had a dozen pairs of gloves, all soft and buttery—the best leather was buttery—and maybe she'd have slipped a pair of peach-colored gloves in among the primrose, just in case Gentleman Jack might like a change.

Mrs. del Salto fished out a dress with lace pockets. Lace pockets? The pockets on the dress of a human-size girl would be about the size of a dining-room table in a dollhouse world. The dining-room table in the dollhouse needed a tablecloth, and the dolls had said the tablecloth should be made of lace.

I remembered how I'd thought the dollhouse table was so bare that it was gritting its teeth. It needed a tablecloth. I'd come back later and cut off one of the pockets.

"This one, I think." Mrs. del Salto held up a dress from the almond shrine. "It never suited Magda. She was too pink for it." But the dress was red—red!—and except for Gentleman Jack's gloves and frills, the Gentlemen wore only black and brown.

"Not red," said the dagger. "Garnet."

Garnet. The background was pale; that might be all right. But the vines and leaves that decorated the fabric were scarlet. I never wore bright things.

I put the dress on over the nightgown. Mrs. del Salto stuck some pins in the dress. "You're not pinkish," she said. "You're ivory and blue. Once it's altered, it will suit you very well." She stuck the pins in her mouth for safekeeping.

I filled up my eyes with Magda's room. A book sat on a table beside Magda's bed. Books are for opening, but this book was fastened with a strap, and the end of the strap went into a lock. In the lock was a keyhole, and in the keyhole was the tiniest key in the world. Later I would come get that key.

First Magda's lace pocket, then the key.

"The key's only tin," said the dagger. "Tin is weak."

It was valuable to me.

I filled up my eyes with Mrs. del Salto. Her mouth was a hedgehog of pins. She knelt beside the wardrobe with its almond-white memories. It must be a kind of Affliction to have memories that made you sad. Memories that made you want everything to go back to the way it had been before. At least I didn't have that kind of Affliction.

"Because you have no memories," said the dagger.

Because I had no memories.

Filling a Drawer

✝ I HAD TO EAT BREAKFAST EVERY MORNING.
I'd been to school eight times, but I'd eaten breakfast more than eight
times, because you didn't go to school on Saturdays and Sundays.

Breakfast wasn't as complicated as dinner, but it was still full of perils.
It was all right to eat cornbread with your fingers, which might make
you think it was all right to eat bacon with your fingers, until you saw
Mrs. del Salto chipping at it with the edge of her fork. You might think
it was all right to use your own spoon to pour gravy over your biscuits,
but you had to use a big spoon, called a ladle. You had to dip the ladle
into a thing called a gravy boat.

"*It's not even a boat!*" said the dagger.

Today was the ninth day. After school, I'd see Gentleman Jack.

"*Sharpen me!*" said the dagger.

"I already sharpened you."

"*Polish me!*" said the dagger, which as always wanted to look sharp
and bright for Gentleman Jack.

I looked sharp and bright, too, but only on the outside—only because I wore a dress with scarlet flowers and a collar with a frill. I wished the inside of my head could also be bright for Gentleman Jack. That's what he really wanted.

My hair was still savage. I still carried the dagger in the sheath, which I wore beneath my skirts. I looked tame but I was secretly wild.

I'd look at the dollhouse before school. School was a bad thing and the dollhouse was a good thing. I wanted to fill up on the good thing before I got to the bad thing. I peered into the dollhouse dining room. I'd awakened the table with beeswax and lavender. I'd dressed it with a lace tablecloth, which had once been a pocket on Magda's dress.

Now the table wasn't gritting its teeth.

I looked at the little table in the foyer. I licked my fingertip, tapping it onto the drawer and popping it open. It was hardly heavier than paper. In it lay a softness of green fabric. On the fabric lay the key.

"The key to Magda's book," said the dagger.

But it didn't belong to the book anymore. "The key to the dollhouse." Magda's book had turned out to be filled with writing that slanted all over the place. I couldn't even read the letters. It wasn't like the neat up-and-down writing in the newspaper the Judge read every day. But that wasn't what mattered. All that mattered was the key.

The father and mother dolls sat at the dining-room table. I pushed the plate around.

"My, how fast the world spins," said the mother doll.

I dragged my finger along the edge of the plate. It slowed, it stopped.

A good thing I liked to think about was how Gentleman Jack would beat his no-account brother. Gentleman Jack would bring five bricks of gold to Grandmother, and then he'd inherit her empire.

"Five bricks of gold, plus a Songbird," said the dagger.

"*Plus a Songbird*," I said. Today I'd tell Gentleman Jack I'd found a Songbird. Today I'd shine like a star.

Mrs. del Salto called me. I had to turn away from the dollhouse. The Judge had already pocketed his key, so he didn't open the drawer and I didn't get to see the keys lying on their comfortable green felt.

But why did I care about seeing them? I had no key. The Judge and Mrs. del Salto kept them for themselves.

"*Sharpen me!*" The dagger was thinking only of Gentleman Jack. "*Polish me!*"

The Chinook had melted Main Street into a swamp of mud and manure. A couple of pigs were splashing around in the muck. A rat scuttled by; the pigs snorted and took off after it. The Judge and I kept to the boardwalk.

School had to be before Gentleman Jack. The walk to school had become horribly familiar. The left turn onto Main Street, the remains of the burnt house, which I never looked at but couldn't help seeing. The sight had tattooed itself on the back of my eyeballs: the blackened rib cage; the rags and tags of its heart; the stairs, like a half-eaten licorice twist, leading to the second floor.

"You don't like it," said the Judge. It wasn't a question.

"It bulges out my eyes." I wondered if Rough Ricky had made it burn. It was the kind of thing Rough Ricky would do; it was burnt with a Rough Ricky sort of thoroughness. I guessed some people must have died in the fire. Why else would there be three gravestones behind the house, and the single white wooden star?

"It was charming, before the fire," said the Judge. "A cottage, a bit larger than ours, with colored glass in the windows. Blue and amber, very pretty."

This stretch of road was the longest in the world. It took forever to pass the house, which was all curled into itself, breathing its gray breath. If you could see my breath, that's what it would look like. Coarse gray breath, belonging to a coarse, gray voice.

"Gentleman Jack tried to smoke them out," said the Judge. "You couldn't pass the house for days, for fear of breathing in corrosive fumes."

I knew what smoking out meant. It's what you do when you want to get into a place that has too many good locks. Smoke makes people open their doors and run out. But it wasn't Gentleman Jack who did the smoking. It was Rough Ricky.

"But he used a lye bomb, which turned to fire. The Starlings perished in the blaze—"

"Starling?" I said. "Like Marshal Starling?"

"He lost his whole family. You might say he was lucky to have been away at the time—"

I'd never say that!

"But he wouldn't have agreed."

The school lay just ahead. The children played in the yard. The girls stood in their circle, singing; the boys flew about in all directions. I was glad I hadn't learned the rules about boys and girls, about blue and pink. I'd rather run and climb trees and throw the dagger. Mrs. Elton rang the bell. Her skirts trembled. I looked at the school; I looked at its Rough Ricky face. I climbed up its mouth-steps and went through its nose-door. Mrs. Elton looked around the schoolroom, and first thing, she called on me. But she knew I never knew anything.

"What is today?" said Mrs. Elton.

"Thursday," I said.

"What is the date?" she said.

"February fourteenth," I said.

"What do we celebrate on February fourteenth?" she said.

What did she mean? There wasn't a new moon. There wasn't a full moon. The Rosati were crazy about the moon. "The middle of February?"

The class broke into laughter. I made my face into a mask. The mask would hide how much I wanted to kill them—kill them! And then came the voice of the person I'd kill most of all, which was Betsy, who explained that February fourteenth was Valentine's Day, which was when people said "I love you" and gave out Valentine's Day cards, which Betsy did. She passed out one to every child.

The others opened theirs. I stuffed mine in my pocket.

I was a little worried about seeing Gentleman Jack. I had good news about the Songbird, but I had no butterscotch for him. I should have asked the Judge for some, even though I knew he'd say no. That was because he disapproved of Gentleman Jack.

Today we talked about punctuation. It was all boring, except for something called an exclamation mark. Molly drew it on her slate, an up-and-down line with an eye beneath. I didn't draw it, but I thought it.

I want to see Gentleman Jack!

I want to see Gentleman Jack!

I want to see Gentleman Jack!

The drawing of Gentleman Jack still hung on the wall of the Sheriff's office. The Sheriff should have taken it down; he didn't need it anymore. There were newspapers everywhere and half-drunk cups of coffee with gray skins. Everything was tired and out of date. The air was stale and half chewed, but I had to breathe it.

It reminded me of the Judge talking about how the Starlings' house breathed out poisonous fumes and how you weren't able to pass the house for days. It reminded me of Mrs. del Salto warning me not to drink lye because it would burn my throat and lungs. I stared at Gentleman Jack's face lying flat against the wall. Five Thousand Dollars. No one else was worth that much, not Rough Ricky, not Doubtful Mittie.

"*Doubtful Mittie's not worth anything anymore,*" said the dagger. "*Being dead and all.*"

They looked just like themselves. The person who drew them knew that Rough Ricky's lips were burnt into a smile. He knew Gentleman Jack's best smile showed only his lips.

A cup of cold coffee sat on a windowsill; beside it lay three squares of paper. The coffee was discouraging, but the paper was encouraging. It was the color of stars.

"Foil," said the dagger. "*To wrap around chocolates.*"

I turned to face the window, folded my fingers around the foil. I felt Gentleman Jack's picture staring at me, watching me steal from the Sheriff.

"*Chocolates are for Valentine's Day,*" said the dagger.

"*But Gentleman Jack likes butterscotch best.*" I wished I had some to give him. I hadn't been exercising judgment not even to try!

The Deputy Sheriff asked if I wanted a cup of coffee. The Judge said it would stunt my growth.

"Not with sugar," I said. "Sugar helps you grow." But I knew it was the wrong kind of growing. It wasn't the slow chicken-pie-ish growing Mrs. del Salto approved of. It was a fast, sugary growing that wasn't good for you.

"Speaking of sugar—" The Judge handed me a small brown bag.

"Butterscotch!" I said.

"Butterscotch," he said.

"For Gentleman Jack," I said.

"For Gentleman Jack," he said.

"Thank you." That was probably the first time since coming to the Indigo Heart that I'd said Thank You and meant it.

At last the Sheriff came to get me. I showed him the bag of butterscotch, which he shook, then handed back without a word. Now to the puckered-ghost-mouth door.

A cell block really was a block. Three cells in a row, with a path in front. The bars were too hard. The cell block was not alive, not like the dollhouse and the attic. In the cell block you could turn around and around like a bird in a nest, but you couldn't make it fit your shape.

Gentleman Jack was still in the middle cell, but he didn't look like himself. They'd let his hair grow, even though in the hideout he kept it short. He said long hair was a disadvantage in a fight. Someone could grab your hair, he said. They could jerk your head back and cut your throat.

Gentleman Jack came to the front. I drew closer, tasted sweat and rust. I gripped the bars, they were cold. Would today be the day he'd say, "This is my girl, returned from the road!

"This is my girl, bright as a star!"

He would say it with exclamation marks!

But Gentleman Jack wasn't thinking about brightness and stars. He was thinking about me, but not in a good way.

"I hesitate to ask, my dear," he said. "And really, I'm sure there's some simple explanation. But it has occurred to me to wonder why you've taken so long to visit again."

"The Judge wouldn't let me," I said.

"Ah," he said, very softly. His voice hardly made a dent in the air. "How, I wonder, might we outsmart the Judge?"

He said the word We, which meant he'd help me outsmart the Judge, even though it was really my problem. Gentleman Jack was nice that way, not saying I was dull, not saying it directly. He was nice that way, sharing the burden of my dullness.

"I'll try to be sharp," I said. But the words tasted like poison. They wilted my tongue.

"Try!" Gentleman Jack hardly breathed the word. The softer he spoke, the duller I got. "Try won't be good enough, not if they find me guilty of murder."

He wrapped his fingers around the bars, even though they'd rust his gloves. He was touching the bars; I was touching the bars. It was almost like we were touching each other.

"Did you try to see Flora?" I knew the word for the way he said Try. The way was called Patient.

But Patient was really just Impatient, with a bubble over it to hide it, like a blister. The bubble is called Sarcasm.

"I saw her twice!" I said. Twice must be extra good.

"Don't mumble," said Gentleman Jack. "Speak up."

Now I spoke too loudly. "Twice!" The words bounced off the concrete walls. Concrete didn't absorb sound. It had no nooks or pores or crannies. Neither did my voice.

Now came the smell of lighter fluid. Now came the flare of the strike lighter, on and off, helping Gentleman Jack think. "You have Grandmother's pocket watch?" he said.

"In my britches pocket," I said.

"And Grandmother's photograph in the watch?" he said.

"I look at it every day," I said.

"Wait until you are quite private," said Gentleman Jack. "Then destroy it."

Destroy Grandmother's photograph? The one that made a safe, silver echo in my head?

"We Royals are famous," said Gentleman Jack. "Someone might recognize Grandmother. They might recognize the watch, too, because of the emblem. Hide it carefully."

I could say I'd try not to be dull, but Gentleman Jack would only pluck out the word Try and blister it again with Sarcasm.

"Say something!" said Gentleman Jack. "Tell me you understand."

"I understand," I said. Gentleman Jack's face was not as familiar as before. His hair was light, but his whiskers were dark. Maybe the jail didn't let him shave. The stubble dragged down his face. But I knew how to make it go back up.

First I gave him the bag of butterscotch. Then I said, "I found a Songbird. We can take him to Grandmother's and she'll be happy."

His face stayed the same. The stubble was too heavy to let it go up. "Who is it?"

"The peanut man, the one who stands outside the Sapphire, whistling."

"No good." Gentleman Jack shook his head. "What's important about a Songbird?"

"A Songbird reminds the Rosati about the Blue Rose so they think about her and worship her and raise their voices in praise, and then she'll grant the boons they crave."

I was right about that, but not about the peanut man. "He came from far away," said Gentleman Jack. "He doesn't worship the Blue Rose."

So he couldn't be a Songbird for Netherby Scar?

No, he couldn't be a Songbird for Netherby Scar.

But there was one more happy thing I could tell him. "Flora and Lord John have a good idea."

"John?" said Gentleman Jack. "John's here!"

I spoke very low. "Flora and Lord John want me to testify at your trial."

"What's John doing here?" he said.

"Playing cards at the Sapphire," I said. "Talking to people with his silver tongue."

"That silver tongue is full of lies," said Gentleman Jack. "John's always trying to steal a march on me."

Steal a march? The Judge would know what it meant.

"But I'm faster," said Gentleman Jack. "And stronger and smarter." He stretched his lips over his teeth. "What did Flora say about my good-luck opal?"

"She says you'll need gold to buy one."

"What did she say about my gold?"

"She said she has no information on that score."

"I'll score her," said Gentleman Jack. I didn't want to ask him what that meant, because asking wasn't a shiny thing to do. "Remind Flora of Lucretia. Remind her of the way Lucretia scores."

Score was a knife-ish sort of word. It meant using something sharp, like a knife, to make a mark in something else, like a bone.

"Flora's idea is about the trial."

It was really Flora and Lord John's idea, but now I didn't want to mention Lord John. I could tell Gentleman Jack didn't like him. I knew that mentioning Lord John's name would be like mixing a lye bomb—which is something that can explode at any time.

I didn't like thinking so much about lye bombs. I wished I could lie down and press the darkness into my eyes—I wished I could cram darkness into everything I knew about smoke and fire and bombs—but that would be dumb. It would be wasting my time with Gentleman Jack.

I hoped he'd get happier when I told him what I'd say about the Fair. There was no time to tell him about the lemonade, or the Belgian horses with their big feet, or how I'd not been sick, but before I finished, Gentleman Jack was nodding.

"Flora always was clever," he said. That was a good word, Clever. But still, he looked far away, with the stubble pulling at his face. He shoved his hands into his pockets and there they stayed, as though they were rusted into place. Now I was the only one holding the bars.

"How will you find Grandmother's house?" said Gentleman Jack. I said that when I got to Netherby Scar, I'd show the bird engraving to the people in the town and they'd tell me the way.

"How can they do that?" said Gentleman Jack.

"Because in Netherby Scar," I said, "people treat you like your last name, which is Royal. Everyone knows Grandmother's emblem and knows where you live."

And now, at last, Gentleman Jack's face went up. He liked talking about how people treated him like royalty. "I want Flora to visit me. Go tell her so, and this time don't delay. Ask her how you might outmaneuver the Judge, so he doesn't keep you away again. Flora's clever that way. I imagine she can shine you up a bit."

I didn't think I could ever get very shiny, but I wouldn't say so, and anyway, my tongue was a dead petal.

Back in the office, with the cups of coffee and newspapers. The news was as cold as the coffee. The poster of Gentleman Jack hardly looked like him now. In the poster he had frills and gloves and the ruby earring. But now his hair covered the earring, and he had dark stubble and a pulled-down face.

Before, I had thought I could bring Gentleman Jack good news about a Songbird, even if I had no butterscotch to give him. But now it was all mixed up. I'd brought him the butterscotch, but there was no good news about the Songbird.

"I wish the Sheriff would steal me," said the dagger. "I'd bite him extra quick before he could give you a penny."

But I thought the Sheriff would be too quick for that. His body was quick enough to handcuff Gentleman Jack, and his mind was quick enough to understand the Whistling.

I asked the Sheriff if I could have the drawing of Gentleman Jack. The Sheriff said he guessed I could take it, if it was all right with the Judge, which it was.

The Sheriff folded the drawing before handing it to me; he folded it twice. Now there would be lines across Gentleman Jack's face. One line going up and down, one line going across.

I slipped the drawing into Magda's pocket, beside the Valentine's Day card. It was Magda's pocket because it was attached to her coat, and also because it was blue, which was a good color for Magda. It was Magda's coat because it had hung in the shrine to Magda. The shrine filled with fabrics, the fabrics filled with memories.

"You don't have any memories!" said the dagger.

That wasn't true. I had memories from when I was around six and had come to live with Gentleman Jack. I knew I had memories from before, but I kept them away by being grateful to Gentleman Jack.

"You use too many exclamation marks," I said.

"That's because I'm pointy!" said the dagger.

Out we went, the Judge and I, into the smells of pigs and muck, which I'd expected, but also into the warm, heavy smell of peanuts, which I hadn't. Then came the peanut man's whistle: "Fresh, hot peanuts!"

"Have you ever had peanuts?" said the Judge.

"Probably," I said, because from the very first, I'd recognized the smell. I'd recognized it even before I saw the peanut cart. And I'd known that the bolt on the attic door was shaped like a peanut.

"*Probably not!*" said the dagger.

"Let's see," said the Judge. We turned toward the peanut cart, which was a cozy sight, the hot red coals bright in the gathering dusk. The Judge passed over some coins, and the peanut man passed back a bag of peanuts. They were delicious, warm and salty. When we had finished, the bag was semitransparent with oil, which sounds ugly but was really very pretty.

I held the bag to the sky. That way you could see the light shining through. "Can you have a Songbird who's not from Blue Roses?" I said.

The Judge said that the farther you got from Blue Roses, the harder it was to find a Songbird. He said that people who lived in faraway towns wanted a Songbird to live in their town, so they could be holy and crave boons of the Blue Rose, but that it didn't work that way. "You can't just march a Songbird away from the Indigo Heart and expect them to sing."

That reminded me to ask about Steal a March. The Judge said it meant getting the advantage of someone by acting more quickly. He said the phrase carried with it overtones of dishonesty. The oil-paper bag shone; the dome of the Shrine shone.

And then a thought came arcing through the air and struck me, quivering, like an arrow.

"*Like a dagger,*" said the dagger.

I could steal a march on Gentleman Jack's no-account brother. I could ask the Blue Rose to bring Gentleman Jack his five gold bricks. That would be the boon he'd crave. Then Grandmother would love him best and give him the empire. I could ask the Blue Rose for a Songbird, and then Gentleman Jack would bring Grandmother everything she wanted. Of course, Grandmother already loved Gentleman Jack the best, but now she'd really love him best.

"I need to tell Gentleman Jack something," I said. But I said it mostly from habit. I knew he'd say I had to wait. That we had to get home to Mrs. del Salto.

Gentleman Jack had said I needed to outmaneuver the Judge, but the Judge wasn't very maneuverable.

"You'll visit him just as soon as you can," said the dagger.

"He'll be so happy," I said.

I had Betsy's Valentine's Day card in my pocket, which I didn't like, but I had Gentleman Jack's face in my pocket, which I did. It turned out the Judge also had something he liked in his pocket, but unlike me, he took it out. It was for Mrs. del Salto. It came in a black velvet box, which he snapped open.

In it was a ring. It looked familiar but not familiar. It was set with dark stones that made a circle all around.

"Opals, for Valentine's Day," said the Judge. "They go with her wedding ring."

"But aren't they supposed to shine?" These opals were dull and dark, not like the stone in her other ring, which swam with brilliant underwater colors.

"Opals come alive when they're with their person," said the Judge, "which in this case is surely Mrs. del Salto, because of how well they match her eyes. Also, opals should be given with love, which these are. Opals are another of the Blue Rose's gifts to us. They're made of stardust and bring good luck and clarity of vision. Black opals are especially precious."

I asked the Judge if it was a rule that an opal had to match their person's eyes. I didn't think Mrs. del Salto's black-button eyes looked very much like her beautiful opal, but the Judge said yes, they had to match. That was a lucky thing to know. Now I knew I had to get a green opal to match Gentleman Jack's eyes. Green eyes were the rarest eye color. Green opals must be the most valuable of all.

Mrs. del Salto gave me a key. My key was not exactly the same as hers. There was the same loop at the top, and a little curlicue inside the loop, but the curlicue was different. That was because my key had been made at a different time than Mrs. del Salto's key. My key was brighter, too, which was because it hadn't been used as much. "But the important part is the same," said Mrs. del Salto. "This bit that sticks out is what opens the door. This bit is the same on both keys because the lock is the same."

I practiced putting the key into the lock and turning it. The bolt slid in and out. It was best when the bolt was in the lock. Mrs. del Salto put her key into the drawer with the green felt lining.

Her new ring shone next to the old one. The Judge had been right: the stones shimmered with life. Mrs. del Salto was their person, even if her eyes were more like buttons than opals. She wore the rings on the same finger. The stones were black and deep and made of stardust. I didn't say anything about them, though, and neither did Mrs. del Salto.

Two keys already lay on the soft green lining. The Judge's key looked like Mrs. del Salto's key. They were different from mine, but it didn't matter. The bit that stuck out was the same. That was the important bit because it was what opened the door.

Now I laid my own key on the green felt. You could tell it was comfortable. There was one shiny key and two not-so-shiny keys.

I closed the drawer.

Now the drawer was full. I had made it full.

A Murmuration of Starlings

✝ YOU DIDN'T GO TO SCHOOL on Saturdays and Sundays. Saturdays were best because you knew you didn't have to go to school the next day, either. On Saturdays, you could wake up before anyone else. You could go down the bright painted stairs to the landing. You could go down the carpet that was held in place by heavy brass rods. That was so the carpet couldn't squiggle away, not with the heavy rods and the pineapples at each end. Then you were on the first floor. You could put on Magda's coat and feel the paper in the pocket. It was Magda's coat, but Gentleman Jack's face was all yours.

On a Saturday, you could walk through the kitchen, above the dreaming cellar. You didn't need to hurry on a Saturday. You could stop in the pantry; you could open a drawer of sweetness. You could catch some on a wet finger and lick it off.

You could open the drawer with the silverware. That's what the Judge and Mrs. del Salto called the forks, knives, and spoons. You could also call them Cutlery. The silverware drawer was divided into long, narrow spaces by wooden walls. They were like long, narrow beds. The walls separated the knives and the forks and the spoons.

Everything was orderly and bright. The spoons were in the middle, which was the way it should be. The knives were on one side, defending the spoons with their sharp edges.

"Not that sharp!" said the dagger.

The forks were on the other side, protecting the spoons with their points. If I could be shrunk into miniature, I'd climb into the middle bed and curl up with the spoons. I'd like the feeling of having the knives and forks protecting me on either side.

On a Saturday, you could go out the back door. The dagger and I had discovered that behind it lay a barn and a chicken coop and a stable and an old doghouse, and beyond that, a forest of indigo trees. Now I knew I could leave the cottage through the back door. Now I knew it was an exit.

I undid the bolt; I flung open the door. Behind the outbuildings stretched the indigo forest, all draped in mist. Today I would explore the forest; today I would follow the path that tramped off between the trees. It was a determined sort of path. It didn't ramble or amble or go chasing after the smells of wet and resin. It marched straight to a clearing in the forest where the sun touched the mist with a white light.

The white light illuminated two pale stones. They were the color of bone and had chiseled writing on them. The dagger and I realized at the same time:

"Magda," I said.

"Isaac," said the dagger.

I knelt before them. I knew which was Magda's grave because of the letter M. I could recognize M and I knew Magda started with an M.

I knew the letter I on the other stone was for Isaac. They had dates for being born and dates for dying. Magda was born in a month that started with an O, and there was only one month that started with an O. It wasn't tricky like, say, a month that started with M, which could be either March or May. Or J, which could be January or June or July.

Magda had been born in October. She'd been born on October sixteenth. Isaac had been born on November third.

There was water springing from everywhere in little rivulets, running off the tops of the gravestones, dripping and twisting and turning. The mist was beginning to lift, but the sun was still white. The light hung on the chiseled edges of the letters and numbers. The children had died in the same year, which was last year. They died in the same month, which was September. The Judge had told me they'd died of the smallpox, and now I saw that they'd died within five days of each other. Their deaths were close as the fingers of a hand.

That was not very long ago. Not even as long ago as when Gentleman Jack killed the Federal Marshal, which had been August twenty-sixth. I remembered August twenty-sixth perfectly. Probably Mrs. del Salto remembered her children's deaths perfectly.

August twenty-sixth was when the Harvest Fair had taken place, which I also remembered perfectly, even though it was all made up.

After the gravestones, the path trickled into indecision. Mrs. del Salto must have made the decided path from the cottage to the graves. I pictured her walking over and over to the graves of her children, gazing at them, eating ashes and salt. Her children had died in just a handful of days. No wonder she was all rusty and sharp.

Why didn't she crave a boon for more children—just the way I was going to crave a boon for a Songbird and gold?

These grave markers were made of stone; there were no wooden stars. Why were some stone and some wood?

On I went, through bars of pale sun, through the shadows of the indigo trees. The trees thinned, then the forest floor broke in half and toppled into a gorge. I lay on my stomach to look. The drop was so steep it made me dizzy. Along the bottom flowed one of the countless rivers of the Indigo Heart, all rushy with spring.

"Not countless," said the dagger. "Not if you count high."

I turned back to the cottage. I passed the graves, the doghouse, the stable, the chicken coop, and the barn. I was beginning to understand that the Judge was rich. He lived in a cottage, which didn't seem like a rich thing, but his horses were the best horses in all of Blue Roses, and he hired workers to tend the horses and the chickens and the gardens. There was even a worker in the cottage. Her name was Veronica. She came on Wednesdays to clean and on Saturdays to make pies and bread.

I smelled the bread first thing. Bread is strong; it has a strong smell. It's so strong, it's alive. You can tuck it away under a cloth, and when you come back, it's grown. I was growing and I was alive. The dough was growing and it was alive.

The kitchen table was bare because making bread would mess up the tablecloth, and also because Veronica washed the clothes and linens. As soon as she saw me, she filled my yellow cup with milk. You could see all the cracks in it, but the glue was strong. I drank down the milk, I drank down the color of the cottage.

I wandered into the Judge's library. It seemed so long ago that I'd thought the walls were made of books. Now I knew they were made of shelves and that the shelves were filled with books. The bottom shelves were taller than the other shelves and they were filled with Magda and

Isaac's books. Books for children were tall because they had to fit in all the pictures.

But I wouldn't look at the books now. I went to the mantelpiece and snatched up the photograph of Magda and Isaac.

"*The photograph isn't worth anything,*" said the dagger.

"*I only care about the frame.*" I was going to fill up all the empty spaces in the dollhouse. The frame would fill up the empty space in the dining room.

"*But the frame's not gold,*" said the dagger. "*Just painted.*"

It didn't have to be real gold to be valuable. It could still be valuable to me, like the little key I'd taken from Magda's book, even though it was only made of tin.

I slid the frame into my coat pocket. The photograph came along with it, of course, even though that wasn't what I wanted. I didn't put the frame in the pocket with the drawing of Gentleman Jack. His face didn't go with a painted frame. His face would only go with a frame of real gold.

The dagger and I paused at the desk.

"*You'll take the coins?*" said the dagger.

"*On May sixth,*" I said.

"*You'll take the inkwell?*" said the dagger.

"*On May sixth.*"

"*When are you going to destroy Grandmother's photograph?*" said the dagger.

I didn't know.

"*You could know if you wanted to,*" said the dagger.

I didn't want to know. I didn't want to destroy the photograph and the safe silvery feeling it gave me. I'd never disobeyed Gentleman Jack before, but maybe it wasn't disobedience if it was a thing you just hadn't done yet.

"*Betrayal!*" said the dagger.

But I was taking a long time to visit Gentleman Jack—another long time—and I wouldn't be able to tell him why. I couldn't say it was because I hadn't destroyed the photograph.

There was something new on the desk, a small square of orange paper, no bigger than the Judge's thumbprint. On it was a picture of an old-fashioned man. His hair was long and bound together at the back. On the square were tiny words I couldn't read, but there was also a number. I could read numbers. It was the number Two.

"*It's a stamp*," said the dagger.

What was a stamp?

"*It's like money to send a letter far away,*" said the dagger.

"*As far as Netherby Scar?*"

"*Farther,*" said the dagger.

The Judge had paper and envelopes and stamps and pens and ink—everything you needed to send a letter. But an envelope was much bigger than a stamp. How strange that such a small thing could send such a big thing traveling thousands of miles.

"*A stamp is little but strong,*" said the dagger. "*If you mail a letter without a stamp, it will come back marked RETURN TO SENDER.*"

I could send a letter to Grandmother in Netherby Scar.

"*You don't know how to write,*" said the dagger.

"*Flora could write it.*" I could send a letter to Grandmother, explaining why we hadn't arrived at her house on Day Zero—on the old Day Zero.

"*You don't know where to send it,*" said the dagger.

That was true. In order to see Grandmother, I'd have to make my way to her house. That's what Gentleman Jack always said, "Make your way." I'd have to make my way by showing Grandmother's pocket watch to the people who lived there. They'd recognize the engraving of the flying bird, which was the Royals' emblem. They'd tell me where to go.

"*Could I send myself to Grandmother's house?*" I said.

"*Don't be ridiculous,*" said the dagger.

I sat in front of the dollhouse. On the floor were all the ingredients I needed to make a mirror: glue, a pencil, scissors, the foil from the Sheriff's office, the frame from the library, and Betsy's Valentine's Day card. The frame was empty; the Valentine's card was good and stiff. The photograph of Magda and Isaac lay on the floor. I traced the shape of the frame on the card, then cut it out, but a little smaller. That was because I had to fit the card into the back of the frame, which was edged with a lip and two metal pivots to hold the back in place.

I only had to use half the card. I used the front part, which had a picture of some roses. I didn't know why I'd kept the part with the words. I'd never know what they said.

It didn't matter that the edges of the card weren't perfectly even. No one would see the edges from the front. I knew about glue now because of the yellow cup. I spread glue on the card, then smoothed the foil over the glue. I folded the foil over the edges. Last, I slipped the whole of it into the frame, set the back onto it, and folded the pivots to keep the back in place.

The mirror fit perfectly in the dining room, under the arch of painted garlands. I unhooked the watch from the library wall and polished the cover. On the outside was the lid with the bird engraving; beneath that was the photograph of Grandmother when she was young; and beneath that was the watch's silent heart.

"*When are you going to destroy Grandmother's photograph?*"

I didn't know. I couldn't make myself destroy Grandmother's photograph and wreck the safe and silvery feeling it gave me.

"Betrayal!" said the dagger. "You can't visit Gentleman Jack until you've destroyed it."

I called out to the dolls. You couldn't reach in and grab them. They might be made of china, but they were real. They were cold on the outside, but they were warm on the inside. Their china hearts were warm.

"Come and look!" I said.

Swish went the mother doll's skirts; tap went the father doll's feet. There came the ticking of Oakheart's feet on the floor, suddenly muted when he reached a carpet, loud again on the bare wood.

"It's beautiful!" said the mother doll.

My stomach floated up like a cottonwood seed.

"Beautiful," said the father doll.

The mother and father dolls looked at everything. At the lace tablecloth—

"Stolen!" said the dagger. "That's good!"

Stolen from one of Magda's dresses. But the dress was just hanging in the wardrobe, doing nothing. The dress didn't need the pocket, not the way the table needed the tablecloth.

At the gold frame on the wall—

"Stolen!" said the dagger.

At the silver paper in the frame—

"Stolen!" said the dagger.

"Don't forget the key in the drawer," I said to the mother and father dolls. "You can lock yourselves in, you can lock others out."

"We won't forget," said the father doll. His eyes were a nice warm brown. It was funny how the father doll had brown eyes, and Betsy had brown eyes, but Betsy's real-person eyes looked like marbles and the father doll's glass eyes looked real.

I had made them happy. "I've seen the baby," I said. I hadn't yet told them about the baby doll in Elton's General Store. It was mixed up with the ugly memory of my sticky fingers and the way the egg-man's arm had dropped to his side. It was mixed up with my sorrows. But I liked the cottonseed feeling of making them happy.

The dolls looked up. Their eyes made the tiniest of clicks.

"Tell us!"

"Tell us!"

I couldn't say he was in a store. They wouldn't understand. "I was in a place with toys for children."

"That's a good place for our baby to be," said the father doll.

"There were jacks and balls and blocks—"

"A ball!" said the father doll. "I should like to have a ball to kick to the baby."

"But he can't stand up by himself," I said.

"Later," said the father doll. "When he's learned to walk."

"By holding on to Oakheart's collar," said the mother doll.

"He's about this high." I showed them a space between my hands, about two inches. "He has brown hair and blue eyes." I wished I knew whether his eyes clicked open and shut. "He's wearing blue pajamas, but his feet are bare."

"We'll have to wrap him up warmly," said the father doll.

"We need a blanket for the cradle," said the mother doll. "There's a cradle in the nursery upstairs."

"Oh, Starling," said the father doll. "You have made us so happy!"

I had made them happy.

"I can get a blanket before May sixth," I said. "I have sixty-five days."

"Hardly any time at all," said the father doll. "Not to get the collar, which is the second task."

The tasks should stop there. Two tasks was the right number of tasks. Grandmother had given Gentleman Jack two tasks.

"Hardly any time at all to perform the third task," said the mother doll, "which is to get our baby."

Even if I had plenty of time, I still couldn't get the baby. I had no money. I'd only told them about the baby so they could be happy. Their being happy was the opposite of a sorrow. It was a joy, and even though it was a lie, I'd still embrace it.

"*You couldn't even steal it,*" said the dagger. "*If you went into the store, they'd be watching you every second.*"

That was true. But still, the rhyme that had begun to spin itself in my mind—the rhyme about the dolls' tasks—suddenly shifted and expanded.

> One is for Oakheart,
> Two's for a collar.
> Three's for a sister,
> Four's for a brother.

"*That doesn't rhyme!*" said the dagger. "*Not Collar and Brother.*"

But the dagger didn't know anything about rhyming, which was why it couldn't understand the Whistling. I knew; I'd tested it.

"*Anyway,*" said the dagger, "*who's the sister?*"

"*The sister sleeps in the green bedroom,*" I said.

"*Where is she?*" said the dagger.

"*She hasn't gotten here yet,*" I said, but I didn't really know what I meant.

"The Indigo Heart will keep you as long as it needs you," said the father doll. "It attracts the people it wants to attract. It keeps the people it wants to keep."

Oakheart was asleep on the parlor carpet. His legs jerked and his tail thumped. He couldn't close his eyes because he was made of wood, but he could sleep and he could dream. Did the wax doll have eyes that opened and closed?

"You said you were going to leave," said the mother doll. "But you came back."

"Because I made a new plan about Gentleman Jack."

"There's always a reason," said the father doll. "That's the way it works."

Fine. If the dolls wanted to believe that the Indigo Heart could keep me here, let them.

"We will sing songs to our baby," said the father doll.

"And read him nursery rhymes," said the mother doll.

"Nursery rhymes?"

The dolls were surprised I didn't know about nursery rhymes. "You speak like a person who knows nursery rhymes," said the father doll. "That's because of the piping in your voice."

But I had no piping in my voice. My voice was thick and heavy as cement. It had one flavor, and the flavor was Ugly.

"The rhymes are in a big book," said the mother doll.

"With a picture of a goose wearing a bonnet," said the father doll.

"Magda's mother used to read them to her," said the mother doll. "And later Magda read them to Isaac."

"Magda could read when she was only four," said the father doll.

"The King was in the counting house, counting out his money," said the mother doll. "That's part of a Mother Goose rhyme."

That was like Gentleman Jack, the King, counting out his money. Except that Gentleman Jack would be counting out his gold.

"The Queen was in the parlor," said the father doll, "eating bread and honey."

The parlor was for Mrs. del Salto, and the bread and honey was for me. I remembered the rhyme, but I didn't remember it. I remembered it like an echo.

"*You don't remember!*" said the dagger.

I thought about Magda, who had learned to read when she was four. I thought about her wardrobe, stuffed with memories. I didn't remember when I was four. I only remembered when I was five, or maybe six, and Gentleman Jack rescued me. Yet there were the echoes in my head.

"*Heads don't echo,*" said the dagger.

But memories could echo. When the dolls told me about the tasks, they made me remember a dog, a collar, and a baby holding the dog's collar. I remembered thinking the baby memory must have been hollow, because inside the memory was a silver echo. And always when I looked at Grandmother's photograph came the same silver echo.

Gentleman Jack had made me come alive. The dollhouse had made Oakheart come alive. You could tell he was alive when you looked at the inside of the dollhouse door. When the dolls left the dollhouse, he banged his nose against it, leaving tiny dents. His nose was real, the dents were real, the loneliness that made him bang at the door was real. Nilsson had given him a real nose, but the dollhouse had brought him to life.

But I was the one who'd dusted the mother and father dolls. And then look what happened! "Did I make you come to life?" I said.

"The Blue Rose made us come to life," said the mother doll. "She made us out of clay and breathed spirit into us."

"But you're made of china!" I said.

"China's made of clay," said the father doll. "And the clay in the Indigo Heart is made of stardust."

Before I left the attic, I hid the photograph of Magda and Isaac in the dollhouse, under the carpet in the parlor. I stuck the leftover half of the Valentine's Day card there, too. It was perfect. You'd never know they were there. Veronica came in to dust the cottage and beat the rugs, but she never cleaned the dollhouse. That was my job.

I left the dollhouse and its apple-seed doorknobs. My feet took me to Isaac's room. There was no dust. The walls were blue; there was a blue cradle with yellow spindles. There was the same kind of horse I'd seen in the General Store, the one that looked like a sleigh; its mane was lavender and yellow ribbons. There were train tracks on the floor.

There was no blanket in the cradle. Isaac must have been cold. It looked too empty. It looked so empty, it would make you frantic.

I didn't care what the dolls said. I was the one who'd dusted the dolls. I'd made them come alive.

Veronica had dusted the room, but she could not make Isaac come alive.

My feet took me down to the library. Magda and Isaac's books stuck out from the lower shelves. Here was one with a picture of a fish-girl on the front, another with a picture of a hut running about on chicken legs. And here it was, a picture of a goose wearing a bonnet.

The pictures were loud with color. One was of a boy dangling long legs from a hayrick, casting a fishing line into a pail. Another was of a boy plunging his thumb into a pie. I almost knew what he was going to pull out.

I stared at a picture of a neat little ship with cheerful sails and white mice in blue coats strolling the decks. I felt I had loved that picture, and the words that went with it, even though I couldn't remember them. I had loved it before I was six, before I went to live with Gentleman Jack.

"You don't remember that time!" said the dagger.

But I wouldn't let the dagger ruin the echo-feeling of having loved the words and the picture. A Mother Goose book could breathe spirit into your memories. The dolls had said the Blue Rose had breathed spirit into them and turned them into stardust. The Judge had said the Blue Rose breathed spirit into all creation.

Breathed Spirit. A memory recaptured is a memory come alive. It's a memory that's had spirit breathed into it. I hid my thoughts under the words Breathed Spirit.

I looked at the words in the Mother Goose book. They looked back. The first word was I. I was easy. But the next word was hard. It started with an S. The words looked back at me. There were lots of S's in the words. The S's curled in on themselves. They held on to their secrets.

Mrs. del Salto came into the library with Veronica and asked Veronica if she knew where the photograph of Magda and Isaac was. Veronica said she had no idea. Mrs. del Salto sighed and said she must learn to be philosophical.

Philosophical?

"Philosophical," said the dagger, "means—"

"It means," I said, "that Mrs. del Salto doesn't suspect I have the photograph."

"It means—" said the dagger.

"It means," I said, "that I don't ever have to think about it again."

I didn't try to hide the nursery rhyme book. I was beginning to understand Mrs. del Salto. She wouldn't like it that I'd stolen Magda's pocket to make a tablecloth or that I'd stolen the photograph to make a mirror, but she wouldn't mind if I looked at Magda's books.

"Magda loved that one," said Mrs. del Salto, looking over my shoulder. She read a bit of it aloud, and all the S's that had lain on the page came sailing out, like waves:

"*I saw a ship a-sailing,*
A-sailing on the sea.
And O, but it was laden,
With pretty things for thee."

I remembered it.

"*You do not,*" said the dagger.

It would be all right to remember the rhyme. It wasn't like remembering my mother, who'd abandoned me. I remembered the rhyme like a dream; I couldn't hold on to it. I had no wardrobe filled with whiteness to weigh down my memories.

And just then Mrs. del Salto said she was going to make me a dress for the Feast of the Blue Rose. That was a coincidence, right when I was thinking about wardrobes and memories. Would we hang the dress in the cupboard bed to keep my memories from floating away?

"Come with me," she said. "I have something for you."

"Good or bad?" I said.

She laughed a little. "Good."

I followed her outside, to the front porch. This was the second time I'd seen her outside. And then she surprised me even more by sitting on the porch.

It wasn't warm, but it was March and it wasn't exactly cold. You could sit on the porch.

"You asked the Judge about jacks," said Mrs. del Salto. She placed a little net bag beside the sunflower carpet. In the bag was a red ball—

"That is a ball for jacks." I heard Betsy's voice in my memory.

But there was more. The bag was filled with stars. Blue metal stars. The stars were the jacks. That's what Mrs. del Salto was telling me. She patted the porch. I was supposed to sit there, too.

Jacks was a game where you bounced the ball, tried to pick up a star, and then tried to catch the ball with the same hand. Mrs. del Salto tried. She missed.

I tried, I missed.

Mrs. del Salto tried and this time she didn't miss. "I used to play when I was a girl."

And looking at her now, her cheeks a little flushed, a tendril of hair escaping its pins, I could almost imagine her as a girl . . . look at her eyes! They weren't flat black buttons anymore. They shone almost as bright as her black opal. What had she been like before she stopped the clocks and started eating ashes and salt?

I thought of Magda's and Isaac's graves behind the house, and then I thought again of the graves behind the burnt house, and again I wondered why some graves were marked with stones and some with wood stars. I wouldn't ask Mrs. del Salto, though. It would make her think about her sorrows and how she could never accept them, and then her eyes would turn back into buttons and her mouth would slide off her face.

I threw the ball, I missed the star. But I didn't care. I understood this kind of game. It was like throwing the dagger. I had practiced throwing the dagger until I could make it hit anything I wanted, and I would practice jacks until I never missed the ball and could pick up all the stars. I took turns with Mrs. del Salto. There was only the sound of the ball hitting the porch and the whisper of our hands across the planks.

Mrs. del Salto must have left her house when she was a girl. She must have gone to school and turned round and round with the other girls, singing the circle song.

Then Mrs. del Salto's hand stopped whispering and she glanced into the sky. I followed her gaze, up and up, to a cloud of birds. No, not a cloud, a ribbon, a liquid ribbon, streaming under and over itself. The ribbon folded over; it twirled around itself, like a candy cane.

The birds swept and moved as though connected by magnets. Maybe they were. Maybe the forces that drew people to the Indigo Heart also drew the birds together.

"Beautiful!" said Mrs. del Salto.

"How do they do that?"

"No one knows," said Mrs. del Salto. "It's called a murmuration. A murmuration of starlings."

But Starling was my name!

"That's the reason I like your name," said Mrs. del Salto.

I reached for the metal stars lying on the porch. The starlings murmured through the sky. The starlings were like the jacks, the jacks were like the starlings. When I learned to play jacks, I'd make the metal stars fly like starlings.

Rough Ricky

✝ I KNEW ABOUT TIME NOW. I knew how the days of the week lined up like the fingers on a hand, always in the same order.

"*There are seven days of the week,*" said the dagger, "*but you only have five fingers.*"

They were always in the same order, but they were different sizes. Monday was usually a thick day, like the thumb. Friday was a shorter day, like the little finger. But like fingers, they could bend. Sometimes a Monday might go quickly, like this past Monday, when an upper-level boy recited a poem called "The Tyger." Then time bent its usual shape. But the pattern of the days was always the same, just like a person's fingers.

"*You don't have seven fingers,*" said the dagger.

"*It's just the idea of a pattern,*" I said. "*Not the actual pattern.*" But I knew the dagger wouldn't understand. It wasn't made of anything bendy.

Five seven-fingered weeks had passed. Prairie crocuses now dotted the sunny side of the schoolyard. They were taller than my hand and of a beautiful lavender. I knew from Mrs. del Salto that lavender was one of my colors. The Judge said crocuses were the first spring flower. He said they lived on the edge of the snow. I knew he meant just the idea of the edge of the snow, not the actual edge, but you could never explain it to the dagger.

Recess was always slow to come and quick to pass. I paid no attention to the big girls, singing their circle song. I wouldn't want to be like a donkey grinding corn, going round and round, always in the same place. I sat on the stoop behind the school. Thunk went the jacks ball. Swish went my hand around the jacks.

Thunk, swish. Thunk, swish. Thunk—

Silence.

A great hand pressed at my mouth. I lunged for the dagger, but another hand grabbed my wrist. That hand squeezed; the other pressed my lips into my teeth.

Now the ball made a different sound. Bumpity-bump-bump, dribbling down the stairs.

"Have you forgotten?" said Rough Ricky's whispery voice. "Never drop your guard."

I knew Rough Ricky would never hurt me, but my heart was like the ball, bumpity-bump-bumping against my ribs. He un-pressed my lips. I smelled ashes and burning, but now my face was cold.

"You need to sleep with one eye open," said Rough Ricky. He thrust a piece of paper into my hand. It was folded, but you could tell it was a map. "Meet me where I've drawn the X."

"After school?"

"After school," said Rough Ricky. "Don't leave early. Stick to your schedule."

I understood. Doing things out of the ordinary would attract attention, and for Rough Ricky, attention would get him arrested.

"After school." He faded into the trees and was gone.

I was covered in Rough Ricky's burning smell. Could anyone else smell it as I walked through the nose-door of the school? As I sat between Molly and Peter, on the too-short bench? But everything was as usual: Peter still drew horses on his slate; Molly's fingernails still shone like moons; there were still words on the blackboard, and if one of them was the word Book, I still couldn't read it. I remembered Agnes's sharp voice: "That new girl don't know nothing."

I'd learned to listen to Mrs. Elton just enough that if she whirled around and asked me what she'd just said, I could repeat a few words. That was all it took to make her believe you were paying attention.

Today we talked about the Blue Rose, because the Feast of the Blue Rose was in two weeks. The sixth level told the story of how the Blue Rose had made roses bloom in the snow, which was why she was the special Guide of unborn children. That didn't exactly make sense until one of the fifth-levelers said that making babies grow was kind of like making roses grow under difficult conditions.

The seventh-levelers said that the Blue Rose was one of the Seven Star Sisters and that it was her light that led the people to Blue Roses, where they could settle, with no one to boss them around or turn them away. Six of the Seven Sisters had star names, like Astra and Estella. The Judge had told me they were mostly from Latin, which was an old language people didn't speak anymore.

But the Blue Rose didn't have a star name. She was named after the marvel she'd performed of making seven blue roses bloom in the snow.

She was the special Guide of the Rosati. People from ordinary places could come and ask for boons, but their places weren't special, like Blue Roses and the Indigo Heart.

The eighth-levelers said the Blue Rose mostly stayed on Earth, which was why you mostly couldn't see her with her sisters at night. Sometimes, though, she went back to visit them, and then she shone brightest of all. If you craved a boon of her then, you could be pretty sure she'd listen.

I already knew this. I knew as much as the eighth-levelers, me, Starling del Salto! There'd been a Dark Moon last night and I'd stayed up late to see if the Blue Rose had joined her sisters in the sky. If she had, then it would have been a good night to crave a boon for Gentleman Jack.

Or maybe I should crave two boons, one for the gold and one for a Songbird. Maybe craving two boons was more polite than craving one boon with a bunch of things in it. But it hadn't mattered anyway: there'd been only six of the Seven Sisters.

There were only two more Dark Moons between now and the new Day Zero. I had to hope that on one of them, she'd be in the sky with her sisters. It would be funny if I could crave a boon of the Blue Rose that she show up and grant my boon.

My thoughts went sliding off to Rough Ricky, how he'd surprised me and pressed my lips into my teeth, and how he smelled of burning, and how the jacks ball and my heart had gone all sideways and bumpity-bump-bumped down the stairs, and then I couldn't think about it anymore.

Betsy was speaking. I listened to her, even though her tongue was usually like a thorn. She said that people ate cinnamon on the Feast of the Blue Rose because the Blue Rose was the Guide to new life and that cinnamon made you live forever.

"*Flesh can't live forever*," said the dagger. "*It's carbon and iron that never die.*"

I'd never tasted cinnamon, but I bet Mrs. del Salto wouldn't have it in the cottage. She wouldn't want to have something that made you live forever. Living forever didn't go with ashes and salt. But then, seconds later, I was back to thinking about Rough Ricky. My heart thudded sideways, and inside my chest I heard the ball go dribbling down the steps.

"*You can't hear inside your chest,*" said the dagger.

I could read a map. That was the important thing about reading. I saw Main Street on the map. You could tell it was Main Street because it was wider than the others, and also Rough Ricky had drawn a star where the Sheriff's office was. But my actual feet were not on Main Street. They were on a street parallel to it. Main Street was the street where everybody went because of the stores, which meant lots of people could see me. That would be attracting attention. So now I was walking on a street where people lived, not where people went.

The houses on the street were smaller than buttercream cottage; their gardens were square and neat. Lots of purplish flowers grew in the gardens. I saw the lively blooms of larkspur, the graceful drooping necks of bluebells. And then, about halfway down the street, in among all the purple flowers, grew two blue roses. They really existed, those blue roses!

Maybe the people who lived in this house were going to have a baby—or maybe two babies. A baby for each rose. That was an interesting possibility.

Or would it be a rose for each baby? Which came first?

You never knew with the Blue Rose.

The map told me to go left on 3 Street. It was good it was called 3 Street, because I could read numbers. Three Street was a shamble of stairs, dragging themselves into the valley. Beside the stairs were shacks, digging their heels into the earth, trying not to fall. There were no buttercream cottages here. There were only shacks, held together by tar paper and spit. There were windows, but there was no glass, only oil paper. You can't see through oil paper.

The stairs were too tired to try to be stairs. They were like a tune that didn't make sense, all scattered notes with no idea to hold it together. The rich people in Blue Roses lived up high, on streets with names like Forest Lane and Indigo Cove. The poor people lived below Main Street on streets that were too tired to have names. The tar-and-spit houses leaned against one another, trying to stand up.

Now the shacks trickled out; the stairs gave up entirely and turned into a muddy path that plunged into the bottom of Blue Roses. The earth fell away into a gulch, and 3 Street gave up being a street and turned into a riverbank. Water swooshed around a bend of the river and rushed on, far as I could see.

Here I was on the bank of the Jordan River, deep and wide. The Judge had said there was milk and honey on the other side. But today there was just a herd of cows. A boy with a switch was tending them. One of the cows raised her head and watched me. She had a red face with a white star on her forehead. She stared at me with calm, dark eyes. The boy raised his switch but not to herd the cows. He was waving. I waved back.

Indigo trees sprang from the sides of the gulch, just barely holding on to crumbs of earth; from the riverbank burst a mass of prairie cro-cuses, dressed in lavender, just as I would be on the Feast of the Blue

Rose. And then a whistle, a regular whistle, with a tune inside of it instead of the Whistling. I knew that tune, but I couldn't remember it. It hovered on the edge of my mind. I tried to grab it, but you can't just grab your memories. You have to pretend not to pay attention to them, which makes them mad. You have to trick them into sneaking up on you from behind.

What if I listened to it sideways?

"You can't listen sideways," said the dagger.

"You said you could listen sideways," I said. "You said it on day ninety-three."

I remembered it very well. I'd been trying to hide my thoughts from the dagger. I'd gotten better at it since then.

I knew the tune, and I knew words went with the tune, just the way I knew the sun was out, even though you couldn't see it through the white eggshell sky. You knew the sun was out because the prairie crocuses were tilting up their faces and opening their mouths to drink in the light. The crocuses knew about the sun, even if they couldn't see it.

"Crocuses don't know things," said the dagger.

The cattle were a red-and-white mass, moving in the opposite direction. I looked over my shoulder. Somewhere in that mass must be the boy with the switch, the boy who had waved, but I couldn't see him. Somewhere in the mass must be the cow with the red star. I couldn't see her, but I knew she was there, just the way the crocuses knew about the sun.

I felt as though the words Father and Mother might be in the song. The song was melancholy, because it had sad spaces between the notes, and the words Mother and Father fit exactly into the sad spaces. And into another of those sad spaces fit the words Milk and Honey.

I skipped in and out of willow roots that laced the bank. I didn't want to remember the Before Time, but I couldn't stop my mind from remembering. I couldn't help hearing the tune the boy had whistled and realizing that once I'd known the words that went with the tune.

"There are no words," said the dagger.

The branches cast shadows on the riverbank. That's another way you know there's sun. There must be sun if there are shadows.

Around another bend of the river, and there he was, Rough Ricky, leaning against a willow. He patted the ground beside him. I sat by the fire, which smelled of burning. Rough Ricky smelled of burning. Rough Ricky and the fire, they smelled just the same.

"You live in the Judge's house?" said Rough Ricky.

"Yes," I said.

"Then you know where the gold is," said Rough Ricky.

"No," I said. I wished he'd said it with a question mark. It was easier to say No to a question mark than to a period.

"What do you mean No?" said Rough Ricky. "Blue Roses is filled with gold."

I tried to think of something I knew about gold. "There never were five bricks of gold," I said. "They were a trick to capture Gentleman Jack."

"Nonsense!" said Rough Ricky.

"Flora said it was a trick," I said.

"Well, if Flora said so . . ." Rough Ricky's voice trailed off. He trusted Flora. "But I need some cash to break Jack out of jail."

"To pay people to help you?"

"Exactly," said Rough Ricky.

"What about the other Gentlemen?" I said.

"The Gentlemen took some serious hits. That Sheriff's a fine shot. We had two lost lives—in addition to Doubtful Mittie—one lost finger, one lost eye, three bullets that still need digging out, and one hundred percent loss of courage. I need fresh men who aren't spooked."

I knew something else Rough Ricky probably didn't know. "Gentleman Jack will be out of jail on May sixth," I said. "That's only sixty days."

"How do you reckon?" said Rough Ricky, and I explained about the trial and how Lord John had a plan to fool the jury so they'd let Gentleman Jack go free.

"John's here?" said Rough Ricky, which was exactly what Gentleman Jack had said when I told him about Lord John.

I explained about the trial and Lord John's idea about the Fair.

The fire burned; Rough Ricky burned. "The story about the Fair is good but too risky. Breaking a man out of jail is unpredictable, but a trial is even more unpredictable. Gold is one hundred percent predictable. There must be some gold at the Judge's house."

I told him about the coins and the inkwell.

"Not piffles like that," said Rough Ricky. Rough Ricky's face couldn't frown, but his voice could frown. "Where's the Judge's safe?"

I said I'd never seen a safe in the cottage. But I knew there was a big door at the bank that led into a vault of valuable things.

"Not a bank," said Rough Ricky. "There's too much security in a bank."

The shadows of the willow branches crept along the ground. Willow was to make a chair; white oak was to make a dog. Now the shadows were bleeding into one another. Soon there would be no shadows, which would mean the sun was gone.

There came a howl, then a long answering howl. The shadows were gathering, the wolves were gathering.

"If I stay any later," I said, "the Judge will ask where I went."

"Quick, then," said Rough Ricky. "What doors do they keep unlatched?"

"What doors?" I said. "Where?"

"Pay attention!" said Rough Ricky. "At the Judge's house."

Rough Ricky, in the Judge's house? He didn't belong there.

"*He can be there if he wants,*" said the dagger.

But I couldn't imagine him there. Anyway, it was too dangerous. He could easily be caught.

"*Rough Ricky likes taking chances,*" said the dagger. "*He likes it as much as gold.*"

"The doors are all bolted," I said. "The windows are all latched. You couldn't creep in, even if you were a mouse."

I shouldn't have said that. Rough Ricky always wanted to do things people told him he couldn't do.

"I can be a mouse," said Rough Ricky. "And I can be a snake and eat the mouse. Tell me about the bolts and latches."

I told him about the doors and bolts. I told him where my room was, in the attic, at the top of the indigo tree.

"But I could meet you back here," I said. Then Rough Ricky wouldn't be taking a chance.

"Keep your window cracked," said Rough Ricky. "Don't worry; I'll get in."

That wasn't why I was worried.

"*Then why are you worried?*" said the dagger.

It was just that I didn't like to be startled. I didn't want to be startled awake when Rough Ricky crept in.

"*You'll have to sleep with one eye open,*" said the dagger.

What if I disobeyed Rough Ricky and kept the window closed? I'd disobeyed Gentleman Jack by not destroying Grandmother's photograph, and I didn't even feel bad.

"*You will,*" said the dagger. "*When Gentleman Jack finds out.*"

I tried to remember the song the boy had been whistling. Bits of the tune lingered in my memory. I remembered the sad spaces where the word Mother fit and where the word Father fit. I remembered the sad space where the words Milk and Honey fit. It was stuck in my head from the Before Time.

I remembered the spaces more than I remembered the notes. Did I know it but didn't know I knew it? Maybe the memory was folded away, wrapped in lavender. But where would the memory be? I had no wardrobe, not like Magda, filled with a whiteness of memories. I didn't know where to look.

"*Anyway,*" said the dagger, "*you don't want to look.*"

Embrace your joys, I thought. The dagger wouldn't understand. The tune and the words were a joy. Embrace your joys, so you do not estrange them.

First I would remember the spaces and then I would remember the words.

One Eye Open

✝ IT WAS THEN I STOPPED SLEEPING.

"*You're sleeping with one eye open,*" said the dagger.

But you can't really sleep with one eye open. It was dreadful waiting for Rough Ricky. I knew how it would happen. I'd be jerked out of sleep but not quite into wakefulness. The smell of burning would fold itself into my mind. I might dream I was running from a fire.

Rough Ricky didn't come the first night. I sat in the rocking chair, looking into the dollhouse. The pocket watch hung on the library wall. I wished I could wind it and make it tick. Grandmother's face and the watch's face were looking at each other; Grandmother wouldn't want her face to look at a face that was dead. When I got to Netherby Scar, she'd help me fix it.

But I'd brought the dolls to life and I'd made them happy. The cradle in Isaac's dollhouse room had had no blanket. But Mrs. del Salto gave me a scrap of flannel, white with blue stars. I cut it into a blanket, a little bigger than the cradle so I could make a fringe all around. The mother and father dolls stood looking into the cradle. If china lips could smile, they'd be smiling.

I'd filled up Magda's dollhouse wardrobe. It's easy to fill a wardrobe that's one-twelfth the size of a human wardrobe. Mrs. del Salto's sewing box was always stuffed with fabrics: sheer organzas and tulles, heavier wools and satins, and even a square of damask. It was mostly gray with silver swirls, but the other side was mostly silver with gray swirls.

Now I'd recognize Grandmother's tablecloth. I knew so many fabrics now.

But not silk. I was saving silk for Grandmother.

Magda's dollhouse wardrobe was a burst of whiteness. It was the inside of an almond. I'd made the dollhouse match up with the human house.

Rough Ricky didn't come the second night.

What if he did something that changed Day Zero again? If he rescued Gentleman Jack from jail, then Gentleman Jack wouldn't go to trial and I wouldn't need to tell my story about the Fair on May sixth. What if Rough Ricky rescued him tomorrow? Then I'd have almost no time to get the dolls' baby.

"You can't get it anyway," said the dagger. "You don't have any money."

I said the task rhyme inside my head:

> One is for Oakheart,
> Two's for a collar.
> Three's for a sister,
> Four's for a brother.

"We can't wait to get our baby," said the father doll.

"What if something happens?" I said. "What if I have to leave Blue Roses before I get the baby?"

"You can't leave before you bring our baby," said the mother doll. "It's the third task."

"But three tasks are too many tasks," I said. "Two is the right number of tasks."

"The third task is the most important task," said the mother doll. "Our hearts will break if we don't get our baby."

The dolls' faces were always the same; china can't move. But I heard the disapproval in the mother doll's voice. If she had a human face, she'd be pressing her lips together and little vertical lines would appear beside her mouth.

"*You have to leave when Gentleman Jack says,*" said the dagger.

"*But Rough Ricky—*" I said. Rough Ricky would have something to say about when we left. I thought of the heat of him, how his hand pressed my lips into my teeth, how my heart went dribbling down my ribs. Rough Ricky was alive and present and burning and dangerous. Gentleman Jack was alive but in jail.

I rocked the cradle with my finger. Willow was for rocking chairs and cradles. That was because willow was bendy and swingy and filled with wind.

The dolls were alive. They couldn't press their lips together, but they could speak.

"*The dolls aren't alive,*" said the dagger.

"*You can't press your lips together,*" I said. "*What if you're the one that's not alive?*"

"*Carbon and iron are extremely alive,*" said the dagger.

"You will not leave," said the father doll. "The Indigo Heart is a magnet. It attracts the people it wants to attract. It keeps the people it wants to keep."

The baby doll didn't matter; magnets didn't matter. I was going to leave on May sixth, or sooner if Rough Ricky broke Gentleman Jack out of jail. I'd take the dagger. I'd take the pocket watch to Netherby Scar and get it fixed. Then I'd wind it and make it come alive.

I'd take the inkwell and the coins. When the time came, I'd creep down the indigo tree and find my way to Rough Ricky's little camp, below the belt line of Blue Roses. I hoped Rough Ricky would be waiting for me. If not, I'd follow the railroad tracks to Netherby Scar.

Why had I told the dolls I might have to leave? They weren't what was important.

Rough Ricky didn't come the third night. But the Judge came knocking at my door, rap-rap-rap. Why did people knock like that? They never knocked just once.

"May I?" said the Judge.

The door had a latch to keep it from swinging open. It was a spring latch, which meant that when you let go of the knob, it would spring out and keep the door in place. And it had a bolt, which meant that even if you turned the knob, you wouldn't be able to get in. But you didn't need a latch or a bolt with the Judge. There was something inside him that was just like a latch or a bolt. The Judge wouldn't open the door unless you let him.

"You may." I tasted the words. They were strong as latches and bolts. They would open the door and let the Judge in.

Now the door was open. Now the lamp from the landing sent a slant of light across the floor. Now the reflection of the Judge's face appeared beside mine in the window. Beyond were the branches of the indigo tree. Beyond them were the stars.

As we looked out into the night, one of them moved.

"A falling star," said the Judge.

"Why do they do that sometimes?" I said. "Unstick themselves from the sky and fall?"

"Like the Blue Rose," said the Judge, "who fell to earth to lead us to the Indigo Heart."

The Judge switched off the electric candle. The window gripped tight at our reflections. "You can see the stars better with no other lights."

He told me all about stars. "The stars look small, but most of them are bigger than our earth. And the stars themselves are part of bigger groups of stars, and those groups are part of even bigger groups." The Judge explained about solar systems and galaxies. He said our galaxy is called the Milky Way and has billions of stars.

He pointed out the constellations. Scorpius, which means scorpion; Taurus, which means bull; Ursa Major, which means great bear.

"Where are the Seven Sisters?" I said.

"As it gets to be spring," said the Judge, "they rise later and later. It's too early in the evening to see them yet."

"So the Blue Rose is a star?" I said. "And she's also a person?"

"She's ineffable," said the Judge, and before I could ask, he explained that Ineffable was when you couldn't describe something.

It was funny to have a word for describing something you couldn't describe.

There were worlds within worlds. The worlds could get bigger, like solar systems being inside of galaxies. Or the worlds could get smaller, like the cottage; and the dollhouse inside the cottage; and inside the dollhouse, a dollhouse of the dollhouse. Or like the Blue Rose. She could be big as a star. She could be small as a seed. She could be both those things and still be who she was.

I said this aloud, and the Judge said that was like the Indigo Heart. The Indigo Heart was the center of the world, and Blue Roses was the center of the Indigo Heart, and the Shrine, where the Blue Rose had made roses grow in the snow, was the center of Blue Roses.

"I would like to be able to see things that are very small," I said.

"I can help you with that," said the Judge.

On the eighth night, the Judge gave me a magnifying glass.

Here's what a magnifying glass looks like: it's a circle of glass in a brass frame. Here's what a magnifying glass does: it makes small things look big. The Judge held it by its handle, which was white and glowed.

"Mother of pearl," said the dagger. "Valuable."

The Judge drew an envelope from an inner pocket of his jacket. "Look at the stamp." It was identical to the orange stamp in the library. The one with the picture of the man with the old-fashioned hair.

The magnifying glass was heavier than it looked. I held it over the stamp, and suddenly the stamp was huge. I saw every detail.

I saw the man's profile, his high collar. I saw that the stamp was made of orange dots and lines on a white background. I saw that the picture was formed by those dots and lines, depending on whether there were lots of them or hardly any.

The magnifying glass held a whole new world. No wonder it was heavy.

The Judge got all the way to the other side of the door, then poked his head in again. "You may keep the magnifying glass," he said. Then he was gone before I could say Thank You, which I wasn't particularly good at remembering anyway.

I stood there holding the magnifying glass. I stood there holding the heaviness of another world.

I couldn't stop thinking about Rough Ricky. About how one night I would wake up, smelling fire, and Rough Ricky would be there. Rough Ricky could get into buttercream cottage. He was not like the Judge, who was filled with latches and bolts. Not actual latches and bolts, of course. Just the idea of them.

Rough Ricky did not believe in latches and bolts. They couldn't stop him.

That night I dreamed about Netherby Scar. I dreamed I was looking for Grandmother's house, but I couldn't find it because there were no street signs. Then I was looking for the magnifying glass, because if I had it, I'd be able to see the street signs. And then I thought that if I'd been able to find the magnifying glass, maybe the magnifying glass would have helped me find its own self. But that was too confusing, and, for that to work, time would have to run backward and forward, as it did with the Blue Rose.

Anyway, you can never find things in dreams.

"What did I say about sleeping with one eye open?" said Rough Ricky.

I was still half dreaming when I sat upright, my heart flapping around like a beached fish. But there was nothing to be afraid of. I'd been dreaming I was lost, and now I was awake and I wasn't lost. But dream fragments still lingered. Why was it so frightening that I'd lost the magnifying glass?

"Tell me about the gold," said Rough Ricky. He made me come fully awake. There was the heat of him, the smell of charred flesh. That was like the real Rough Ricky, not a dream. He sat on the bed beside me, which made my side of the bed go up. That was like a real person, not a dream. He leaned over me so he could speak quietly. That was like a real person, not a dream.

"We need the gold," he said.

But I'd already told him about the gold, which was that there wasn't any. Not in buttercream cottage, anyway.

"Of course there's gold," said Rough Ricky. "Gentleman Jack's reliable source knows the Judge has a substantial share in a gold mine."

"He keeps it in a bank," I said. Rough Ricky didn't know the Judge the way I did. He didn't know that the Judge was careful, and that he was filled with locks and bolts, and that he'd keep his money in a place like a bank that was also filled with locks and bolts.

Needle-sharp barks came from the dollhouse. Oakheart had heard Rough Ricky. Or maybe Oakheart smelled the fire on him. "Danger! Danger!" said his barks. Usually the dolls didn't pay much attention to the human-size world.

"Where's the safe!" Rough Ricky's voice got hotter.

There was no safe.

"He's hiding it." Rough Ricky's voice leapt and licked. "We'll creep about the house and you'll show me all the Judge's special spots." In the moonlight, his face was a scrumble of scars. He paused, put up a finger, which meant, Quiet!

From the other side of the door came the faintest of clicks. Rough Ricky's finger, which had said Quiet, turned sideways and made itself into a revolver.

I nodded. Yes, the Judge did have a revolver.

For all his scars, Rough Ricky could move fast. He was out the window before the door smashed open. The Judge leapt forward, but all that was left of Rough Ricky was a burst of breaking glass and singeing.

The Judge wheeled round, pushed past Mrs. del Salto, who stood in the doorway. I hardly recognized her. For one thing, it was she, not the Judge, who was holding the revolver. She must be the one who'd made the click. It had been the click of the revolver's hammer. It meant the revolver had been getting ready to shoot.

"*A knife is quiet.*" The dagger didn't like my thinking of the revolver. "*A knife doesn't click.*"

The revolver shone silver in her hand. There was scrollwork down the muzzle and a golden eagle on the backstrap. She was hard to recognize, with a revolver in her hand. Also, she wore a white nightdress, which made her even harder to recognize. If I'd ever thought about it, I'd have assumed she wore black to bed. Black was her color, not white.

The Judge wasn't going to catch Rough Ricky. Rough Ricky had a head start; Rough Ricky had lots of practice running; Rough Ricky knew how to fade into the night. Rough Ricky had left so fast, he'd broken the window.

"*You sound as though you wish the Judge could catch him,*" said the dagger.

"I don't sound like anything." Of course I didn't want the Judge to catch him. "*Thoughts don't have sounds.*"

"*That's what you think,*" said the dagger.

If Rough Ricky were caught, there'd be no one to tell me what to do, except Gentleman Jack, and what if I couldn't get Gentleman Jack out of jail?

The wind through the window smelled of spring and wet indigo. Beneath was the tang of the oil the Judge used to clean his revolver. Did he clean it every day? Had he been waiting for Rough Ricky, sleeping with one hand on the ivory handle, sleeping with one eye open?

The smell of coffee came wafting upstairs. Mrs. del Salto and I looked at each other. We both knew: the Judge hadn't caught Rough Ricky, or else he wouldn't be making coffee. Mrs. del Salto laid the revolver on the floor, pointing the muzzle toward a corner. Now she couldn't shoot someone by accident. "I'll ask Marcus to make it safe again," she said. She didn't know as much about guns as Flora did.

Together, we went downstairs. The Judge had already set out three cups. Mrs. del Salto lit all the kitchen lights. She liked the dark, but still, she lit the lights. That was nice of her.

The glinting copper pans and silver curves of the stove looked just the way the coffee smelled, strong and bright. It reminded me of my first evening at buttercream cottage. How ignorant I'd been. Now I knew how to use a fork; now I knew the curly knife was only for butter.

"*You couldn't use it for anything else,*" said the dagger. "*Whoever heard of a knife without an edge!*"

But I liked the idea that the butter had a knife just for itself. I liked the idea of the butter waiting in the cellar, dreaming of its very own knife with the curly edge.

"How did Rough Ricky get in?" said the Judge.

"Through my window," I said.

"Why was the window open?" said the Judge.

"I like the smell of indigo," I said.

The Judge looked down his long beak nose. "What did he want?"

I could answer truthfully. "He thinks you have gold in the cottage."

"I wouldn't be that foolish," said the Judge.

"That's what I told him," I said, which was not exactly untrue.

"'Not untrue'?" said the dagger. "'*Not untrue' means False. Just say it. Say False!*"

But I knew from the way the Judge talked that "Not untrue" had a different flavor than just saying False. "Not untrue" was filled with echoes. The word False was a cement block.

"*You're talking like the Judge, all in circles,*" said the dagger.

Mrs. del Salto set a bowl in front of me.

"*A bowl of coffee!*" said the dagger. "*She must think you're a baby.*"

Mrs. del Salto had mixed in sugar and frothed the milk so the top was foamy. I figured it must be all right to stunt my growth just for tonight.

"*Don't forget your tin cup in the hideout,*" said the dagger. "*Don't forget you liked drinking coffee from your tin cup.*"

I hadn't forgotten, but that didn't mean I shouldn't drink from the bowl. It was so unusual to wrap your hands around a bowl of coffee. It warmed the whole surface of your palms.

"*Tin is metal,*" said the dagger. "*Metal holds heat. Your hands were warmer with the tin cup.*"

I looked from the bowl to my yellow cup. The coffee was sweet and milky and hot. You could smell it so much better from the bowl. The sweetness came from the drawer in the pantry.

But next time I'd drink from the yellow mug. Then the mug would be equal with the bowl.

"We need a dog to guard the house," said the Judge.

I heard him but I wasn't listening. Rough Ricky had come, and he had gone, and now I could think about other things. I could think about drawers filled with sweetness. I could think about the butter down in the dreaming cellar.

"The dog will be Starling's dog," said the Judge. "It will protect her from Rough Ricky."

Now I was listening. "I don't need protection from Rough Ricky."

The Judge sighed and said I had remarkable tenacity of mind, which made Mrs. del Salto laugh. She seemed brighter than usual. Maybe it was because she'd had something to do. She'd had to hold the revolver, she'd had to protect me.

She'd had to make sure she didn't shoot me by accident.

"The dog will guard the house," said the Judge. "The dog will sleep in Starling's room and stay at her side always."

Even in school? Would the dog come into school with me and lie beneath my feet? But there'd be no room, because the bench was too short and my feet didn't dangle. I thought of the doghouse, nestled among the outbuildings behind the cottage. "You used to have a dog?"

"We did," said the Judge. "A bulldog. Great temperament, face like the back of a pan."

Mrs. del Salto produced a lovely, creamy cake soaked in milk and syrup. You could eat it with a fork or a spoon. I chose a spoon. I knew how to use a fork, but you could trust a spoon.

It was past midnight, and the Judge said that today was the Ides of March, which was supposed to be unlucky, but he said that right now he felt quite lucky. Mrs. del Salto said I'd never sleep after all that coffee, and the Judge said he'd go upstairs and bore me to sleep. Mrs. del Salto actually laughed again.

But what the Judge really did was to bring some planks and nails to the attic so he could cover the broken window. He asked if I'd be afraid to sleep, even with the planks.

"I'd never be afraid of Rough Ricky," I said. "But I'll miss looking at the stars."

"We'll replace the glass soon enough," said the Judge. "And with the dog to protect you, we won't worry about anyone breaking in." He reached for a plank, then paused.

"Look! It's late enough—or early enough—to see the Seven Sisters." He reminded me how to locate them, gliding your eyes from the three stars in Orion's belt, to the bright, reddish star in the Taurus constellation, to the Seven Sisters. The Sisters were a tight blue cluster. The Judge reminded me I'd probably only be able to see six of them. He was right; I counted twice.

He reminded me of their names. I liked Astra and Estella. But Sidra was also pretty and it also meant Star.

"What about your name?" I said. "Does it mean anything?"

The Judge said that Salto was a word from the language they used to speak and that it meant Jump, or Leap. That's what his ancestors had done when they followed the Blue Rose to the Indigo Heart.

"Like a leap of faith," said the Judge. "We had faith that the falling star was to lead us to our true home."

I thought about the name del Salto. I thought about the star names. The names matched up with their owners. I wondered if Starling would ever match up with me.

"Since there are only six stars," I said, "that means the Blue Rose is on earth?"

The Judge said Yes.

"When does she visit her sisters?"

"We, here on earth, tend to notice it during the Dark Moon," said the Judge. "That's because we can see the stars better with no moonlight to distract us. When you see the Blue Rose as a star, with her sisters in the heavens, you must climb the star steps to the Shrine to thank her for granting you a boon."

"But what if she hasn't granted it?" This was one of the things I just couldn't understand about the Blue Rose.

"You should do so anyway," said the Judge. "The Blue Rose can see backward, into the past. She can see forward, into the future. You could thank her for something she hasn't done yet. She'd know how to appreciate that."

I knew about time—this wasn't the way time worked. And anyway, what a waste of a perfectly good Thank You! "Do you mean she won't grant your wish if you don't thank her first?"

"It's not as simple as that," said the Judge. "It's hard to describe. Her ways are mysterious."

"Ineffable," I said.

"The perfect word!" said the Judge.

I had said a perfect word. The Judge knew a lot about words. If he said so, it must be true. The Judge knew about a lot of things.

"One thing we know for sure," said the Judge, "is that she prefers to be thanked through a Songbird."

"You used to have a Songbird," I said. I didn't need to say it with a question mark.

"Before she died," said the Judge, "she used to whistle our praises to the Blue Rose, which meant that all of us in the Indigo Heart could hear and raise our voices with her. She united us in thanking the Blue Rose. Three times daily we'd raise our voices, and together, sing out our thanks."

"But now," I said, "you have to say the words yourselves."

"Exactly," said the Judge. "We cannot hear each other. We have to wait for the bells to ring, and only the stars know what a stumbling and a bumbling we make. We worry that she'll fade away."

"She'll fade away if you don't sing to her?"

"She sang the Indigo Heart into existence," said the Judge. "And we sing her into existence. Each of us keeps singing to the other—it's our life blood, so to speak."

That seemed like an example of the crazy, mixed-up way that time passed for the Blue Rose.

"How did you know Rough Ricky was here?" I said. "Were you sleeping with one eye open?"

"I sleep with one ear open," said the Judge. "I've been expecting something like this for a while."

He hammered the planks into place. He hammered the Sisters out of sight. Goodbye, Astra. Goodbye, Sidra. Goodbye, goodbye, Estella and Marien.

The Judge could do big clumsy things, like nailing planks. He could do smaller things, like building the plate-wheel beneath the dollhouse.

"You say you're not afraid of Rough Ricky," said the Judge, "but I think you should be. You should be afraid of him, and you should be afraid of Gentleman Jack. There's no shame in being afraid. It's smart; it protects you from dangerous people. If Gentleman Jack indeed cared for you, and cared for you well, as he claims, I can't understand how he could allow Doubtful Mittie in among the Gentlemen."

"What's wrong with Doubtful Mittie?" I said.

"His hands," said the Judge. "It shows he's not safe with children."

"Maybe he killed a child by accident," I said.

"That would be manslaughter," said the Judge. "Manslaughter is when you kill someone by accident. But a person can only acquire that particular Affliction when he kills a child on purpose. And as you know, that's what we call Murder."

I did know that, but I wouldn't think about it.

But I owed Gentleman Jack my gratefulness, not fear. The next time I told him I was grateful, he'd smile his best smile again.

The Shrine

✝ I HAD A NEW DRESS for the Feast of the Blue Rose. I'd tried
it on a lot of times so Mrs. del Salto could sew it just right, and after all
the trying on, Veronica washed it. The dress was clean and bright, and
I took a bath so I could be clean and bright, too. It was pleasant to take
a bath in the morning, with the sunshine creeping across the floor, the
pots and pans smiling from the walls. The floors in the kitchen were
relaxed; they didn't mind a little water. Mrs. del Salto squeezed lemon
juice into my hair. For extra shine, she said.

"You leave the shining to me," said the dagger.

Mrs. del Salto led me to her bedroom. I'd peeked in before, but
I'd never been inside. It was filled with big pieces of furniture painted
blue and white. On the chest of drawers was something draped in black
cloth. It must be a mirror, covered so Isaac's and Magda's souls wouldn't
get stuck. But the rest of the room was all blue-and-white patterns—
tiles with paintings of boats, and stripes with flowers in between, and
funny blue dogs running along the top of the walls.

There were little tables on either side of the bed, just like in Flora's room, but Flora kept a derringer on top of hers. Probably the Judge kept his revolver in the drawer. He was tidy that way.

I stood with my arms up so Mrs. del Salto could pour the dress over my head. It took ages to float over and down. It was pleasant to be extra clean and put on an extra-beautiful dress.

"Those colors become you," said Mrs. del Salto.

By colors she meant lavender, which the dress mostly was, with just enough ivory background to show off the flowery design. There was a lavender velvet collar and a lavender velvet sash, and if you ran your fingernail through the velvet, you'd leave a shining silver line. The shoes had been bought specially for me, too, and had never belonged to Magda. They were laced with grosgrain ribbons that matched the dress.

Lavender was also something you put in a wardrobe to make the clothes smell good. I liked the idea of that—lavender-colored dresses hanging in lavender-scented wardrobes.

"I'm suffocating in here!" said the dagger.

"But you don't breathe." I'd stuck the dagger down the inner thigh of my stocking and tied it round with a ribbon. Mrs. del Salto would never find it there.

I sat on a tall stool, in front of the black drapery covering the mirror.

"Hmm," said Mrs. del Salto. She looked at our non-reflections for a long time. "It's March twenty-first," she said, "which is the first day of spring. And it is on this day we celebrate the Blue Rose, because she is our Guide to growth and new beginnings."

Mrs. del Salto and I looked at our non-reflections for a while longer. "Here's to spring!" she said, and whisked the cloth away. The room jolted into brightness. The mirror was in a frame, mounted onto the chest, and when you swung it back and forth, the wall leapt with light.

Mrs. del Salto's face appeared in the mirror. She paused, as though waiting for something, then said, "It didn't even crack!"

She laughed. That was nice. She usually only laughed when the Judge said something funny. It's good to be able to make yourself laugh.

Mrs. del Salto swung the mirror to reflect me, then worked out the snarls in my hair. The mirror reflected the black opals in her ring, and her eyes looked like her black opals, just as they'd done on the day we'd played jacks. I thought about how different Magda and I looked. Magda was gold and pink. You could see that in the photograph, even though the colors were only shades of tan and brown. But everything about me was pale, except for my hair and also my eyebrows, which flew up like dark birds.

Mrs. del Salto stopped brushing and looked at me. "Your skin is lovely." Her voice trailed off, as though she were surprised. As though she were looking at me for the first time. "Like the moon, or a pearl." That was good. Later, in Netherby Scar, Grandmother would let me try on her pearls, and the pearls and I would match.

The top of the chest was fascinating. There was a glass bowl filled with dried flowers. They smelled like dust and sunshine. There were beautiful little bottles with lots of sides and glimmering angles. They were filled with liquid the color of straw. A straw color went well with blue and white. It was like the cottage, buttercream with blue trim. The cottage went well with itself.

Mrs. del Salto hesitated her finger over a little china box, then fished out a chain. On the chain swung a gold oval with a stone in the middle. "A star opal," she said. "It belonged to Magda."

"It doesn't shine like your opals," I said.

"The light went out of it when Magda died," she said. "Maybe it's time to find it a new home." She fastened it around my neck. The mirror reflected the opal. The mirror reflected how it warmed to me. It shimmered with light, then blazed into blue fire.

"It's certainly the right color," said Mrs. del Salto. "You've made it come alive, which means it belongs to you. It will bring you good luck and protect you and give you the gift of clear sight."

"I already have good sight," I said.

"I mean a different kind of clarity," she said. "Such as knowing what to do if you're confused. Knowledge like that will bring you good luck."

I had good sight, but I didn't have good luck. Neither did Gentleman Jack, because he was in jail. Gentleman Jack needed good luck more than I did. Maybe I should give him my opal.

"Am I the only one who can wear the opal?" I hoped the answer would be No.

I hoped the answer would be Yes.

"You are now," said Mrs. del Salto. "The opal's warmed up to you. It belongs to you and wouldn't warm up to anyone else. You must never wear an opal that doesn't warm up to you. It's terribly bad luck."

"I can feel you being happy," said the dagger, "happy you can't give the opal to Gentleman Jack."

"Why don't you just go back to being smothered!" I said.

The star opal shone at my neck. The black opals shone on Mrs. del Salto's hand. They matched our eyes. Gentleman Jack had valuable green eyes. I'd have to give him a valuable green opal.

It was a long time before I said, "I forgot to say Thank You."

"You don't need to," she said. "I can see it in your eyes, which are bright as the opal."

It was such a big present, and I didn't even have to say Thank You!

❨ ✳ ❩

Later, in the library, the Judge said I was dressed in style. He looked at the opal and said how well it matched my eyes.

"That's another reason not just anyone could wear your opal," said Mrs. del Salto. "The color of the opal has to match its owner's eyes with a fair degree of precision."

"Or else it's bad luck?" I said.

"Very bad luck," said the Judge, but he was looking at Mrs. del Salto. He looked at her for a long time, then said she was dressed in style, too. I saw what he meant. There was nothing rusty about her today. Her black silk dress was almost as bright as her black opals; her buttons caught the light. They were made of jet, she'd said. I was learning lots of things this morning.

We squished up in the carriage; I sat in the middle. I kept my hands on my lap so I wouldn't touch Mrs. del Salto's dress by accident. If I did, I'd know what silk felt like before I touched Grandmother. I wanted to touch Grandmother first.

Crows cawed all around us as we rode toward town. When you see big clumps of crows, it means winter's over. The Feast of the Blue Rose meant spring was beginning.

We passed some carriages, and the Judge called out Good Morning and Happy Feast Day, and they called the same thing back. The del Saltos' horses were the most beautiful and the quickest. They lifted their knees the highest, shaking jingles out of their harnesses.

We were going the long way round, which was what you had to do when you drove into town. You couldn't drive on the scatterbrained steps with the unsteady bannister. As we dipped toward town, there began a sort of murmuring, which grew into a rush and roar.

"*Like water,*" I said.

"*Like people,*" said the dagger, which turned out to be right. The square was crammed with people, more people than I'd ever seen at once, a spring melt of people—

"Not water!" said the dagger.

The Judge handed the reins to a couple of boys who, for a penny, would walk and water the horses. He explained we had to leave the horses here and walk. You couldn't drive to the star steps on the Feast of the Blue Rose. Main Street ran straight and narrow to the foot of the star steps, where only a couple of carriages would fit.

I followed the Judge closely. I was afraid of getting lost, even though that wasn't a wild thing to feel. But wherever the Judge went, the crowd melted away—

"Not melted!"

Now I could be wild and also not get lost.

All through the square stood tables laden with shiny things and rose-shaped things and blue things and good-smelling things. People everywhere were pushing coins at the merchants, eager to celebrate the Blue Rose with a blue feast-day flag with rose-shaped cutouts, or a balloon twisted and folded to look like a star, or an opal—

There were tables of opals—vast fields of opals—just waiting for their person to bring them to life. I looked at Mr. Elton's tables. He had plenty of green opals, but none of them was quite the right color. None of them was quite the most valuable green of Gentleman Jack's eyes.

Children dressed in blue robes stood on overturned crates, piles of blue roses at their feet. But how could that be? Blue roses were marvels. They didn't grow naturally. The Judge explained that they were dyed. "If you set white roses in a mix of dye and water, the roses will turn the color of the water."

He bought three blue roses, the stems wrapped in paper to protect from the thorns.

"*Roses should be red!*" said the dagger.

Everyone around us carried a blue rose.

"*Bloodred!*" said the dagger.

The Line between the genteel and disreputable ends of Main Street ran through the middle of the square, and before long we'd drifted into the disreputable end, where all the fun was to be had. This was the part where the Sapphire was, the part that ten-year-old girls weren't supposed to know about. But I did. That's because I belonged to Gentleman Jack. That's because I was wild.

There were lots of people I didn't recognize. The Judge said they were pilgrims who'd walked to the Indigo Heart from other parts of the Territories. He said that walking a long way showed the Blue Rose how very much you wanted the boon you craved. Riding and driving were less convincing because they were so much easier.

This part of Main Street was awake and alive. The windows had flung up their shades and rubbed the darkness out of their eyes. The signs on the doors invited you in with their big friendly O's. The Sapphire was so open that its double doors were pressed all the way to the walls, the sideways music spilling out.

All the children were welcome here on this feast day, and no one worried about the saloons and roulette parlors. The shops had opened their doors, giving out paper roses with bendy stems. Mrs. del Salto showed me how you could wrap the stem around your wrist, so it looked as though the rose were growing from your skin. She said the stems were made of lengths of flexible wire, with fuzzy fabric wrapped around them so your wrist could be comfortable.

The peanut man was out with his cart, but he wasn't whistling. He was selling peanuts just as fast as he could. I asked Mrs. del Salto why he always whistled and never spoke.

"He comes from a place where the people in charge don't like other people disagreeing with what they say. They made sure he'd never speak again."

That was a terrible thing to think about. But I hoped he wouldn't want to talk to me more because I was almost the only person who understood him. No, what would be even worse would be if he wanted me to talk back.

It was so exhausting to talk to people.

Other carts along the road sold something that smelled rich and sweet. "Horns!" said the Judge. They were crispy fried pastries sprinkled with cinnamon and sugar. Custard spilled from their open mouths.

"Named after the Horn of Plenty," said the Judge. "The Blue Rose has always given us an abundance of blessings."

This was the first time I'd had cinnamon. It had a deep taste, as though you had to mine it from the ground, like gold. No wonder it made you live forever.

We passed Betsy in the crowd. Her chin was smeared with cinnamon and sugar. I wiped at my own face. I refused to look like Betsy. You could have surface eyes like Betsy, marble eyes, brown and dead. Or you could have alive opal eyes, like me. Mrs. del Salto said I had star opal eyes, and she never said anything but the truth, not even to make you feel good.

Betsy glanced at me, then stared. It wasn't polite to stare; I knew that now.

"You began your stay in Blue Roses," said the Judge, "by discomfiting Mr. Elton. And now I believe you are doing the same to Betsy."

"Discomfiting?"

"Make them feel uncomfortable."

I guessed it wasn't very comfortable to see someone you'd called an ignorant robber girl wearing a velvet sash and collar. Betsy wanted my clothes, you could tell. She wanted lavender and velvet and grosgrain laces.

I thought about what Gentleman Jack or Rough Ricky would think if they saw me now. Probably Rough Ricky wouldn't notice. He didn't pay attention to beauty, not like Gentleman Jack. Gentleman Jack would notice all the beautiful things I wore.

We passed through the piano music; we passed out of it. We walked along a little twisty road that rose out of the gorge. We crossed a bridge over one of the many branches of the Jordan River; we crossed another bridge over a riot of indigo trees. In the distance, great pink needles poked up toward the clouds. The Judge said they were the spires of the Shrine. The tallest spire was called the belfry, because that's where the bells hung, the same bells that rang morning, noon, and night.

Now we came to the star steps. So many steps! Many more than from Main Street to buttercream cottage. I asked how people who were old or sick could come to the Shrine, and the Judge said there was a road going up the far side of the mountain, and that if you were infirm, you were allowed to drive.

"So if you're firm," I said, "you have to walk?"

The Judge laughed and said Yes.

Up we went, up and up. It was good I was wild and used to climbing and running. The Judge and Mrs. del Salto were slowing and getting slower. The Judge said I could go ahead. I would be safe, he said—safe from people like Rough Ricky—because there could be no violence on the star steps. "That is one of the Blue Rose's immutable rules. No violence near or in the Shrine."

I didn't ask what Immutable meant. My feet were too itchy. They wanted to go. It was nice to be alone but not alone. To pass people on the steps and feel them looking at the back of my beautiful dress. To have them see my wild, dancing feet.

As I climbed, the bells began to ring. I imagined what they'd look like—long lily throats, wide joyful mouths. I imagined what it would be like to climb into the belfry and ring them. The big sound would shine through you. You would sing and ring like a bell.

As I neared the top, the steps grew narrower, and the line moved more slowly. The line was stringing itself out—now we were walking in threes, now in twos, now single file. It was then that I saw three women standing at the top of the star steps. They wore blue gowns and spoke to each person who passed.

"*Priestesses*," said the dagger.

The line went slowly. I heard snips and snatches of what the priestesses said. They said words like Weapons, Surrender, Prosper. I was three steps away when I heard all of what they were saying. "No weapons shall be allowed in this place dedicated to the Blue Rose," said the middle priestess. "Surrender them here, or they shall fail to prosper."

"Fail to prosper," said the other priestesses. "Fail to prosper."

Another step up revealed the pile of weapons lying at their feet. There were knives and guns and bullwhips and even a slingshot. "Fail to prosper," said the priestesses.

What should I do?

"*They don't know you have me*," said the dagger.

"*They can't know, can they?*" I said. They were priestesses, but that didn't mean they could see the dagger in my stocking. That didn't mean they could see the thoughts about the dagger in my head.

The pendant grew suddenly cold. It went through no in-between stages. All at once, it lay like a chip of ice against my chest. Except that a chip of ice would melt and the opal did not melt. The inside of my head grew gray, and cold. It was so cold it hurt my teeth. I pulled the pendant up and turned it upside down to look at it. The blue light was gone. It was like a gray fish eye, except that fish eyes are alive and this was dead.

Had I killed it? How could I get it to light up again?

Now I was first in line. Now the priestesses said the words they'd said to everyone else: Weapons, Blue Rose, Surrender, Fail to Prosper.

The middle priestess stretched out her hand. "Fail to prosper," said the priestesses. "Fail to prosper."

I walked past the priestesses. They did not stop me. They didn't know about the dagger, even though they were priestesses. They were just regular people.

I waited for the pendant to warm up again. I waited until the Judge and Mrs. del Salto had caught up with me, which took a long time. But the pendant remained chilly and aloof.

We walked along a path that led through a cemetery to the Shrine. Beside the path stretched an untidy line of people. The Judge said the people were waiting to crave a boon of the Blue Rose.

A massive statue of the Blue Rose loomed on the face of the Shrine. The wiggly line of pilgrims stretched away into the distance. If I were to crave a boon right now, I'd ask that the pendant go back to its blue fiery self. I'd ask that the pendant warm up to me. That it not lie against my chest like a chip of fish eyes.

We stood and gazed at the statue. It was carved into the stone above the doors of the Shrine, with roses carved all over the rest of the front. The Blue Rose wore a crown of stars, and her head was turned to the side so you could see the front and back.

"She has an eye at the back of her head!" I said.

"She is our Guide to endings and beginnings and middles," said the Judge. "She can see backward and forward."

"What you can't see," said Mrs. del Salto, "is the eye on the top of her head. There's no point seeing the past and the future if you can't also see the present."

On went the bells, and on and on. We went into a dim, hollow space. The bells made extra echoes inside the Shrine "This is our row," said the Judge. We slipped onto a polished bench with a high, straight back.

The Shrine felt just right. Everything was the center of everything else. The Indigo Heart was the center of the world. The town of Blue Roses was the center of the Indigo Heart. The Shrine was the center of the town of Blue Roses. And at the center of the Shrine was the foundation stone, which was the very first stone they put into place when they built the Shrine.

First we all sat down. The polish on our bench was so hard it pressed into that place you weren't supposed to talk about, which is opposite another place you're not supposed to talk about.

A priestess called us to the front, row by row. We took turns filing past the foundation stone and laying our roses upon it. The foundation stone was where the seven roses had grown when the Blue Rose led her people to the Indigo Heart. It wasn't big enough for all the roses lying in drifts and piles of cream—

"Not cream!" said the dagger.

"I'm not talking about the color," I said. "I'm talking about the feeling of cream."

"The feeling should be bloodred," said the dagger.

I added my rose to the piles. The roses together smelled of a wild, sweet wind. Before you returned to your row, you were supposed to take some of the rose seeds that lay in a number of small bowls scattered about the foundation stone.

The Judge collected a few and skittled them into my palm. "It's symbolic," he said. The seeds were brownish and irregular. They didn't match up with an important word like Symbolic. It was hard to believe that a beautiful thing like a rose could grow from them. The foundation stone was in the center of the Shrine, the rose was in the center of the seed. That's where the rose slept, dreaming of the future.

Roses weren't uncomplicated, not like daisies, say, which spilled out all their secrets at once. No, a rose was made up of frill upon frill of mystery, becoming more profound and dense until you reached its heart.

I liked the idea of the rose, sleeping in the seed, dreaming of the future.

The bells stopped. A priestess came to the front. The Judge pressed a penny into my hand. "For the collection plate," he whispered. But I'd never heard of a collection plate and I didn't like the word Plate. You could sit and stare at a plate and not know how to eat the food on it.

"*You hang on to that penny*," said the dagger.

The priestess talked about roses. Her voice made a big, joyful sound, like the bells. She said that certain kinds of roses grew naturally in the Indigo Heart. They were wild mountain roses, which could grow in extreme temperatures. But the ones that grew for the Blue Rose, the ones that had grown in the snow, ordinarily only grew in mild climates or in hothouses. That was why these roses were marvels, in addition to their blueness, of course.

"What does the Blue Rose bring us?" said the priestess.

"She brings us marvels," said the assembled in a single voice. "She brings us the gift of children."

The priestess told of her marvels, of women who'd traveled to Blue Roses, climbed the star steps, and craved the boon of a child. And whenever the Blue Rose sent a child, she caused a blue rose to bloom outside the family's door.

"Does the Blue Rose always bring us what we crave?" said the priestess.

"She is wiser than we," said everyone together. "She brings us what we need."

"How, then, must we receive her marvels?" said the priestess.

"We must receive her marvels with an open heart," said everyone together. "We must seek to know why we need them. They will otherwise turn against us."

"What must you do on the night of the Dark Moon?"

"We must look to the night sky," said the assembled. "It is thus we may see the Blue Rose visiting her sisters."

Mrs. del Salto had said something similar, hadn't she? That it was on the very darkest nights you could see if the Blue Rose had returned to the sky. I glanced at her opal rings. They were made of stardust. And it then occurred to me that maybe the black opals were a special gift from the Blue Rose. You could see the Blue Rose better during a dark moon. You could see the underneath colors in an opal better when the opal was black.

"And when she visits her sisters?" said the priestess.

"That is the time to thank her," said the assembled.

"We must thank her for whatever gift she might have given us," said the priestess, "or might be going to give us." It was so confusing when you had time running in both directions.

"It is also a propitious time to crave a boon of the Blue Rose," said the priestess.

There came a series of standings up and sittings down and openings and closings of a songbook. Music was playing from flutes and pipes.

The Judge had told me about them. He said they played flutes and pipes to celebrate the Blue Rose, because they made a sound kind of like the Whistling and the Blue Rose liked it when you sang her praises in the Whistling. The music didn't go sideways, like the slippery music at the Sapphire. But it wasn't straight-ahead, either. It was delicate as silk—

"*You don't know about silk!*" said the dagger.

It was delicate as moonlight on water.

I held tight to my penny. I looked at the stained-glass windows. They were very pretty with the sun shining in. I remembered that the Judge had said the house down the street from school had had colored glass in the windows before it burnt. I remembered eating peanuts with the Judge, way back on Valentine's Day. I remembered how, when we'd finished, the bag was semitransparent with oil. It was a little like the stained-glass windows in the Shrine.

Now the collection plate came around. People were dropping coins into it. I stood up; I sat down. I smelled the penny, warm from my hand.

"*Keep the penny,*" said the dagger.

The collection plate came down our row.

I thought about giving away the penny. The opal grew suddenly warm—yes, warm! I touched it. It warmed my fingers, and also the inside of my head. My brain crackled with blue fire. It was a friendly fire, it helped me think.

The Judge now held the collection plate. I could see it without turning my head. I had very stretchy eyes. I'd never seen so many coins at once.

"*Pennies,*" said the dagger. "*Worthless.*"

The opal grew warmer still. It was helping me decide, in a friendly way. I held my hand over the plate. I felt the heat of all those coins. Money is power and power is hot.

Or maybe it was more that an opal is lucky and luck is hot.

I let go of the penny.

"That was stupid!" said the dagger. "You might need that penny."

"I thought you said pennies were worthless," I said.

The Judge smiled at me and passed the plate over my lap to Mrs. del Salto.

"What did the Blue Rose give us?" said the priestess.

"She gave us the Indigo Heart."

"How did she create the Indigo Heart?" said the priestess.

"She sang it into existence," said the assembled.

"What do we do to thank her?" said the priestess.

"We sing her praises," said the assembled. "Over and over, three times a day."

"How do we sing her praises?" said the priestess.

"We sing her praises through our Songbird."

"But we have no more Songbird," said the priestess.

"We have no more Songbird."

I thought about Gentleman Jack trying to get a Songbird for Netherby Scar and wondered if someone was trying to get a Songbird for Blue Roses. Someone like the Judge, maybe, or one of the priestesses. I was going to crave a boon of the Blue Rose of a Songbird for Netherby Scar. Could you crave a boon of the Blue Rose for a Songbird for the Indigo Heart? It was hard to think about clearly. The people in the Indigo Heart wanted a Songbird to thank the Blue Rose in the best way possible, so she'd grant the boons they craved. But if there was no Songbird to help thank the Blue Rose in the best way possible, how could she grant the boon of a Songbird?

This was another example of time running in both directions, like trains on a track. Wouldn't they just crash into each other?

We rose for the final time. The flutes and pipes played again. It was the music that went with the words of praise to the Blue Rose. Finally, something I recognized!

> *"The bird sang like a star,*
> *Exalting near and far*
> *The brightest Sister Seven.*
> *With grateful joy we raise*
> *Our voices in her praise:*
> *A melody to heaven."*

I mutter-said the words, like the Judge, because I had an ugly voice and I couldn't sing. But how had I even been able to say the words with my Affliction? Maybe the priestess had been speaking to me—to me alone—even though she was also speaking to everyone else. That would be very priestess-y.

It had felt a long way walking up to the Shrine, but it was all downhill back to the square. The Judge passed coins to the boys who had watered and walked the horses. Off we went again, the horses lifting their beautiful, delicate legs higher than the other horses, shaking bells into the air.

A heavy moon sat just above the horizon. "A full moon!" I said. How strange it was that the Feast of the Blue Rose should be on the night of the full moon, when what the Blue Rose really liked were nights of the Dark Moon.

I tried to express this, and the Judge said that maybe the word I wanted was Ironic. That Ironic meant something happening the opposite way from how you thought it should.

My eyes started puffing in and out, which is what happens when you're tired. Or maybe it's that your eyes stay the same and the scenery keeps puffing in and out. My eyes closed themselves, and my head bobbled of its own accord against Mrs. del Salto's shoulder. I thought maybe she wouldn't like that, but my head was too heavy to lift. The Judge must have thought I was asleep, because he said a sort of personal thing to Mrs. del Salto, the kind of thing he'd never say in front of me. He said that the Blue Rose's ways were mysterious and that Mrs. del Salto shouldn't turn her back on the Blue Rose for not having granted her boons.

Then the Judge corrected himself. "For seemingly not having granted your boons. You have to remember to keep your heart open to whatever the Blue Rose may bring."

Mrs. del Salto lost the nice voice she'd had all day. "I don't want to open my heart, Marcus," she said sharply, as though she was still fitting me for the lavender dress and her mouth was still a hedgehog of pins. "And I most certainly don't appreciate being used in a game of Russian roulette—"

The Judge hardly ever interrupted, but he did now. "And don't close your eyes to whatever the Blue Rose might already have brought."

"Russian roulette," said Mrs. del Salto. Her shoulder had gone stiff. My head joggled against her bones.

Russian roulette? I knew what roulette was, although it was hard to imagine the Blue Rose playing it, bending over the spinning wheel, looking at it with all her eyes, including the one at the back of her head. But if she did play, I'd bet she'd win. The Blue Rose was probably pretty good at roulette.

"It's humiliating," said Mrs. del Salto. "Crawling to her to crave that

Magda and Isaac be spared from the pox. Then begging her to bring them back—"

Her words swam like minnows, in and out of my ears. I wanted to listen, but I was too tired. Mrs. del Salto had craved boons of the Blue Rose. This was something to think about when I had more light in my brain.

I woke up just as we neared the cottage, and as we made the last turn, a murmuration of starlings swirled into the sky.

"Look at them!" said the Judge.

They were like the bells that rang from the Shrine. They lit you up from inside. How did they know how to twirl themselves into a ribbon, to fan across the sky, to pleat themselves into the folds of an accordion?

They were like metal filings, drawn in the same direction by a magnet. Now the magnet tugged in one direction; now the magnet tugged in another. And then I thought of what the dagger had said about iron in blood, and what the dolls had said about the Indigo Heart attracting the people it wanted to keep, and about how the Indigo Heart was filled with magnets.

I kept thinking about Magda and Isaac and how Mrs. del Salto had craved two boons for them to live. And then I thought that babies were also like magnets and that the Blue Rose made them stick to you.

And then I wished I had more magnets so I could fly with the Judge and Mrs. del Salto, fly as the starlings flew, always swooping in the same direction, seeming to know when the others would move.

"No, you don't," said the dagger, which shook me into wakefulness.

The dagger was right. I was no starling. Starlings went about in murmurations with thousands of other starlings. I did not swoop about with thousands of other people. I went about only with Gentleman Jack.

The Brewster Boy

✝ I STILL HADN'T VISITED GENTLEMAN JACK.

"Because you haven't destroyed Grandmother's photograph," said the dagger.

I'd tried explaining myself to the dagger, but it could never understand how the photograph rang a pearly bell inside my mind. How I couldn't bear to think of losing that bell. But Gentleman Jack had been asking for me again. I had to go now.

"Sharpen me!" said the dagger, which always wanted to be sharp for Gentleman Jack.

I wanted to be sharp, too, but I couldn't sharpen myself, and now I couldn't even sharpen the dagger. I'd slid both edges of the blade over a whetstone. I'd slid it at the correct angle, which was twenty-two degrees. But the dagger wouldn't sharpen.

"You're not doing it right," said the dagger.

"I've sharpened you a million times," I said.

"Not a million," said the dagger.

First, I raided the pantry for butterscotch. The good thing about the Judge was that he'd bought butterscotch for Gentleman Jack—enough for a long time. The bad thing about the Judge was that maybe he was keeping an eye on the level of the butterscotch, watching to see if I was visiting Gentleman Jack in secret.

It would be like a butterscotch thermometer: the more the butterscotch went down, the more time I'd been spending with Gentleman Jack.

But that didn't sound like the Judge. He wasn't sneaky that way.

I had to slip off in secret because the Judge didn't want me going about on my own. Not until the guard dog arrived, anyway. But it took a long time to train a good dog, and we were still waiting.

What if the dog arrived after Day Zero? Would they send the dog to Netherby Scar to find me? Maybe that would be what the Judge called Ironic. What if the dog brought me back? It would be extra ironic if the dog stopped me from stealing myself.

Nothing in the Sapphire had changed, not the curling piano music, not the bulgy glass eyes of the moose. How did the moose manage always to be looking at you no matter where you were? There was the yellow smell of old cards and the raw smell of pink gin.

Flora sat in a deep chair, wearing a black dress with a pattern of gold horseshoes; the ribbon around her neck was gold. Her baby bulge was bigger. The horseshoes climbed up and down the bulge. I went over to her, and when Lord John saw me, he did, too. Flora wrapped an arm around my waist. "What's on Jack's mind now?"

"He said to remind you about Lucretia," I said. "He said to remind you that Lucretia is sharp." He'd actually said to remind Flora about the way Lucretia scores, but it meant the same thing.

"I remember," said Flora. "What do you think, John?"

"I think," said Lord John, "that we should be very afraid."

They both laughed.

No one laughed at Gentleman Jack. No one made fun of him. Their laughter struck me like one of the great bells in the Shrine. But the bells could stand being struck. A bell is made to take the strike and transform it into a great golden voice. I didn't have a golden voice, though. If you struck me, I'd just fall down.

"He wants you to visit him in jail," I said. "He wants to talk to you."

"I appreciate the invitation," said Flora, "but tell him I'll pass."

"He sure doesn't give up," said Lord John. "You can say that about Jack."

"You should call him Gentleman Jack," I said.

You couldn't call Gentleman Jack just Jack, and laugh at him, without a storm of fire and lightning. Rough Ricky's bombs were firestorms. One of them would make Lord John stop laughing.

"Jack doesn't mind a little informality," said Lord John. "Not between friends." But Lord John didn't have a friendly voice. I wished I was wearing the opal pendant. Maybe it would tell me if Lord John was really friendly. But the opal didn't speak clearly. It grew hot, it grew cold. Hot, cold. What did it mean? Anyway, I could only wear it after the guard dog arrived. Then I wouldn't have to worry about someone stealing it.

Someone like Rough Ricky.

"What's Russian roulette?" I said.

"My stars!" said Flora. "What put that in your head?"

"Mrs. del Salto said that when she asked for her children back, the Blue Rose played Russian roulette with her."

"Hmm," said Flora. "John, see if your silver tongue can fashion an explanation."

"Tell me," said Lord John, "how many chambers does a revolver have?"

"Six, usually," I said.

"What if you loaded the revolver with one bullet, leaving five empty chambers. Then you spun the cylinder, held the gun to your head, and pulled the trigger. Your odds of survival are one in six. It's a game of chance, which some find exciting."

"I bet they change their minds if they end up dead," I said.

"I bet they do, too," said Lord John.

"But what did Mrs. del Salto mean?" I said. "About Russian roulette and the Blue Rose."

"She might mean," said Flora, "that the Blue Rose appears to act randomly. Sometimes she grants the boon you asked for. Other times she gives you something else entirely. I can see that a person would be mad if she asks the Blue Rose to save someone she loves and the Blue Rose lets that someone die." Flora set her hand on her stomach. On the baby, really. "But she always gives you what you need even if it's not what you want."

"Why do you want a girl?" I said. Most everyone—including Gentleman Jack—would rather have a boy.

"That's a big question," she said. "One thing I like about women is that they're generally better at compromise than men."

But compromise was tame. Compromise was giving in.

"Gentleman Jack never compromises," I said.

"My point exactly," said Flora.

"Why do you want a baby?" I said.

"It's someone to love," said Flora. "It's someone to share with another person." Her voice was different than usual. It was a love-and-share voice.

"Are you sharing it with Lord John?" I said.

"I am," said Flora. "And if it turns out that we didn't get what we expected, we will try to be philosophical and discover what it is that we need."

Philosophical. That was the word Mrs. del Salto used. "Does Philosophical mean to accept your sorrows?" I said.

"That's a very neat explanation," said Flora, which I think meant Yes.

"Do you remember the story about you and Gentleman Jack going to the Fair?" said Lord John.

Of course I remembered. It was something that hadn't happened, but it felt more real than anything.

"You need to practice telling the story," said Lord John. "You want to be word perfect for the trial."

"Not word perfect," said Flora. "That's unnatural."

I didn't think I'd be word perfect. None of my words had ever been perfect. But I practiced the story. I described the great horses with the hair falling over their feet, and the lemonade, and the shells and the peas, and the gingerbread.

"Here comes a part we haven't talked about," said Lord John. "At the end of the day, you and Jack walked to the edge of the fairgrounds to rest. And in the dust . . ."

He paused. "Don't forget the dust. It was at the end of the day and very hot and dusty."

"Which was after I had not been sick," I said.

"Which was after you had not been sick," said Lord John. "That's when you found these."

He poured a string of beads into my palm. They were yellow, green, and blue. "They were scattered in the dust."

"Later," said Flora, "when you got back to the hideout, you strung the beads on this string."

I nodded. I pictured myself stringing the beads. I pictured myself wetting the end of the string with my tongue, pulling it to a point with my fingertips, easing it through the little openings in the beads.

"It's a good detail, those beads," said Lord John. "There were several peddlers at the Fair, selling beads and tins and other whatnots. A judge and a jury will believe a child found beads in the dust."

I let the beads slide through my fingers. It was not a long strand, not even long enough to go around my wrist. I would remember the story. My mind scurried about, nailing the details into place. Peddlers—that was one detail. Bang! Dust—that was another detail. Bang! I tucked the beads into my pocket; I tucked the story into my mind.

"What should I tell Gentleman Jack?"

"Tell him I remember," said Flora.

I was just pushing through the swinging doors when a voice said, "Hey, Girl!"

I turned around. The owner of the voice stood at the bar. He made a shadow in the mirror.

"It's Robber Girl to you!" I said. I could say that here, in the Sapphire. Flora and Lord John would stand up for me. I could say whatever I liked.

I stood a little apart from him. He turned out to be a biggish boy. "You tell Gentleman Jack something for me." A biggish boy with a biggish ambition. "You tell him the Brewster Boy is wanting to join the Gentlemen."

"You tell him." No boy was going to tell me what to do—especially no half-baked boy. That's what the Brewster Boy was, mostly raw, with red wrists that stuck out of his sleeves and little face-pricks of hair trying to be whiskers.

"You're the one can tell me how to join up." He stood beneath the moose head, but his gaze was as exactly unlike the moose's as it could be. Instead of looking at everything, his eyes looked at nothing in particular, now shambling off in one direction, now another, now stumbling in to focus on me.

A thought like a dark plum dropped into my mind. I remembered standing right here, beneath the moose head, hating Betsy Elton, vowing to get even—

"*Revenge at last!*" said the dagger.

Yes, revenge—revenge and estrangement. Betsy would be sorry for everything she'd said to me. "There's a girl at school," I said. "Betsy Elton. Gentleman Jack hates her." That wasn't exactly untrue. He'd hate her if he knew her.

"*Not 'Not untrue' again!*" said the dagger.

"You find out what she looks like," I said. "She lives above the General Store and has yellow hair." I would not say the word Ringlets; I refused to say it! "Then you come to school and give her a scare. It has to be at school, so I can see it." Not to mention that there'd be no adult other than Mrs. Elton to protect her. "So I can tell Gentleman Jack what you did."

"Done and done," said the boy. "I'll scare her real good, and you can tell Gentleman Jack the Brewster Boy is wanting to join the Gentlemen."

"The Brewster Boy," I said, as though memorizing his name. But it was a dumb name. It was too dumb to forget.

"Then I'll get in with the Gentlemen," said the Brewster Boy. "I'll get me some bloody hands, just like Gentleman Jack."

"Gentleman Jack doesn't have bloody hands!" I said. "He'd never kill a child. No hurting, just scaring. If you hurt Betsy, Gentleman Jack won't let you join the Gentlemen."

"Do you got any of Gentleman Jack's gloves?" said the Brewster Boy.

"Twenty dollars a glove," I said. I turned away from the Brewster Boy. I had to see Gentleman Jack.

For once, I didn't have to wait in the Sheriff's office. The Deputy rose when he saw I'd come alone. He smiled his big, easy smile and said he could guess why I was there.

I showed him the bag of butterscotch. He opened it briefly and said, "No axes in there!" Then we were through the ghost-mouth door and into the cell block.

Gentleman Jack rose when he saw me. He gripped the bars, hard. His gloves were filthy, stained with rust and grease and plink water. The silence was terrible. Please, Gentleman Jack. Ask me what my name is. Ask me who saved me in the wilderness. Ask me what I owe you, and I'll say I owe you all my gratefulness.

"Don't tell me the Judge kept you away again," said Gentleman Jack.

That was my plan. "Butterscotch." I passed the bag through the bars. That was all I'd tell him about the Judge, which was nothing.

Gentleman Jack smiled. It was a cat-smile. I'd never quite seen it that way before. Cats smile over their teeth. Cats smile over mouthfuls of cream.

"Tell me about Flora," said Gentleman Jack.

"I told Flora to come visit you," I said.

"And?" said Gentleman Jack.

"She said thank you for the invitation but that she'll pass."

"And?" said Gentleman Jack.

"I reminded her about Lucretia."

"And?" said Gentleman Jack.

"She said she remembers." These were all the wrong questions.

"Where's Grandmother's photograph?" That was especially the wrong question.

"I destroyed it."

"Liar!" said the dagger.

"What do they call you?" said Gentleman Jack.

At last—the familiar question about my name. "I said I have no name."

"Is that what I asked?" said Gentleman Jack. "I asked what they call you."

I hadn't exercised judgment. This wasn't one of the old questions, after all. "They call me Starling," I said.

There came a silence, hard as glass. Gentleman Jack clasped his hands behind his back. Hold the bars, Gentleman Jack! I thought. Then I could hold them, too, and we'd each be holding on to the other. "What is Grandmother's emblem?" he said.

"It's a bird," I said.

"What kind of bird?"

I didn't know, so Gentleman Jack had to tell me. "It's a starling."

I should have realized. I'd seen enough starlings. Starlings are distinctive, with their short tails and long, slender beaks. I remembered how the engraving traced the outline of the starling's wings, short and pointed, so when it flies, it looks like a star.

"What's my last name?" said Gentleman Jack.

"Royal," I said.

"Does it match me?" said Gentleman Jack.

It did.

"Does the name Starling match up with you?"

I understood what he meant. If Grandmother's emblem was a

starling, that meant it was too fancy for me. It was too Royal for me. In Netherby Scar, people treated Grandmother and Gentleman Jack like royalty. Everyone knew their emblem and where they lived.

"It's just for here," I said. "Just so I can go to school."

"I said I'll give you a name," said Gentleman Jack. "A proper name. A name that matches up with you."

That meant it would be ugly.

"Don't use that name," he said. "Promise!"

I promised. It was another promise I'd break. So I had to say something extra good.

"I can climb the star steps for you." Now the words were out. "I'll crave the Blue Rose to bring you the gold and a Songbird."

"No!" he said, not even bothering to keep his voice low. "The Blue Rose is tricky. Years ago, I craved a boon of her, but she turned around and spat in my eye."

Maybe that's kind of what Mrs. del Salto had been saying, in the carriage ride home, on the Feast of the Blue Rose. Maybe she was saying that she'd craved some boons and the Blue Rose had spat in her eye. I was sure both Mrs. del Salto and Gentleman Jack knew that the Blue Rose doesn't bring you what you want, that she brings you what you need. But that didn't mean they couldn't be mad about it.

It was then I saw the problem with my plan. It's funny how saying something aloud makes you understand it better. I had only to tell Gentleman Jack about it in order to realize I couldn't ask the Blue Rose for anything. It would take far longer than three breaths and a swallow to climb the star steps, and unless the Blue Rose was the sort of Guide who spoke to you first, my Affliction would keep me from craving a boon.

Ask me, Gentleman Jack. Ask "Who rescued you in the wilderness?"

"You rescued me," I'd say.

"Why did your mother leave you?" Gentleman Jack would say.

"Because of my Affliction," I'd say.

"What did you do to get your Affliction?"

"I don't know," I'd say, which would get me thinking about what terrible thing I might have done to get this Affliction. It meant I couldn't crave a boon of the Blue Rose. It meant I had an ugly voice.

Ask me, Gentleman Jack! Ask me who saved me in the wilderness.

Gentleman Jack did not ask.

Ask me, Gentleman Jack! Ask me what I owe you.

I'd tell him I owed him my life. I'd tell him I owed him my gratefulness. But Gentleman Jack didn't ask. That was the way I had to leave him, pressed into himself and wanting Flora and gold bricks and a Songbird, but not wanting me.

The Judge and I stood in the kitchen. He was making a door so the guard dog could go in and out. It was really just a flap in the bottom half of the kitchen door. The flap locked automatically when it shut so people like Rough Ricky couldn't scramble in. The dog would have to learn to hit a lever to unlatch it before it could go outside, and then it'd have to learn to wait outside until somebody let it back in.

The Judge could do big, clumsy things like hammering planks over a window or making a dog door. But what about the dollhouse, which was little and delicate? "Hand me another nail, would you?" he said.

"Did you build the dollhouse?" I said.

The Judge said Yes.

"Did you build the cottage?"

The Judge said Yes, with a lot of help.

"Which did you build first?"

"The cottage," said the Judge. "I built the dollhouse last year, for Magda's birthday."

"You mean the one when she was going to turn eleven?" I said.

"That's the one," said the Judge.

But Magda had been dead on that birthday, on October sixteenth. He'd built the dollhouse for a dead girl?

"I promised her," he said. "I started in early summer, because I knew it would take a long time. And then along came the smallpox—"

He puffed out a breath. "There seemed no reason not to finish it."

That seemed like an extra-good thing to have done. I suddenly saw the actions people chose to take as a long string of decisions. I saw them as beads, trembling on a wire. On one end of the wire were the really bad deeds, the kind that would give you an Affliction. Like killing a child. Then your hands would be stained with blood. In the middle of the wire were regular deeds. Some might be a little bit bad, like Betsy saying I was an ignorant robber girl. Some might be a little bit good, like the Sheriff giving me Gentleman Jack's wanted poster.

I thought of the bag of peanuts the Judge and I had shared so long ago. I remembered the exact day. It was the day Mrs. Elton had embarrassed me in front of the whole class for not knowing about Valentine's Day. It had been a Thursday, and it was also Day Eighty-One in the countdown to the new Day Zero. I remembered how the bag had been semitransparent with oil, like the stained-glass windows in the Shrine. I thought about how the dolls wanted a baby and that giving them a baby doll would be pretty good.

"Some say," said the Judge, "that promises are like piecrust, which means they're made to be broken. But I could not believe that and still be a judge. One must keep one's promises."

The Judge was good in a stained-glass kind of way. I was good in an oiled-paper kind of way.

"The Blue Rose instructs us to keep our promises," said the Judge. "It's her second precept."

My ear was getting ready for something un-fancy, like the first precept. My ear was right. The second precept went like this:

> Keep your promises:
> T'was you that made them.
> Let not others say:
> T'was you betrayed them.

At the very far end of the wire were the really good deeds, like the Judge keeping his promise to a girl who was dead. I'd never do that. What was the point?

"You will bring our baby?" said the father doll.

"I will bring your baby."

"You will not leave?" said the mother doll.

"I will not leave."

I was making piecrust promises. Why not? I was no judge. I might as well make the dolls happy while I was here. I might as well complete the tasks I was able to complete. I might as well pretend I'd bring the baby, even though that was impossible.

"The baby is made of wax," said the mother doll.

"He cannot crack," said the father doll.

"He's perfect."

But the baby was in the General Store, behind a glass window, on a shelf too high to reach. It didn't feel bad to lie to them. It didn't feel good. It felt like nothing.

I reached for the pocket watch. Looking at Grandmother's photograph would make me feel something. But the photograph didn't work as it usually did. My eyes kept getting stuck on unimportant things, like the bonnet of eyelet lace and the tiny embroidered letters—too tiny to read.

"You can't read anyway," said the dagger.

"I brought Oakheart a collar," I said. Can a person feel nothing?

"A collar!" said the mother doll. A person can feel nothing if she's a robber girl.

"A collar!" said the father doll. "You are a wonderful girl."

A robber girl can feel nothing if she squeezes her stomach so her stomach flap doesn't float open. So her bitter stomach juice doesn't flow into her heart. I reached for the string of beads Lord John had given me. I wound it twice around Oakheart's neck and tied it. It made a wonderful collar.

"A dollhouse dog doesn't need a collar!" said the dagger. *"A collar is to tame a dog, but a dollhouse dog isn't wild."*

The beads were supposed to make the judge and jury believe Gentleman Jack had been at the Fair when the Federal Marshal was killed. I was using the beads as a collar right now, but it wasn't a betrayal of Gentleman Jack. That's because Gentleman Jack had taught me to hide things in plain sight. The beads were in plain sight, and when the time for the trial came, I'd unwind the beads from Oakheart's neck and bring them with me.

"*A dollhouse dog isn't even alive!*" said the dagger.

"The collar's the right size," said the father doll, "and so many beautiful colors."

The baby was the last task. But I'd made a piecrust promise. I had no money. I couldn't get the baby.

"Best of all," said the mother doll, "there's only one more task."

For Want of a Penny

✝ THE NEXT DAY, the schoolyard wasn't separated into groups of boys and girls. It wasn't separated into groups of small, medium, and large children. All the children stood in a mixed-up lump, holding lunch pails and books and satchels.

The Brewster Boy's hands were empty and stuck out from his grubby shirt sleeves. They hung from his raw, knobby wrists. He looked like the indigo trees along Main Street, undergrown and spindly from too much coffee and too many cigarettes. Was that the way I'd looked on my first day of school?

"This is exciting!" said the dagger.

It was exciting. The Brewster Boy was here to give Betsy Elton a scare.

"You hate Betsy," said the dagger.

"I hate Betsy."

There was no throwing of balls or wrestling in the dust or singing in circles. No climbing into the cottonwood tree or playing jacks on the solitary stoop behind the school. There was only the schoolyard and the children and the Brewster Boy.

He looked at me. I turned away. I didn't want the others to think I knew him. Once I had been like him, with my broken nails and sticking-out wrists and scratched-up thumb. But even on my first day of school, my hands hadn't been empty. The Judge had given me a slate and a lunch pail. Even then I'd not been quite alone. The Judge had been with me.

My wrists did not stick out now, and my cuffs were garnet. Garnet is two things. It's a color, and it's also a precious stone. The color of both is the same: garnet is not quite as bright as crimson, but it's still bright. When I'd arrived in Blue Roses, I'd not been used to wearing bright clothes. But now I felt like myself in this dress. Glass buttons ran down the front, and because they were a deep red and sparkled, they looked like garnets.

"*Look beneath his jacket,*" said the dagger. It meant the jacket of the Brewster Boy. I saw what I'd already known would be there; I saw what the dagger saw. No, that wasn't right: the dagger could only see what I saw, but sometimes it noticed things first. Buckled around the Brewster Boy's waist was a belt. From the belt hung a sheath; in the sheath rested a knife.

Even though I could see only the handle, I knew what kind of knife it was.

"*A bowie,*" I said. Garnet made me feel like myself. I clung to that thought.

"*A bowie,*" said the dagger. But it was hard to remember about garnet, with the dagger so pleased and the handle of the bowie so big.

You could tell it was a bowie because of the handle. You could tell because of the guard at the bottom of the handle, right above where the blade began. It was meant to protect the Brewster Boy's hand from slipping onto the blade and losing a finger.

"*Because he's clumsy,*" said the dagger.

"*He doesn't need a knife to scare Betsy.*" Why had he brought a knife?

"*A knife will scare her, all right,*" said the dagger.

Mrs. Elton rang the bell. Usually the children pretended not to see her or hear the bell so they could go on wrestling and picking dandelions and singing and climbing trees, and today was a good day for climbing because the air was extra blue. But now they weren't doing anything. There was too much time before Mrs. Elton rang the bell. Too much time to do nothing.

"*I want to bite the Brewster Boy!*" said the dagger.

"*No blood today,*" I said. "*Just scaring.*"

The Brewster Boy strode toward the school. He made a hole in the blue air.

Mrs. Elton was ringing the bell when she saw the Brewster Boy, and now the bell was ringing, ringing, and the Brewster Boy passed her and entered the school, and the children filed silently up the stairs, and the bell kept ringing, even though there was no need.

Everybody was already inside.

Mrs. Elton came in now. She passed the Brewster Boy, who stood against the back wall. We all sat in our places. She passed the bigger children and the medium children. She was no longer ringing the bell, but the echo was loud in my head. She passed the small children, then turned, shaking her pointer.

"How many times have I told you not to fidget?" The pointer jabbed at Peter, but Peter wasn't fidgeting.

"How many times," said Mrs. Elton, "have I told you to direct your gaze to the front of the classroom?"

But Peter was directing his gaze.

"What are you allowed to do, Peter?" said Mrs. Elton. "You are allowed to look at me, and where else are you allowed to look?"

"At my books," mumbled Peter.

"What's that, Peter?" said Mrs. Elton. "Speak up!"

"At my books, ma'am."

Mrs. Elton said she would hear the lowest level first.

"A bowie knife," said the dagger, *"is an all-purpose knife."*

That was true. Gentleman Jack's Lucretia was a bowie knife. Gentleman Jack sometimes said that Lucretia was long enough to be used as a sword, sharp enough to be used as a razor, and heavy enough to be used as a hatchet.

But the Sheriff had taken Lucretia and given Gentleman Jack a penny so Lucretia wouldn't bite him.

"I'm a single-purpose knife," said the dagger. *"You can't use me for skinning."*

No, you wouldn't use a double-edged blade for skinning, because you'd cut off your fingers.

Mrs. Elton asked the first level what we were supposed to have studied last night. No one in the first level said anything. The Brewster Boy was too big; he squeezed the thoughts out of my head.

"You can throw me better than a bowie," said the dagger.

Mrs. Elton called on the second, third, and fourth levels, but no one knew the lesson. They sat behind me; I heard their voices mostly as a scratching at my spine. Now came a scraping of footsteps. The first-level children looked around, only to see the second- and third-level children looking around, only to see the rest of the children looking around, only to see the Brewster Boy shuffling down the aisle. Mrs. Elton stood on the platform. The Brewster Boy stood on the floor. He was spindly, but he was as tall as she was.

"Do you have a slate?" said Mrs. Elton, even though you could see he had no slate. I hated Mrs. Elton, but I had to admit it was brave of her to pretend this was an ordinary day of school.

The Brewster Boy had no slate.

"Do you have chalk?" said Mrs. Elton.

The Brewster Boy had no chalk.

"I don't got a lot of learning," he said in his almost-man's voice. He slouched up the aisle, stopping at Betsy's row. No, he slouched down the aisle. Going up the aisle was for getting out of school. "But still and all, I reckon I'm going to sit here and ain't nobody going to stop me."

He took the empty seat next to Betsy. He slid the bowie from its sheath. It sounded like rustling silk. "I got this beauty here, and I got me enough learning to scrawl this little gal's name on her face."

But he was only supposed to scare her.

"*Scrawling will scare her,*" said the dagger.

The Brewster Boy slashed the knife, he slashed too close to Betsy's face. He was not supposed to hurt her.

"How do you write your name, little gal?" said the Brewster Boy. "I don't spell too good, and it would be a shame to get it wrong."

I hated Betsy. I hated Mrs. Elton. You'd think it would be delicious to see them being scared, but it wasn't. You'd think you could count on your feelings, but no: they scurry around like mice, leaving horrid droppings wherever they go. You're always having to clean up behind them.

"*I can count on my feelings,*" said the dagger. "*Vengeance is delicious, so hot and raw.*"

The Brewster Boy was slashing again, and so close to Betsy's face! Had he misunderstood me, or didn't he care if he went beyond scaring into hurting?

At least I had my garnet dress, my bright courageous dress. I stood up. The dress stood up. I squeezed down the first-level aisle, and so did the dress. Together we turned our backs on Mrs. Elton and walked up the center aisle—yes, up, up!—toward the door. I stopped when I reached the Brewster Boy. I stood as tall as I could; the brightness helped me be tall. The glass buttons burned with cold flame.

Betsy had pressed herself against the back of the bench. Her brown-marble eyes were very dark, or maybe it was that her face had gone pale. I was glad, which Mrs. del Salto would say wasn't nice. But I liked not being nice.

The Brewster Boy's gaze shambled over to meet mine. He hadn't expected me to approach him, shining with buttons. This wasn't part of our plan. But I had to speak to him, which meant someone had to speak to me first.

Speak to me, Brewster Boy! He didn't speak.

"Throw me!" said the dagger. "Then he'll speak, all right!"

"But Mrs. Elton will see you, and the Judge will take you away."

There came the sound of someone being sick. I looked toward the front row. There was a space beside Molly's head, but I'd expected that. It was the space where my head should have been. There was another space on the other side, though, where Peter's head should have been. Peter was leaning over the floor.

That was all right. I didn't think I'd be going back to my seat today.

I reached into my pocket, my fingers closed around the ball for jacks. I'd make the Brewster Boy speak.

The ball bounced off his head. It was too small to hurt him, but it surprised him.

"What the hell!" he said.

All the children gasped, quick and sharp; they weren't used to words like Hell. I was, though, and I had no need to gasp, no time to waste. Three breaths and a swallow are quickly gone.

"I challenge you to a knife-throwing contest," I said. "First blood wins." The jacks ball dribbled to the floor, rolled under the desks. I remembered how it had dribbled before, down the steps, when Rough Ricky came to school.

"That was a great day!" said the dagger.

"You can't have a throwing contest without both people got knives." The Brewster Boy had wet, tired eyes with hollows beneath, as though scooped out with a spoon.

I shrugged. "I'll let you throw first if you're scared."

Did he see how bright I was, how much I felt like myself in the garnet dress? Time stretched like elastic as I waited and watched the Brewster Boy, and strange thoughts came to me. What did I mean by Myself? Did I mean the Robber Girl who lived with the Gentlemen? Did I mean the girl who lived with the Judge and Mrs. del Salto? Were they different people, those two girls?

"What about it?" I said.

"I got twice the reach you got," said the Brewster Boy. He swung out his arm. It was pretty long.

He hadn't exactly accepted the challenge, but I pretended he had. "Let's go outside. A person who rides with Gentleman Jack would never fight in a schoolroom."

I turned my back on the Brewster Boy. He'd have to follow me or else he'd seem scared. Yes, there he came, shuffling up the aisle behind me. There were four more rows of children—all the way up to the eighth level—and then the very oldest children, who were not really children but studying to graduate from high school. It didn't matter how old they were, though: they all looked at their desks, but as we passed their row, they stood and followed.

"Keep your seats!" said Mrs. Elton. But I heard the children following me, tramping up the aisle, rushing down the mouth-steps, where they clustered at the edge of the yard. Only Betsy stayed behind with her mother. They squashed together in the doorway.

There were dandelions to be picked and dandelion necklaces to be made, but no one picked the dandelions. No one made the necklaces. No one stuck their thumbnail into the stem, let the milky stem-blood ooze to the surface. No one climbed the cottonwood tree into the blue air.

"I'll ride with Gentleman Jack, sure enough," said the Brewster Boy.

The Brewster Boy and I faced each other. The others were too far away to hear me shout-whisper at him. "You're supposed to scare Betsy, not hurt her!" Some scraggly hairs prickled from the Brewster Boy's chin. He needed more practice growing a beard.

"But Gentleman Jack—" said the Brewster Boy.

"Gentleman Jack would never hurt a child!" I said.

The Brewster Boy shrugged. "I aim to get me them bloody hands."

How could I not have known my plan would go so wrong? When you're wild, you can tell when an animal is going to attack. There's something about the tension of the muscles, the way the animal looks at you, the way its fur goes up or down, the way it smells.

I had to make myself wild again.

The Brewster Boy grabbed his bowie and got ready. His shoulders were slightly hunched, his wrist was bent. When your body is out of line, it's hard to throw true.

The Brewster Boy wasn't able to throw his knife any better than the men in the Sapphire. I knew exactly where the bowie would land just from the way he bent his wrist.

It took him ages to throw, which gave me plenty of time to calculate, and then jump. I jumped toward the bowie rather than away because I'd have to snatch it up fast. I couldn't let the Brewster Boy get it again.

The bowie wobbled past me, thudded to the ground. I leapt for it, the big bowie with its single edge and the smells of rust and moist leather. The blade was about ten inches long, far bigger and heavier than the dagger. But here we were: I had the bowie without ever having reached for the dagger. That was good for lots of good reasons and one bad reason. The bad reason was that the dagger had lost its edge. Maybe I couldn't have stuck the Brewster Boy with it.

"Gentleman Jack won't like it that you don't take care of your knife," I said. "You haven't kept it clean and dry and sharp. But I bet it's sharp enough to slice into you. What do you want to bet I could hit your stomach?"

The Brewster Boy didn't want to bet. "You tricked me!" he said.

"Outsmarted you, more like," said sharp-voiced Agnes.

I raised his bowie, held it properly, backward facing, thumb on one side of the handle, which lay in the scoop of my thumb and forefinger. How heavy it was. The Brewster Boy backed up.

"She springed away," said Agnes. "Dead away from the knife."

Right now I didn't have room in my head to despise Agnes and her terrible voice. I would have to despise her later, and anyway, I'd sprung toward the knife, not away.

It's good to show people you know how to throw a knife. It's good to have a straight, solid wrist. It's good to let the knife lie in the cradle of your thumb and first finger, to hold the blade facing behind you, so it will somersault through the air.

The Brewster Boy saw I could hit him if I chose. He had no reason to believe I wouldn't aim for the belly. He might have been thinking of belly wounds, how they turned green and you swelled like a toad, for he turned and ran. He cut across Main Street, through the property with the burnt house, and vanished into the indigos behind.

"Does anyone have a penny?" I said.

The children understood. You mustn't take someone else's knife unless you paid them for it.

No one had a penny. I'd once had a penny, but I gave it to the collection plate.

"*I told you to keep that penny!*" said the dagger.

I should have kept the penny.

And then Mrs. Elton was ringing the school bell. She rang it so hard, the bell lost all its echoes and vibrations. She rang it so hard, it sounded like a slap in the face. Discomfited, I thought. The Brewster Boy had discomfited Mrs. Elton, and now Mrs. Elton was discomfiting the bell.

Too much time was passing. Even if I had a penny, I'd have to catch up with the Brewster Boy to give it to him. I was running now. I'd run as fast as I could and give him back his bowie before it leapt out and bit me.

But would that work? I wished I'd worn the opal pendant. I needed the gift of clear sight, except I didn't understand what it meant when the opal grew cold and what it meant when it grew hot. Could you give a knife back to its owner and escape being stung and mortified? I knew how un-bendy the rules were. You could put the knife in a drawer, but it would get out. You could even lock the drawer, and it would still leap out and bite you.

I ran fast, but a knife is faster than a girl, even a robber girl. I followed the Brewster Boy across Main Street, leaping the burnt bones of the house—not breathing in case there were any lingering pockets of lye—sprinting through a patch of indigo trees. The bowie twitched. I hadn't thought I could run any faster. I was wrong. A gully yawned in the distance, spanned by a pink stone bridge. There was only one way the Brewster Boy could have gone. I was within spitting distance of the bridge when the bowie twitched again.

I closed my fingers tight around it, but the rule of knives was stronger than my fingers. The bowie arced through the indigo shadows. It didn't shine, it smelled of rust and damp, but that didn't matter. It carved its way down my forearm. I'd known it was going to leap and bite, but I was still surprised. I found myself sitting back on my heels, looking at the inside of my arm. I watched the blood fountain from the pale underside. I'd run so fast, I felt sick. Or maybe it was because the bowie had cut so deep.

I knelt beside the grave markers, three of stone and one of wood. Sunlight glanced off the edges of the wooden star. The star shape pressed itself into my eyes. Was it Ironic that the Brewster Boy's bowie had bitten me just when the dagger had lost its edge—just when I was no longer able to sharpen it?

I turned to the side and was sick on a carpet of indigo needles. I crawled to the gulch to get away from the pool of sick. It hurt more than I'd imagined. It was funny how I felt the gash more in my stomach than in my arm. My blood was streaming out, but even when it's fast, you can't feel it. You can't feel the flow of your own blood.

Thoughts pressed in on themselves. They were too crowded. I had no room to think. The gash, the gush, the red blood—they surprised me. They didn't seem real. The bowie slid from my fingers. I didn't seem real, either. Was I truly on my knees now, stretching out on my stomach, looking down into the gully? You could tell there'd been a fire here. The treetops prickled up from the bottom like the ashy stubble on an old man's face.

I did not so much throw the bowie as let it go. One minute my fingers were wrapped round it; the next minute they were not. It slid down the side of the gulch, caught on a bit of root, then bounced away.

I didn't hear it land.

I closed my eyes and lay there, my good arm draped over the edge of the gulch. Waves of shock crashed through my skull, and I thought crazy, disjointed things. I thought about Oakheart and how he could sleep without closing his eyes. I thought about my own self and how I was closing my eyes but not sleeping.

I thought of the dolls' baby, and how he was waiting for me in the General Store. I thought of how I had no money to buy him. I thought of how Gentleman Jack had craved a boon and the Blue Rose had spat at him.

I should get up and go to the Sheriff's office so he could see the blood and help me. But waves of shock crashed on the shores of my thoughts. The heart of the earth beat beneath my ear. The earth was alive and breathing.

"There you are," said Betsy Elton's voice. "Tilda and Gabriel have gone to fetch the Sheriff."

I could hardly hear my voice under the crashing of the shock waves. I asked Betsy to take the sheath and dagger and hide them for me. "If the Judge knew I had the dagger, he'd take it away," I said. "But I need it."

"I'll have to give you a penny," she said.

How could I have forgotten that? I couldn't think anymore. My mind was all crash and quake, and I was cold, so cold. I tried to tell her it didn't matter, that the dagger was hardly sharp enough to hurt her, but my voice was too far away.

Betsy pressed a cool round object into my palm. I felt her search for the belt and the sheath. I felt her pull the belt tighter before she unbuckled it, then it got looser, and then—

"Here's the Judge!" said Betsy.

Somebody picked me up, somebody walked me through the trees, their feet loud on the indigo needles.

I looked up into a face with a beak nose and chicken-scratch eyes. It was all right now; the Judge was here. The Judge was a person who would always keep his promises, even to a dead girl.

Aŋ Epidemic of Bells

† I HEARD TICKING. It was the pocket watch, ticking from the dollhouse. Its clear, sturdy voice was counting out the time, counting down to Day Zero. In my head were bells and ticking. The ticking was steady, the bells were all crash and slam. The ticking was cool. The bells were hot.

I saw the room as though I were floating on the ceiling. I saw the roof of the dollhouse. It had four chimneys. I saw the waggling fish tail of the electric candle. I saw a pool of light. A pool of light, a pearl of light. Grandmother wore pearls, and when we went to live with her, she was going to let me wear them.

I saw the top of Mrs. del Salto's head, but her hair wasn't rusty. It should be rusty to match her dress.

"Hush now," said Mrs. del Salto.

But I hadn't said anything. Mrs. del Salto's hand made a familiar pattern on my forehead. But how could I recognize it? She'd never touched me.

Tick, tick, tick. "She's so hot!" said Mrs. del Salto. Tick, tick, tick.

"The infection's set in bad," said another voice. The voice smelled of ironed shirts; I smelled the heat trapped inside the cotton.

Mrs. del Salto's hand reached for mine. This time I recognized the pattern of her hand. Then came a heavier hand. It belonged to the smell of ironing. It didn't have a familiar pattern.

"Infection," said the ironing voice.

"Bergamot," said the ironing voice.

"Poultice," said the ironing voice.

Bergamot. That was a new word. I didn't like having it in my head. It was too loud. It had been fried in color and made my eyes hurt. Poultice was a new word, too. It was a terrible word, filled with the sounds of poultry and lice. What if the new words crowded out the old words I knew, the words from when I lived with the Gentlemen? What if my thoughts were being rearranged, like puzzle pieces? Where would the old words go?

I tried to un-think the new words, but I couldn't. They made a parade through my head. Organza, star steps, discomfit, poultice, galaxy, magnifying glass, RETURN TO SENDER—

"Drink this," said the ironing voice.

I shook my head, which clanged the bells inside my skull. I didn't want to drink down poultry and lice.

But the hand insisted, and Mrs. del Salto said to let the doctor help me get better. Liquid dribbled in the side of my mouth. It was too hard to struggle. The doctor said it would make me feel better. His voice went slow, then dissolved and trickled sideways.

He was right. Not hearing him was better.

His voice made me think of the Federal Marshal, how one minute he'd been sitting on his horse in the middle of the street. How the next minute his face fell open, how he'd sat very still for a long time, his hand on his stomach. How at last he, too, had trickled sideways.

Beneath the Federal Marshal's job name was a personal name. His name was Marshal Starling. I had a personal name, which was Starling. Good thing I wasn't his daughter, because then my name would be Starling Starling.

If the dagger were here, it would say something about the name Starling. It would say that Gentleman Jack told me not to let people call me Starling. That I was too un-fancy for the name.

Where was the dagger? I knew somehow that it wasn't here, in buttercream cottage, but I couldn't remember why. The poultry and lice had made me thirsty. My tongue was a slice of old leather. "I need some water."

"She's too hot," said Mrs. del Salto in her new faraway voice. It was the opposite of a magnifying-glass voice, an anti-magnifying-glass voice.

It was a mini-fying-glass voice.

I couldn't think of the old words. When the dagger came back, it would remind me.

Then I had the notion that I'd asked for water even though no one had spoken to me first. But that couldn't be. An Affliction has strict rules, just like the rule of knives. An Affliction doesn't change just because you're sick.

If you killed a child, you couldn't wash the blood from your hands. If you burnt something, you couldn't peel away the scars. And now all I could see were Gentleman Jack's gloves inside my head. I saw the initials GJR, embroidered so beautifully by Grandmother.

Usually I loved thinking about the gloves. But now my hands longed to fly up and push the darkness into my eyes. Maybe it was because the color primrose is pretty much just yellow, and the pinto's ribbons had been yellow, and the revolver spit had been yellow. One of my hands could move, but the other couldn't, which meant I couldn't push at my eye jelly, which meant the primrose gloves hung right in the center of my mind.

"I wonder at her voice," said Mr. Poultry-and-Lice. "I believe she must have sustained some damage to her vocal apparatus—"

But I didn't want to hear about my voice. I refused to hear!

Time had gone all funny. First it went slow. In the slowness, Mrs. del Salto said I was hot, and then I asked for water. In between, someone must have spoken to me, but I couldn't remember. Finally, time went from being stretched out, like taffy, to being concentrated, like life in the dollhouse. The dollhouse felt more real than the twelve-times-bigger world all around. The space inside the dollhouse was more concentrated and real than the outside space. It was a dreaming space.

My teeth chattered against the water glass. I was hot but my teeth chattered. Someone leaned over me. A cup pressed itself to my lips. I smelled bitterness. I smelled poultry and lice.

The cup made an unfamiliar pattern. "Where's my yellow cup?"

Now came the cracked edges of the yellow cup. It was comforting, even in its yellowness. Why did I like it, though, and not the yellow ribbons and gloves? Maybe it was because the yellow cup made me think of fairness. I had broken it and the Judge had treated me fairly, even though it hadn't seemed so at the time. What did the gloves make me think about? It was too tiring to figure it out. When I woke up, I'd like the color primrose again.

《 ✳ 》

I awoke to an intensity of roundness. Roundness hugged me from all sides. The round attic room, the curl of the dollhouse, the wheel upon which the dollhouse spun. The curving ceiling, the round nest of my bed, even though the bed-roundness was all inside my mind. Circles within circles within circles.

Something cold and wet snuffled at my neck. I wanted to be startled, but I was too tired. I tried to push myself up, to see what the cold, wet thing was, but one of my arms shrieked. I stopped; the shrieking stopped. I turned my head to the side; I came face-to-face with a long black wolf muzzle.

A wolf in a person's bedroom is a startling thing, but I was so tired. You need energy to be startled. Then I looked at it more closely and I knew it was no wolf. It was the dog the Judge had promised, the dog that would protect me from Rough Ricky and keep him from stealing my opal pendant. It was a gift from the Judge. I'd wait for him to talk to me, and then I'd have to remember to thank him.

It was so easy to forget to thank people.

The dog was black and tall and lean, with pointy ears and a narrow face. It stood quite still, and when I spoke, it sharpened its ears, twitching them toward me. That meant it was alert; it was listening. That meant it was wild. It didn't look like the kind of dog to let a baby stagger around holding on to its collar.

Footsteps sounded on the stairs. The footsteps were attached to feet; the feet were attached to the Judge and Mrs. del Salto. They came into the room; they talked too loud. They said how much they had worried about me and how glad they were I was better. Even Mrs. del Salto said so. Worried. Glad.

Frantic.

But I couldn't really listen. The dog kept pacing the attic floor. Tick-tick-tick went its nails. Of course the ticking hadn't been the pocket watch; the pocket watch didn't go. The ticking had been the dog's nails. How strange that the dog's nails should sound the same as a watch. The watch was wound down, the dog was wound up.

I closed my eyes.

The dog was not like the dog I'd expected. For one thing, it was not a boy. You'd think a guard dog would be a boy.

"A girl dog can be just as good as a boy dog," said the Judge. "Some people think a girl dog is more protective of her person. Some people think a girl dog tends to roam less and stay closer."

The dog was not like Oakheart, rough and bouncy and shaggy. She was narrow and aloof. She was altogether a sharpish sort of dog, but she had a softish sort of name, which was Paloma. Her name started off with the popping P sound, but it didn't live up to its beginning. It grew mushy on the L, and by the time you got to the M, you were bored to death.

The Judge and Mrs. del Salto talked and talked. I closed my eyes and let their words swim all around me. I only opened my eyes when they said I should never have fought the Brewster Boy.

"But I won!" I said.

"Did you?" said the Judge. "Let's look at the outcome: the Brewster Boy is unscathed and you are wounded." He'd already told me my forearm had been badly cut. He'd already told me I might not regain the use of my hand, which was my right hand, and also my dagger hand.

I should feel terrible about it, but I'd save it for later. I'd save feeling terrible for when I had energy.

But I remembered all the conversations with Gentleman Jack and the dagger—was it better to kill someone or to hurt them? Bits of these conversations tumbled through my head. Being more sure, cutting tendons, getting into more trouble.

"Did I cut a tendon?"

"Well—" said Mrs. del Salto.

"Yes," said the Judge.

Later, I would care.

"What's the date?" I said.

"April seventh," said Mrs. del Salto.

"What's the date?"

"April seventh," said the Judge.

I had missed the Dark Moon. But it didn't matter. Gentleman Jack hadn't wanted me to crave a boon of the Blue Rose, anyway.

"What's the date?"

"April eighth," said the Judge.

"Twenty-eight days to Day Zero," I said.

"What do you mean?" said the Judge.

I shouldn't have said that aloud, but it's hard to be careful with bells and ticking in your head. "Nothing," I said.

"Can there be such a thing as a Day Zero?" said the Judge.

"There can be the idea of a Day Zero," I said.

"There once was a time," said the Judge, "back in the very old days, when the number zero hadn't even been invented."

I asked how that was possible. The Judge said that ancient people went merrily along, counting the things they had—wool and wine and wives—without making the depressing discovery that they could also count the things they didn't have.

I wished I'd never heard of zero. What was the point of anything?

I slept too much, and my sleep was smeared with dreams. A lot of them were about the Federal Marshal. In my awake life, I tried not to remember the Marshal, but you can't not remember things in dreams. I dreamed that Gentleman Jack killed Marshal Starling. He'd shot him in the stomach, which meant it was a belly wound, which usually meant death. And then I'd dream that when I woke up, the dream would turn out to have been true, which it was. It was a dream within a dream.

It was during one of these dreams that I heard the dagger, sharp and cool. "*It's no dream!*" But I knew the dagger wasn't with me in the cottage, so I must have been dreaming. It was a dream within a dream within a dream.

"*I'm no dream!*" said the dagger.

I woke up.

"*A double-edged blade is no dream,*" said the dagger.

But where was it? I heard it but couldn't see it. I was confused about where the dagger had gone.

"*Six inches of carbon and iron is no dream.*"

On the bed lay a square package. It was beautifully wrapped in cream-colored paper with a raised pattern you could trace with your fingers. Some of Betsy's Valentine's Day cards had raised patterns. Molly had let me touch hers. The ribbon was the same color, and it also had a raised pattern, which felt like velvet.

"*Open the box!*" said the dagger. "*You'll see I'm no dream.*"

I pushed myself up on the pillows with my left arm. I tugged at the ribbon with my left hand. My right hand would hurt too much. It

was funny how I didn't really care that I'd wrecked my right arm—
my throwing arm. I didn't care that all the moving parts under my skin
had been tightened, like screws. They had no stretch.

"Hurry!" said the dagger.

In the box was the belt and the sheath, and in the sheath was the
dagger. I slid out the dagger. It looked the same as always, but why
shouldn't it? The dagger never changed.

"*That's because I'm perfect,*" said the dagger.

I remembered now: I'd asked Betsy to hide the dagger for me. She'd
been clever to wrap and send it to me like a present.

I pictured Betsy, standing before the rolls of wrapping paper in
the General Store, choosing the fancy one with the pattern you could
touch. She had stood before the spools of ribbon and chosen the velvet
one to match. They were different patterns, but they were meant to
go together.

She hadn't sent a card, though. I remembered how pretty her
Valentine's Day card had been. Maybe she'd stood in front of the cards,
choosing the one with the roses for me. I hadn't looked at it since
Valentine's Day. It had lain beneath the dollhouse carpet all this while.

"*Are you listening?*" said the dagger. "*Are you alert?*"

I hadn't heard anything.

"*Footsteps!*" said the dagger.

It was easy to hide the dagger. There were drawers built in right
under the bed.

"*A wild thing would have heard them approach,*" said the dagger.

In came the Judge and Mrs. del Salto. "We come bearing gifts," said
the Judge. He held the yellow cup; Mrs. del Salto carried a plate. That
was like fixing a tray. There was no actual tray, but it meant I could
eat in bed, so the idea was the same. The del Saltos saw I'd unwrapped

Betsy's present, but they didn't ask what was inside. They were like that. They let you be private.

"No more of that poultice stuff?" I said.

"Far from it!" The Judge raised the cup. "Nectar."

Mrs. del Salto raised the plate. "Ambrosia."

The yellow cup made a familiar pattern in my hands. It smelled of hot chocolate. Was that nectar?

That was nectar.

Ambrosia was a cinnamon roll.

"Now I'll live forever?" I said.

"Precisely!" said the Judge.

A cinnamon roll is like a secret: there's a length of pastry, which is sprinkled with cinnamon, then coiled up like a snake, and baked, and iced. You unroll it and discover secret deposits of cinnamon. Then you eat it.

But I would wait to eat it because I didn't like people watching me eat.

Paloma sat beside me. Her nose twitched, but she didn't so much as sniff at the cinnamon roll, even though it smelled so dark and gooey and not-too-sweet.

"She's very well trained," said the Judge. "We let her into the kitchen, with a great ham sitting on the table. She never touched it."

"A dagger would touch the ham," said the dagger. *"A dagger would touch it a million times."*

"Not a million times," I said.

"It's her training," said the Judge. "It's so no one poisons her. She'll only eat food we give her." He looked at me. "You give her, that is. It should be you."

If I was the only person who could feed Paloma, how would she eat when I was gone? "How did you feed her when I was sick?"

"We know the command that allows her to eat."

I couldn't drink the nectar with my dagger-throwing hand. My skin was winched up around my fingers.

There was another way I knew they'd fixed me a tray, which was that they spent lots of time behind the closed door of the person who got the tray, talking to that person. I know, because that person was me.

"Betsy owes you a great deal," said the Judge. "You were brave to have saved her."

It wasn't bravery. Don't you have to be scared to be brave? Anyway, it was my fault the Brewster Boy had tried to scrawl her up.

"How can you be wild?" said the dagger. *"Now that you can't throw me?"*

What if I was losing my wildness? This notion snagged at unpleasant thoughts—memories of how I'd felt about my garnet dress, of how I'd felt like myself in it. How I'd then wondered what it meant to be Myself. Whether there was a new Myself and an old Myself, and if so, whether the new Myself had been tamed.

If I thought about getting the baby doll for the doll family, did that mean I was tame?

"You could steal it," said the dagger. It didn't like the idea of the dolls, but it liked the idea of stealing.

What if the dagger was right and I was losing my wildness? What if I didn't actually care about throwing the dagger? Why did I feel the trickling-honey sense of relief?

"Thank you for bringing me Paloma," I said. I'd stored it up for so long that I said it without thinking. Did that mean I was tame?

Paloma's ears made little cradles to catch her name.

"You are most welcome," said the Judge.

You were supposed to thank the Blue Rose, even if she hadn't given you anything yet. Even if you hadn't even craved anything yet. "What if you crave a boon of the Blue Rose but she sends you something terrible?" I said.

"Then you have to consider," said the Judge, "whether you accepted what you were given with an open heart. The thing that appears to be terrible may in truth be the answer to your dearest wish."

"Gentleman Jack said the Blue Rose spat in his eye," I said.

"I've often thought the iron has entered his soul," said the Judge.

But iron and souls didn't go together, did they? Iron was a dagger-ish thing and souls were a shrine-ish thing. The Judge said it was just a useful image, like the image of restoring the yellow cup's bloom. He explained that when the iron enters someone's soul it means he gets disillusioned with life. The Judge thought Gentleman Jack believed the world was out to cheat him, so he had to get what he wanted by stealing.

The Judge remembered about Steal a March. "If the iron's entered your soul," said the Judge, "then of course you'd think you need to steal a march to get what you deserve."

When the Judge and Mrs. del Salto left, I took the dagger from the drawer. I ate the ambrosia and drank the nectar. Because of my right hand not working, I'd have to start all over learning to eat neatly. I gave Paloma bits of the cinnamon roll. I scooped up a fingerful of the not-too-sweetness and held it out to her. She took it with her lips, like a fish. She barely touched me with her fish lips. I was the only one who could feed her. That was so Rough Ricky couldn't poison her.

"*Tell me the old words,*" I said. "*The ones from when we lived with Gentleman Jack.*"

The dagger would never forget. "*Gold, Primrose, Stagecoach, Grateful.*" Its memory was made of iron and carbon, which was stronger than flesh and blood.

"*Primrose, Stagecoach, Grateful,*" I said.

I would turn my memories of Gentleman Jack into cold metal.

"*Stagecoach, Grateful,*" I said.

"*Grateful,*" I said.

Gold, Primrose, Stagecoach, Grateful.

Primrose, Stagecoach, Grateful.

Stagecoach, Grateful.

Grateful.

I lay in bed, remembering to be wild. The dagger had said I'd forgotten. The dagger said I'd forgotten to listen, and listening was part of being alert, and being alert was part of being wild.

But it's hard to be alert when you're sick. "*Wild things get sick,*" I said.

"Yes," said the dagger. "*And then they die.*"

I lay in bed, wondering if Paloma was wild. She'd been trained, but what did that mean? Training and taming—were they the same things?

"*Exactly the same,*" said the dagger.

But I wasn't sure. "*Do you think learning to read is a taming thing?*"

"*Extremely taming,*" said the dagger.

"*Do you think Gentleman Jack is wild?*" I said.

"*Extremely wild,*" said the dagger.

"*But Gentleman Jack can read,*" I said.

The dagger didn't like that. It liked to win every argument. "*That's because he's a man. You can train a man but not tame him.*" Its voice was cool and sharp. That's what happened when it got angry. When I got angry, I grew hot.

I grew hot all at once, just the way the Judge turned a handle and the lamps sprang into life. One minute they were cold and dark, the next minute they blazed with fire.

"*Are boys better than girls?*" I said.

"*Ten times better,*" said the dagger.

"*The Judge said a girl dog is more protective of her person.*" But the Judge and Gentleman Jack were different. If Gentleman Jack were to have a child, he'd only want a boy.

I rolled over and slid open the drawer. Before, it had been a hiding place for the dagger, from the Judge and Mrs. del Salto. I would turn it into a prison for the dagger. But instead of bars there were piles of petticoats and drawers and stockings. The dagger would call them taming things.

I imprisoned the dagger beneath the taming things. Serve it right.

"*Don't leave me here!*"

But I was sick of the dagger. I left it in piles of petticoats and drawers and stockings. I left it to be tamed.

The Valentine's Card

✝ I CURLED UP IN BED. I was inside a seed.

"*Don't be stupid,*" said the dagger. "*A person can't get inside a seed.*"

I was inside a rose seed.

I curled myself into an egg. I was a seed, I was an egg.

"*Make up your mind!*"

I would bloom into a bird. I would turn around in my nest.

"*You can't be a seed and an egg and a bird,*" said the dagger.

But I could. That's because I was bendy.

Paloma followed me wherever I went. She followed me down to breakfast. Her nails made clicks on the attic steps, then little sighs on the pink-cheeked carpet with the brass rods and pineapples.

On the way back up to the attic, her nails went click again. Click, not tick. I must have been very sick to mix up the clicking of her nails with the ticking of a watch, especially a watch that had no tick inside.

I knelt on the floor, my chin resting on the edge of the spinning platform. I was too tired to hold up my chin. I was cold and tired because I'd been sick. Paloma sat beside me, but she didn't rest her chin anywhere. She was too noble for that.

The dolls sat in the parlor, folded into the wings of a dove.

"Not *real* wings," I said, before the dagger could say anything. "*Just the idea of wings.*"

I unhooked the watch from the library wall. You could open the watch with one hand. That was lucky, because even though I could no longer use my right hand, I could still use my left. I looked at the photograph of Grandmother and thought about being with her. I was glad I'd disobeyed Gentleman Jack. Her photograph helped me think about how I'd sit in a crimson velvet chair, and the watch would be ticking, and our hearts would be beating.

"We like it when the house is open," said the father doll. "Then we can see the indigo tree through the window."

"And the blue sky behind the indigo tree," said the mother doll. "We also like it when the house is closed and we can be cozy and private."

"Do you think," I said, then I wondered what I was going to say. I started again. "Do you think you should be grateful to me?"

The mother doll and the father doll turned to look at me. Their eyes clicked when they closed, but they also clicked when they opened. The father doll's eyes were brown, the mother doll's eyes were blue.

"Grateful?" said the mother doll.

"Grateful?" said the father doll.

"To me." Now I wished I hadn't asked, but I had started and I couldn't stop. "Grateful for bringing you mirrors and tablecloths and clocks. Grateful for bringing you Oakheart?" The words turned to rocks in my mouth.

"Gratitude has to spring up of itself," said the mother doll. "It has to spring up freely."

"Sometimes," said the father doll, "gratitude can be a burden."

The dolls were stupid.

I discovered a wonderful thing. I could speak to Paloma without being spoken to first. Or maybe Paloma really was speaking to me, and it was just that I couldn't understand. "You've never seen the second floor," I said. She clicked down the attic stairs behind me.

I showed her Isaac's room. It was the same as before: blue walls, blue cradle, yellow spindles. Except in the cradle there now lay a blanket—blue stars, white background, a fringe all around. It was exactly like the blanket I'd made for the dollhouse cradle. What an interesting coincidence.

I led Paloma to the dining room. There was the painted garland, and beneath the garland hung the mirror. But where was the black drapery? The mirror now reflected the sunlight. It reflected the lace tablecloth that lay on the dining-room table.

This could be no coincidence. I might even have expected it. The dolls in the dollhouse were alive, and the dollhouse was alive, and the dollhouse made things come alive. I'd made a blanket; I'd made a mirror; I'd made a lace tablecloth. It stood to reason that the things I brought to the dollhouse had come alive in the cottage.

The Judge would say it better. He'd say that the things I brought to the dollhouse had breathed spirit into the cottage.

Last, I showed Paloma the human-size library. She sat beside me in front of the bookshelves. "I'll show you my favorite picture," I said.

The Mother Goose book opened of its own accord at the page with the sailor mice in their blue suits.

Mrs. del Salto came into the library. First she looked at the mantelpiece, which she always did now upon entering the library. She looked at the place Magda and Isaac's photograph used to be. She asked about the photograph, as she always did, and I said what I always said, which was that I didn't know where it was.

"*I like it when you lie to her,*" said the dagger.

"Things go missing sometimes," she said. "I must try to be philosophical."

Was she being philosophical? Was she accepting her sorrows?

I pretended to read the first line of the poem. "I saw a ship a-sailing," I said.

Then I was sorry I'd spoken aloud. It made Mrs. del Salto lean over my shoulder and say, "Reading?"

I stared at the page, at the white silk sails and the golden mast.

"You're at loose ends," said Mrs. del Salto. "That happens sometimes when you've been sick."

Loose ends. That was interesting. It was as though I'd been neatly knotted into myself. Then I got sick and all my knots came undone. I was just a length of flyaway string.

"*That's bad,*" said the dagger.

"That's bad." A person was strong when she was knotted into herself. A knot for me and Gentleman Jack. A knot for me and Grandmother.

"*A knot for you and me,*" said the dagger.

All those knots had made me strong. Now I was at loose ends—

"*What happens with loose ends?*" said the dagger.

"*They fray,*" I said.

"You know how Magda could read when she was four?" I seemed to be asking Mrs. del Salto a question. But I was really talking about myself. I was talking about a loose end of myself.

Mrs. del Salto stood motionless behind me. Of course she knew about Magda.

"I am ten," I said. Or probably I was eleven. "And I can't read."

"No?" said Mrs. del Salto.

There followed a long silence. I got more and more frayed.

"Would you like to learn?" said Mrs. del Salto.

"Mrs. Elton says I'm too stupid," I said. I was frayed, I was afraid.

"Really?" said Mrs. del Salto.

I nodded. I swallowed down the taste of varnish. But it was too big to swallow.

"We'll see about that." Mrs. del Salto walked across the floor; she walked back and forth. Her dress was angry. It lashed itself this way and that.

I thought of the needle that had sewn that dress. Such a small thing to make all that heavy fabric hold together. Such a small thing to hold all that rage.

"Let's prove Mrs. Elton wrong," said Mrs. del Salto. "Wouldn't that be satisfying?"

I believed it would be satisfying, but I didn't believe it would be possible.

"What would you like to read?" said Mrs. del Salto.

Mrs. Elton made me not remember what I knew. I could never read in front of her. I remembered how she'd made me feel foolish for not knowing about Valentine's Day. I remembered Betsy's Valentine's Day card and how I didn't like to look at it because I didn't know how to read.

And then I knew what I wanted to read. I'd told Mrs. del Salto I'd be right back. I tried to run up to the attic, but my legs were frayed. There was the card, just where I'd left it, in the dollhouse, beneath the parlor carpet.

It had been fifty-four days since Betsy had given it to me. Such a long time ago. It felt like a lifetime.

Back in the parlor now. I stood in front of Mrs. del Salto, beside another photograph of Magda on a small side table. Mrs. del Salto looked at it, and I could tell she was wondering about the photograph from the library and trying to be philosophical. Then Mrs. del Salto patted the cushion beside her, and I sank into it. I sank into the dove softness, while all around were sparks of color—the cream-and-rose tiles, the crimson fire, the rug, all pink and gold.

Mrs. del Salto looked at the leftover half of the card, the half with the words on it. "All it takes is practice," she said. "Remember how you practiced jacks until you could pick up all six at once?" I did remember, but I knew she was wrong. Learning to play jacks was one thing. You just bounced the ball and you snatched at the jacks. You bounced the ball again and again, and at first you mostly missed the jacks and missed the ball, and then you mostly got the jacks and caught the ball.

That was one kind of practice. It wasn't the same as learning to read or learning to write on a slate. Those were things that were as mysterious as stars falling from the sky or blue roses growing in the snow.

There were only ten words, but that doesn't help when you can't read any of them.

"You know where every word starts and stops?" said Mrs. del Salto. That was one thing I'd learned in school. There was a space when a word ended. Sometimes there were commas or periods or exclamation marks.

"You read the first word, then I'll read the second," said Mrs. del Salto. "See how short the first word is?"

The first word was only one letter. It was the letter A. The problem was that you could say the letter A in two ways. You could say it like the sound Uh, or you could say it like the A sound in Way.

"I'd say it like the Uh sound," said Mrs. del Salto.

The second word was a complicated tangle of letters. "Friend," said Mrs. del Salto. But there were too many letters just for the word Friend. The spelling made it look as though it would make a lot of sounds, but when you said it, it made only one sound.

"A friend is someone special," said Mrs. del Salto. "Maybe it deserves to have an extra couple of letters."

The third word was short, but it ended with the tricky letter Y. Mrs. del Salto gave me a hint. "We talked about the word Way. This word rhymes with Way."

The word started with an M. I made the M sound with my lips, then added the end sound of Way.

"May?" I said.

"Excellent!" said Mrs. del Salto.

So far the valentine read, "A friend may . . ."

The next word started with a W. The letter W had always seemed friendly. Maybe because I knew it was in the friendly word Swing. That made sense because it made a sound like a swing.

"Weh . . ." I said.

"Very good," said Mrs. del Salto. "Now just add the L. It doesn't matter that there are two of them. You say it the same way."

"Well?" I said.

Mrs. del Salto nodded.

"Well!" I said.

Mrs. del Salto looked at me. "Who says you can't read? Can you think of a word that rhymes with Well?"

"Tell," I said.

"Wonderful!" said Mrs. del Salto. "What letter does Tell start with?"

That was easy. It was the generous, smiling T.

"T," I said, then I saw it all at once. "F-E-L-L is for Fell."

"Yes!" said Mrs. del Salto.

"B-E-L-L is for Bell." And I thought of the bells that rang from the Shrine morning, noon, and night. How amazing that four little letters could make you think of the swinging, reeling Shrine bells.

"My stars!" Mrs. del Salto's cheeks had gone pink. "Don't you think you can read?"

"I can read Well," I said. "W-E-L-L." And we laughed. I had made a kind of joke. Who would have thought you could make a joke out of reading?

The message in the card said, "A friend may well be reckoned the masterpiece of nature." I read the words Be, Of, and Nature, which is not the easiest word in the world.

"Nice," said Mrs. del Salto. "Not too sentimental."

I fixed my gaze on the crazy word Friend and tried to make it look familiar. It didn't look like a friend, but maybe we hadn't gotten to know each other yet.

"I think that maybe you already knew how to read," said Mrs. del Salto. "But then you stopped practicing and forgot."

It didn't seem possible that I'd once known how to read. But how else would some of the words be unlocking their secrets, smiling at me from the page?

I liked the valentine; I liked what it said.

"I bet you could read when you were four," said Mrs. del Salto.

And suddenly it was like opening Magda's wardrobe shrine. There were layers of memory, the tissue-paper memories and the lace memories, and there were also the heavier woolen memories, all folded softly onto shelves. I didn't know what the memories were, not exactly. I tasted them more than I saw them. I remembered the taste of reading, how the word Soap had a soft lemon flavor, how the word You was just a silver breath over your tongue.

I looked at Magda's photograph, at her ordinary girl face, neither pretty nor plain. Magda had been able to read when she was four. Maybe I had been able to read when I was four. That was in the Before Time, before my memories started with Gentleman Jack.

Mrs. del Salto's skirts lay draped on the sofa beside me. I stared at them for a moment. "Your dress is purple," I said. "Not black."

"It was time," she said. "Wearing black is a way to show how sad you are. But as time passes, you wear lighter colors to show that you've begun to forgive the Blue Rose."

"For what?"

"For not granting the boon you craved."

"Did the Blue Rose send you what you needed, not what you wanted?"

"It's difficult to think of it like that," said Mrs. del Salto. "But I can say I've begun to accept what she sent me."

Mrs. del Salto was being philosophical. She was accepting her sorrows.

"Maybe," said Mrs. del Salto. "Maybe something that first appeared to be a sorrow can turn into a joy. Maybe it turns into a joy when you almost lose it."

That also went with the Blue Rose's first precept.

> Accept your sorrows,
> If you cannot change them.
> Embrace your joys,
> So you don't estrange them.

It also went with the Blue Rose and how time was all mixed up with her. How she could grant a boon you hadn't craved yet. How joys and sorrows could be the same thing, depending on when you see it. If you see it before you almost lose it, it's a sorrow. If you see it after you almost lose it, it's a joy.

Mrs. del Salto was becoming extremely philosophical.

"You wear lighter colors," said Mrs. del Salto, "to show you're returning to the joys and sorrows of the regular world."

Joys and sorrows. I knew what the sorrows were, but what were the joys? Then I answered myself. The joys were in the dollhouse. That's where the baby would be. Life was joyful as long as it unfolded in miniature. And sometimes the joys in the dollhouse breathed spirit into the cottage.

"*Stop liking the cottage!*" said the dagger. "*You have to like Grandmother's house best.*"

If I had forgotten how to read, what other important things had I forgotten?

"You begin," said Mrs. del Salto, "to accept what you've been given with an open heart."

If Mrs. del Salto could give up ashes and salt and start accepting her joys and sorrows, I could start saving my memories. I remembered reading and I already knew reading would be a joy. But if I remembered the joys, I probably had to remember the sorrows, too—like maybe remembering my mother. But they went together, the joys and sorrows. Maybe I'd forgotten the feeling of silk. Maybe there was joy in touching a silk dress.

"Is your dress silk?" I said.

It was.

"Can I touch it?"

"Of course!" said Mrs. del Salto.

"You have to wait for Grandmother!" said the dagger.

I brushed the front part of my fingers across the silk. It was cool and smooth. It was like water. I waited for the dagger to say silk wasn't water, but it was too busy telling me I had to wait for Grandmother, and that I had to think about Grandmother, and that I had to like Grandmother best of all.

"I can think about anything I want." I hid my thoughts from the dagger. I buried them under my new words, Ambrosia and Nectar. The dagger wouldn't like to know I was going to start saving my memories. It thought my memories of Gentleman Jack were enough.

Ambrosia. Nectar. Hot chocolate was Nectar, a cinnamon roll was Ambrosia. Mrs. del Salto and the Judge had fixed me a tray of Nectar and Ambrosia when I was sick. They were the food and drink of the gods, which meant they were joyful.

"You don't want to remember," said the dagger.

"I don't want to remember," I said, just to avoid getting into an argument. But inside my head I thought, Nectar and Ambrosia. Joys and sorrows. I wanted the joys, even though it meant I also had to have the sorrows.

A New Collar

✝ THE NEXT DAY, the Judge brought a collar for Paloma. It was red, which looked nice on her black fur. There was a brass nameplate on it, which said Paloma. The bright popping P was big and swirly.

"*You shouldn't put a collar on a dog,*" said the dagger. "*Just like you shouldn't send a girl to school. It tames them.*"

"But if I don't go to school," I said, "they won't let me see Gentleman Jack."

"*I suppose the dog thinks it can't eat if it doesn't wear the collar,*" said the dagger.

I unbuckled the collar. It had pressed a band of flatness into Paloma's fur. Her fur was not exactly curly, but wavy, with feathers at the haunches and tail. Why had I taken it off? She wasn't going to grow wilder now that her collar had been removed. The dagger made me think crazy things, or it tried to. It tried to make me think that there was nothing so very bad about Gentleman Jack's not teaching me how to read. But however much the dagger stuck me with its exclamation points, I got mad every time I thought about it. It rubbed at a raw, sore place in my chest.

When something happened in the dollhouse, it often also happened in buttercream cottage. It made the human-size cottage more alive— a blanket had appeared in Isaac's cradle; the mirrors were suddenly uncovered; and now that Oakheart had a collar, Paloma had one, too.

I wondered if the dollhouse called out to the human-size cottage: "Tablecloth! Mirror! Blanket! Collar!" And then the cottage got the same things. Maybe it even called back to the dollhouse: "Collar! Blanket! Mirror! Tablecloth!"

"*That's crazy*," said the dagger.

I was tired of the dagger.

I wanted to fill up on reading before I had to leave. Mrs. del Salto said I had burst into reading. I discovered a curious thing in the Mother Goose book. Mother Goose had already made up the rhyme-pattern about the tasks. My underneath mind must have remembered it from the Before Time, and my over-and-above mind had changed it to fit the dolls' tasks.

> One for sorrow,
> Two for joy,
> Three for a girl,
> Four for a boy.
> Five for silver,
> Six for gold,

Seven for a secret
Never to be told.

It wasn't even as different from mine as it seemed. Mine had Sister and Brother; this had Girl and Boy. And all the things in the rhyme were things I'd thought about, like joys and sorrows—that the joys were concentrated in the dollhouse and the sorrows in the human-size world.

But maybe that wasn't true anymore, now that Mrs. del Salto had started being philosophical about her sorrows. I could see her being philosophical when she looked at the lamps and didn't turn them off. I could see it on the day she wore lilac, which was brighter than purple.

Silver was for the inkwell, and gold was for the five gold bricks. I hadn't thought about a secret, but maybe that was because it was an especially secret secret: it was never to be told.

I discovered another curious thing, which was that some words were made up of words within words. The second verse of the sailor mice poem, for instance:

There were comfits in the cabin,
And apples in the hold;
The sails were made of silk,
And the masts were made of gold.

I knew the word Discomfit but not the word Comfit. The Judge sat at his desk while I sat on the floor. He never minded being interrupted, but he had to speak to me first.

I knocked on the leg of his chair.

"Yes?"

He was very easy to train.

"What are comfits?"

"It's an old-fashioned word for something sweet."

If Comfit was something sweet, then Discomfit must mean something not sweet. Comfit was a word inside the bigger word of Discomfit.

Mr. Elton had discomfited me. He'd accused me of stealing the green candy, which meant I'd felt the opposite of sweet.

Discomfit meant to make someone feel not sweet.

I mentioned this to the Judge, who said it was a most perceptive observation. That was the second time he'd said those very words to me.

I thought more about Discomfit. You'd think someone would only be discomfited with a bad thing, but I saw you could also be discomfited with a good thing. I'd done a good thing when I'd saved Betsy from the Brewster Boy, but—

"I discomfited Mrs. Elton when I saved Betsy," I said. "That's because she didn't want to be grateful to me."

The Judge laughed and said he wished he could have been a fly on the wall.

He always said such strange things.

"I have to talk to Gentleman Jack," I told Mrs. del Salto. "I want to tell him I can read." Maybe then he wouldn't say I was dull.

"When you're better," she said.

"I have to talk to Gentleman Jack," I told the Judge. "I want to tell him I can read."

"When you're better," he said.

"But Gentleman Jack will be mad if I wait too long." And once I'd said that, a thought floated from my undermind to my over-and-above mind. That was really the reason I wanted to see him: I didn't want him to get mad.

"He already knows you've been ill," said the Judge. "He already knows you can't visit him."

That was just like the Judge. To tell Gentleman Jack I'd been ill before I'd even thought of it myself.

I believed the Judge more than I believed Mrs. del Salto. He'd kept his promise to Magda to build her a dollhouse, even though she was dead. That was the kind of person he was. He'd keep his promise.

Every evening the Judge asked me about what I'd read. I told him about bears that turned into men and huts that ran around on chicken legs. I told him I'd found the number three in almost every story—three tasks, three sisters, three talismans—which made me wonder if the dolls were right about three being the proper number of tasks. Not that I said this to the Judge, of course.

"No!" said the dagger. "*Two is the right number. Grandmother's number of tasks is the right number.*"

"Three is an exceptional number," said the Judge. "A triangle, with its three sides, is the strongest shape there is."

The Judge was very smart. He knew all about numbers. He knew about the number zero. He knew about the number three.

We were silent a moment while I thought about this, then the Judge said, "It's a wonderful thing, reading. Just think of our brains. They weigh only a few pounds, but when you read, they're as big as the whole universe."

There was the Judge, at it again, making small objects like your brain look big, so you could understand them. And making big objects like the universe look small, so you could understand them.

"I'm better now," I said. "I need to see Gentleman Jack."

"Not until the trial," said the Judge. "We're transferring him to Buffalo Bend."

Now that I had been to school, I knew more about Buffalo Bend. I'd known it was the capital city of the Territories. I'd known it was where they took the gold. Now I knew it was where they sent people to be hanged.

"But you said I could see him when I was better." The Judge and Mrs. del Salto exchanged glances. They had forgotten. It was not like the Judge to forget.

The Judge said he was sorry but it was quite impossible to see Gentleman Jack. "He won't get angry," he said. "He knows you've been ill."

The dinner table turned slightly unreal. The lamps sucked in their breath. The steam rising from the stew stood still. The Judge's lips opened and shut, opened and shut. Funny how naked they looked inside his black whiskers.

The Federal Marshals were coming to get Gentleman Jack. They were going to put him on a stagecoach on April twenty-sixth and drive him away to stand trial in Buffalo Bend.

April twenty-sixth was four days away. It was also to be my first day back at school.

"But you promised," I said.

May sixth was the new Day Zero. The last Day Zero.

"I'm so sorry," said the Judge. How funny mouths were, two pink worms, squiggling and talking and eating, opening and closing and eating and squiggling.

"You kept your promise to make a dollhouse for Magda," I said. "Even though she died."

The flames held their breath. When you don't breathe, you grow pale. The flames grew pale.

Mrs. del Salto laid her fork on her plate. "You're picking at your thumb," she said. "You haven't done that for a long time."

I glanced at my thumb, which had sealed itself up without letting me know. It was such a strange stump of a thing, all whorls on one side and ridges and folds on the other. Maybe I'd never looked at it before.

But I picked at it; I was good at picking my thumb. I found a loose end of skin. Now I could make it bleed.

The Judge said that Gentleman Jack had to stand trial outside the Indigo Heart. It was the law, said the Judge, because of where Gentleman Jack was supposed to have killed Marshal Starling.

Gentleman Jack, leaving the Indigo Heart? I could not seem to understand this. The steam hung motionless. The flames were pale.

"You'll go, too, of course," said the Judge. "So you can testify at his trial."

"In the carriage, with Gentleman Jack?"

But the Judge said that he and I would go in the del Saltos' carriage. He said the stagecoach would be too full of Federal Marshals, plus the Sheriff, so Gentleman Jack couldn't escape.

Gentleman Jack—escape? There, that was something to think about. That was real. Escape. The word made the world real again. The flames started breathing. The candlesticks reflected them with their round brass cheeks. The steam went back to rising.

"*Escape!*" said the dagger.

"*Escape!*" I said.

I walked about the cottage. Walking helped me think. I passed through the library. The Judge was sitting in his armchair, as he often did after dinner. I didn't look at the desk, just the way I always didn't look at the desk, in case it made me steal the inkwell and the coins. But Paloma was supposed to keep people from stealing things. Would she protect me from my own self?

Escape! It was funny to think the word Escape so loudly and clearly with the Judge sitting right there. But he couldn't read my thoughts, not like the dagger. He couldn't know I was making a plan. He couldn't know I realized Rough Ricky could help Gentleman Jack escape. That Rough Ricky could hold up the stagecoach, and this time he wouldn't be stealing gold. He'd be stealing Gentleman Jack.

"*Gentleman Jack is more valuable than gold,*" said the dagger.

It was a little like deciding whether to hurt someone or to kill someone. Hurting gets you into less trouble, but killing is more sure. Helping Gentleman Jack escape would get me into more trouble than lying at his trial, but helping him escape was more sure.

With Gentleman Jack I had to be more sure. I remembered thinking that when I helped Gentleman Jack escape, I'd be giving him back to himself. It would be my gift to him. A wonderful gift he'd get on April twenty-second.

I could forget about the dolls and the last task and the trial. What a relief to know what to do. What a relief the Judge had forgotten his promise. He'd betrayed me; I'd betray him.

My thumb was bleeding again. I licked it clean. I licked up the iron in the blood. Now I could be strong and cold.

The moon was still almost full. It shone off the star steps and the roof of the Shrine. The moonlight was kind to shadows, stretching them on the ground, crisp and clear. But there'd only be a half moon on April twenty-sixth, which was good. That meant it would be a lot darker on the night Gentleman Jack was to escape. It's harder to find someone in the dark.

I took the street parallel to Main Street, so I wouldn't risk running into anyone who knew the Judge or Mrs. del Salto. I neared the garden in which the two blue roses had been blooming when I'd last run down this street. In the garden was a swing, and in the swing was a woman with a baby in the crook of each arm. There! I saw the letter W in action. The letter W was in the word Swing, and the letter W was the swingiest of all the letters. I couldn't think of anything swingier than swinging babies to sleep.

I was glad when the woman wished me good evening; I could ask her about the babies and the roses.

Had she wished for the babies?

She had, although she hadn't specified two.

"I saw the blue roses in your garden," I said, "on . . ." I thought about the date. "On March seventh."

"My stars!" said the woman. "That was just when they were born."

"Did you thank the Blue Rose?"

The woman said you bet she did, on the Feast of the Blue Rose. And that also, every time the bells rang, she sang the song of praise extra loudly. "I know it's not like having a Songbird," she said, "but I hope my words of praise reach the Blue Rose."

I said I was sure she would—because, suddenly, I was sure. I had a good feeling about the Blue Rose. And then I was off to meet Rough Ricky.

I wished I felt wild. But I hadn't been outdoors since I'd fallen ill. I wished I felt the iron course through my blood, cold and strong. But I was stumbling. I had to stop to catch my breath and organize my feet.

Here, on Main Street, the roofs covered the sidewalks, and the pillars held up the roofs, and the metal basins fixed to the pillars leapt with fire. There the shadows lost their edges. The firelight caught at the shadows of passing people, smudging them like charcoal.

I turned off Main Street and went down 3 Street, down the skitter of stairs that led to the river. I passed the tar-and-spit houses, the oil-paper windows. Everything was paper down here, oil paper, tar paper. The moon glistened off the moisture on the stairs.

Down and down. I heard the rush of the river; I heard the rustling of the willows and their papery sighs; I heard a faint whistling that fit into the spaces in my brain that I'd kept empty, on purpose. It was the cattle boy's song, and here was the cattle boy, although he wasn't herding cattle because it was night. He was whistling the same song as before.

There was enough moonlight for us to see each other. We stopped, the cattle boy touched the brim of his cap. "Evening," he said.

I said Evening back, and then, "Can you tell me the words of that song?"

Not only could he tell me, he could sing them. He sang the notes clearly; he said the words clearly.

"My mother dear will unto me
Fetch milk and honeycomb.
My father dear will for us three
Build our enduring home."

I'd been right. The words Mother and Father fit into the sad spaces
of the song. And so did the words Milk and Honey, except that the
word that fit the rhyme was Honeycomb. But you could slurp honey
off honeycomb. They were kind of the same thing. This was the song
I'd recognized when I'd first met Rough Ricky by the river. This was
the song I'd recognized, I'd recognized it in the way crocuses recognize the sun.

The cattle boy went on his way, and at the very next turn of the
river, there was Rough Ricky, waiting.

He spoke to me so I could speak to him. I sat beside the fire and
told him about the stagecoach. Rough Ricky was quiet for a while. Then
he said that the Federal Marshals were going to construct the stagecoach
very carefully so Gentleman Jack couldn't escape.

Rough Ricky told me about another man who'd been transferred to
the jail in Buffalo Bend. This other man was like Gentleman Jack, quick
and tricky, with a history of escaping, so the Federal Marshals took
great care in the construction of his coach. They'd do the same with
Gentleman Jack's coach.

"Here's what they'll do," said Rough Ricky. "The blacksmith will
bolt a sheet of metal to the floor of the stagecoach. He'll rivet leg irons
and a chain to the metal plate. The chain will run from Gentleman Jack's
handcuffs, through the leg irons, to the metal plate."

The Judge hadn't told me about any of that.

"*He doesn't trust you,*" said the dagger.

I didn't trust him, either. He had broken his promise, and now I saw that maybe he had lied, just a little, about the reason I couldn't go on the stagecoach. It wasn't only that the stage was too full. It was also because he didn't want me to know about the sheet of metal and the leg irons and the handcuffs and the chain.

"*You can't lie just a little,*" said the dagger.

It was hard to imagine Gentleman Jack with irons on his wrists and ankles. Not Gentleman Jack, with his frills and ruby earring and primrose gloves.

Rough Ricky said I did just right to tell him. He said they'd rescue Gentleman Jack from the stagecoach. "We'll bring crowbars and metal saws and chisels," he said. Those were all tools to break metal.

I wanted to carry a crowbar. I wanted to break metal. But Rough Ricky said I couldn't ride with him and the others. "If you disappear on the very day Gentleman Jack is due to be transferred, that Judge of yours might suspect something."

But the Judge wasn't my judge.

Rough Ricky said that if I went missing, the Judge would sound an alarm, and they'd change their plans about how and when to transport Gentleman Jack, and this time the Judge wouldn't tell me about the new plans.

"First," said Rough Ricky, "leave your coat here, by this willow. It's warm in Blue Roses but it will be cold in Netherby Scar. You won't have so much to carry. You can get it when we meet on Friday." Friday was April twenty-sixth. "Right here, no later than five o'clock."

"Don't you need gold to help you stop the stagecoach?" But Rough Ricky said that stopping a stagecoach wasn't a tricky thing, not like getting Gentleman Jack out of jail with no one catching them and no one dead. He said that he and the few other Gentlemen who remained could rescue Gentleman Jack.

In four days, I'd creep down the indigo tree and meet Rough Ricky by the Jordan. Finally I had something to do.

"*Finally!*" said the dagger.

"No later than five o'clock," said Rough Ricky.

Reading at School

✝ IT WAS MY FIRST DAY BACK AT SCHOOL. It was April twenty-sixth. It was my last day back at school. It was April twenty-sixth. It was a day of knowing things the other children didn't know. I knew that today Rough Ricky and the remaining Gentlemen would ride out with saws and chisels and crowbars. I knew that today they'd free Gentleman Jack. I knew that today I'd meet Rough Ricky at five o'clock sharp.

I had everything I needed. I couldn't put anything in a suitcase. All I had were my pockets. Gentleman Jack's face was already packed. It was folded into quarters. My coat was waiting for me on the banks of the Jordan.

And I knew one more thing. I knew that today I'd read aloud and that I would discomfit Mrs. Elton.

The dolls were seated in the parlor. Their china heads jerked up. Their lips couldn't smile, but their voices were filled with smiles.

"Starling!" said the mother doll.

"Starling!" said the father doll. "We long for our baby."

"We long to see him learn to walk," said the mother doll.

"Holding on to Oakheart's collar," said the father doll.

Would their hearts break if I didn't bring the baby? I'd told them I'd bring the baby, but I hadn't meant it. It had been a piecrust promise, just to keep them quiet.

"I have to leave tonight," I said. "I can't get the baby."

"You can't leave!" said the mother doll.

"You can't leave without bringing us our baby," said the father doll.

"I can leave," I said. The dolls didn't care about me. They only cared about the baby. "I will leave." All the magnets in the world couldn't stop me.

"But you promised," said the mother doll.

I'd promised, but that was just to make them happy.

"You can't break a promise," said the father doll.

Yes, I could. People broke promises all the time. But I tried to explain. I explained about Gentleman Jack and how the Gentlemen would stop the stagecoach, and how stopping the stagecoach was more sure than going to trial.

"The Indigo Heart will bring you back," said the mother doll.

She was wrong. I was no starling to swoop and twist in their dance. I only swooped in Gentleman Jack's dance.

The dolls clicked their eyes shut. It shouldn't work that way. Their eyes should only click shut when they lay down.

"I only care about Gentleman Jack," I said.

The dolls said nothing. Their eyes were closed. I laid the back of my forefinger against the mother doll's cheek. It was cold, but she was always cold. She was made of china.

Your heart can break when you're made of china. Were they dead? Did you die when your heart was broken?

I laid them down. Their eyes stayed closed.

I pushed their eyelids open. But their eyes weren't alive. They had dead glass eyes. There would be no opals that could match their eyes.

"Talk to me!" I said. "I brought you a dog and a collar."

The dolls said nothing.

"And a clock and a mirror and a tablecloth and a key," I said. "You didn't even ask for them."

The dolls said nothing. The dolls were dead. Maybe it was the Judge who'd made them come alive by keeping his promise to build the doll-house, even though Magda had died. Maybe the dolls were dead because I'd made them a piecrust promise.

The Judge was going to walk me to school, just as he'd done on the first day. How long ago that had been! It was even longer ago that I'd first seen him open the drawer in the little table in the foyer and lay his key on the green felt. And now I had a key. It was shinier than his, but the important bits were the same—the sticking-out bits that jaggled down the side, those were the ones that opened the lock.

We stepped out the cottage door. I now knew the sunflower carpet wasn't really a carpet; it was a doormat. I knew that the letters on it spelled WELCOME. And for the first time, I thought maybe it was facing the wrong way. The word WELCOME was right side up when you were leaving the cottage, but upside down when you approached. You didn't need a WELCOME sign when you were leaving. That would be ironic.

It was funny how everything was the same. Only I was different. The star steps still rose up to the Shrine; the Shrine still rose into the clouds. The banister down to Blue Roses was the same unsteady character. The bridge was familiar, as was Main Street, as was the black skeleton of the house, as were the grave markers, three of stone, one of wood.

"Why aren't they all of stone?" I said.

"Usually," said the Judge, "when someone dies, you know they've died. You have their body." I wondered if he was thinking of Magda and Isaac. "That means you give them a grave marker made of stone, which is permanent. But what if someone has disappeared?

"They might still be alive. You wouldn't want to weigh them down with something permanent. You wouldn't want to weigh them down with stone."

"They all died from Rough Ricky's fire?" I said.

"It was Gentleman Jack's fire," he said. I looked at the stone markers. Into each was carved the same word: Starling, Starling, Starling.

"Like Marshal Starling?" I said, even though the Judge had already told me that Marshal Starling and his family had lived here. I was just making sure.

"Mrs. Starling was our last Songbird," said the Judge, "the one who whistled praises to the Blue Rose. She and her children died in the fire. And now we have no one whose words of praise can, with certainty, reach the Blue Rose."

I read all the names on the gravestones. The Marshal's first name was Aldo. The Judge said it means Honorable, which is a good name for a marshal. The Songbird's name was Lyra, which is a good name for a Songbird. It comes from the word Lyre, which is an old-fashioned kind of guitar. But the name on the third stone was confusing because it had too many of the same letters.

"Darrell," said the Judge. "Their little boy's name was Darrell."

Darrell had another good meaning. It meant Beloved.

"Why doesn't the wooden marker have a name?"

"Names are the most lasting things of all," said the Judge. "We only put them on stone."

But what about my name, my original name? That hadn't lasted.

"*You didn't take the coins!*" said the dagger suddenly.

"*I took a penny,*" I said, although I'd really just asked the Judge for a penny. It was less risky than stealing. I knew the Judge pretty well now. I knew he'd be appalled if I stole something but he'd be delighted if I asked him for something. He liked giving me things.

"*You didn't take the inkwell,*" said the dagger.

"*Because the Judge or Mrs. del Salto would notice,*" I said. "*Remember how doing things out of the ordinary attracts attention.*"

Everything I needed was in my pockets: Grandmother's watch, the magnifying glass—

"*Why do you want a magnifying glass?*" said the dagger.

The dagger didn't know the word Talisman. I could think it loud and clear without the dagger saying that talismans were taming. I was setting out on a journey, just as people did in fairy tales, and I was filling up on the exceptional number three. I was bringing three talismans: the watch, the magnifying glass, and the opal pendant. I also had the rest of the butterscotch, but that wasn't a talisman. It was just to sweeten up Gentleman Jack.

We reached the schoolyard. Now the cottonwood tree filled the air with pale fluff; now fireweed and coneflowers blazed purple in the schoolyard, and dandelions were everywhere.

The Judge talked to Mrs. Elton. "We must insist," he said, "that the dog accompany Starling inside."

She rang the bell, which was her way of saying "Fine!" and as usual, the mouth of the school fell open and gobbled up the children.

I watched the Judge leave, and as I did, a kind of sickness crept upon me. The word for that sickness is Regret. Regret is when you know you'll never see the Judge again. Regret is a worm that curls up in your stomach and lashes its tail.

None of the newness had worn off the classroom. There was still the smell of varnish, but I guessed I was used to it. It no longer scraped the back of my tongue. There were lots of things that were new. No one sat where they were supposed to. Why was there a new boy in my old seat?

"Starling del Salto," said Mrs. Elton, using all my names and looking over my head as though searching for me in a crowd. "I hear you think you're ready to move up to the fifth level." I saw now that Betsy, Tilda, and Gabriel were in the fifth-level row. Everyone had moved up while I was sick. Even Peter had moved up to the second level.

Mrs. Elton gave me a passage to read. I stood at the front with Paloma. How nice to have her stand with me! The passage was filled with easy, cheerful words like Well, Tell, and Bell. How could I not have known them before?

Mrs. Elton did not say if I read well or badly. She only said, "Do you think you're ready to move up?"

I didn't know.

"Do you think so?" said Mrs. Elton.

Mrs. Elton made me not know what I thought.

"You may join the fifth level," she said. "Provisionally."

Even though Betsy, Tilda, and Gabriel sat in the fifth-level row, they sat in the same order as before. Betsy and Tilda shared a desk and a bench, and there was a space on the bench beside Gabriel, which was where the Brewster Boy had sat, slashing at Betsy's face. That meant I'd have to sit next to Gabriel. Gabriel moved to the outside edge of his side of the bench, as far from me as he could get. I sat on the outside edge of my side, as far from Gabriel as I could get. Paloma lay at my feet.

The lid of the desk slanted downward. Gabriel lined up his pencils and chalk along the middle of the slant. They made a wall between us.

And now Mrs. Elton skipped right over the third and fourth levels and called the fifth level to the front. The fifth level had been studying a poem, and the poem had ten verses. "Three verses each for Betsy and Tilda," said Mrs. Elton. "Two verses for Gabriel and Starling."

I was to read the last verses. Mrs. Elton was saving me up, like dessert after dinner, so she could enjoy my failure. Didn't she remember how I'd saved Betsy from the Brewster Boy? Shouldn't she be grateful?

I read through the verses. I knew all the words, but there must be a trick. Mrs. Elton would not allow me to read well.

Betsy and Tilda read smoothly. The poem was about a father who knew his daughters were going to take him by surprise and give him lots of kisses, except it was no surprise because he already knew about it.

I'd never really listened to Gabriel read before. He read as though he was riding a bicycle down Main Street, which I'd seen one of the big boys do. It's all bumps and dips, and then an oncoming horse makes you careen off to the side.

"That was barely adequate," said Mrs. Elton. "You need to work on your inflection."

Inflection? Did Betsy have inflection? I probably didn't have inflection.

I had a sudden startling thought. Mrs. Elton didn't like boys. She didn't like Peter, she didn't like Gabriel. She thought boys were rough and stupid, which was why they couldn't read well. Mrs. Elton made them not know what they knew—just like me. She didn't like me, either, because I was more like a boy than a girl.

That was because Gentleman Jack had always wanted a boy. What if I were really his child and he was testing me to see if I could be an excellent boy?

"You were an excellent boy," said the dagger, "until we came here and you started wearing all those taming things."

In Netherby Scar I would go back to being an excellent boy. I would never make any compromises.

It was my turn. Time for the saved-up dessert. Time for the girl who was rough and daring, like a boy. Now Mrs. Elton would enjoy my discomfiture. But my verses were the best, and Paloma stood beside me, which was also the best. The verses said that the father wants to put his daughters in the round-tower of his heart. He finishes by saying:

> "And there will I keep you forever,
>> Yes, forever and a day,
> Till the walls shall crumble to ruin
>> And moulder in dust away!"

I could read the verse. I read all the words; I didn't stumble. What was Mrs. Elton's trick? What had I done wrong?

"You have memorized it!" said Mrs. Elton.

How could I have memorized it? I hadn't seen it until just now.

"Mrs. del Salto helped you memorize it," said Mrs. Elton. "That's cheating."

But Mrs. del Salto would never cheat. She was the Judge's wife.

I walked back to the desk. The smaller children looked at me from the front. I didn't look at them. They were almost too small to see. The bigger children looked at me from the back. I didn't look at them. They were almost too big to see. I sat on the bench, on the outside edge.

But at least I had a desk. I had to enjoy it. I'd only have it for today. The desk was varnished to a clear, hard shine. There was a space beneath the top of the desk, in the front, where I could put my books and slate. There was a groove running along the top where I could put my pencils and chalk.

There was a round hole in the desk, which was meant to hold an inkwell, but there was no inkwell. I held my hand beneath the hole. I could see my hand inside the desk. Paloma fit beneath the desk, and I didn't even have to squish up my legs.

Tilda leaned across Betsy and whispered—whispered to me, even though you were not supposed to whisper! "You read with inflection," she said. "Lots of inflection."

That was all Tilda could say, or else Mrs. Elton would catch her and whip out the ruler. But it was enough. No girl had ever whispered to me before, except Molly, and Molly was too young to count.

What should I do at lunchtime? I had my jacks, but I no longer had the red ball. I'd thrown it at the Brewster Boy. As I stood in the school-yard, with the cottonwood fluff drifting all around, Betsy came up to me. She handed me a square of thick, creamy paper. On it was written the word Starling.

"It's an envelope," said Betsy. "You open it like this."

I knew about envelopes, which was how I knew what to ask. "Where's the stamp?"

"You don't need a stamp," said Betsy. "Not if you're delivering it yourself."

"So you're like the stamp?" I said.

"I am not like a stamp." Betsy snatched back the envelope and took out the paper, which was covered with slanted, curly writing—the exact kind of writing that's hard to read. So I didn't mind Betsy reading it aloud. Once she had read it, I could read it, too. It was an invitation to Betsy's birthday party. There was only one word on the paper I didn't know. "RSVP?"

"It's French," said Betsy. "It means you're supposed to say if you can come."

I said nothing. I couldn't come; I would have left by then. But I couldn't tell her so.

"Thank you for the Valentine's Day card," I said.

"So, can you?" said Betsy.

"I'll ask at home." Home. How strange to say that word. I really only said it so I wouldn't have to say I'd ask the Judge and Mrs. del Salto. It was embarrassing to call them by such formal names, as though I didn't really live there.

But I wasn't going back, so maybe I didn't live there anymore. Maybe I was between spaces. Or maybe I already lived in Grandmother's house, but I just hadn't gotten there yet.

I fished out the Judge's penny and handed it to Betsy. "Thank you for hiding the dagger." Now we were even.

If all had gone as planned, Gentleman Jack was already free. Rough Ricky and the Gentlemen had held up the stagecoach. They'd have pried Gentleman Jack from his shackles. They'd have taken him from the stagecoach, just as they'd planned to take the gold on the first Day Zero.

I'd meet Rough Ricky at five o'clock. Not a moment later.

After school now, trotting down Main Street, past the burnt house and its smell of ashes and the burning feeling that made my throat clench itself into itself. But that made it hard to breathe. It was hard to choose between breathing and burning.

"Peanuts!" came the whistle of the peanut man. "Fresh, hot peanuts!"

His whistle drew me toward him, outside the General Store. There he stood, with his close-set eyes and corrugated face. "Hello!" he whistled, just the way a bird would sing it. The music of the word started up and went down. You could hear the soft sounds—the Eh and the Oh. You could hear the soft slide of the L's, you could even hear the H. A whistle can make the breathy sound of an H.

I wanted to try it myself, but whistling was bad luck, and anyway, I was sure to make a fool of myself. Which was mostly what happened when I spoke.

What about whistling for Paloma? She was coming with me to Netherby Scar. It might be useful to be able to whistle her name, and no one would think it was foolish to whistle for a dog.

"How would you whistle the name Paloma?"

There were three notes to the name Paloma. They went low, high, medium—One, Three, Two. And there were three sounds to the name: Pa-oh-ah.

I was sure I could whistle it—even though I was never sure about being sure. But I'd just be whistling for a dog, which people did all the time.

No one but the peanut man would know if I got it wrong.

It was easy. I whistled it clear and bright.

Paloma came to me in one bound—she'd only been about three feet away. She sat, which was what she was supposed to do when I called her. She also wagged her tail, even though it wasn't required.

I extended my hand and she snuffed it. She liked the Whistling. I liked the Whistling.

There came a rapping at the glass inside the General Store. It was Betsy. Was it nice of her to rap at me? I didn't know. But now she was beckoning me inside.

But even if she was being nice, I couldn't go inside. I had to keep track of the time. I had to meet Rough Ricky at five o'clock. I waved and walked on. But the opal grew heavy and cold. It was so cold, I could feel it through the smocking on my dress, even though smocking is a kind of sewing that gathers a bunch of fabric together and sews a decoration on top, which makes it thick.

I didn't need to glance down at it to know that the opal had turned dull and gray, like dirty ice. What was I not seeing, even with my excellent sight? Did the opal not like what I was doing?

Then I would do the opposite of what I was doing, which was walking away. It was only three thirty; I had time to enter the General Store.

I pulled at the door, the bell tinkled. Mr. Elton was piling cans of peas into a fearsome tower. His face was a blank. Maybe he was angry I'd hit him with a hammer. That would mean he was saving up his sorrows. But maybe he was grateful I'd saved Betsy. He'd have to be twice as grateful, though, to make up for the ungratefulness of Mrs. Elton.

Betsy and I said nothing to each other, but we found ourselves walking to the toy section. We passed the balls; I didn't look at the red ball, which was for jacks. I wasn't taking the jacks to Netherby Scar. They weren't a talisman. There was Betsy's doll from France; there was the baby doll in the blue pajamas. The mother and father dolls would never have their baby.

I'd left the dolls in the parlor; the dolls were dead. I'd broken their hearts. They'd stay dead, just as they'd been when I found them, unless someone else found them and wiped the dust from their eyes.

I'd always known I couldn't bring the baby. What I hadn't known was that making a piecrust promise would kill them. My head didn't care about killing them, but my feet did: they were taking me to the front of the store, to Mr. Elton and his tower of peas.

Betsy followed, calling after me. She watched as I made a nest of my hands and held them out to Mr. Elton. The pocket watch was an egg in the nest.

"Don't give him the watch!" said the dagger.

But Mr. Elton was already easing it from my hands, just as though it were a real egg. I'd given him the watch before I quite realized what I was doing. Or thinking of doing.

What if I could bring the baby doll to the mother and father dolls?

"You don't have time!" said the dagger. "You can't bring the doll all the way to the cottage and still meet Rough Ricky at five o'clock."

"May I help you?" said Mr. Elton.

"Can I buy something with this watch?" I said.

"Trade it for something?" said Mr. Elton.

That's what I'd meant. "Trade it for a doll." The watch was valuable, and it hadn't been stolen. It was surely worth enough to trade for a baby doll who was only made of wax and not even from France.

The dagger was right. I couldn't possibly be thinking about failing to meet Rough Ricky at five o'clock. Of thinking about walking to Netherby Scar alone.

But the opal had an opinion. It grew warm. I'd forgotten how it not only warmed my skin, but also the inside of my head. The friendly blue fire crackled in my brain.

I saw that I'd betrayed the mother and father dolls. I saw that I'd killed them with my piecrust promise, and that now I had to bring them back to life.

"They're not even alive!" said the dagger. "Don't leave Rough Ricky waiting because of something that's not alive."

Piecrust promise, I thought. I'd create a screen of words the dagger wouldn't understand. The words Piecrust Promise made one screen. The second precept of the Blue Rose made another screen. The dagger didn't understand things that rhymed.

> Keep your promises:
> T'was you that made them.
> Let not others say:
> T'was you betrayed them.

The worm of Regret lashed its tail. Did it regret that I'd be leaving buttercream cottage and the dolls and Mrs. del Salto and the Judge? Did it regret that, even now, Rough Ricky would be waiting for me by the river; and that first he'd wonder where I was; and then he'd get mad; and that finally, he'd ride off, leaving me to walk to Netherby Scar.

I could regret both things—leaving buttercream cottage and leaving Rough Ricky waiting. And then I'd have to accept my sorrows.

"Where did you get the watch?" said Mr. Elton.

"It's Gentleman Jack's," I said. "It wasn't stolen." How extremely ironic it would be if Mr. Elton thought it had been stolen, because it was the one thing I knew for sure hadn't been stolen.

Mr. Elton flipped open the watch, and—

"Do you see why you shouldn't have given it to him?" said the dagger.

I saw why. Mr. Elton was going to recognize Grandmother. He wouldn't recognize Gentleman Jack from when he was a baby—babies all look the same—but everyone knew what the Royals look like, and when Mr. Elton realized who she was, he would . . .

He would what?

All he did was draw in a soft, whistling breath. He looked at the photograph for a long time, and finally he said, "Do you know who she is?"

I knew that she was Gentleman Jack's mother. I knew she was going to be my grandmother.

"She used to live here," said Mr. Elton. "She used to be our Songbird."

That made a little earthquake inside my head. I felt I could not have understood correctly. "Here in Blue Roses?"

"Here in Blue Roses," said Mr. Elton.

"*Don't be so surprised,*" said the dagger. "*Grandmother's lived a long life and done a lot of things.*"

"But the Songbird died!" I said.

The dagger's voice was almost always the same. It could sort of shrug—mostly by slowing down the words it was saying—but its voice never really revealed what it was thinking.

There came the tiniest click of time before it said, "*She was the Songbird ages before Lyra Starling was the Songbird. She left to go to Netherby Scar. She left to get free of the tameness of Blue Roses.*"

But if Grandmother was a Songbird . . . "*Why would she want a Songbird if she's a Songbird?*"

"*Being a Songbird is like being a servant to all the Rosati, and also to the Blue Rose. But Grandmother's no servant. She's an empress, who's going to run an empire.*"

"You look remarkably like her," said Mr. Elton.

I did? I looked like Grandmother! I wished Gentleman Jack had told me—it was so extremely excellent.

Mr. Elton yo-yoed the watch up and down in his palm as though he were weighing it. "The watch is worth more than any of our dolls, and I don't have near enough change."

"Even though it doesn't go?" I said.

"Let's take a look," said Mr. Elton.

I'd always thought Mr. Elton was completely different from the Judge, but I now saw he could do little, delicate things, too. He produced a worn leather case, snapped open the fastenings. Inside gleamed tiny tools. He picked a little screwdriver, twirled at a screw, and off came the back of the watch's case. There were its insides, three wheels and lots of screws, all very small.

"You've got to clean a watch regularly," said Mr. Elton. "Otherwise the pivots get gummed up and will seize. We'll clean it and oil it." He took the whole watch apart and cleaned it with something that smelled like turpentine. He let the pieces dry, then dribbled oil on them from an eyedropper. Finally, he screwed the case back on.

"Will it go now?" I said.

"Let's see," said Mr. Elton.

"Can I wind it?" I'd had the watch all these months, and all these months I'd imagined winding it.

Mr. Elton told me to twirl the little knob on top. I wound it, I gave the watch a minute to come back to life. I held it to my ear.

"It's ticking!" The watch was warm and alive. I weighed it in my hand like a yo-yo, just as Mr. Elton had done. It was heavier now that its heart was wound up and beating.

"Perhaps," said Mr. Elton, "you'd also like to set the time."

I did want to set the time. Mr. Elton told me to pull up the knob at the top of the watch. When the knob was down, you wound it; when the knob was up, you set it.

"It's four forty-five," said Mr. Elton.

I'd known I was going to miss Rough Ricky, but still the words "four forty-five" came as a kind of thunderclap. The thunder clapped the two sides of my head together and made crumples in the part in between. My thoughts got lost in the crumples.

Mr. Elton asked if I'd like to keep the photograph. I said I would, and that I also wanted to make a copy of the emblem. I was going to have to walk to Netherby Scar. "Four forty-five!" said my brain crumples. "Four forty-five." I'd have to have a picture of the emblem so I could find Grandmother's house. Mr. Elton gave me a piece of paper and a pencil. I laid the paper on top of the watch and, with the side of the pencil, scribbled over the emblem. When I was done, I had a picture of the emblem on the paper. That was because the lines of an engraving are dug into the metal, which means that the pencil doesn't make a mark where the lines are because there's only emptiness beneath.

"Which doll do you want?" said Mr. Elton. And the way he said it felt a little as though he was saying, "Sorry for thinking you stole the candy."

"The baby doll," I said, which was a little like saying, "Sorry about the hammer and your elbow."

I wondered why Mrs. Elton didn't like me, even after I'd saved Betsy. She didn't know it was my fault I had to save her. Maybe the iron had entered her soul the minute I hit Mr. Elton.

"We have several baby dolls," said Mr. Elton.

"He's a little longer than my fingers," I said. "His pajamas are blue and his feet are bare."

"Better show me," he said.

We came first thing to the glass case of opals. The good-luck case, Betsy had told me. I turned; I stopped. I asked Mr. Elton, "Would I have enough change to buy an opal?"

"Which one would you want?" said Mr. Elton.

It was so hard to look at all the opals—not just at all the opals but at all the colors of the opals.

Mr. Elton collected all the greens for me. It took me ages to look at them all . . . but I had ages because it was already after five o'clock, sharp.

"It has to be a very valuable opal," I said.

"Green opals aren't especially valuable," said Mr. Elton.

"It has to be the greenest opal," I said.

Mr. Elton knew his opals. He selected three for me to look at. They were all green . . . but green could be so many colors. There was sea green, which was green with a dash of gray. There was teal, which was green with a dash of blue. And there was lime green, which was green mixed with a dash of sour.

"I can't tell you which to choose. You'll have to decide," said Mr. Elton.

"What green do people like the best?" I asked.

"Probably emerald green," said Mr. Elton.

Emerald green was a beautiful green. Emerald green was just the way Gentleman Jack said his eyes looked.

Mr. Elton said I could take the emerald green opal—although it wasn't truly emerald green, he kept saying—and that I'd still have some change that was due me.

Then we came to the tables of fabric. We came to the wall of knives. I'd once thought I knew everything about knives. Why some knives had jagged blades. Why some knives had curved bellies. But I couldn't understand about sharpening the dagger. The dagger couldn't be sharpened, even though Sharp was how it liked to look, especially for Gentleman Jack.

We came to the mirror. Neither of us looked at the other. That would be too embarrassing. I saw myself, though. Wild robber-girl hair, but with the snarls taken out. Bird-wing eyebrows, a face that went down into a triangle—an upside-down triangle. That meant my face was strong. I really did look like Grandmother. I couldn't feel the opal growing warmer through the scarlet smocking on my dress. I saw it in the mirror, though, And most important, the opal lay against the scarlet smocking, blinking and winking a fierce, crackling blue, as though it were smiling at me.

The opal wanted me to bring the baby doll to the dollhouse.

Mr. Elton and I passed the table of boots and turned toward the table of tools and the barrels of candy, which meant we definitely didn't look at each other. We passed the hammer with the red handle, which meant we definitely kept not looking at each other.

Now past the buckets and shovels to the toys. We passed the blocks and the purple yo-yo. We passed the balls and the jacks. We came to the bears with the outstretched arms that said, "Come feel how soft we are."

Above the bears, on the highest shelf, stood the baby. Even Mr. Elton had to stand on a stool, and a moment later, the baby was smooth and warm in my hands. That's because he was made of wax. Wax was warmer than china.

He still wore his blue pajamas, his feet were still bare. I was glad they were bare. That meant I could warm him up in the blanket with the blue stars and the fringe all around.

When we went to the front again, Mr. Elton said, "A parcel to make up, Betsy."

Betsy looked at me, she looked at the doll. She said nothing about china or France or wardrobes full of clothes. She measured out brown paper and a length of string to make the doll into a little parcel. She knew just how much paper to tear from the roll, just how much string to cut from the spool. I pictured her, again, wrapping the dagger, choosing the white-on-white paper and the white-on-white ribbon.

"Don't forget about the RSVP," said Betsy. Betsy really loved France.

"I hope I can," I said, which wasn't entirely a lie. I would have liked to; I just knew I couldn't.

Then the package was in my hands, and the baby was in the package. I no longer had the watch, but the seconds started to tick away inside my head. "Hurry, hurry," said the seconds.

☾ ✳ ☽

Later, when I crossed the bridge, I dropped the invitation over the edge. It was spring, the river was fast. It swept the invitation round the bend and out of sight. The current would soon pull it under. The river overflowed its banks, running up to the willows and pooling in their roots.

I thought about the song with the mother and father. Soon I'd be leaving the Indigo Heart, which was where my mother and father lived—if they still lived. But I didn't care. They'd wanted me to die. Soon I'd be leaving the River Jordan and the milk and honey. I didn't care about that, either. The River Jordan was deep and wide, but the milk and honey was always on the other side, so you could never get it. When I got to Netherby Scar, Gentleman Jack would let me have coffee and sugar. That was better than milk and honey.

But first, I'd look at Grandmother and see my face, and Grandmother would look at me and see her own face.

I picked at my thumb. The blood from my thumb was inside my mouth. It was full of cold iron. I was bright and alive.

Crowbars and Chisels

✝ I OPENED THE FRONT DOOR. I didn't have to step in to know that the cottage was empty. That's because it was extra cold. Neither the Judge nor Mrs. del Salto was inside. When people are inside the cottage, they warm it up with their beating hearts and breathing lungs.

I didn't like it being cold. I tried to warm it up. I turned the welcome mat around. Now the word WELCOME was right-side up to any visitor. Now the sunflower was smiling. That felt warmer, but it was still pretty cold. The cottage felt the cold, you could tell. Its timbers whined, huddling themselves closer, for comfort.

Paloma and I stood in the foyer, listening to the voices of the timbers. They strained against their own nails. "I wonder," I said. Paloma pressed against my leg. Thank the stars I could speak when Paloma was there. It's easier to work things through when you can speak aloud. Paloma gazed up at me. She was a very good listener. "When you bring blankets and keys and tablecloths to the dollhouse, they appear in the cottage. But what if you take something away from the dollhouse?" The pocket watch, I thought, but I didn't want to say its name aloud. "Will the same thing disappear from the human house?"

The grandfather clock was the human-size version of the pocket watch. What if the grandfather clock had vanished?

"Such nonsense!" said the dagger.

But I had to look, so into the corridor we went. I scraped myself around the gleaming library moldings. There was the clock, quite un-vanished and even more present than usual. The pendulum was swinging and the clock was ticking. As I stood gazing, it struck the half hour. The chimes were out of tune with themselves, but what can you expect when you haven't spoken for so long?

Mrs. del Salto must have gotten happier and set time going again. Setting time going wasn't the kind of thing you did when you were sad. When you were sad, you wanted to keep everything the same. You didn't want to move ahead.

The dolls lay in the dollhouse parlor, still and dead, just as when I first found them. What had I done to make them come alive, way back on the first Day Zero? I'd picked them up. I remembered how the mother doll had lain in my hand, slack jointed and dusty.

Would her eyes open if I sat her up? I'd better dust her first. She wouldn't want dust in her eyes. I wiped her eyes, then licked my finger and dabbed at the dust in the corners. Was that what I'd done before?

I sat her up, but her eyes didn't open. I'd killed her too completely. The father doll's eyes didn't open. The two of them sat side by side, heavy and dead.

"I brought you a dog." I could speak because of Paloma.

They did not come alive.

"I brought you a collar."

They did not come alive.

"I brought you a baby."

Click. The mother doll opened her eyes. "Starling!" she said.

Click. The father doll opened his eyes. "Starling!"

I'd said what they wanted me to say.

"Our baby?" said the mother doll.

"Our baby?" said the father doll.

I pulled the parcel apart. Gentleman Jack's green opal tumbled out first. It didn't glimmer like my star opal, but it would when Gentleman Jack put it on. The green opal hung on a long chain, way too long for me but it would be just right for Gentleman Jack.

After the green opal, the baby boy tumbled from the package. His feet were bare. His eyes were closed. I tilted him up. His eyes opened. He was perfect. His eyes opened and closed.

"I long to hold him." The mother doll swung her right arm up, then her left arm.

I laid the baby in the mother doll's arms. He was almost too big for her.

"He's a fine big boy," said the father doll. "Our very own boy."

"He's beautiful," said the mother doll.

"His eyes open and close," I said.

"They open when you tilt him up," said the mother doll.

"He has real eyelashes," said the father doll. "Not painted."

"My heart is about to shatter," said the mother doll.

I'd thought it was only sadness that could shatter a heart. "He's made of wax. He's not fragile; his heart can't break."

The dolls walked up the stairs to the baby's room. In the human world, it was Isaac's room. In the doll world, it was the baby's room.

They took an age. I could have lifted them so quickly, but you couldn't just grab and lift a doll, not when it was alive.

"Not *alive!*" said the dagger.

I reached into the parlor and peeled back the carpet. There lay the photograph of Magda and Isaac I'd hidden, back when it was still winter. Back when I'd broken the yellow cup and learned about glue. I'd leave the photograph on the bed, where the Judge would be sure to see it. Even though Mrs. del Salto had started accepting her sorrows, she'd probably never climb the attic stairs again.

But she'd like to have the photograph. Then she wouldn't have to be philosophical anymore.

The mother doll laid the baby in the cradle; she rocked the cradle, and it called out, light and rushy with air. Willow was good for a cradle. The word Willow had the sound of wind in it. The wood was light and resisted shocks easily. It was weak for its weight, but that didn't matter. It was good for a baby, because babies were light.

The baby liked the cradle. You could tell because that's when he came alive. He kicked and stretched and opened his little rosebud mouth.

"He has real hair," said the mother doll. "He has a face like a peach."

"Peaches and cream," I said.

The father doll tucked the blanket in around the baby, especially his feet.

"Do you want me to shut the house?"

"Please," said the mother doll. "We would like to be alone together."

Alone together. Those were very strange words to say at the same time. They contradicted each other. *Alone together.*

It was ironic that you could say them both and they made sense.

☾ ✳ ☽

"May I?" said the Judge from behind the door, even though the door wasn't locked. Even though he could turn the handle and push the door open.

"You may," I said.

This was really the last time I'd see the Judge. Later, I'd creep out the window and down the indigo tree.

The Judge opened the door but didn't come in. He spoke from the landing. He spoke across the threshold.

"Gentleman Jack has escaped," he said.

"Oh?" I sounded surprised.

"I told you Gentleman Jack was to be conveyed by stage to the capitol."

I was surprised I sounded surprised.

"I told you what day the Marshals were going to take him."

The Judge was going to tell me to leave. I knew from the poking feeling in my stomach. I was going to leave anyway, but I still had the poking feeling.

Paloma raised her head and sniffed the air. She was sniffing the Judge's voice. It sounded different and it must have smelled different, too.

"The stage was held up by a gang of men wearing masks," said the Judge. "A gang of men with crowbars and saws and chisels."

Outside the window, against the sky, unfurled ribbons of starlings.

"I knew about the stagecoach and so did Mrs. del Salto," said the Judge. "So did the Sheriff and the Deputy."

The starlings furled like a fan. The fan opened and closed, opened and closed. The starlings exploded themselves into the sky, bursting into fireworks. No, not exactly like fireworks. Once you explode fireworks, they can never be un-exploded. They can never come back together.

"Only one other person knew," said the Judge.

But an explosion of starlings could un-explode itself. The starlings could come back together, like iron filings drawn to a magnet.

The Judge didn't step out of the room; he'd never entered it. The doorknob was for arriving, but it was also for leaving. The Judge turned the knob; the door clicked shut.

I stared at the cool, blank face of the door. The Judge had opened my door but he hadn't come in. The starlings outside were attracted to one another by some unknown force, just as iron was to magnets or planets to the sun. But I wasn't attracted to anybody. Maybe I had no round-tower in my heart, not like the father in the poem. The Judge had turned the doorknob and closed the door. There was no force holding us together. There had used to be, but it was broken.

I'd broken it.

No one called me for dinner. The room grew dark. The starlings melted into the night.

I thought of how I'd turned round and round in the attic, making it fit my shape. I thought of the great craggy spaces of the hideout. I could turn around in it a million times, but it would never fit me. Soon I'd come to Grandmother's house. I'd have to make it fit my shape. I'd have to start all over again.

I wore my britches now. They had good pockets. They held Grandmother's photograph and the copy of the emblem. But my coat pockets were better. They were deeper. They wouldn't crumple something like a photograph. My pockets were waiting for me by Rough Ricky's willow, packed with Gentleman Jack's wanted-poster face, the magnifying glass, and the rest of the butterscotch. I wore the opal pendants beneath my blue robber-girl shirt.

The Judge would check the butterscotch-thermometer. He'd see that the butterscotch-mercury was down to zero. Maybe he'd think that when your mercury is down to zero, that means you're dead. Maybe he'd think that was about right, because to him and Mrs. del Salto I was as good as dead.

I couldn't bring Paloma with me. Now I knew the Judge slept with one ear open. His open ear would hear me creeping downstairs, which also meant he'd hear Paloma.

"I wish you could climb down the tree, Paloma," I said.

Paloma tilted her head into a question mark. I wouldn't tell her I had to leave her. I knelt and rubbed her ears, and she licked me. She was getting friendly, just as I was leaving.

It was my fault. I hadn't exercised judgment. If only I'd left her downstairs, she could have pressed the anti-Rough-Ricky lever and left through the dog door.

I felt my voice go liquid. I swallowed my next words, even though I didn't know what they were going to be. Funny how sometimes you don't know what you have to say until you say it. If I spoke, my voice would run out of my eyes.

I opened my cupboard-bed door. At the end was the wardrobe bit, where there was a space for hanging clothes. The wardrobe burst with scarlet frills and lavender velvet and garnet buttons; but despite the scarlet and lavender and garnet, the whole of the wardrobe shone like the inside of an almond.

Mrs. del Salto had filled up the wardrobe, which made it hard to think cold, hard thoughts. But I had to. Hard cold thoughts would keep my voice from running out my eyes.

I'd opened the window earlier so the Judge couldn't hear me pull at the sash. I climbed into the indigo tree and dislodged a chorus of small birds. Surely the Judge couldn't hear that! I'd betrayed the Judge by telling Rough Ricky about the plans to transfer Gentleman Jack. I'd betrayed Rough Ricky by buying the doll. And now I had to walk to Netherby Scar alone, which probably meant I'd betrayed myself.

The clay road was red because it was filled with iron. My blood was red because it was filled with iron. Iron is magnetic. But I was stronger than magnets.

Usually when you pull, you have something to pull on. But the road tugged me in the wrong direction, so I had to pull at myself. The red road tugged at me like a giant elastic—

"*It's not an elastic!*" said the dagger.

It didn't matter what it was. I was strong. I pulled until I gained the far side of the road.

The dolls had been wrong. I was stronger than the Indigo Heart. I'd snapped the elastic.

"*Not an elastic!*" said the dagger.

It took six days to walk to Netherby Scar. Or, really, six nights. It was safer to travel at night and hide myself in the bluestem grass by day. It wasn't safe to be a girl alone in the Territories. Was this why Gentleman Jack wanted a boy, so his son wouldn't have to dive into the grass whenever he heard voices or when a train barreled by? I wasn't exactly sure why it was dangerous to be a girl. You could knock a boy on the head just as easily. You could bloody his nose; you could rip off his opal pendant.

"*Can you tell you're getting wilder?*" said the dagger.

"I can tell I'm getting hungrier," I said.

Sometimes I thought about my talismans and wondered if I'd chosen the right three. Maybe I should have brought Oakheart's collar, just in case—

"In case of what?" said the dagger.

In case I was caught again and taken straight to Buffalo Bend to testify. I'd need the beads as proof I'd been to the Fair.

Maybe I should have brought my key to buttercream cottage, just in case—

"In case of what?" said the dagger.

I didn't answer. I'd never go back.

Was this what it was like to go on a pilgrimage? Walking for days and days to get to a sacred place? Usually people went to Blue Roses, but I was going away. Maybe I was going on an anti-pilgrimage.

That would be wild.

I followed the railroad. I hid in the grass. I slept in my coat. I was glad Rough Ricky had suggested I bring it with me. I was warm enough during the days, but it was chilly at night. I'd decided to make fires only in the middle of the day, when it was too light for anyone to notice. But it turned out I couldn't make any fires at all. It would be too easy to set the grass on fire. I didn't have the tools to dig a clearing and I couldn't pull up the grasses. Their roots went down longer than I was tall.

I caught grasshoppers. A person can eat grasshoppers when she's really hungry. She has to skewer them, then rotate the legs and the wings until they come off. Legs and wings can choke a person.

The person slashes at the legs and wings with the dagger, but the dagger has grown dangerously dull. The person cannot sharpen it, even when she holds the whetstone at twenty-two degrees.

The grasshoppers make her chew hard. Raw grasshoppers are mostly crunch. She has to listen to the dagger saying, *"There's a lot of iron in grasshoppers."*

She is sick of iron.

My britches had been too small, now they were getting big again.

"It's you, getting smaller," said the dagger. *"Just like you were with Gentleman Jack."*

Why was I smaller with Gentleman Jack? Was it because he didn't fill me up with information, like about Grandmother being a Songbird?

"No one cares anymore," said the dagger. *"No one cares that Grandmother was a Songbird."*

But I cared. All the times I'd recited the task rhyme, wondering how to get a Songbird, and there she was—she had always been tucked away in the lid of the pocket watch.

It was strange to think that Grandmother had been a Songbird—no, she was still a Songbird, even if she no longer whistled praises to the Blue Rose.

She'd been hiding in plain sight.

You couldn't see Netherby Scar right away. You couldn't see it until you came to the edge of it, which was because Netherby Scar did not go up. It went down. It was built into a canyon.

It was the opposite of what the Judge had said about Blue Roses: that a city set on a hill cannot be hidden. Netherby Scar was very hidden.

I saw only one person. He was pacing the edge of the canyon, smoking a cigar. When it got dark you'd be able to see the glowing ash. The land that surrounded the canyon had no trees or mountains; you'd be able to see the cigar a long way.

The railroad didn't go into the canyon, though. It turned into a bridge and flew over. That made sense. A train would have a hard time climbing into a canyon and out again. I drew near the railroad bridge. Great wooden trestles pierced the mouth of the canyon; the tracks sat on top of them.

The cigar man stopped me. "This is a path." He had a black eye. You could tell he'd had it for a while. It had turned yellow and sulky.

He didn't mean the path the railroad made over the canyon. He meant a path that led into the canyon. It was broad and smooth, flowing from the canyon's edge, past the trestles. You could ride a horse down the path, or even drive a carriage if you were a very good driver and kept the wheels dead center. You could drive right into the town of Netherby Scar, which hulked on the canyon floor below.

"I built the path," said the cigar man. "I get paid for the path."

But I had no money. I didn't even have the penny I'd put in the collection plate. I should never have given it away. I had my opal pendant, but I couldn't trade away my good luck.

I had Gentleman Jack's opal pendant, but I couldn't trade away his good luck, either.

"Two cents," said the cigar man.

I didn't have two cents.

The man shrugged and went back to pacing.

I'd have to climb. I had gravity on my side. I walked along the edge of the canyon, peering over. Perhaps the town had once fit into the palm of the canyon, but now it had grown too big. The newer buildings heaved themselves up the canyon walls, where they lay sprawled and gasping.

The good thing was that the canyon walls weren't straight up and down. They angled out as they went toward the bottom. I turned around and eased myself over the edge. I slid my feet onto little crumbles of stone. I held on to scrubby trees and roots that grew from the canyon walls.

When the walls became too steep, I had to move sideways, like a crab. But crabs scuttled and scuttling was fast. I was slow.

I felt the cigar man's eyes on my back. They pressed at me, until a sound came hallooing and bouncing into the Scar, reverberating in fingernail crevices, off razor-blade shelves. The sound doubled and tripled and clapped at my ears.

It was the cigar man, laughing. He'd seen what I'd just seen, which was that I couldn't climb out again even if I wanted to. I had gotten to where I was by hanging from a root-hand, dropping to a scribbly shelf, and pressing my fingers into a cleft. The root-hand had bent down with me, but once I let it go, it sprang up. I couldn't reach it anymore.

I pressed my cheek into the rock face. It panted back, cold and greasy. I un-scuttled just a little farther. My feet were amazed to find a shelf generous enough to hold them both.

My heart pounded against the rock. But I felt no answering heart-beat, as I had in the Indigo Heart. Maybe this place wasn't really alive. Maybe it was the place of the dead.

I lay against the wall of the Scar. The slant was now less steep. The wall lay at about a forty-five-degree angle; you could rest at forty-five degrees.

I was lucky to have gotten there, because that's when the train arrived. It shrieked a warning and rattled the tracks and shook the flesh off the canyon walls. The train was a streak of darkness; it was sparks flashing from the rails; it was bursts of earth and rock. A couple of stones hit me, hard. I flung my arms over my head. You could do that at forty-five degrees.

The train screamed and shrieked itself away. I lay for a few more minutes against the rock. The rock was yellow rather than the beige and pink of the first and second floors of the world. It smelled like rotten eggs, which was also the smell of sulfur, which was the smell of the underworld, which was appropriate because Netherby Scar was built into the underworld.

I ducked beneath a ledge and came face-to-face with a cluster of nests. They were cliff swallows' nests, hanging like grapes from the underside of the ledge. They were empty, even though it was May. The cliff swallows should have returned already. They were probably late because this place—the place of the dead—was very cold. It was the kind of cold that got into your bones. Rough Ricky had been right about bringing a coat.

By the time the cliff swallows returned, I would have met Grandmother. By then I'd be at home.

Now I was near. I was very thirsty. When I reached the bottom, I'd have a long, refreshing drink of sulfur. I climbed among the houses that bloomed from the canyon walls. They were fine brick houses, the color of sin.

"*Sin doesn't have a color!*" said the dagger.

Past the yellow houses now and toward a tower, which I thought must mark the center of town. The tower turned out to be a shrine, which was not so surprising, although the rest of the town center did surprise me. It looked nothing like Blue Roses. But why should it be like Blue Roses? It wasn't a city on a hill. Why should it be made of neat parallel streets fronted with pink stone buildings? Why shouldn't it be made of tilty wooden structures crammed along alleyways? Why shouldn't the alleyways wriggle every which way? Why shouldn't they be a howling of mangy dogs and gangs of half-naked children?

In one way, though, it was like Blue Roses: it had a Main Street. There were no street signs, but I recognized it right away because it was wider and less wriggly, and because the buildings were bigger and most of them were shops, and because it was the only street lined with sandbags to keep people out of the muck.

But there were no street signs, not that it mattered. I didn't know the name of Grandmother's street, but the picture of her emblem was in my pocket. When I showed it to someone, they'd tell me where Grandmother lived. That's because Grandmother was Royal, and everyone knew them. I'd ask at one of the saloons, even though they had no names, just the word Saloon painted onto the walls themselves. Everywhere I looked, the word stared out at me with its two owl eyes: SalOOn.

I chose a saloon at random, pushed through the door, and found myself wishing Paloma were with me. I wished for her hot, wet breath. I wished for her kisses, which she doled out as sparingly as silver dollars.

But if wishes were horses, beggars would ride, which meant there was no point wishing for what I couldn't have.

"*Wishes can't be horses!*" said the dagger.

"*They can if I want them to,*" I said. "*Anyway, stop sticking me with exclamation marks.*"

"*You stick someone with a blade,*" said the dagger.

The saloon looked different from the Sapphire. It was made of splintery dark wood that had shriveled into itself, like a plum left sitting too long. There were plenty of women walking about. They were young enough, and pretty enough, but I felt as though someone had crumpled their faces like paper bags, then smoothed them out again. You couldn't really see the creases but you could tell the women were old, beneath their skin.

I stopped the prettiest one. She'd be the most like Flora. I took out the picture of the emblem and waited.

"No begging!" she said.

I wasn't begging! I was probably doing the exact opposite, since I was looking for the Royals, and the Royals lived like kings, not paupers. "The design is my Grandmother's emblem."

"I don't know about no emblem," said the woman. She stretched her lips into a smile. She had surprisingly nice teeth, but her smile was too rubbery.

"Can you tell me where she lives?" I said.

"Beats me," said the woman.

"But everyone knows my Grandmother," I said. "Her last name is Royal. Everyone knows her emblem."

"You sit here a spell," she said, "and wait for my boys to come visiting. There's nothing they don't know about emblems."

I didn't like the way she said this. I stepped back, but she grabbed my wrist, stretching her lips again into that rubbery smile. This was one of the things about being a girl I didn't understand: girls had to be careful of boys who came visiting.

I couldn't throw the dagger anymore, but I could reach for it. My right hand was still very quick. The dagger all but leapt from the sheath. I pressed it to the woman's wrist. Now came the thin line of blood; now she didn't smile.

"*See!*" said the dagger. "*I'm still sharp!*"

"*You're not,*" I said. "*It's just that the skin on people's wrists is thin.*"

I chose one more person to help me find Grandmother. I chose an old man sitting on the street because he had only one leg. I could outrun him and out-kick him, and out-everything him. I showed the old man the emblem but held it out of reach.

"Can't see it too good," he said.

But I wasn't going to lean in closer, not so he could grab me.

"Where can I find the Sheriff?" I should have thought of this before. The Sheriff here would know Grandmother and Gentleman Jack, just the way the Sheriff in the Indigo Heart knew the Judge.

"Sheriff?" said the old man. "The last Sheriff got his badge at eleven o'clock in the forenoon and he was dead by lunch. T'ain't too healthy to be sheriff around here."

Quick as a lizard's tongue, his hand snapped out and grabbed my ankle. I swallowed back my surprise. I turned my surprise into a boot to the face. I turned my surprise into a crunch. But he laughed—he laughed! His crab-apple fingers caught at the blood streaming from his nose. He lapped it from his fingers and laughed.

There I was, stuck in Netherby Scar. I was in the town center, and the town center was in the palm of the canyon. And the palm of the canyon was a scribble of lines, like the palm of a hand, but not nearly as organized. Think, Starling! Grandmother's house was made of yellow bricks. I'd passed through a clump of yellow-brick houses on my way to Main Street. I could walk back to the clump, or I could—

It was easy to find the Shrine in this town of humpback houses. All I had to do was look up. It was easy to slip inside the Shrine, easy to talk to the priestess, because she spoke to me first. "No weapons shall be allowed in this place, dedicated to the Blue Rose," she said, in a bored sort of way. "Surrender them here, or they shall fail to prosper."

The opal blazed into warmth. That was how it spoke to me, wasn't it? It had spoken to me three times before, twice on the Feast of the Blue Rose and once in the General Store. It spoke by growing cold and also by growing hot. Cold was for Stop. Warm was for Go.

It had grown cold when I'd been deciding to sneak the dagger into the Blue Rose's Shrine. Cold was for Stop: don't sneak in the dagger!

It had grown hot when I was deciding to drop the penny into the collection plate. Hot was for Go: give up the penny!

"You think the opal wanted you to put the penny into the collection plate?" said the dagger.

"Yes," I said. "It kept growing hotter when I hesitated."

"But now we know you can't trust the opal," said the dagger. "We know you should have kept the penny."

"Because of the cigar man?" Of course, the dagger didn't want me to trust anyone except itself, and Gentleman Jack and Rough Ricky of course.

"Because of the cigar man."

"But the cigar man wanted two pennies," I said.

"You should have kept Betsy's penny, too," said the dagger.

But Betsy had given me the penny in exchange for the dagger. The rule about knives and pennies was immutable, which now I knew meant it wasn't a rule you could change. I didn't know what would happen if someone returned your dagger and you didn't give them back their penny, but it was bound to be bad.

The opal had grown hot when I was deciding whether to trade the watch for the baby doll. Hot was for Go: bring the baby doll to the mother and father dolls! And now it was hot again and blue flames lapped at the margins of my mind.

I reached for the dagger.

"Don't leave me!" said the dagger.

"But you're failing to prosper." I handed the dagger to the priestess.

She was monumentally unsurprised. She accepted it, her face as bland as rice pudding, and directed me to the stairs that led to the tower. There were slim, pointy openings all around the tower, so I could look in any direction. I looked back the way I'd come. I saw the houses at once, the clump of yellow bricks, panting up the canyon wall. Now to find eleven chimneys, all streaming with smoke. But it was dusk, and dusk and smoke look a lot alike. Quick, before it got too dark.

Four chimneys, three chimneys, eleven chimneys—good! Quick now, look at the streets. There was a street parallel to Main Street that went straight to the house with eleven chimneys.

Back to the priestess now, who returned the dagger. *"Please be sure to inform me when I start to prosper,"* said the dagger bitterly.

Back on the streets, glancing up at the canyon rim. There was the cigar man, his mouth making a hot, glowing O.

I looked away, but the glow had attached itself to my eyes. On I walked, through a maze of scummy streets. The red light stayed in my eyes like a stain. These streets were worse than the streets below the belt line of Blue Roses. They were gray and sticky and clogged with people who seemed only half alive.

I made my way toward Grandmother's house. I couldn't easily lose sight of it, because it peered over the crookback shoulders of the other houses. It stood very still, as though its bones ached.

"Houses don't have bones," said the dagger.

But something was wrong. None of the chimneys were puffing with smoke.

"No smoke when it's warm," said the dagger.

"You said they were always puffing." And anyway, it wasn't warm. It was spring on the first floor of the world, but not here, not in the cellar of the world. Or maybe the cellar below the cellar.

Or maybe the underworld.

There were only two steps up to the door. I pressed the doorbell. The aching bones shook themselves, gave a tinny ring.

Feet came to the door. The door opened but only a crack: it was on a short chain. A face peered through the crack.

"So?" said the woman, but when she saw me, she unchained the door and opened it a little farther so I could see all of her face. She had black hair, like the photograph of the woman in the pocket watch. But she couldn't be Grandmother. Grandmother was old and would have white hair.

She stepped back and opened the door wider. "You might as well come in," she said.

Grandmother's House

✝ THE WOMAN AND I STOOD IN THE FOYER. We
stood on the floor I'd imagined so often. It was black and white, all
right, but it wasn't marble. It was paint. You could see the grain of the
wood through the black-and-white squares. I'd never seen marble, but
I'd never confuse it with paint. Marble is shiny.

There was no marble, and also, there was no table.

"Where's the table?" I said.

"There is no table," said the dagger.

"Where's the drawer?" I said.

"There is no drawer," said the dagger.

"Where's the key?"

"The key's in Grandmother's pocket," said the dagger.

"Where's Grandmother?" I said.

"That's Grandmother," said the dagger.

Grandmother looked different from what I'd imagined. She had young hair but an old face. Beneath her oldness, though, she looked familiar, with her square jaw and quick, round eyes. Maybe she looked familiar because I looked like her. Mr. Elton said I did. I was recognizing myself when I got older.

The floor was painted and Grandmother was painted. There were pink rouge circles on her cheeks—I knew rouge was a kind of people paint—and her lips were dark as damson jelly. She had two moles, which she had blotted out with beige paint.

She wanted everything that was pale on her face to be bright and everything that was bright on her face to be pale. But you couldn't really blot out moles that stuck up from your chin like little hills.

Was that what Songbirds did? Did they paint their faces? That seemed surprising.

"Come on, Girl," said Grandmother. "I don't have all day."

I followed her out of the foyer, which went straight into the sitting room. I knew it was the sitting room because of the crimson velvet sofas and chairs. But there was no corridor leading there.

"Where's the corridor?" I said.

"There is no corridor," said the dagger.

"Don't you need a corridor?"

"You don't need a corridor."

The sitting room was full of people, and aside from me and Grandmother, the people were all men. Some sat on the floor because there was no more room on the sofas or chairs. Everything was different from what I'd expected. I'd expected a table, but there was no table. I'd expected a corridor, but there was no corridor. I'd expected a chair, but they were all sat-on. I didn't expect the men, but there they sat—and lounged and lay—pouring drinks from cut-glass decanters and playing cards and billiards.

"*Who are the men?*" I said.

"*They pay for living in Grandmother's house,*" said the dagger. "*She's practicing for when she builds her Grand Hotel and the rest of her empire.*"

I'd expected Grandmother to touch my hand; I expected her hand to feel like silk. I expected her to say, "This is my girl, returned from the road. This is my girl, bright as a star."

Instead, she said, "Go sit with your friend."

I had no friends, but my gaze traced the direction of her pointing finger. There sat Rough Ricky, the Brewster Boy, and a couple of the Gentlemen near a small, sullen fire. "Keep him company," said Grandmother, "and in the name of the stars, keep him quiet."

Grandmother meant the Brewster Boy.

It was a long walk to the end of the room. Lots of people had walked on the carpet. It was scraped down to the matting, scraped down almost to zero. The Brewster Boy stood up before I reached him. His words tumbled out every which way.

"I went to see Gentleman Jack," said the Brewster Boy. "Just like you said, and I got me in with Gentleman Jack. I ain't so dumb as what you think."

"That would hardly be possible," I said, and as I spoke, I heard an echo of the Judge's voice, except mine was meaner. I'd never seen the Brewster Boy without a hat. I hated his thin, slippery hair.

"I'll get me some bloody hands, too." The Brewster Boy's eyes were shiny and out of focus. They went every which way, just like his words.

"Gentleman Jack doesn't have bloody hands," I said.

"Why does he wear them gloves?" said the Brewster Boy.

"Because he's fancy," I said.

"I bet he has bloody hands," said the Brewster Boy.

"The boy's very enthusiastic," said Rough Ricky. "He'll learn."

I didn't want the Brewster Boy to learn. He was too enthusiastic. He was enthusiastically sitting in a crimson velvet chair, which meant I had to sit on the floor. I leaned my forehead against Rough Ricky's chair. The velvet poked against my forehead. Velvet in Netherby Scar wasn't as soft as velvet in Blue Roses.

The sitting room was crimson. The dollhouse dining room was crimson. The father doll had said that crimson is a happy color.

I waited to be happy.

"I thought we agreed," said Rough Ricky. "Five o'clock, by the river."

I'd have to wait until later to be happy.

"I couldn't get free," I said.

"Lies and betrayal!" said the dagger.

But the dolls would call it something else. They'd say that the feeling of wanting to get the baby doll was a magnet. They'd say the feeling of wanting to make them happy was a magnet. They'd say that's what made me stay longer in the Indigo Heart.

"Gentleman Jack told me to find you," said Rough Ricky. "I went all the way back to Blue Roses."

"You did!" Maybe Gentleman Jack really wanted me! Maybe when he saw me, he'd say, "This is my girl, bright as a star."

"We couldn't leave you behind." Rough Ricky's kerchief lay in an ashy band around his neck; the bottom half of his face was cleaner than the top. "It would be asking for trouble." Behind him, the fire gnarled at a half-chewed log. His face was heavy; his mustache was dark; his scars were white.

"What trouble?" I said.

"Trouble from the Blue Rose," said Rough Ricky.

"Why does the Blue Rose care about me?" I said.

"Ask Jack," said Rough Ricky. "He's the one who craved a boon of her."

"She spat in his eye," I said.

"She did more than that," said Rough Ricky.

"What else did she do?" I said.

But Rough Ricky wouldn't say.

"What kind of trouble?" I said.

Rough Ricky wouldn't say.

I must have been asleep, but I couldn't remember. There was a blank of time, then someone dragged me to my feet. Someone wrenched my arms behind me.

"Where were you on Friday?" said Gentleman Jack. "When you were supposed to meet Rough Ricky?"

I stood on my tiptoes, easing the wrench in my shoulders. It was the same kind of wrenching the Sheriff had done to Gentleman Jack on that first Day Zero, when Gentleman Jack tried to escape.

Everything was the same in the sitting room. "I have enough trouble without you up and disappearing." The candles still burned, the men still played cards and drank and spat. Except now Gentleman Jack was here.

"You are never," he said, "to leave this house without telling me where you're going."

Was it because of the trouble from the Blue Rose? But why would the Blue Rose give Gentleman Jack trouble about me? Why would anyone care where I was? No one had ever cared before, back when we lived in the hideout.

I was just the Robber Girl. I was just the girl who'd been abandoned in the wilderness. "I have something for you," I said. Gentleman Jack dropped my arms; I turned to face him. He ruffled his fingers—ruffled them toward himself. "Give it to me!" said his fingers. His fingers knew I'd brought butterscotch.

I fished the bag of butterscotch from my pocket.

"Late as usual," said Gentleman Jack. "Don't tell me the Judge delayed you again."

"I have something even better for you." I would not talk about the Judge and lateness. I twitched the green opal pendant up and over my head. "It's the most valuable opal in all of the Indigo Heart." That was so it would match his valuable green eyes.

"It's your good-luck opal," I said. Gentleman Jack reached for it.

When people are surprised, their eyebrows go up and their eyes go wide. Gentleman Jack's eyebrows went up. Gentleman Jack's eyes were already so round you wouldn't think they could get any rounder.

You'd be wrong.

I liked seeing Gentleman Jack being surprised. It showed I'd done something good. When people are surprised, they drop their jaw. The more they're surprised, the more they drop their jaw.

But Gentleman Jack didn't drop his jaw. Of course—I hadn't been exercising judgment. How could I have forgotten that Gentleman Jack's best smile never showed his teeth?

Gentleman Jack stared at the opal. "An opal should be bright."

Gentleman Jack was surprised, but he was surprised in the wrong direction. I could fix that, though. "It needs to warm up to you," I said. How strange to know more than Gentleman Jack. "It matches your eyes, which means it will get warm and bright when you wear it."

I wouldn't think about how green opals were especially common. How they weren't especially valuable.

Now at last, Gentleman Jack dropped the chain around his neck. The opal remained cool and dull and gray. It was like a fish eye.

We waited. The opal was a fish eye.

What made a fish eye so fishy? Maybe it was because the pupil in a fish's eye never changed, which made them seem as though they didn't care about anything. You couldn't even always tell if they were dead or alive.

But you could tell that the opal was dead.

It was a fish eye.

A fish eye.

A fish—

Gentleman Jack made a sort of shrug with his mouth. He turned around. He walked away from me. The opal was a dead fish eye, but still he wore it. Still, he walked away from me.

I awoke to a rattle and growl that sent me sitting upright, my heart thumping against my ribs. It's only a train, I told myself as my thoughts caught up with my heart. I was still in the sitting room; Gentleman Jack and Rough Ricky were asleep in their chairs; the Brewster Boy lay asleep on the floor.

It was almost light. I rose and stretched. My shoulders remembered Gentleman Jack. *"Let's find the exits,"* I said.

"You don't need exits in Grandmother's house," said the dagger.

"You always need exits," I said.

The sitting room led to the dining room. It had dark wood walls and a dark wood table. There was a door off the dining room, but I didn't open it. It was set with heavy panels that said "I'm private. Keep out!" The dining room led into the kitchen. I hardly recognized the blue enamel stove Gentleman Jack had described so often. It was all smeary with grease and chicken carcasses. At the end of the kitchen was a door, set with a window. It overlooked a weedy yard, strewn with bottles and a couple of mismatched boots.

Except it didn't open. It was nailed shut.

The house was more straight-ahead than I'd imagined. No, not straight-ahead. It was narrow. I thought about what made it seem so narrow, and then I realized: except for the foyer, there were no in-between spaces. There were no corridors or landings. There were no spaces to help you get used to the next space.

You couldn't be a thief in this house. It was a good house to live in if you expected an attack. There were no places to hide.

There came a swish of skirts and Grandmother's voice. "Already up, Girl? Excellent."

I liked the word Excellent.

"You'll help with the morning chores."

Chores were excellent. They were like orders. I liked it when

Gentleman Jack gave me orders. I liked knowing what to do.

Grandmother led me to the door with the heavy panels. The door that said "I'm private. Keep out!" Grandmother lit a candle because her house didn't have fire running in its walls. The candlelight glinted off blue and silver bed hangings.

"I keep it ready with all the things he likes," said Grandmother. "A bar of his favorite soap. You can smell it if you like. But don't touch the cravats. He's very particular about his neckwear."

Gentleman Jack was particular about his neckwear, but he wore frills, not cravats.

"Who's He?" I said.

"John," said Grandmother. "Who else?"

"Lord John?"

"Don't play dumb with me, Girl," said Grandmother.

But I didn't need to play dumb. Gentleman Jack said I came by it naturally.

Grandmother showed me Lord John's razor. "It has an ivory handle, see? I strop it every day and keep it clean, sharp, and dry."

Clean, sharp, and dry. That was just the way I'd always kept the dagger, except that now it refused to sharpen. Funny that Gentleman Jack had used those exact same words, over and over; and then Lord John, in exactly the same way; and now Grandmother—

Lord John and Gentleman Jack were brothers. I should have realized; they looked so alike, and they both looked like Grandmother, not to mention Grandmother looking like them. They all had round, quick eyes and square jaws. Lord John had a shrine, but he was the no-account brother.

"Do you keep a room for Gentleman Jack?" I said.

This was not a new thought. I'd imagined Grandmother making a shrine for Gentleman Jack. Making sure his lace was beautifully clean. Maybe slipping a pair of peach-colored gloves in among the primrose. Maybe pinning a little ruby brooch onto his neck ruffles as a nice surprise.

"Jack makes too much of a mess." Grandmother waved me out of the shrine-room with the back of her hand. She'd wanted to show off the excellence of Lord John, and now she was going to tell me about the excellent morning chores.

"I suppose I'll have to show you how to set the table," said Grandmother.

But I already knew. I laid the fork on its napkin, to the left of the plate. I laid the knife to the right of the plate, the sharp edge turned inward. There was something about setting the table that was bright and clean and orderly. I hoped it would make my thoughts orderly, because I needed to figure out what was tugging at the edges of my mind. It had to do with Gentleman Jack and Lord John looking like each other, and Grandmother looking like both of them.

And since I looked like Grandmother, I looked like them, too. That was a good thing, wasn't it? Why didn't I have a Good Thing feeling in my stomach?

I'd give myself a Good Thing feeling. I'd think about how much I loved setting the table. How wonderfully orderly it was except . . .

Except you were supposed to place the spoon outside the knife. If I were in charge of the rules of cutlery, I'd say the knife should go outside the round, childish spoon. Wasn't it obvious that the round, childish spoon should be guarded by the fierce, watchful knife?

I didn't have a Good Thing feeling.

I laid the butter knife diagonally across the bread plate. In the cottage, the butter lay dreaming in the cellar. But what did the butter do here, in Netherby Scar? What did the butter do in the cellar below the cellar of the world?

Morning came slowly in Netherby Scar, or at least the light came slowly. The canyon walls were too close to let you see the stars slide down the sky. The walls were too close to let you see the sun rise.

Somehow, though, the birds knew it was time to wake up and start singing. I recognized their voices—there a lark, there a robin—but their accents were thick and strange.

Grandmother handed me a squat bowl with round sides. It was a sugar bowl. I knew because of the little feet. I took it through the kitchen to the pantry. My tongue was getting ready for sugar. It prickled at the edges with sugar juice.

All the drawers in buttercream cottage opened like butter.

"Not butter again!" said the dagger.

But there was nothing buttery about Grandmother's sugar drawer. It was cranky and saggy, running downhill and tilting into its own corners. There was no white sugar, only brown, and it was too hard to scoop. You'd have to excavate it with a pick, like gold.

Nothing was the way I'd thought it would be. There was no marble floor. There was no trying on Grandmother's pearls or touching her skin. It was good I'd touched Mrs. del Salto's dress. Otherwise I'd never know the feeling of silk.

"Then quit thinking about it!" said the dagger.

Now the men came to eat, not all at once, but in little groups. I waited for Gentleman Jack. Where would he sit? Would he sit at the end of the table? It wasn't a democratic table. It was long and narrow.

The regular people would sit at the long sides; the important people would sit at the ends.

I asked Grandmother where Lord John sat. She said he sat at the end.

I asked Grandmother where Gentleman Jack sat. She said he sat at the side. He never did come to breakfast, though. He slept the whole morning in one of the velvet chairs.

I ate in the kitchen. That was the way I liked it, sitting alone, no one watching me eat. Not the Judge, not Mrs. del Salto. No one watching me put the knife outside the spoon, turning the sharp edge outward so the spoon would be safe.

The father doll had said that people ate more in a crimson room. But the kitchen wasn't crimson. I would have to wait until later to eat more.

Everything was heavy. My coat was heavy, but I couldn't take it off. Grandmother's house was too cold.

My insides were heavy, but I couldn't take them out.

My pockets were heavy—at least I could empty my pockets. I set the magnifying glass and Grandmother's photograph on the kitchen table. I unclasped my pendant and set it beside them.

Once I saw them all together, I realized they belonged to each other. They were all about seeing. The opal made you see the right thing to do. The magnifying glass made you see things that were small. And the photograph made you see I looked like Grandmother.

I had three talismans. The number three was strong. I had a strong triangle of talismans.

I reached for the photograph and studied it. I didn't need the magnifying glass to see that the woman in the photograph had long eyes. They did not look like Grandmother's round eyes. I didn't need the magnifying glass to see that the woman had birdsong eyebrows. They did not look like Grandmother's straight-ahead eyebrows. Or to see that the woman in the photograph had a triangle chin and that Grandmother had a square chin.

Or to see that Grandmother had looked familiar because she looked like Gentleman Jack and Lord John. But I needed the magnifying glass to see the baby. I held it over the photograph, over the baby's bonnet, over the grayish embroidery that was all but invisible against the eyelet fabric. I drew the glass away, adjusting it to get the best focus.

The word on the bonnet said Darrell.

Darrell.

Darrell meant Beloved.

Darrell.

The word was too heavy. It lay in my mind like a stone.

Darrell meant Beloved.

It was too much to know.

My pockets had been heavy and made me tired. My insides and my thoughts were heavy and made me tired. I laid my forehead on the table, pressed my knuckles into my eyes. I wanted to make my brain go dark, but the word Darrell was too full of letters. They kept my eyes bright.

Darrell. It had so many extra letters. Beloved was a big idea; it needed a lot of letters. Just like the word Friend.

"*Sharpen me!*" said the dagger.

"*But you don't sharpen,*" I said.

"*Polish me!*" said the dagger.

"*But you don't polish,*" I said.

"*Sharpen me!*" said the dagger.

"*But you don't sharpen,*" I said.

"*Polish me!*" said the dagger.

"Oh, *for stars' sake!*" I said. But I borrowed Rough Ricky's whetstone, just to shut the dagger up. I ran the whetstone along the blade and . . . and I felt the friction! I felt the grit in the stone catching at the dull bits of the blade.

"*I told you!*" said the dagger.

But the dagger hadn't told me anything.

I wished I could sharpen myself for Gentleman Jack. But you can't take a whetstone to your mind the way you can to iron and carbon. You can't angle a whetstone against your brain—angle it at twenty-two degrees—and sharpen up your mind.

From the sitting room came crashes and yells and the sound of breaking glass. I was running before I was quite awake. I squeezed myself through the narrows of the house. Dark pressed at the windows. I'd slept through the whole day and into the evening.

Gentleman Jack stood in the sitting room. He held a chair by the legs. I knew he was going to throw it. You can throw a chair harder when you hold its legs because you can swing your arms. The chair hit another man in the chest. The man staggered back. Now the glimpse of a black eye, now the whole of his face, now a shiver of recognition: it was the cigar man!

"Fight!" yelled a couple of men. "Knife! Fight!"

Knife? I saw then that the cigar man held a blade. It was only a dumb cigar cutter, but I still wished Gentleman Jack had his Lucretia, or another good knife, like the dagger. I thought about giving the dagger to Gentleman Jack, presenting it to him, my palms side by side, the dagger laid across. I thought of how Gentleman Jack would examine it. I imagined how he'd say:

"You have kept it clean.

"You have kept it dry.

"You have kept it sharp."

And then he'd pay me a penny.

"I am Jack Royal," said Gentleman Jack. "I do not pay to enter my own town. I gave this mutt one black eye already, and now—" He curled his fingers into his palm, where he had another black eye, waiting.

"Knife! Fight!" Everyone was yelling now. The words got all mixed up. They didn't exactly rhyme, but when you yelled them, they started to sound the same.

Gentleman Jack leapt. He kicked the cigar man's blade hand. The kick made a crack, the kick made the cigar cutter go flying. The cigar man was backing up now, backing up, almost in the foyer, turning to run, which was hard because of having no exits. And Gentleman Jack running after him, scattering chairs and tables, clenching the second black eye in his fist.

"I love Netherby Scar!" said the dagger.

I'd thought I'd love it, too. But it was different from what I'd expected. I thought of how the cigar man had tried to charge me to use the path. Of how I'd thought about my opal pendant and how I'd never give it away so I wouldn't give away my luck. I'd thought then that I was walking toward my luck, but now I wondered if instead I'd walked away from it.

The men settled down again. They seemed to be agreeably surprised by the fight. I couldn't tell what kind of men they were. They wore suits and ties, like the Judge, but they acted like the men in the Sapphire, drinking, smoking, swearing, spitting. Except that Grandmother's house had little silver cups for spitting.

"Not real silver," said the dagger.

Why had Gentleman Jack told me I'd have to be quiet in Grandmother's house? The men were explosions of loudness. Even their spit was loud.

Was this Grandmother's empire, all spit and tilt and no brown sugar to sweeten it?

Grandmother gave me a broom and told me to sweep up the broken glass, which I did, while she picked up the overturned chairs and tables. "What did I tell you," said Grandmother. "Jack always makes a mess." I swept up other crumbs from the fight—bits of splintered wood; a couple of coins; a white porcelain knob with a silver screw in the center; and a brown tooth that probably should have had a screw in the center but had only a hole.

Now Gentleman Jack returned, stretching his cat-smile over his teeth, his black-eye fist open and relaxed.

"There will be no fights in my house, Jack Royal," said Grandmother. "How many times do I have to tell you?"

Gentleman Jack didn't say anything, but he didn't have to. It was what the Judge would call a rhetorical question.

Grandmother herded us to the velvet chairs, and then we were all sitting, the three of us, around a little table. This was the first time I'd sat on one of the chairs, which should have meant that Grandmother would let me try on her pearls. But I knew now that would never happen. Nothing would ever happen.

"*Lots of things are happening,*" said the dagger. "*Good things like fights are happening.*"

"Let's see what Jack has told you, Girl," said Grandmother. "What are the tasks I asked of him and John?"

At least I knew the answer to this.

"*Fetch unto me the mountain's gold,*
To build our city fair.
Fetch unto me the wingless bird,
And I will make you my heir."

And then I saw that it was just like the cattle boy's song. When you put the Mountain's Gold words to the melody of the cattle boy's song, they fit exactly. Which had come first? Had the Rosati stolen it from Grandmother, or had Grandmother stolen it from the Rosati?

But that was a dumb thing to think. You can't steal words.

"*You can steal anything,*" said the dagger.

"Why do we want the gold?" said Grandmother.

"To build your empire," said Gentleman Jack.

"I thought this was the empire," I said.

"Not this dung heap, Girl," said Grandmother. "Once I have the gold, I'll transform Netherby Scar into a glittering town that will draw people from hundreds of miles."

I thought of the Judge talking about Blue Roses and how a city on a hill cannot be hidden. But no matter how much Netherby Scar glittered, people would never see it from hundreds of miles.

"Tell me, Jack," said Grandmother, "why did I choose Netherby Scar?"

"It's on the railroad line," said Gentleman Jack. "People can get here quickly and comfortably. We'll run a trolley from the railroad station direct to the Grand Hotel."

"Why do we want the Songbird?" Grandmother was exactly like Gentleman Jack. She liked asking questions.

"The Songbird will sing praises to the Blue Rose," said Gentleman Jack. "And that will call the Blue Rose's attention to Netherby Scar."

An hour ago, I might have said to Grandmother, "But I thought you were the Songbird." That was because of what Mr. Elton had said, that the woman in the photograph had been their Songbird. It would be hard to un-know what I'd thought for so long, that the photograph was of Grandmother. But the woman held a baby. The baby's name was Darrell—

I might still have tried to believe it was Grandmother in the photograph. After all, anyone can hold a baby, and things you've thought for so long are hard to un-think. But Mr. Elton said I looked like the woman in the photograph, and I knew I didn't look like Grandmother.

I refused to look like Grandmother.

"The Songbird will praise the Blue Rose, so she'll bring us marvels," said Gentleman Jack.

"We'll sell the marvels," said Grandmother, but I didn't understand.

"Why doesn't the Girl know about the empire?" said Grandmother.

"She's a little dull, Mother," said Gentleman Jack.

"Then sharpen her up!" said Grandmother.

"Here's what we care about," said Gentleman Jack. "We want people from all over the Territories to spend their money in Netherby Scar. People will come from miles around to crave boons of the Blue Rose."

"And why will they stay?" said Grandmother. "Even after having craved their boon?"

"Because," said Gentleman Jack, "we will have built casinos with crystal chandeliers, and dance halls with marble floors, and hotels with mahogany reception desks, and everywhere you turn you'll be able to purchase lobster dinners and sirloin plates and pink champagne and opals, and every opal will come with our pledge: 'Good Luck Guaranteed!' We'll attract gentlemen with heavy pockets and diamond stickpins who will pay, and pay well, to play—and play hard—with no interference from the law."

I suddenly saw it all very clearly. I was getting horribly good at seeing. Netherby Scar would be selling luxury and pleasure. Netherby Scar would be selling lawlessness.

"*No one likes a town with a sheriff,*" said the dagger.

"So, Jack," said Grandmother, "what do we need first?"

"The gold," said Gentleman Jack, "to build the casinos and hotels."

"So, Girl," said Grandmother, "where's the gold?"

"In the Indigo Heart," I said.

"So, Jack," said Grandmother, "where do we get a Songbird?"

"We crave the boon of a Songbird from the Blue Rose."

"What happened the last time you craved the boon of a Songbird?"

"The Blue Rose sent me the Girl," said Gentleman Jack.

"The Blue Rose sent me?" I said.

"How did you know she was no Songbird?" said Grandmother.

"She couldn't be a Songbird," said Gentleman Jack. "Not with that voice."

"The Blue Rose sent me?" I said.

"Then why did the Blue Rose send her?" said Grandmother.

Gentleman Jack shrugged. "Sometimes the Blue Rose sends you a burden, to see if you accept it with an open heart. And when she sees that you do—that you've honored what she sent—she sends what you really want."

I was the spit in Gentleman Jack's eye.

"I've cared for the Girl for many years," said Gentleman Jack. "I've proved myself to the Blue Rose. It's time to crave another boon."

"Who inherits my empire?" said Grandmother. "You or John?"

"Whoever brings you the gold and the Songbird."

"And if you each bring me one?" said Grandmother.

"We have to split it."

I'd dreamed for so long of living in Netherby Scar with Grandmother, but I'd arrived now and already I had to leave. Was that ironic? Netherby Scar was filled with irony, and it was also filled with iron. "The iron has entered his soul," the Judge had said. Maybe the iron had entered my soul, too. There was iron in my soul about Grandmother, iron in my soul about Gentleman Jack. The iron told me I had to go back to Blue Roses.

I'd become so good at seeing that I knew exactly what to say. I knew the exact words that would get Gentleman Jack to take me back to Blue Roses. They'd be lies, of course, but I figured I owed Gentleman Jack a few lies. "Lord John already craved his boon. He asked the Blue Rose for a baby—a baby for him and Flora. He asked that the baby be the next Songbird."

"Why didn't you tell me!" said Gentleman Jack.

I didn't answer. It was a rhetorical question.

A great silence fell among us. I heard only the fire chewing at the log. I had to break the silence before it was too late to speak. "The Blue Rose granted the boon he craved."

"How do you know?" said Gentleman Jack at last.

"Because of the blue rose that bloomed," I said, "just outside the Sapphire."

"When did you start to lie so much!" said the dagger.

"And besides," I said, "Flora has a bump that shows you she's having a baby."

Gentleman Jack paused, then said, "That's why she refused to visit me in jail. She reckoned I'd figure out their plan and steal a march on her and John."

"But as usual," said Grandmother, "John's way ahead of you."

"Not for long," said Gentleman Jack. "I'll get the baby. I'll smoke them out! Flora will appreciate that. It's my signature touch."

No, it was Rough Ricky's signature touch.

Gentleman Jack shouted for me and the Brewster Boy to stir our bones. He shouted that we were going back to Blue Roses. He shouted that Rough Ricky was too recognizable to come with us. He shouted that the Brewster Boy and I should get our things together.

I'd leave the copy of the emblem and the wanted poster behind, but the rest of my things were already together—the photograph of baby Darrell, the magnifying glass, and my star opal. I wore the opal; the other things were in my coat pockets. And then it struck me: I'd been in Netherby Scar for one night and one day, and then part of another night, and I still hadn't taken off my coat.

The Dark Moon

WE LEFT BEFORE DAWN. The darkness seemed absolute, but I knew it could get still darker. It would get darker tonight. Tonight was the night of the Dark Moon.

Gentleman Jack gave the Brewster Boy a lantern. "Hold it high," he said.

Back on the old Day Zero, Gentleman Jack, Rough Ricky, and I had ridden first, the three of us making the points of an arrow. But now, on the almost-last Day Zero, Gentleman Jack, the Brewster Boy, and I straggled along in a row. We didn't make a triangle. We made a line. A triangle is strong, a line is weak. I rode last, in the coattails of the lantern light. The light glanced off the streets, which were sticky as flypaper.

It glanced off a few spindly fly-people, struggling in the muck. They buzzed as we rode by. They buzzed for pennies, for crusts of bread, for scraps of blankets. It was cold in Netherby Scar. It was hard to remember it was spring in the world above. One fly-person buzzed at us louder than the others. He bumbled his way free of the muck. He had a stinger. He came stumbling and stinging toward us.

Gentleman Jack beat him off with his whip.

It was still dark when we reached the two-cent path that led to the first floor of the world. The walls leaned into us, just as the ravine walls had done on the very first Day Zero. But there had been twelve of us then, an arrow of us, with Gentleman Jack, Rough Ricky, and me making the point.

"Me too," said the dagger. "I have the best point."

Now there was no more Rough Ricky. Now there was no more point.

We ducked beneath rocky ledges, scraped past swallows' nests. I'd first seen the nests when I climbed into the canyon. I'd thought I'd be here for a long time. I'd thought I'd see the cliff swallows return.

But I was already leaving. Maybe the nests were empty because it was still so cold in Netherby Scar. Maybe the swallows would return when it got warmer. I wouldn't, though. I would never return.

We crested the two-cent road. We gained level ground. The cigar man looked up. There was only one of him. There were three of us, plus Gentleman Jack's whip.

"Plus me!" said the dagger.

The cigar man watched from his lopsided face: he still had his old black eye, smeary and yellowing, and now a new black eye, pouchy and purple. Gentleman Jack danced his horse sideways, toward the cigar man. The cigar man danced sideways to avoid it. Gentleman Jack danced the cigar man right up to the brim of the canyon. He waited until the cigar man yelled before wheeling his horse around.

We set off again in our weak, scraggly line. "That was amusing," said Gentleman Jack.

The horses made it seem as though I'd never walked to Netherby Scar. They ate up the hungry miles of the outward journey. I thought about the long road beside the railroad tracks, about hiding in the tall grass, about eating grasshoppers. But at least my britches had gotten bigger. They no longer squinched at my middle.

"*You've gotten smaller*," said the dagger.

It was funny to think I'd gotten bigger with the Judge and Mrs. del Salto and smaller with Gentleman Jack. But wasn't that the way it always was? Didn't I always get smaller with Gentleman Jack?

That was a strange new thought, and with it came another. John was a bigger name than Jack. Each name had just one sound, but John was the real name, and Jack was the short name.

I remembered what Gentleman Jack had said about liquids that were distilled and liquids that were diluted. When you distilled something, you boiled it until all the extra water evaporated. Then the liquid became more truly its own self. John was the strong version of the name. John was the distilled version.

When you diluted something, you poured extra water into it. It became less its own self. Jack was the weak version of the name. Jack was the diluted version.

"*Jack's not the weak version*," said the dagger.

I was tired of the dagger listening in. I hid my thoughts from it the way card players hide their cards. They hold them close to the chest. I thought about holding my cards close to my chest. The dagger couldn't understand something like hiding your cards.

I had other new thoughts. I thought that Gentleman Jack had no shrine but Lord John had a shrine. I thought that Grandmother had given

Gentleman Jack the weak version of the name he shared with Lord John. I thought that Gentleman Jack could bring Grandmother a hundred gold bricks, but she'd never love him best.

"*You're crazy,*" said the dagger.

We arrived near evening. Gentleman Jack said it would be dark by the time we reached Blue Roses, which was good. "We'll operate under cover of darkness."

"*I like darkness!*" said the dagger.

It would be extra dark because of the Dark Moon.

"*I like extra darkness,*" said the dagger.

I let the red clay road tug me into the Indigo Heart. I was tired of so many things now. I was tired of the dagger jabbing me with exclamation marks. I was tired of resisting the magnets in the Indigo Heart. Maybe the dolls were right. Maybe the Heart kept pulling me back because it wanted me.

Or maybe because I belonged here. Had I made a Leap of Faith, just as the del Saltos' ancestors had done when the Blue Rose first appeared? The Leap had been to follow the falling star through forty days and forty nights. The Faith had been the del Saltos' belief they'd find their true home.

Which they had.

We followed the uphill branch of the Jordan River. The Jordan roared at us with its big, spring voice. Now the riverbank leveled out, now came another sound, a sweet, sad whistling. It was the cattle boy. He didn't have his cattle, but, as always, he had his song. He raised his hand, I waved back. I remembered the words of the song, I remembered them along with the tune.

My mother dear will unto me
Fetch milk and honeycomb.
My father dear will for us three
Build our enduring home.

Before, in Netherby Scar, I'd thought how similar the task rhyme was to the cattle boy's song. But now I thought it wasn't all that similar. There was still some fetching going on, but the fetching in the cattle boy's song wasn't in the form of tasks. The fetching was in the form of gifts.

Surely the gift song had come first and Grandmother had stolen it to make it into her rhyme. Giving people tasks was the diluted version. Giving gifts was the distilled version.

We angled up and over toward Main Street, up splay-fingered steps, through crook-fingered alleys. Up and over, up and over, until the sideways music of the Sapphire slid downhill to greet us.

That's where we left the horses, across from the Sapphire in a sip of darkness. The Dark Moon was munching up the last light by the time we slipped past the billiards hall and onto Main Street. The pillars held up the roofs as usual, and the metal bowls were attached to the pillars as usual, but no fires burned in them. That was so you could see if the Blue Rose was in the sky.

But the Sapphire was bright. It was all burning candles and glowing cigars and the greasy light of oil lanterns. Hot coals glowed from the peanut man's cart. He whistled from across the street. "Hello!"

I could whistle Hello back to him; I knew I could. It seemed so easy—the breathy H, the slippery L's, the easy sounds of the Eh and the Oh. But even though Gentleman Jack was already halfway across the street, he'd hear me because the Whistling is meant to be heard over long distances. He'd hear me and get mad.

I waved, instead.

A huge man stood outside the Sapphire. The doors were open, but you had to pass the man in order to get in. The music tried tugging you inside by the earlobe, but the man was stronger than the music. He was stronger than an earlobe. He looked like a bull, with his thick neck and huge chest. He stepped in front of the door.

Gentleman Jack came up to him. He jutted his chest forward. That was his way of showing he was the boss of everyone. But the Bull had a different way of being the boss. He slammed his hand into Gentleman Jack's chest. Gentleman Jack flew backward and tumbled off the boardwalk.

He took his time getting up and brushing off his clothes. He came back to us, smiling his crescent cat-smile. "Time for plan B."

The Brewster Boy produced a bottle filled with liquid. The liquid, of course, was lye.

"And the fuse?" said Gentleman Jack.

"Right here, boss."

It wasn't really a fuse, but that's what Gentleman Jack liked to call it. It was one of several metals you could mix with lye to make it explode. Rough Ricky called it a catalyst. You didn't add it until the last minute, in case the mixture got too eager.

I couldn't warn anybody. No one had spoken to me for too long. I wouldn't think about the bad luck that came with whistling, or about Gentleman Jack getting mad. I'd think about Flora, and Lord John, and all the others, trapped in the Sapphire as it burst into flame.

"Fire!" I whistled. I would make the peanut man hear me, even though he was busy scooping peanuts into a brown paper cone. I whistled the two tones in Fire—the first high, the second lower. I whistled the two sounds in Fire—first the Eye, then the Ur.

The peanut man jerked round to look at me, then sprang away from his cart. The Bull stood aside to let him into the Sapphire. Gentleman Jack shook the bottle; he raised his arm.

The bottle was small, but the noise it made was big. The Sapphire screamed as the front walls convulsed with flame and smoke. I stood in an explosion of lye. I knew the smell, of course, but how did I know the coughing and choking that came with it? How did I know the way your throat seizes up, like the pivots of a watch?

"Your throat's not like a pivot!" said the dagger.

People came streaming from the Sapphire, coughing and choking, too, yet also looking back to make sure the danger was real. To make sure they hadn't left their cards on the table for nothing.

The fire was stronger than the Dark Moon. It lit up the night. I knew the strength of fire—

"You don't know about fire!" said the dagger.

I knew the smell of lye—

"You don't know about lye!" said the dagger.

It was the smell that tugged at the strings of my memory. Smells are like that: they can open a door to the past. In the past, a house had been alive with flame. In the past, fire had skittered along the walls, then buckled the window frames and shattered the glass.

"You don't know about anything!" said the dagger.

I knew how the house cried out, how its voice popped and cracked. How it exhaled hot, sharp breaths, smelling of resin.

"It's not a house," said the dagger. "It's a saloon."

The dagger hadn't realized that I'd walked through a door into the past, a past in which a house was alive with flame. That I remembered blue glass and amber glass. That I remembered how the flames had admired themselves in the glass, then gobbled them up, both colors at once. I remembered a child screaming. I remembered that there were words, hot in my mouth, but that the pivots of my throat had seized. I couldn't make a sound. I remembered Doubtful Mittie.

Now I remembered the strength of the fire. I remembered the strength of the smoke and lye. I remembered Doubtful Mittie scooping me into the crook of his elbow, where I dangled upside down, where I saw the floorboards breathing flame, where the flames reached for my face as we leapt, where he yelled—

"*Not yelled!*" said the dagger.

Then we were outside, where there was wind and there was smoke and there was air and there was lye. The wind was in the air; the wind was in the smoke. The smoke was in the wind, and the lye was in everything. You can't turn your back on air. Even if there's smoke and lye in it, you have to keep breathing.

Your throat hurts, your chest hurts. Then everything goes dark for a while, and when you wake up, you taste vomit and blood. All this I remembered—

"*Not remembered!*"

—I remembered, while the Sapphire blaze unfolded before me. I was in the past and I was in the present. Flames leapt to the indigo trees in front of the Sapphire. Indigo burns with more snap than other trees. They smacked and snacked with a bright, smoky flame.

"The horses!" said Gentleman Jack.

If the fire leapt Main Street, it would first snack on the indigo trees that grew at the edge of the gulch, and then it would reach our horses, which we'd tethered in the gulch. Probably it couldn't snack on the horses because horses aren't quick and gobbly enough.

It would just plain eat them.

"Quick, boy!" said Gentleman Jack, and then the Brewster Boy was gone.

The fire would keep running and chewing, although sometimes it might choke on a rock, the way a careless eater might choke on a chicken bone. But finally it would reach the river. It would stub its toes on the river's edge and drown.

The fire burned so bright, it turned people into shadows. Gentleman Jack had smoked everyone out, including Lord John and Flora, and—and Flora's baby! She wore it swaddled to her front. I wanted to look at the baby. I wanted to touch the baby. But too much was happening.

First, there was the derringer that appeared in Gentleman Jack's hand. The only reason to carry a derringer is to be able to conceal it until you're ready to shoot. A derringer isn't much good for anything else. It's famous for shooting every way except straight.

Second, there was Lord John, who took a step back. "Are you planning to shoot me, Jack?" he said. "Shoot an unarmed man?"

Third, there was Gentleman Jack. "Don't tell Mother." The derringer raised its muzzle.

"Have a care, John!" cried Flora. But there was nothing Lord John could do. The derringer sniffed the wind. Click! It licked its lips.

The world reduced itself to revolver sniff and throat burn. I remembered the throat burn from the other fire. My throat still burned from the other fire. The indigo trees danced with flame.

The derringer cracked.

Lord John exploded away from it. He exploded toward the Sapphire.

Flora bent over him. "John!" she said. "John!" It was Lord John who had the real name. Gentleman Jack had the diluted name.

Lord John raised himself to his elbow, which was not the smartest idea, because it showed Gentleman Jack he was still alive. Gentleman Jack fished into his pocket. I knew he was searching for a new cartridge: a derringer can only shoot once. Gentleman Jack was going to reload, then finish Lord John off, just as the Judge had finished off the pinto.

I found I'd already made my plan. I'd made it long ago, I just hadn't realized. I ran to Gentleman Jack, holding the dagger on the open book of my palms. I thrust it toward him.

"Is that for me?" he said.

"You don't have Lucretia anymore," I said.

I hid my thoughts from the dagger. "Breathe spirit," I thought. I was going to breathe spirit into Lord John.

Gentleman Jack paused a moment. You could almost hear him thinking that a dagger was more accurate than a derringer. That a derringer was for ladies because it didn't shoot straight. That you didn't have to reload a dagger. He snatched it up. "You have kept it clean," he said. With the other hand, he dug into his pocket. "You have kept it—"

I whipped around. I'd never take his penny. I bolted down Main Street. I bolted toward the Shrine.

"Wait!" called Gentleman Jack. His feet pounded behind me, faster and faster, trying to outrun the rule of knives and pennies.

Gentleman Jack was faster, but I was lighter. Sometimes light things are stronger than heavy ones. Some light things, like willow branches, can bend but not break. The indigo trees along Main Street were light, like willows, from all that coffee and all those cigarettes.

Thank the stars the wind was blowing east. If it shifted, the trees on the gulch side would sizzle up, like Gentleman Jack flicking his switch lighter.

I reached a tree, I leapt. The branches bent beneath me, but I was light and windy and rushy, and indigo bark is scaly, which is excellent for climbing. Gentleman Jack was only seconds behind me. He grabbed a branch, and for a long, suspended moment I thought it might support his weight. But there came a snap; the branch broke. Gentleman Jack stood in the street for just the pinprick of a second. Then he launched himself at the trunk and shook it, as though I'd fall like a ripe apple.

I found myself remembering the story of the Fair. I remembered Flora saying I couldn't have eaten apple pie because there were no apples in August. But there were no apples in May, either, which is what it was, May fourth. Gentleman Jack couldn't shake me to the ground. I clung to the excellent clingy bark.

"What are you playing at?" said Gentleman Jack. He reminded me of Grandmother saying, "Don't play dumb with me." It was the kind of thing the Royals said.

I didn't answer. Soon the rule of knives and pennies would play out. I remembered how fast I'd run the day the bowie had bitten me. I'd been fast, but the bowie had been faster, leaping and biting and . . . and . . .

And now it was happening! The dagger twisted from Gentleman Jack's hand. It streaked away; it sliced through drifts of smoke. But it didn't go far. It flipped around and arced back toward Gentleman Jack. A comet of silver struck his shoulder. It was bright and beautiful. It was bright and brutal.

Gentleman Jack had made Lord John stagger back. Now I made Gentleman Jack stagger back. He stumbled against the rise of the boardwalk. He lurched his palms to the boards, eased himself down.

Such a liquid honey feeling ran through me: the dagger had stuck Gentleman Jack. It truly was sharp again. It had struck and it had stuck. Down the road, the fire crunched at the Sapphire, just a cottage length away. It chewed on the indigo trees, but so far it hadn't crossed Main Street. If it did, it would blow downhill, where it would have to cross a couple of stone bridges—unless it drowned first. Maybe it would bite into them, maybe it would break its teeth.

"Get some help," said Gentleman Jack. "Someone who won't call the Sheriff." His voice was tight, stretched over the pain beneath.

"What about my Affliction?" I said. Bells clanged in the distance. "Someone will have to talk to me first." They weren't the Shrine bells with their long lily throats. They were the tinny tone-deaf bells of the fire engine.

Gentleman Jack still hadn't realized I'd meant the dagger to strike him. Maybe the thought that I could betray him made such a new shape—all lumpy and jutting out—he couldn't fit it in his mind.

"The Brewster Boy will talk to you," said Gentleman Jack.

"He's seeing to the horses," I said.

Gentleman Jack sat for a bit without speaking. The indigo trees burned in distinct spires of flame. He reached for his striker. I imagined him commanding his striker: "Let there be light!" And of course there would be light.

The striker flame showed that his lips had gone gray. The dagger was a plug, keeping in the blood, but he was bleeding from inside. It was funny how separate from the Sapphire we seemed, even though we were no more than a stone's throw away.

I waited for the dagger to say something sharp, like *"Depends on who's throwing!"* But it was silent.

"There is no Affliction," said Gentleman Jack.

His words punched the fabric of the night. Of course I had an Affliction! His words weren't real, but they stayed in my mind: no Affliction. No Affliction.

"I invented the Affliction to protect you," said Gentleman Jack.

No Affliction.

"You were so young," said Gentleman Jack, "I couldn't trust you to keep the secret."

He wanted me to say, "What secret?" but I wouldn't. Quick, think about something real. Think about the dagger—it was real. *"When you have edges and a tip and carbon,"* it had once said, *"you're as real as anything."*

"The secret," said Gentleman Jack, "that your father was Marshal Starling."

Marshal Starling? No, don't believe him. Keep thinking about real things. Think about the fact that the dagger was buried about three inches in Gentleman Jack's shoulder. That was real. Think about the fact that it takes only an inch to make a person bleed to death. That was real.

"The Marshal drove lots of people away from the Indigo Heart," said Gentleman Jack, "not just me. People who wanted the gold, people who had a right to the gold, people who were his enemies. They'd have killed you if they knew he was your father."

But the Federal Marshal was Gentleman Jack's enemy. Did that mean Gentleman Jack was protecting me from himself?

The night was stretched all out of shape. I watched the flames running faster and faster to keep up with themselves. They were running out of things to eat. I kept thinking of real things. I made my mind into a magnet so the real things wouldn't slip away.

Real: beneath the job name of Federal Marshal was a person name, Starling.

Real: my own name was Starling.

Real: people in the same family had the same names.

"Quick!" said Gentleman Jack. "Before the Sheriff finds me. I can't even use my good hand."

He meant his right hand, his knife-and-gun hand. He meant if the Sheriff, or the Deputy, came along, he wouldn't be able to protect himself.

The dagger was stuck in his shoulder, not his hand. But I knew now that things in your body were all connected with other things. Things that could be severed. If you hurt your forearm, you could wreck your dagger hand. If you hurt your shoulder, you could wreck your knife-and-gun hand.

Bits of information lay scattered about, like puzzle pieces. I was beginning to put some of them together: if Marshal Starling was really my father, then Mrs. Starling was my mother, which also meant my mother had been the Songbird.

I tried to be surprised, but my surprise was all used up.

I'd lived with Marshal Starling and the Songbird in the cottage with the blue and amber windows. I thought about the pocket watch. Of course, Gentleman Jack had taken it from the Marshal after he'd killed him. It was hard to think of the Marshal as my father, but I'd get used to it. I'd make myself get used to it. I remembered Gentleman Jack picking through my father's pockets. Gentleman Jack had taken the watch in plain sight—the sight was extremely plain. Why hadn't I realized?

It should have been easy to realize. For one thing, he'd given it to me on August twenty-seventh, which was the very day after he'd killed the Marshal. Also, the photograph in the watch was of my mother, which was why I resembled her. Lots of the puzzle pieces had been lying right in front of me, but I'd been so addicted to my version of the truth, I couldn't take in any other possibilities.

I thought about the graves behind the cottage. One wooden star for me, because my body had never been found. One stone marker for my mother, Lyra Starling. One stone marker for my father, Aldo Starling. I thought about the Sheriff—it had probably been the Sheriff—boxing up the Marshal's body and bringing it to Blue Roses to be buried beside the graves of his family. Beside the stone marker for their little boy—

My brother, Darrell Starling. My brother, who'd worn a little embroidered cap when he was a baby.

The graves were in plain sight. The names were in plain sight on the markers, except for the wooden star. The wooden star belonged to me. It was good there was no name on the marker, because now I had a new name. My old name would probably have been pretty and have had a good meaning. But now I was used to Starling.

Another thing in plain sight was that I matched up with my name. Starlings were warrior birds that would fight for their families. So would I. Starlings were feathered iridescence, and so was I, with my opal pendant and opal eyes.

It was time to climb down now, even though the excellent indigo bark wanted me to stay. I shimmied down the trunk. The bark was scaly, except for a raw, pale patch where a branch had once grown. Gentleman Jack had broken it trying to launch himself into the tree. I picked it up.

"Find someone sympathetic toward us Royals!" said Gentleman Jack.

I waited for the dagger to demand that I find help for Gentleman Jack. But it was silent. Maybe that's because it was stuck in Gentleman Jack, and Gentleman Jack was the kind of person who made you be silent.

Gentleman Jack was the kind of person who gave you white wounds. Gentleman Jack was the kind of person who made up an Affliction. Gentleman Jack had said he'd give me a name, but it had only been a piecrust promise. I was glad of it now. He'd have found a name he thought fit me, which meant it would be ugly. Not a name like Starling, which belonged to the Starlings' emblem. It didn't belong to the Royals, which meant the name Starling with its melodies and murmurations wasn't too fancy for me.

It belonged to the Starlings. I belonged to the Starlings.

I crossed Main Street, sizzling the branch through the air. The dagger had once said Starling del Salto was a quarter inch too long. But a quarter inch can make a big difference. It can make the difference between whether someone bleeds to death or lives.

Starling. The name sang inside my head. It was just the right length. I listened to the fire engine's tin-can voice. I listened to the hoses hissing out water. I listened to the flames gasping for air.

I listened to Gentleman Jack yelling at me to get help. "Why are you just standing there?"

Someday I'd forget all about Gentleman Jack. Someday I'd push his memory to the backwater of my mind. But first I had to notice what things were in plain sight, before they disappeared. I had to look at things as though I'd never seen them before. Gentleman Jack's gloves were in plain sight. I noticed them especially because they were dirty and torn and soiled with plink water. Grandmother had no shrine for him filled with extra frills and piles of fresh, clean gloves.

I bet she'd never embroidered the initials GJR on his gloves. Of course she hadn't.

I found a safe spot on the boardwalk, about two Starling lengths from Gentleman Jack. It was too far for him to grab me. I waited until three breaths and a swallow had passed. I would bring my Affliction into plain sight.

"Take off one of your gloves," I said. Out came my words, plain as plain.

My voice was in plain sight.

"What?" he said.

I swished the branch through the air, and it made a sound like Gentleman Jack's whip. "Do it, or I'll unstick the dagger."

"What?" said Gentleman Jack.

I tipped the branch against the dagger. "Then you'll bleed to death."

Gentleman Jack hissed with pain. He hissed back his lips. He bared his teeth. His mouth was an abandoned cemetery. His teeth were tombstones of decay. I tried to be surprised again. I'd forgotten I'd used it all up.

"Go on," I said.

Gentleman Jack used his left hand to tug at his right-hand glove. His eyes flickered sideways. He wanted you to call his eyes Green. Green eyes were uncommon and precious. But his eyes were really the color of mud, which was everywhere. That's why the green opal hadn't warmed up to him. He flicked the glove onto the boardwalk.

I wouldn't have been surprised if Gentleman Jack's hand looked like Lord John's, long fingered and elegant. I wouldn't have been surprised if it looked like Doubtful Mittie's, all raw liver-splat. I'd told the Brewster Boy that Gentleman Jack would never harm a child. I'd believed it then, but now I wasn't sure.

It turned out I hadn't used up all my surprise. Gentleman Jack's hand was worse than Doubtful Mittie's, worse than Rough Ricky's face. At least Rough Ricky's burns had turned to scars, but Gentleman Jack's flesh was raw and bubbling. It was mostly white—but not a fresh white, not like snowdrops, say, which are so alive they can grow when it's snowing. It was a flat, dead white, marked with red rivulets and canyons and yellow ooze and drip. The fingers were tenements of raw flesh, staggering up and down. He had only two fingernails. Strange that this made me think of Molly and her pale moon-nails. His index finger was a melted candle. It wept yellow tears.

There were no surprises left. I remembered the Mother Goose rhyme, the one I made into the task rhyme. It talked about a secret.

How had I known that Gentleman Jack had a secret?

> One for sorrow,
> Two for joy,
> Three for a girl,
> Four for a boy.
> Five for silver,
> Six for gold,
> Seven for a secret
> Never to be told.

Here was one of them: Gentleman Jack had said he couldn't use his good hand, but those words hid another secret:

Gentleman Jack didn't have any good hands.

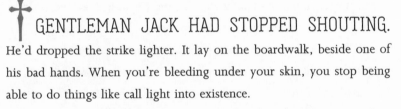

In Plain Sight

✝ GENTLEMAN JACK HAD STOPPED SHOUTING.
He'd dropped the strike lighter. It lay on the boardwalk, beside one of
his bad hands. When you're bleeding under your skin, you stop being
able to do things like call light into existence.

I couldn't call light into existence, either, but it came to me when
I needed it, which was now. Warmth burst from the opal. I glanced
down. My shirt was buttoned over the pendant, but the blue fire flashed
through. Warmth and light meant Go!

But where was I supposed to Go? What was I supposed to do? If I
had the dagger, it might tell me not to do something, and then I'd know
that was the very thing I should do. It had told me not to learn to read,
because reading is taming, but it turned out that reading is a joy.

If a taming thing is joyful, I'd choose tameness over wildness.

I could think of all the things Gentleman Jack or the dagger had
told me to do, or not to do. Then I'd do the opposite, especially if the
opposite was joyful.

Then I'd Go!

Gentleman Jack had forbidden me to show the pocket watch to anyone. But it was too late for that. Mr. Elton had seen the Starlings' emblem on the case.

Gentleman Jack had ordered me to destroy the Songbird's photograph so no one else could see it and realize I looked like her. But it was too late for that. Mr. Elton had seen the photograph. He'd seen that I resembled my mother. My face was in plain sight, being as it was on the front of my head.

Gentleman Jack hadn't wanted me to speak without being spoken to first. But it was too late for that. I'd turned against Gentleman Jack, which had forced him to reveal that my Affliction was a lie. Why had he created the Affliction in the first place? Perhaps because he wasn't sure how much I remembered about my family and the fire. He wasn't sure what I'd be able to tell other people and get him arrested.

Gentleman Jack had forbidden me to whistle—

That I could still do! I would do whatever he'd forbidden. I'd whistle for the Sheriff, and it wouldn't be any old whistle. I'd call out to the Sheriff in the Whistling.

There was music in what I wanted to say. There was always music in words. The name Gentleman Jack was a little song: high, medium, low, high.

Three, two, one, three.

It would be difficult to whistle the hard sounds, like the T in Gentleman. I'd have to whistle around them. But I thought I could make the softer N sound, and I knew how to make the softer L sound from the way the peanut man taught me to whistle Paloma.

I would need to whistle the words South and Sapphire, but they only contained soft sounds. Vowels were the easiest to whistle, and next easiest were the soft sounds.

I licked my lips and made a little practice whistle, which Gentleman Jack would say was bad luck. He'd be right, too. It would be bad luck for him.

"Gentleman Jack," I sang out in the Whistling. "South of Sapphire."

Speaking the Whistling was a little like learning to read. You felt that you'd never be able to read, and then all of a sudden, the squiggles on the page turned into friendly, smiling words, like Well, and Bell, and Tell.

I must have known how to speak the Whistling in the Before Time.

Gentleman Jack found his voice. "You're the Songbird," he said.

"In plain sight," I said.

"Tell me again about the Songbird," said Gentleman Jack. "It never was Flora's baby?"

"It never was Flora's baby," I said.

It turned out that Gentleman Jack didn't have excellent vision, like me. It turned out that even when things were in plain sight, he didn't see them.

Like this: "You have such an ugly voice," said Gentleman Jack. "How could you be the Songbird?"

"Breathing smoke and lye damages your voice," I said.

Like this: "Why did you turn against me?" said Gentleman Jack.

"You were supposed to accept me with an open heart," I said.

Like this: "You owe me all your gratefulness," said Gentleman Jack.

"Gratitude has to spring up naturally," I said, which is a thing in plain sight if you have any brains.

It was Flora who found us first. I recognized her from pretty far away by the shape she made in the air. She had the same baby bulge as before, except now it was strapped to her outside. Her fierce, clear voice reached us before she did. "At last you found a Songbird, Jack!" It was the voice that made the men in the Sapphire sit up and shut up.

But Gentleman Jack could not sit up.

But her voice grew soft when she talked to me. "The Sheriff got your message," she said. "He's still busy with the fire, so he sent me on ahead to keep an eye on Jack."

Keeping an eye on Gentleman Jack meant taking out a revolver and pointing the eye part at Gentleman Jack.

It turned out Flora already knew about the casinos and the diamond stickpins and the marble floors and the champagne dinners and the opals that came with a Guarantee of Good Luck.

Here's what else she knew: "You craved the boon of a Songbird," said Flora, "and the Blue Rose sent you Starling."

"Don't call her Starling!" said Gentleman Jack.

"The secret's out, Jack," said Flora. "The whole town knows who she is. The whole town knows that the name Starling belongs to her."

I had the peculiar thought that I'd had a name vacuum, because Gentleman Jack hadn't kept his promise to give me a name. A vacuum is kind of like a magnet. A vacuum will attract something to fill it up.

"Anyway," said Flora, "the Blue Rose isn't going to follow you to Netherby Scar just because you stole a Songbird. You can't simply transplant her like—like some prize tomato!"

I thought about this. "The Blue Rose is made of stardust," I said, "and the Indigo Heart is made of stardust—"

"Just so," said Flora. "You can't separate them."

You couldn't take the Blue Rose away from the Indigo Heart. If you put her in an envelope and sent her to Netherby Scar, the envelope would come back marked RETURN TO SENDER.

That was why people from other parts of the Territories made pilgrimages to the Indigo Heart. They even walked to the Indigo Heart. You couldn't worship the Blue Rose in a place with no stardust. Which was why you had to take care of it and not dig it up. You had to keep it knotted into itself so it wouldn't be at loose ends.

My own loose ends had knotted themselves up. A knot for me and the Judge. A knot for me and Mrs. del Salto. A knot for me and Flora, even though Flora had tricked me into thinking she wanted to help Gentleman Jack. Now I knew the truth. She wanted to get Gentleman Jack arrested and convicted.

"You're Gentleman Jack's reliable source?" I said it with a question mark, even though I knew the answer.

"I am," said Flora.

"But not very reliable," I said, because she had lied to him about the five bricks of gold.

"Not very reliable," said Flora.

I remembered the story about the Fair she and Lord John had come up with. "But what about the Fair?" I said. "What about the peas and the shells and the beads?"

"I'm sorry we misled you," said Flora. "There was no truth to the story. The details were all wrong."

Flora and Lord John had been going to let me be caught telling a lie in court! But what about the apple pie and how they'd changed it to blueberry because of no apples in August? It had made me think they were so kind and clever.

"No one would have blamed you," said Flora. "You're just a child and everyone knows how persuasive Gentleman Jack can be."

Yes, a knot for me and Flora. I understood why she'd tricked me. She had to make sure the jury would convict him.

No knot for me and the dagger. No knot for me and Gentleman Jack. He'd never wanted me. If the Blue Rose had put me in an envelope and sent me to Gentleman Jack, he'd have sent it back with the message DEFECTIVE: RETURN TO SENDER.

No knot for Flora and Gentleman Jack. She'd only pretended to have been knotted up with him. But a sturdy three-way knot for Flora and Lord John and the baby.

"Is the baby a girl?" I said.

The baby made a mewling sound. Flora jiggled the baby, which was like saying "Yes, a girl!" And suddenly Gentleman Jack didn't matter. Flora and the baby were about life and love. Gentleman Jack and Grandmother were about disappointment and death. I inched closer. "Can I look at her?"

Flora peeled back a bit of blanket. She wasn't what I'd expected. She was red and creased, as though she'd been folded away in a drawer for too long. She opened her mouth like a blind kitten.

I brushed my finger down her cheek. She turned toward my touch and opened her little red cave of a mouth. How did she know how to do that? How intelligent she was!

"Later," said Flora, "I'll let you hold her."

I knew exactly how to hold her. I'd have to lay my hand beneath her head. I remembered that about a baby—such a weak stem of a neck, such a heavy flower of a head.

"What's her name?" I said.

"Aria," said Flora. "Do you remember it?"

"Why would I remember it?"

"It was your name," said Flora. "Before Gentleman Jack carried you away."

Aria! I tried to remember it, but I couldn't. When I got back to the buttercream cottage, I'd look in my almond wardrobe and weigh down the memory.

It was a pretty name, I thought, and it had a pretty meaning. Flora said that an aria was a kind of lyrical song. And then she had to explain that Lyrical meant beautiful and imaginative.

She also said a pretty thing, which was that she was proud for her daughter to have my name and that I matched up with my name.

"You mean I'm beautiful and imaginative?" I said.

"Precisely!" she said, sounding for a minute like the Judge.

"And good at compromise?"

"You're getting better and better at compromise," she said.

I thought that the word Compromise was sort of like the word Discomfit. Discomfit had the word Comfit in it. The word Compromise had the word Promise inside of it. I had used to think that compromise was tame, but keeping your promises was important, and compromise was important.

Flora spoke in a voice I'd only heard once before. It was the voice she'd used when she said she wanted a baby to share and love.

"I can never thank you enough for saving John," she said.

I especially hadn't expected her to say that. I'd saved Lord John, and at last someone was grateful to me—and I hadn't even thought about it! Was it better to have it come as a surprise?

It had never come when I wanted it.

A knot for me and Flora's baby. And now—yes, I was sure of it—I'd had a knot with another baby, in the Before Time. Ever since Gentleman Jack had given me the watch, my head had been filled with half-dreamed opal glimmerings of a baby, who'd grown gradually into a little boy. He'd held the collar of a great dog and staggered around. With the memory came a smell. The smell of lavender. The smell of wardrobes filled with whiteness. The smell of memories.

You could have good memories and bad memories. But if you were going to have any memories, you had to have them both, didn't you? You couldn't just keep the good ones and bury the bad.

The memories of my brother were both good and bad. If I wanted the good ones about his flower head, I had to have the bad ones, too. The memory of the two of us, in a room filled with fire. Of a great timber falling and of—

There my memories stopped. But that was all right because almost everything was in plain sight. Doubtful Mittie's bloody hands had been in plain sight. "Doubtful Mittie murdered my brother," I said.

"Not murder," said Gentleman Jack. "It was manslaughter, because he didn't mean to. He was trying to save you both."

"If a person gets bloody hands," I said, "it means he meant to kill the child."

"It was just that the fire got out of control," said Gentleman Jack. "Doubtful Mittie couldn't go back for your brother or for Rough Ricky."

"The Judge told me that bloody hands mean murder." The Judge knew everything, and Gentleman Jack knew the Judge knew everything. He fell silent.

Rough Ricky's scars were in plain sight. "Rough Ricky never had an Affliction," I said.

"No," said Gentleman Jack. "He was injured in your fire."

"It wasn't my fire," I said.

"Your fire" and "my fire" reminded me of the Judge explaining the difference between the Judge and the Sheriff setting a trap for Gentleman Jack and Gentleman Jack setting a trap for Marshal Starling.

Gentleman Jack broke the law and fell into the trap. Marshal Starling obeyed the law and fell into the trap. They were pretty different things. Gentleman Jack's fire had been a trap. Gentleman Jack had broken the law by setting the trap.

All this from a wardrobe filled with whiteness and a phantom sniff of lavender.

Flora waited with me until the Sheriff and Deputy arrived. They bent over Gentleman Jack. They yanked out the dagger, which made him yell. They applied pressure to the wound, which made him yell. But he wouldn't bleed to death, not with the dagger out and the pressure on. They snapped on the cuffs, which made him yell.

Then, finally, the Sheriff turned to face me. "Thank you!" he said. "Thank you for calling us to arrest Gentleman Jack."

That made the second time someone was grateful to me. I was surprised. My surprise buds had started to work again.

I was more used to saying Thank You than You're Welcome, but I said it pretty well anyway, and then I mentioned that Gentleman Jack was wearing a pendant that belonged to me. The Sheriff took it from Gentleman Jack and gave it to me without a word, but he was smiling a rusty sort of smile.

Flora handed me the dagger. "It's a nice piece," she said in her usual "sit down and shut up" voice. Her voice was like vinegar, sharp but bracing. "Use it well."

It fit in the sheath as usual, but nothing could ever be usual between me and the dagger, not now.

The Sheriff and the Deputy propelled Gentleman Jack toward the Sapphire. Gentleman Jack was handcuffed, so the Sheriff didn't need to wrench his arms behind him.

I walked the other way. I walked until the buildings trickled out and a stone wall ran along the gulch. I hoisted myself onto the wall. I wore both pendants again, the green opal hanging so far down that it lay in the place where my ribs didn't meet. I wasn't really wearing it, though, not the way the opal's owner would wear it. I don't know why I was so certain it wouldn't bring me bad luck. Maybe it was all about intention—I just meant to take care of it until I found the opal's true owner. I knew I didn't own it. But Gentleman Jack had meant to own the opal, even though it had never warmed to him. Even though it didn't match his eyes. It was bad luck times two.

The sky was beautifully bright. Now that it was spring, Orion would rise in the east, just before dawn, which it must have been because I found the three stars of Orion's belt. From there it was an easy eye-hop to the reddish star, and then another eye-hop to the tight blue cluster of the Seven Sisters. I said their names: Astra, Estella, Sidra, Marien, Izar, Vespera, and—

"The Blue Rose!" She had joined her sisters in the sky. Tonight was the night to climb the star steps and thank her for granting the boon I craved, even if she might not have granted it yet.

Even if I might not have craved it yet.

The Seven Sisters were clear and bright, but they weren't bright enough to help me walk the star steps. I knew who could help me, though. I needed only to whistle three notes: low, high, middle.

One, Five, Four.

I needed only to whistle three sounds: Pa-oh-ah. I whistled, I waited. She wouldn't be long.

It was easy to walk with Paloma. I could hold her collar without stooping. She nudged me around a bend in the stairs. We curled round jetties of rock. I brushed against it, felt the weight of it: a thousand-thousand tons of pink stone. It smelled like the beginning of the universe. It smelled like the wardrobe of space.

The moon was black, but Paloma could see with her nose. I couldn't see with my nose, but I could see inside my head, where there were more half-remembered opal glimmerings. I saw my mother's bird-wing eyebrows. I heard her sing the song about milk and honey. I knew I was in bed because I could smell the sheets and I could feel the satiny trim on the hem. I was in bed and she was singing to me. I felt her lips press at my cheek.

The stars hung so close, like the cliff swallows' nests, that I felt I might reach out and pluck them. Stars weren't cold and distant. They were warm and friendly and smelled of cinnamon.

It's good to return to a place where you can call a dog from the other side of town and she'll come running and snuffling your fingers and lick you. It's good to return to a place where a dog has a collar and the collar is just the right height for your hand. It's good to return to a place where there are star steps and where there can be no violence.

It's good when the dagger doesn't say a word.

I thought about Oakheart's collar. I'd thought about taking it with me, just in case we ended up in a courtroom and I could produce it as evidence that I'd been to the Harvest Fair. But when I'd given Oakheart his collar, the Judge gave Paloma her own red collar. If I'd taken Oakheart's collar, maybe Paloma's collar would have disappeared.

It was excellent that I hadn't taken it.

I also thought about the coins I'd given away, despite the dagger's insistence that I keep them. What if I'd kept the coin that was intended for the Shrine? Maybe that would have displeased the Blue Rose. What if I'd kept the Judge's penny instead of repaying Betsy? Maybe the dagger would have been forced to attack me.

The dagger said nothing.

There was no more Day Zero. It turns out there can never be a Day Zero because nothing can be the way you expect. If you keep expecting and counting, you start to count into negative numbers. That's the way to unwind your life. But I was going to wind it up.

Candlelight glimmered at the top of the star steps. When there's a Dark Moon, you can see a burning candle a mile away. But you can't see the person holding the candle until you reach the top of the stairs. The person handed me a candle and lit it with her own candle. There she stood, in her robes; I waited for her to speak.

"No weapons shall be allowed in this place dedicated to the Blue Rose," said the priestess. "Surrender them here, or they shall fail to prosper."

I liked how things kept being in plain sight. No wonder I hadn't been able to sharpen the dagger after I'd failed to surrender it on the Feast of the Blue Rose. It wasn't prospering when it couldn't get sharp. But then I did surrender it to the priestess in Netherby Scar and I was able to sharpen it again.

The opal grew warm; blue fire ate at the darkness. I drew the dagger from the sheath. "May I leave it here?" I said to the priestess. I didn't need the dagger. I un-needed the dagger.

"You may," said the priestess. That was all she said, but she looked at me for a while before she took the dagger.

"Come back for me!" cried the dagger. *"Don't leave me here!"*

The dagger had been stuck in my mind for about five years, and then it had been stuck in Gentleman Jack for about half an hour. The effect was the same: it was a plug. For Gentleman Jack, it kept his blood from leaking out. For me, it kept my memories from leaking out. But when the dagger had been stuck in Gentleman Jack, memories had come to me. Memories contained in smells and feelings and pictures and words.

I would start saving my memories. I would fold them carefully. I would wrap them around lavender. I would tuck the most delicate ones in tissue paper. I would add them to the memories that were already in my wardrobe.

I would rebuild my memories shelf by shelf.

I walked the path to the Shrine. I stopped when I reached the statue of the Blue Rose. I held up the candle; it shone on her face. It turned her cheek into a silver pear. The eyes in the back of her head let her see into the past. The eyes in the front let her see into the future.

She was the Guide to beginnings and endings. She was at the center of everything. I would crave a boon.

"Please bring the del Saltos a baby boy."

I had said Please, and I had gotten pretty used to saying Thank You. It would be all right to thank her, I thought. All right to thank her for something she hadn't yet done but might do. Something she might make happen in the past and let it bleed into our future.

But you couldn't just say a regular old Thank You to the Blue Rose. You had to raise your voice, you had to praise her in song. And I was a Songbird—

I was *the* Songbird.

I stood at the edge of the cemetery, looking down at the town. I raised my voice in praise of the Blue Rose. I whistled the delicate, melancholy tune. I whistled it once through, in order to call the people to their windows, so they too could raise their voices.

Lights flickered on in the houses below. The windows filled with smudges. The smudges didn't look much like people, but you knew they were people because you could hear them. From all around came voices raised in praise of the Blue Rose, together with my whistle. With the words in my whistle.

"The bird sang like a star,
Exalting near and far
The brightest Sister Seven.
With grateful joy we raise
Our voices in her praise:
A melody to heaven."

From all around came a melody to heaven.

And then came the bells, the great, lily-throated Shrine bells. They were ringing out the Dark Moon. The birds were already up and singing, but you couldn't hear them over the bells. They flew in silent bundles of darkness against the dawn. I rang with echoes, I rang with the bells. I burst into a shower of sparks.

Morning stars eddied round me, pale moths winking into dawn. Such strange things I thought! I thought about wildness and tameness. I thought that maybe wildness wasn't all about sharp edges and chilly nights. My feet could be wild, walking the star steps, but I could also still curl up in a room. I could turn around and around, making it fit my shape. Birds turned round in their nests and birds were wild. Wolves turned round in their dens and wolves were wild.

I could be wild and still have a home.

Now light leaked from the Shrine. People came pouring out. Each carried a candle, a white wax candle like mine, burning with a steady yellow flame. I waited. The Judge and Mrs. del Salto came first. Mrs. del Salto wore a light summer dress with pale embroidery. Only once before had I seen her in white, and that had been her nightgown. I was surprised all over again.

"Our Songbird!" they cried as they drew near. "Our Songbird!"

The light in their faces pulled me toward them. They were magnets, I was a magnet. I couldn't help it. The Judge caught me, wrapped his arm around my left shoulder. Mrs. del Salto wrapped her arm around my right shoulder. Her dress was soft and smooth. It was silk.

She pulled me round to face her and there came a familiar warmth. It was the warmth of an opal calling out to me, telling me to open my eyes, to see the world clearly.

But it wasn't my star opal. It was the green opal that hadn't warmed up to Gentleman Jack. It warmed the hollow place beneath the meeting of my ribs. It pressed against Mrs. del Salto's midsection.

It was where Flora had had her baby bulge.

The Blue Rose must have looked backward and given Mrs. del Salto a baby, and then looked forward and known I was going to crave a boon for a baby. Maybe Mrs. del Salto didn't even know she was going to have a baby, not yet. But the opal knew.

The opal belonged to the baby. It warmed to the baby, even through Mrs. del Salto's fluttery dress. Even through her skin. In a few months, the baby would start to make a bulge, and then it would be in plain sight. But there might be something that was already in plain sight, which would be a blue rose growing in the garden for the baby. I smelled it in my memory, wild and sweet.

And then—yes, I thought: I was the sister. There would be a blue rose for me, too.

Mrs. del Salto kissed my right cheek. "This is our girl," she said, "returned from the road."

I wouldn't have to race to tell them about the baby before three breaths and a swallow passed by. I could tell them when I wanted to, which was pretty much Now. I would make them so happy. I would tell them the baby would have green eyes.

The Judge kissed my left cheek. "This is our girl," he said. "Bright as a star."

ACKNOWLEDGMENTS

With deep appreciation for Gaston Bachelard's The Poetics of Space, without which this book could not have been written; and many thanks to Rosaria Munda, for her loving and careful reading of the manuscript, and in particular, for saving me from dozens of saintly errors.